About tl

Lori Wilde is the *New* bestselling author of over is a three-time RITA® a Romantic Times Reviewers' Choice nominee and has won numerous other awards. She earned a bachelor's degree in nursing from Texas Christian University and holds a certificate in forensics. An animal lover, Lori is owned by several pets, and lives in Texas with her husband, Bill.

New York Times and *USA Today* bestselling author **Barbara Dunlop** has written more than fifty novels for Mills & Boon, including the acclaimed WHISKEY BAY BRIDES series for Mills & Boon Desire. Her sexy, light-hearted stories regularly hit bestsellers lists. Barbara is a four-time finalist for the Romance Writers of America's RITA® award.

USA Today bestselling Author, **Maxine Sullivan**, credits her mother for her love of romance novels, so it was natural for Maxine to want to write them. This led to over twenty years of submitting stories and never giving up her dream of being published. That dream came true in 2006 when Maxine sold her first book to Mills & Boon Desire. Maxine can be contacted through her website at http://www.maxinesullivan.com

The Bosses

COLLECTION

August 2019
Forbidden Nights with the Boss

September 2019
Becoming the Boss

October 2019
Seduced by the Boss

November 2019
Flirting with the Boss

January 2020
Desired by the Boss

February 2020
Claimed by the Boss

March 2020
Taming the Boss

April 2020
Ruled by the Boss

Ruled by the Boss

LORI WILDE

BARBARA DUNLOP

MAXINE SULLIVAN

MILLS & BOON

First Published in Great Britain 2020
By Mills & Boon, an imprint of HarperCollins*Publishers*
1 London Bridge Street, London, SE1 9GF

Special thanks and acknowledgement to Maxine Sullivan for her contribution to the *Dynasties: The Jarrods* series.

ISBN: 978-0-263-28126-2

0420

MIX
Paper from responsible sources
FSC™ C007454

This book is produced from independently certified FSC™ paper to ensure responsible forest management.

For more information visit: www.harpercollins.co.uk/green

Printed and bound in Spain
by CPI, Barcelona

ZERO CONTROL

LORI WILDE

To Kathryn Lye, who always makes me look good.

1

"YOUR AGENCY HAS THE JOB, but only under one condition."

Taylor Milton Corben, owner and CEO of Eros Airlines and Fantasy Adventure Vacations, folded her arms and leveled a look at former Air Force Captain Dougal Lockhart. Taylor was a sophisticated redhead with chic blond highlights threaded through her stylish hair, unwavering chocolate brown eyes and dynamite legs. She was also the new wife of Dougal's best friend, Daniel Corben.

Dougal drew himself up to his full six-foot-two-inch height and held Taylor's steady gaze. He should have known there would be a catch. In his experience, there was always a catch.

Did her stipulation have anything to do with the reason he'd left the military and started his own private duty air marshal service? Daniel had probably told her what had happened to him in Germany. Instinctively Dougal stuck his hand in his pants pocket and ran his fingertips over the 9mm slug fragment that he'd had turned into a key chain precisely so he wouldn't forget. The bullet scar at his upper right thigh—at the very same level as his pocket—throbbed at the memory.

Dougal steeled himself for a proviso he couldn't live with, but he wasn't in any position to be choosy. He needed the work. He was trying to get his fledgling business off the ground and it was a struggle. Last month he'd been forced to take out a loan just to make payroll. But there were some things he simply wouldn't do. No matter how badly he needed the money.

"What's the condition?" He fisted his hands.

"I want you and your team to go undercover—"

"That's a given."

She ignored his interruption and went on smoothly. "As tour guides."

"Tour guides?" She caught him off guard with that one.

"Tour guides," she repeated.

"Why?"

"I need you and your men not just on my planes, but at my resorts, as well." She leaned back in her chair, crossed her legs and angled her head to size him up.

"The Lockhart Agency is an air marshal service, not resort security," he said.

"Should I take that to mean you don't want the job?"

Dammit, he did want the job and she was well aware of it. At least she hadn't made any reference to Germany or Ava. He shifted his weight, his feet shoulder-width apart, hands resting on his hips.

Taylor laughed. "You look like an old West gun-slinging sheriff staving off a lynch mob, Dougal. Relax, have a seat."

He forced himself to drop his arms by his sides and settle into the plush leather couch across from Taylor's expensive mahogany desk. He did have a tendency to brace for battle even when there was nothing to brace for.

"What does the job entail?" he asked.

"You'll work for the entire first two weeks in May," she said. "It's a fourteen-day tour."

He nodded. "No problem there."

"You and your men will take tour guide training with the rest of my employees. You've got four men. We have four new tours starting next month and I want air marshals on all the planes and at the facilities."

"Okay," he said cautiously. "What else?"

"You'll be required to wear costumes."

"Excuse me?"

"I'm sorry, but it's nonnegotiable." Taylor might look like a pampered supermodel, but she was a sharp business woman. "In fact, if you decide to take the job, you should start growing your beard now."

"Beard?" Involuntarily his hand went up to stroke his jaw. He'd never worn facial hair in his life.

"You'll be playing the Bard."

"Who?"

"Shakespeare."

Dougal frowned. "I'm not following you."

"I'm concerned that the saboteur is targeting the Romance of Britannia tour next, and the lead tour guide on that junket dresses as Shakespeare. Or rather the *Shakespeare in Love* version of what he dressed like."

"Why are you so sure the saboteur is targeting that particular tour?"

Taylor opened up her desk, took out a green file folder and passed it across her desk. Dougal opened it and read the letter inside.

> You thought those little incidents at your Venice resort was trouble? You haven't seen anything yet, bitch. Just wait until one of your planes falls from the sky. Wouldn't that set tongues wagging? Do you have any idea how vulnerable your air fleet is? Just take a look.

Attached to the anonymous letter was a schematic of the inside of a Bombardier CRJ200. In the margins, written in red, was a detailed listing of the numerous ways a saboteur could cripple the private jet.

His blood chilled.

Dougal raised his head and met Taylor's gaze. For the first time, he saw real fear in her eyes and he was strangely comforted. If she was afraid, that meant she was taking the threats seriously, and the fact that she'd laid her cards on the table made him feel instantly calmer. He was the kind of guy who liked to have a map of the quicksand bogs before he ventured into the jungle. "What did the police say when you showed them the note?"

Taylor plowed a hand through her hair. "I didn't."

"Why not?"

"I don't want any more negative publicity than I've already gotten. I prefer to keep this in-house."

"We should have it dusted for prints."

"I already sent it out to a private lab. There were dozens of prints on the envelope, none on the letter beyond mine and the temp who's been filling in since my executive assistant decided not to return from maternity leave."

"What happened in Venice?"

Taylor inhaled audibly. "A few months back my Venice resort experienced a series of…problems."

"Meaning?"

"Malfunctioning smoke alarms that allowed a fire in the laundry room to go undetected until it had done several thousand dollars' worth of damage. It was suspicious because the smoke alarms had just passed inspection the week before."

"Cause of the blaze?"

"Undetermined."

"Go on."

"After one of the scheduled banquet feasts, a few guests contracted food poisoning, sending them to the hospital for treatment. And finally a Renoir was stolen. The security system had been turned off, and the police suspected an inside job. I fired the manager, hired someone new. Taken one by one it seemed like mere coincidence, but then I learned an exposé reporter was following me."

"The incident between you and Daniel in Spain," he said.

"Yes." She nodded. "Once the reporter aired his piece, I thought the sabotage was all over. Apparently—" she waved at the letter Dougal was still holding "—I was wrong, and the guy was just lying in wait, lulling me into a false sense of security."

"You believe it's a man?"

She shrugged. "Aren't men usually the ones who do these kinds of things?"

Dougal thought of Ava. "Not necessarily."

Taylor pulled her lips back in a pensive expression. "I hadn't considered a woman."

"What makes you think this saboteur is going to strike the Romance of Britannia tour?"

"That diagram is not just any generic Bombardier schematic. It was torn from the handbook of the plane that services that specific tour." She pulled the handbook from her desk and tossed it to him.

Dougal opened it to the back where the schematics were located and saw the jagged edges where the paper had been ripped out. It didn't take a crime scene investigator to see that the torn segments matched. "Any clue as to who could be behind this?"

She shook her head. "I'm no stranger to controversy, you know that. There have been outspoken religious fundamentalists picketing my resorts, condemning them as hedonistic and wicked. Then there are the superkinky customers who threaten to sue me because Eros refuses to fulfill their illegal fantasies. My competitors are jealous of the way I've taken my father's dated commuter airline model and given it a very profitable new millennium makeover. But many on the board of directors are unhappy about this new direction. Making enemies is all part of doing business in the tourism industry."

"This feels more personal." He fingered the torn pages. "For one thing, how did they get access to the jet's handbook?"

"I don't know. That's where you come in."

"I'm not sure how my men are going to like dressing up and playing tour guide."

"I understand it's asking a lot. I'm willing to sweeten the deal." She named a figure so high it was all Dougal could do not to blink in disbelief. "What do you say?"

He smiled. "How can I refuse?"

Taylor reached across the desk, rested her hand on Dougal's forearm. "I want this person caught and I want my guests kept safe."

"We'll take care of it."

"I'm counting on you."

He got to his feet, thought about what happened in Germany and swallowed hard. He could do this. He had to do this. He'd learned from his past. He wouldn't be played for a fool again. He met Taylor's steady gaze and made her a promise. "You can depend on me. I won't let you down."

At that moment, a knock sounded on the door and before Taylor could say, "Come in" the door opened and a heavyset older gentleman, with a straight-shouldered military bearing, stepped over the threshold.

Immediately, Dougal saluted the former general who had once been his superior officer. "General Miller, sir."

"Please." The general waved his hand. "There's no need for that. We're both retired."

Dougal relaxed his stance.

"How are you, Uncle Chuck?" Taylor asked and got up to give the general a kiss on his cheek.

"I'm just fine, princess." He wrapped an arm around her waist.

"How's Aunt Mitzi?"

"Blowing through all my money on a spa day with her friends."

He grinned at her, and then looked at Dougal. "Are you in the middle of something here? I thought I'd take you to lunch and you could tell me what's going on with that sabotage business."

"Actually, I just hired Dougal and his team to augment my security staff. I just received another threatening letter. This one targeting my air fleet."

"Oh?" The general canted his head.

"I've started my own private air marshal service, sir," Dougal explained.

"Ah." Miller nodded. "Applying the lessons you learned about security after that mess in Germany."

Was that a personal dig? The man's tone made Dougal squirm in memory over what had happened. "Yes. And I'm going to do everything in my power to ensure that Eros Air stays safe."

"See that you do," Miller said curtly. "See that you do."

"HEY, HANDSOME, YOU CAN SHAKE your spear over here anytime you want."

In light of that sexy remark, Dougal forced himself not to roll his eyes as a group of women filed onto the Bombardier CRJ200, chatting, giggling and finding their seats. The majority of them were young, rich and attractive. The red-haired woman who'd cracked the suggestive comment briefly met his gaze, then lowered her eyelashes, licked her lips and murmured, "*Yummm-o,*" before moving down the aisle.

It didn't help matters that Dougal was dressed like Joseph Fiennes from *Shakespeare in Love* right down to the artsy, beatnik beard he was itching to shave.

After all, this was Eros Airlines and Fantasy Adventure Vacations and Taylor's company's catch phrase was Something Sexy in the Air. Other than the pilot and copilot, who were both pushing sixty, Dougal was the only male employee aboard. He felt like the last cut of prime beef in the meat market on the Fourth of July.

He was going to have to talk to Taylor. The puffy-sleeved shirt and skintight leather breeches were bad enough, but the facial hair simply had to go. Resisting the urge to scratch his jaw, Dougal greeted each guest with the requisite smile, welcoming them aboard with an affected British accent. It was going to be a long two weeks.

Look at the side benefits. You stand an excellent chance of getting laid.

Except he and his men had signed a contract with a morality clause. While they were encouraged to flirt with the guests, sexual contact was strictly prohibited. Dougal watched a provocative young woman with a great ass wiggle away and he hissed out his breath.

Damn that morality clause.

That was the moment Dougal spotted her.

The last one to board.

The one who didn't belong.

She stood out like a single red rose in a field full of dandelions, all genteel and otherworldly, an escapee from the pages of *Grimm's Fairy Tales.* He half expected to see unicorns and songbirds and butterflies trailing after her.

Her hair was raven's-wing black, her skin pure alabaster, her eyes a stunning shade of ice-floe blue. She must be wearing contact lenses; no one's eyes were that color naturally. She was dressed in a butter-yellow sundress made out of some soft, frothy material that caused his mouth to water. Dougal could taste the sugar-coated marshmallow bunnies and chickens his mother had put in his Easter basket when he was a kid.

Unbidden, he found himself imagining what she looked like underneath that springtime sundress. Did she have on white cotton panties with a sensible underwire bra? Or would he find a delightful surprise? Maybe a wicked scarlet bustier and G-string panties?

Dougal tilted his head. No, he decided. Pink satin tap pants and a matching camisole. Sweet yet sassy. A good girl longing for adventure but nervous about reaching out and grabbing what she desired.

And yet it was more than her ethereal beauty that set her apart from the others, and Dougal was trained to notice subtle differences. It was the serious, "all-business" slant to her slender shoulders and the determined set to her chin, as if she had something to prove. It was the perceptive expression in her eyes, the purposeful way she moved and the manner in which she was sizing him up just as intensely as he was measuring her.

No mere vacationer, this one. Not a woman simply looking for a good time. This enigmatic lady had an agenda.

Alarm bells went off in his head. Until he knew exactly what her agenda was, Dougal was keeping a close eye on her.

Another thing that didn't fit—she was traveling solo. Everyone else on the vacation had traveling companions, but this mysterious miss appeared to be all alone. No doting husband or fiancé or boyfriend at her elbow. No best buddy yapping her ear off. No mother or sister or cousin.

Perhaps she also worked for Eros, maybe she was an actress paid to help set the stage for the Romance of Britannia tour the group was embarking upon and it was her first day on the job. If you put her in historical garb along the lines of the ridiculous outfit he'd been forced to wear, she'd be a shoo-in.

Except that Taylor hadn't told him about any new employees joining the group, and he'd made it quite clear that he was to be kept in the loop regarding anything to do with passenger safety. Odd, though, that while his brain and experience were warning him to watch out for her, his gut was telling him something startling and stupid.

She's the one you've been waiting for.

Why the hell was he giving himself mixed messages? The last time this had happened he'd ended up with a bullet in his thigh.

The woman reached the top step of the metal mobile stairs and their eyes met. Quickly she glanced at his outfit and when her gaze found his again, a slight grin tipped her lips. She was laughing at him.

He cocked an eyebrow, gave her his best Joe Cool expression and stretched out his hand. "Welcome to Eros Airlines, where *your* pleasure is our only concern."

The greeting might have been prescribed, but the emphasis was all his. Dougal didn't know why he extended his hand as she stepped into the cabin. He hadn't shaken any of the other women's hands. Impulse motivated. That bothered him because he struggled so hard to control his impulses.

For the longest moment she said nothing, merely stood there staring at his outstretched hand. It was damned unnerving.

"Hello," she murmured in a husky, breathy voice, and then turned her back on him and started down the aisle.

"Wait," he said and touched her shoulder, stopping her. *Hold up, you're coming on too strong. You don't want to blow your cover.* "What's your name?"

She turned back, raised an eyebrow. "My name?"

Why was she being so cryptic? Did she have something to hide or was he too hypervigilant?

"For our exemplary customer service." He blurted the first excuse that came into his head and manufactured what he hoped was an earnest smile. "We didn't earn our five-star rating by calling our guests 'Hey You.'"

There it was again, that sly, amused grin, as if she found him extremely comical. "I'm Roxanne Stanley. But my friends call me Roxie."

"Roxie." He extended his hand again.

"You're assuming we're going to be friends."

"Not assuming, just hoping."

The minute their palms touched, a shudder shot straight down his spine. His stomach squeezed and his balls pulled up tight against his body and he was just...*rocked.*

The intensity of his reaction disturbed him. Resolutely he shook off the feeling. By nature he was a guarded man. It was the way he'd been born—cautious, cagey, always on the lookout for trouble, seeing the world though the eyes of a troubleshooter. Life circumstances had added to his innate wall, one emotional brick at a time. The one time he'd opened himself up, let down his guard, chipped a few bricks off the wall and—*wham!*

His old bullet wound ached at the thought. *Fool me once, shame on you. Fool me twice, shame on me.*

"And you are..." Roxie tilted her head.

"Here to make your every fantasy come true."

"Ah," she said. "Is that so?" Her smile widened to reveal a double dimple deep in her left cheek. God, he'd always been a sucker for dimples, and look here, she had two.

Key word being sucker. *Keep your testosterone in check, Lockhart. You're on the job.*

"Let's see where you're sitting." Dougal leaned closer, ostensibly to read her boarding pass, but he already knew where she was sitting. He'd memorized the passenger manifest, and he recalled that Ms. Stanley was seated in the first row, near the window, while he had the aisle seat beside her. Handy coincidence.

What he really wanted was to see how she'd react to his proximity. Would she flirt like a single woman on a sexy vacation retreat? Or would she act guilty like someone up to no good?

When it came down to it, she did neither.

Instead, with an unflappable expression, Roxanne Stanley said silkily, "You're blocking my way, Mr. Fantasy Man. Now if you'll excuse me..."

He moved aside, but the passageway was small and he was

large. She had to squeeze past him to get to her seat and in the process her hip grazed his upper thigh. It was the slightest contact, barely there, and yet Dougal's cock stirred instantly inside those damned leather breeches as surely as if she'd stroked him.

This was crazy. He didn't lose control like this, not with so little provocation. He took a deep breath, trying to cool his heated blood. Wanting a woman—hell, who was he kidding, he was *craving* her—brought risks and vulnerabilities.

Think about something else. Whatever you do, do not watch her ass as she walks away.

The woman moved past him and his gaze homed in on her ass like a heat-seeking missile. She swiveled her head and caught him staring. Her steal-your-breath blue eyes locked onto his and sucked the air right out of his lungs.

In that moment it was as if they were totally alone on the airplane. The noise of dozens of voices humming in conversation faded away and Dougal's focus narrowed to only her.

Her gaze was steady, but he saw a faint tinge of pink color her cheeks and she lowered those long, thick black lashes. His heart knocked. She looked at once strong and extremely vulnerable, and he wondered what secrets she was keeping.

Had she been sent by one of Taylor's enemies? An irate stockholder or a competitor? Or was it a personal agenda? Was it revenge against Taylor? Was she a straitlaced saboteur deeply offended by Eros Airlines and its sexually adventuresome vacations, or was he totally off the mark about her altogether?

Dougal couldn't deny that his instincts were telling him she wasn't what she seemed, but did he trust his powers of deductive reasoning? Getting close to her was the only way to find out, but something told him if he flew too near the flame of her hot blue eyes he was going to get singed.

He clenched his teeth to keep from scooping her into his

arms and carrying her away to some secluded corner of the expensively decorated airplane and stripping off her clothes in a hungry effort to discover if her flesh tasted as sweet as it looked. He wanted to cup his palm around her breasts, to thread his fingers through that mane of lush black hair, to press his mouth against her ripe, rich lips.

"Is there something you need?" she asked.

You.

"No," he answered mildly.

He could almost hear her heart thumping, could feel his own heart slamming against his chest.

"Okay, then."

"Okay." Behind him, the flight attendant closed the door, but he didn't look away.

Roxie broke their stare. Ducking her head, she scurried toward her fully reclining, plush leather seat beside the window. Leaving Dougal feeling as if he was flying into the eye of a storm, and his instrument panel had just frizzed out.

2

ROXIE'S BOSS, PORTER LANGLEY, the owner and founder of Getaway Airlines, had seriously underestimated Taylor Corben. Roxie doubted that Porter realized how much money the woman lavished on her airline, nor did he have any idea that she was hiring gorgeous macho men as tour guides. Of course, that was the very reason Mr. Langley had sent her on this trip—to get the lowdown on Eros. Her boss hungered to follow in Taylor Corben's footsteps and open his own destination resort in Ireland, along the lines of Eros's version in Stratford.

The lavishness of the accommodations was the first item going into her report, after she got her hands to stop sweating and her pulse to quit pounding, following her encounter with the hunk in Renaissance attire. The way "Shakespeare" had stared at her caused Roxie to fear that he'd guessed her secret.

She was a mole.

Roxie hadn't been happy about the whole go-spy-on-the-competition assignment her boss had cooked up, but she was loyal to the bone when it came to people who'd given her a break, plus she desperately wanted the head of public relations position that her boss had dangled in front of her. Pulling off this little piece of corporate espionage would cinch her promotion.

The job was not only one she coveted, but the bump in salary would also allow her to put her kid sister, Stacy, through college. Roxie didn't want Stacy to end up like her, forced by circumstances and lack of money to give up on her dreams of becoming an actress.

She peered out the window. Even though she worked for an airline she wasn't a comfortable flyer, and heading to London twisted her stomach. Crossing miles and miles of ocean held little appeal.

She blew out her breath, ran her palms over the front of her thighs and then dug her BlackBerry from her purse to distract herself. She started to type in her impression of the big man in the Shakespeare costume and the lavish interior of the plane—mahogany wood paneling, cocktail bar at the back of the plane with a gleaming granite countertop, opulent carpeting—but then he came over and strapped himself into the last empty seat on the plane.

The seat right beside hers.

Unnerved, Roxie shut off her BlackBerry and returned it to her designer knockoff handbag she'd picked up at a yard sale. She definitely did not fit with this crowd, but her childhood had taught her to be someone else whenever she was in a dicey situation. Slip under the skin of an invented character. For the duration of this trip she was a smart, sharp, infinitely calm, corporate spy. She just had to keep reminding herself of that.

Inhaling, she caught a whiff of his spicy, masculine cologne and felt herself come undone. Fear revved her pulse rate. *Did* he suspect she was not typical of Eros's well-heeled clientele?

Play the game. Be the role.

To boost her confidence, she reached up to run her fingers over the gold-and-silver comedy-tragedy mask necklace she always wore. It was the last gift her parents had given her before they were killed two weeks after her eighteenth birthday.

"Hello, again." His deep voice rumbled, rolling over her ears like a gathering storm.

She felt something shake loose in her chest, a tearing-away

sensation like a boat breaking free from its mooring and drifting out to sea.

Be cool. You are an expert spy. Think Mata Hari, Antonia Ford, Belle Boyd.

"Hi," she said casually.

"I'm Dougal, by the way. Dougal Lockhart. Sorry about stonewalling you earlier. It's part of the flirtatious role-playing Eros requires from tour guides."

Role-playing she understood. It was how a shy girl from Albany made it in New York City. "So I deduced. Are you sitting here for the entire flight?"

Oh, damn, her voice had come out high and reedy.

"Yep. Does that distress you?"

"You're the one who should be distressed," she countered. When she'd first started working for Porter he'd coached her on how to go on the offensive diplomatically whenever she found herself backed into a corner, but the skill didn't come easily. By nature she was open, expressive, a people pleaser, and she had to fight against her tendency to be overly accommodating. It was only when she pretended to be someone else that she was able to change her behavior.

"Oh?" He cocked his head.

"I gotta warn you," Roxie amended. "I'm a nervous flyer. I get fidgety."

"And yet you're traveling alone."

"I am."

"Vacationing by yourself?"

Was he fishing for details? Fear hopscotched through her and she dug her fingernails into her palm. "What's wrong with that?"

"Nothing. It's brave."

"I like traveling alone," she lied. "I'm accountable to no one's agenda but my own."

"Touché." His gaze skimmed over the naked ring finger of her left hand. "I take it you're not married."

"Astute conclusion."

"Snarky." His eyes twinkled. "Unexpected but engaging."

"I'm happy I could provide you with some free entertainment." She took a peek at his ring finger. "You don't look married, either."

"Astute conclusion."

"Now you're just mocking me."

"Trying to keep your mind off takeoff."

"I appreciate the effort."

"If it would help any, feel free to grab hold of my arm," Dougal invited.

She dropped a glance at his strong forearm, poking from the rolled-up sleeves of his puffy white shirt. His forearms were ropy with muscles and thick, dark hair. She curled her fingers into fists and forced herself to breath normally.

"I've got to warn you, I tend to babble when I'm nervous." She scrunched her shoulder blades together.

"Babble away."

"You're too kind."

"Not at all. I have earplugs."

She had to laugh. Strange as it seemed, she was having fun.

The plane taxied from the gate.

"Quick," Roxie said. "Say something to distract me. Take-offs and landings freak me out the most. That and looking out the window when we're over water."

"Looking out the window freaks you out?"

"Sort of."

"So why the window seat?"

"Because looking out the window keeps me from feeling claustrophobic."

"You're claustrophobic, too?"

"Only when I feel closed in."

He laughed again, the corners of his brown eyes crinkling. "You're funny."

"I'm happy that you find my terror amusing."

"It is a seven-hour flight. I have to take my amusement where I can find it." The teasing expression in his eyes warmed her from the inside out.

The plane rushed down the runway, gathering speed, the tarmac whizzing by in a gray-black blur. Roxie gripped the armrest.

Dougal held out his palm. "I'm here if you need a hand to hold on to."

Gratefully she took it, but the minute his fingers closed around hers, Roxie realized she'd made a grave mistake. His grip was firm, his palm calloused. His scent, a complicated aroma of spicy cologne, leather and sunshine invaded her nostrils.

Madness.

The plane was airborne, soaring.

Treetops fell away. Vehicles crawling along the freeway in rush-hour traffic glimmered like spotted stones. The early-morning sun burned orange against the clouds. Roxie jerked her gaze from the window to stare at the man beside her.

The warmth inside her kicked up to a sultry simmer. A labyrinth of emotions pummeled her. Overwhelmed, Roxie had to remind herself to breathe. What was going on here? Why was she feeling so…so…what was she feeling?

Attracted.

Yes, that was the word. She was attracted to him and the feeling scared her.

He held on tightly to her hand, and she closed her eyes so he couldn't read what she was struggling to hide.

The landing gear came up with a bump. Her eyes flew open. The sound never failed to send her heart lurching into her throat. Dougal squeezed her hand. A sexual tingle shot all the way up to her shoulder.

Think about something else.

But that was difficult to do, considering how delicious he smelled and how his quick-witted banter reminded her just how long it had been since she'd had sex.

Roxie tried to concentrate on the luxurious surroundings. The state-of-the-art flat-screen television sets at each seat were so sophisticated they'd make a techno geek weep with happiness. There were the elaborate meal menus that could send a gastronome into paroxysms of epicurean delight and the butter-soft, oversize leather chairs with enough legroom to satisfy the long-legged man beside her.

"How long have you been a tour guide?" She searched for something neutral to talk about, something that wouldn't inflame the feelings burning through her. Or result in her inadvertently giving herself away.

"I just started," Dougal explained. "In fact, this is my first trip."

"Really?"

"Yep."

"You seem so self-confident."

"It's all an act," he confided. "Inside, my knees are jelly."

"You fooled me."

"How so?"

"You don't look like you're scared of anything."

"Looks can be deceiving." The way he said it, the penetrating expression on his face made her feel as if he'd whipped off all her clothes and she was sitting there stark naked.

"What did you do before you took this job?" she asked.

"Variety of things."

"You seem a little old to still be finding yourself."

"Some of us are late bloomers."

"Late-blooming jelly knees? I'm not buying it."

He stroked his bearded chin. "No?"

"How old are you?"

"Thirty-three. You?"

"Anyone ever tell you it's impolite to ask a woman her age?"

"You brought up the topic," he pointed out.

"I guess I did. How old do you think I am?"

"That's so not fair. If I guess that you're older than you are, then you'll never speak to me again and that would be such a shame because you're definitely a woman worth speaking to. So let's see. You're sixteen going on seventeen?"

Okay, so she was flattered. Roxie didn't get this kind of talk from men very often. Mainly because she avoided situations where such talk could spring. To be honest, she avoided men and any hint of romantic relationships, but she wasn't dumb. She knew it was part of his tour guide please-the-customer shtick, so she relented and let him off the hook. "I'm twenty-eight."

"And you've got your life all figured out?"

She shrugged. "I guess."

He reclined his seat, crossed his ankles. "What do you do for a living?"

"Executive assistant," she said, wanting to lie as little as possible.

"Is this your first trip to Europe?"

"Yes. You?"

"Been many times. Twelve years in the Air Force."

"I guess that's why you became a tour guide? You know your way around the world."

"I've been around the block a time or two." He narrowed his eyes, his smile turned wicked and for a moment he looked positively hawkish. A calculating raptor analyzing the habits of his prey just before he swooped in for the kill. Suddenly she felt like a field mouse who'd ventured too far from home. What on earth had made her believe she could pull off something like this?

"Do you like music?" he asked.

"Sure." She shrugged. *Act nonchalant, sophisticated.* "Doesn't everyone?"

"Not everyone. I ask because Eros Airlines has satellite radio piped in. Listening to music might help you relax."

He leaned over her to reach for the console containing the small flat-screen television. She tried not to notice that his broad chest was mere inches from her lap. He opened a drawer, pulled out a headset and handed it to her. "What do you want to hear? I'll dial it in for you. Rap, country, classic, pop? You name it, we've got it."

"Emocore," she said.

The corners of his mouth turned down in a surprised, "Who knew?" expression. "Seriously?"

"You got something against emocore?"

"Matter of fact it's my favorite, but I really don't like the emo label," he said.

"It's dumb, I know. Why don't they just call it poignant punk rock? Who are your favs?"

"Rites of Spring, Embrace, Gray Matter."

"Oh, oh, don't forget Fire Party and Moss Icon."

"What do you like about it?"

"Emo is so raw, you know. Primal." Roxie pressed her palms together. "But it's also deep and expressive and soulful." Some people thought the music was loud and chaotic, but to Roxie the sound represented a part of herself she was afraid to explore any other way. The part of her that longed to flaunt convention, throw back her head and just howl at the moon.

Dougal shook his head. "I wouldn't have pegged you for an emo fan."

"Same here."

They grinned at each other.

Dougal shifted in his seat, angling his body toward her. "Okay, so what's your favorite food?"

"Italian."

"Me, too. What dish do you like best? Lasagna?"

"Always a crowd-pleaser, but my hands-down fav is chicken Marsala."

"No kidding? It's my favorite, as well."

"Wine, mushrooms, chicken in cream. What's not to love?"

"I couldn't agree with you more."

"What's your favorite dessert?"

"Brownies."

"With nuts."

"Absolutely."

"Pecans or walnuts?"

"Either will do, but I like walnuts best."

Roxie narrowed her eyes. "You're just telling me what I want to hear. That's your job."

He grinned, shrugged. "I like seeing you smile."

"Ha! I knew it. Flatterer."

"Doesn't mean that I'm lying. Slap some Fugazi on the MP3 player. Whip up a batch of chicken Marsala. Promise walnut brownies for dessert. Sit you across from me and it's the stuff of dreams."

Sudden silence sprouted between them, and Roxie felt an anxiety of a wholly different kind. "You can let go now," she whispered.

"What?"

"My hand. May I have it back? We're in the air. My takeoff terror has passed."

"Oh, yeah, sure." He let go of her hand.

She dropped her hot, damp palm into her lap and averted her gaze. Her pulse galloped. "Thanks," she said. "You make a good distraction from fear of flying."

Now all I need is something to distract me from the distraction.

The captain turned off the Fasten Seat Belt sign, and Roxie, anxious to put as much distance between herself and Dougal as she could get, decided to visit the lavatory. A splash of cold water in her face to calm her racing pulse. She unbuckled her seat belt and got to her feet. "Excuse me, may I slip by you?"

Dougal moved his long legs into the aisle just as the plane lurched. Roxie hissed in her breath. The plane pitched again, thrusting her forward onto his lap. His arms closed around her, Roxie's fanny snugged against his thighs. She peered into his face, glanced away, and then looked back again.

Sharp, dark eyes stared straight into her, holding her motionless. "Are you okay?" he asked, his voice sounding husky and strange as if someone was tightening a wire around his throat.

"What was that?" she asked.

"Turbulence. It'll be fine."

A sudden stillness settled over her. She sighed deeply and all the air fled her lungs. She felt a million different things at once. Safe, desired, happy, confused. The shock of recognition passed through her. He was a stranger and yet it was as if she'd known him her entire life. How could that be?

In that split second of surprise, she felt as if she'd met her match, identified the other half of life's jigsaw puzzle. She was like a lost traveler, wandering in a foreign land, who'd stumbled upon a field of flowers indigenous to her homeland. No, not just the flowers of her homeland, but the same glorious mix that once grew in her own backyard. She gave no thought to whether he was friend or foe. Her impulse was simply to rush to the sweet smells of home.

Roxie's heart surged toward Dougal, and she knew in that moment she'd totally lost all control. How in the hell was she going to pull off corporate espionage when all she could think about was pulling off Dougal Lockhart's clothes?

"YOU CAN LET GO OF ME NOW," Roxie said.

Dougal loosened his grip, and she struggled to get to her feet. The plane lurched again sending her right back into his lap, and a small gasp of surprise escaped those perfect pink lips. He wrapped his arms around her waist again. "Maybe you should just sit tight until we get through this turbulence."

Even as he said it, he had to clench his teeth to fight off his stirring erection. Getting a boner with her on his lap might be totally natural, but he was certain it would alarm her. It alarmed him. He was supposed to be in charge of passenger safety on this plane, not coming on to a guest.

He took a deep breath and immediately inhaled her heavenly scent. Her delicate aroma encircled his nose, played havoc with his brain cells. The fragrance, coupled with her body heat, slicked his mind with desire and he couldn't think of anything but her.

Bad idea. *Okay, no more breathing.*

She wriggled in his lap, and Dougal swallowed a groan. This was crazy. He had to put a stop to it. "Um, maybe we should get you back into your seat."

"But you said—"

"Buckle you down tight. That's what you need. Buckled down." Why had he said that? Now he had an image of her, seat belt resting against her lower abdomen, the buckle right at the level of her—

Stop it!

Before she could feel the erection he could no longer control, Dougal transferred her quickly into her seat, settled back against his own chair, plucked a glossy magazine from the pouch on the side and plunked it into his lap as camouflage. He prayed she hadn't spied the overt evidence of his desire. He cast a glance over at her. She stared at him, wide-eyed.

His pulse jumped. Her gaze searched his face for a long

moment. Stunning blue eyes, full of innocence. She smiled coyly, lowered her gaze and then turned to look out the window.

What was that look all about?

The plane jerked, shuddered. Several of the other passengers gasped out loud. Roxie splayed a hand at the base of her throat.

He rested a palm on her shoulder. "You hanging in there?"

The tremulous glint in her eyes told him she was frightened, but the firm jut to her chin suggested she was toughing it out. Her vulnerability tugged at him.

"Are you sure it's just turbulence?" she whispered.

Until Roxie had asked the question, he was almost positive the lurching of the plane was nothing more than turbulence, but now she had aroused his suspicion. Could there be something amiss with the aircraft?

He thought of the death threats Taylor had received. Immediately his mind conjured disturbing scenarios. Taylor had hired him because she feared someone might tamper with the planes, and he'd agree with her that the possibility existed. To that end, he'd been with the pilot when he'd done his preflight check, and Dougal had personally searched the private jet, but he wasn't a mechanic. An expert saboteur could have rigged something up that neither he nor the pilot had detected.

The plane vibrated.

This time the collective let out more than just gasps.

Concern for passenger safety got Dougal's mind off his attraction to Roxie and back on his job. He unbuckled his seat belt and stood.

"Is something wrong? You look worried."

"I'm going to speak with the pilot about the turbulence." He gave her a reassuring smile.

"Thank you." She exhaled an audible sigh.

Dougal made his way up the aisle toward the cockpit. He was forced to pause and brace himself each time the plane pitched like a boat in a tropical squall. He tapped on the cabin door with a coded knock and the copilot let him in.

"Problems?" he asked, shutting the door behind him.

"Something's wrong with the autopilot," said the pilot, Nicholas Peters, a heavy-browed, stern-faced man with jowls that hinted at Russian ancestry. "Every time we try to switch over the plane pitches."

Uneasiness rippled over Dougal. "Any idea what's causing the glitch?"

Peters frowned, shook his head.

"Do you think someone could have tampered with the autopilot?" Dougal recalled the detailed schematics of the plane's electrical system that had accompanied the most threatening of Taylor's letters.

"It's not likely," Peters hedged. "I'm ninety-nine-percent sure it's nothing more than a stuck valve."

It was that one percent Dougal worried about. The pilot's reassurance didn't lessen the thread of anxiety pulling across his shoulder muscles. "Should we turn back?"

"Not necessary," said the copilot, Jim Donovan. "We can fly manually. We've already contacted the control tower and reported the problem. They gave us the thumbs-up to continue on to London. It just means Nick and I'll have to work a little harder on the transatlantic flight. But it's nothing we can't handle."

That might be true, but Dougal was calling Taylor when they got to England and having her put a team of mechanics on the Bombardier, just to make sure there'd been no sabotage. Yes, he might be overreacting, but it was better to be safe than sorry.

"To keep from alarming the passengers, we'll blame it on turbulence. I was just about to make the announcement when you came in," Peters said, and then he hit the button that allowed him to deliver the message throughout the cabin. "Ladies and gentleman, sorry for the bumpy ride. We've hit a bit of turbulence, but we're taking her up a few thousand feet, and all should be clear from here on out, so sit back and enjoy the ride."

"Let me know if anything comes up that needs my input," Dougal said.

"Will do." Peters nodded.

Dougal made his way back down the aisle. Roxie looked at him with eyes that could break a man's heart. He stood there for a moment as if held in place by a wire strung from the middle of his back into the plane's ceiling, staring back, blood thick as paint chugging through his veins.

"Everything's okay," he said, forcing himself to slide into the seat beside her once more and noticing she had a death grip on the armrest. "You can relax."

Take your own advice, Lockhart.

"Thanks for checking," she murmured. "I feel better now." Soft, light, feminine, seductive, she possessed the sexiest speaking voice he'd ever heard.

Do not start that again, stop being so aware of her.

Far easier said than done. She wasn't the kind of woman you could choose to ignore.

"No problem," he croaked.

"Not everyone would have taken the trouble to reassure me."

Dougal could hardly think. Talk about eye candy. Perfectly arched eyebrows the same bewitching ebony shade as her hair. Long, lush lashes. A straight, slender nose with delicate nostrils. Her strawberry colored lips tipped up in a slight smile. Fascinating.

He fisted his hands. Roxie wasn't for him. For one thing he had a job to do, and for all he knew she could be a saboteur. Never mind that she looked sweet and innocent. She'd probably be sweet and innocent in bed, as well, and who needed that kind of sex? He liked his women experienced and uninhibited when it came to lovemaking. He didn't fancy himself as anyone's teacher.

Who cares? You're not going to find out what she's like in the sack. That would break all the rules.

Besides, clearly they came from different worlds. The girl-next-door types didn't mix well with burned-out Air Force captains who'd witnessed too much of the dark side of life. He'd seen terrorists' bombs take out entire villages, had watched women and children starving in refugee camps, had heard of other atrocities he didn't want to think about.

Yep, he was going to keep his libido locked up tight. No matter if he had to take a dozen cold showers a day until this trip was over. Not just for his sake, but for hers, as well.

3

HER BODY'S INVOLUNTARY reaction to the bothersome Mr. Lockhart worried Roxie more than she cared to admit. Not only that, but she was drawn to him on an emotional level—they had a lot in common. They liked the same music and the same food. And then there was that odd feeling she got whenever he touched her, as if she'd come home after a long journey.

Ever since he'd come back from the cockpit, she felt encased in a protective bubble, as if nothing could harm her as long as he was beside her. The thought was ridiculous, but she couldn't shake it. He was so tall and strong, so commanding and reassuring.

Some corporate spy you are. Seriously, stop thinking about the dude. Keep your mind in the game or you're going to get caught.

And if that happened, Mr. Langley would have no choice but to fire her and then who would put Stacy through school? Okay, no more noticing how those pants fit so snugly to his thighs. No more imagining what his chest looked like beneath that puffy-sleeved shirt. No more sliding surreptitious glances.

Her gaze drifted over him. Wow, but he was a muscular guy. Not bodybuilder physique, but hard clean through his core. He didn't have an ounce of fat on him. His forearms were sinuous. His powerful hands bore the nicks and scars of a man who'd done manual labor. His fingers were long, his nails clean and trimmed.

His compelling profile drew her attention. He possessed

firm, no-nonsense features. Sturdy, sharp nose, angular jaw that his beard couldn't hide, lips shaped like a crossbow.

He turned and caught her studying him. His dark brown eyes, intense as an eagle's, drilled right through her. His gaze was proud and commanding, yes, but there was more. She saw compassion beneath the rough edge and a kindness he couldn't cloak. She didn't question that he would catch her if she fell; he already had.

"How does a guy like you stay single?" she asked.

Good lord, why had she said that? She couldn't have anything to do with him. He worked for Eros. She was a spy for Getaway. Not an auspicious way to start a relationship.

You're not starting a relationship. Stop thinking like that!

He arched an eyebrow and the corners of his mouth tipped up. "Pardon?"

Great, now she was going to have to repeat the question. "How come a guy like you is still single?"

Shut up! What was wrong with her? Someone should put a ball gag in her mouth.

The eyebrow shot up higher. "A guy like me?"

She could hear the chuckle in his question. "You know. Good-looking, big, strong, all protector-y?"

"Protector-y?" Amusement lit his eyes.

"I'm just saying you don't look like your typical tour guide."

"No?"

"Not so much."

"What do I look like?"

"A cop or a soldier or a fireman. Something rugged and tough."

"What about a mercenary?"

The way he said *mercenary* lifted the hairs on her forearm. "Are you a mercenary?"

"Aren't we all?" His eyes darkened and all traces of humor left his face. "In one way or another?"

Panic squeezed her lungs, snuffing out her breath. Anxiously her hand stole to her chest and she pressed her palm against her heart. Did he somehow suspect what she was up to?

Don't freak out. There's no way he can know what you're doing.

No, but if she didn't stop overreacting she was going to give herself away. "Have you ever been married?" she asked, trying to appear supercool even as she felt sweat trickle down the back of her bra.

"No."

"Ever been engaged?"

"Almost. Twice."

"What happened?"

He shrugged. "The first time we were too young, kids fresh out of high school. Luckily we both came to our senses before it was too late. The second time…"

"The second time?" she prodded. Why didn't she just pluck that romance novel out of her purse and start reading and pretend he didn't exist?

Why? Because ignoring him would be like ignoring the sun in the Sahara. He was that dominant, that powerful. And yet she couldn't help feeling he hid a vulnerable side. Had he lost someone important to him? She thought of her parents and bit down on her bottom lip.

"Let's just say that I was blindsided."

"Oh." So his ex-fiancée had cheated on him? Who would betray a guy like this? If he was her man—

Don't even go there.

But how could any woman cheat on him? In spite of the theatrical costume he wore, Dougal Lockhart was, in every sense of the word, *masculine.*

"Have you ever been engaged?" he asked.

"Me?" She shook her head. "No, no."

"You say that like the idea is preposterous."

She almost opened her mouth and told him about her parents and Stacy, but then she bit down on her tongue. She was supposed to be a spy. Spies were quiet and unobtrusive. They didn't blather. They got *other* people to talk. She shrugged.

"Not the marrying kind?" he supplied.

"Something like that."

He unbuckled his seat belt. "I've enjoyed talking to you, Roxie, but now that we're airborne and the flight has evened out, I need to schmooze with the other guests. A tour guide's work is never done."

"Oh yeah, right, sure." *Dolt, you've made him uncomfortable.*

He got out of his seat, walked back to talk to the other passengers. Instantly the sound of flirtatious laughter drifted to Roxie's ears. Who was he talking to?

Don't do it, don't look over your shoulder.

She turned to peek over the back of her seat. Dougal was leaning down, talking to two gorgeous young women a few seats behind her. He was speaking in an old English accent that should have sounded dorky, but in his deep baritone it came off sexy as sin and had Roxie wishing she'd been born in sixteenth-century England.

One of the women wore a low-cut blouse, and she was doing all she could to make sure he got a good view of her ample cleavage. The other woman was gazing at his crotch and practically drooling. These women weren't subtle. They were making it perfectly clear what they were after.

Roxie gritted her teeth.

You're jealous….

She wasn't. She was embarrassed by the flagrant way the women were throwing themselves at him. She was peeved that he seemed to be having more fun talking to them than he'd had talking to her. She was…she was…

Oh hell, she was jealous.

Why him? Why now?

It was, she decided, Eros Airlines that had pumped her up. From the buttery leather seats cushioning her fanny, to the free alcohol the flight attendants started distributing throughout the cabin, to the way Eros provocatively dressed their tour guides. She thought of the brochure in her purse, recalled the opening blurb: *Eros: where all your fantasies come true.*

The fantasy had taken hold and made her long to behave in ways she would never behave back at home. Eros had woven a spell over her, and Roxie hadn't even been aware of the spinning. Until now. Until she tried to dissect why she was feeling the way she was—lusty, jealous, greedy and intrigued.

Make notes. You need to get this down.

She reached for her purse for a pen and paper, but stopped herself. What if Dougal came back and caught her making notes? She glanced over her shoulder again. He'd moved on down the aisle, leaving twittering females in his wake. Roxie rolled her eyes.

Jealous.

Okay, so she wanted him all for herself. She wanted to kiss those commanding lips, wanted to slide her arms around that honed waist, wanted…oh, the things she wanted.

Maybe it was more than just Eros's effective marketing campaign. Maybe part of this sudden and intense desire was due to the fact she'd put her personal life on hold for the past ten years while she raised her sister. Now that Stacy was in college, Roxie finally had the opportunity to explore her sexuality.

She'd had a couple of lovers, but both relationships had ended because she wouldn't put the men above what was best for her sister. After the last relationship went sour, she'd made a promise to herself that she'd avoid romantic entanglements until Stacy was grown. Now Stacy was a college freshman, and Roxie was free to pursue a romance.

This wouldn't be a romance. This would be all about having a good time. Great sex and nothing more.

The thought of it made Roxie's ears burn. She'd never had casual sex and she had no idea how to handle something like that.

She couldn't.

She wouldn't.

Could she?

ROXIE SPENT THE REMAINDER of the flight with her nose buried in her book, doing her best to ignore Dougal's presence beside her.

They landed at Gatwick Airport around six in the evening. The minute Roxie stepped onto British soil, a fresh surge of excitement pulsed through her. Even though she worked for an airline, she'd never traveled overseas. For one thing, she hadn't wanted to be away from Stacy that long. For another there was the money issue. Although she got free flights, lodging, transfers and food didn't come cheap. Every extra bit of cash she got she stashed aside for Stacy's college tuition.

While the group waited for their luggage to be unloaded, Roxie checked her watch and subtracted the time difference. Perfect timing to call. Back at home, her sister would be in between classes, headed for lunch.

"So," Stacy answered, "how's London?"

"Right now we're at the airport. Looks pretty much like any other airport."

"Meet any cute guys yet?"

"I just got off the plane."

"Planes have been known to harbor cute guys."

"Uh-huh," Roxie said, distracted by the sight of Dougal bending over to help an older woman with a ginormous, red plaid, attack-of-the-tartans-style suitcase. The man's butt looked absolutely ferocious in leather. Absentmindedly, Roxie traced the tip of her tongue over her lips.

"Rox? You still there?"

She blinked. "Um…yeah, sure still here."

"You didn't say anything for a couple of seconds. I thought I lost you."

Resolutely she turned her back on Dougal. "Nope, you didn't lose me. I'm here. Rock solid."

"Rock-solid Roxie," Stacy echoed. "So you never did answer my question. Meet any cute guys yet?"

"I'm not here to meet guys, I—" Roxie broke off. She hadn't told her sister the real reason she was in England. She'd let her believe she was taking a vacation. Guilt nibbled at her. "I'm here for adventure."

"Guys qualify as adventures."

Roxie made a dismissive noise.

"Come on," Stacy wheedled, "when was the last time you had a date?"

"I went out with Jimmy last week."

"Listen to yourself. Jimmy is sixty-five, our second cousin, and he took you to play bingo just because he thought you needed to get out of the house. That is not a date."

"I shaved my legs for it."

"Doesn't make it a date."

"You know I decided to put my dating life on hold since things with Marcus didn't work out."

"Um…" Stacy made a disapproving sound. "I was a freshman in high school when you were going out with Marcus."

"Okay, so I haven't had much of a love life lately, I—"

"You've never had much of a love life," her sister corrected. "I've dated more guys than you and I won't turn nineteen for another three months."

"How's school?" Roxie tried changing the subject.

"Same as it was yesterday. You've only been gone for a day, Rox. Chill out. Have some fun. Find a guy. Get laid, for heaven's sake."

"Stacy!"

"Don't act so scandalized. You're young, you're hot, and you deserve to have all kinds of adventures. I thought that was the reason you picked Eros. I mean, come on, why else would a single woman sign up for an erotic fantasy vacation if she wasn't interested in indulging her erotic fantasies?"

Why indeed? She couldn't cop to being a corporate spy, so she was left with admitting that she was here for romance.

"That's why I was so happy when you told me you'd booked yourself on the Romance of Britannia tour. I thought, at last, Roxie is going to get some sex."

It felt weird having this conversation with her sister. In many ways they were more like mother and daughter than siblings. Not only was Roxie ten years her senior, she was also a lot more conservative in her outlook. Where Roxie treasured a quiet evening at home with a bowl of popcorn and a romantic comedy on DVD, her sister was the life of the party who collected friends the way some people collected shoes.

"Let's say I'm second-guessing my reasons for being here. I worry about you being home alone." That was true enough.

Stacy sighed.

"What?" An airplane took off, the noise halting their conversation for a minute. "What is it?"

"It's time you stopped using me as an excuse for putting your life on hold. I appreciate everything you've done for me, Roxie, you know that, but I can't keep being the thing that's holding you back. I feel guilty and—"

"Don't ever feel guilty," Roxie said fiercely. "Raising you has been the joy of my life."

"I'm not saying this to hurt your feelings, but you need a new joy in your life. I'm grown. I have my own friends, my own interests."

The stabbing sensation deep within her heart hit Roxie. She knew everything her sister said was true, and yet, she couldn't let go of the identity she'd taken on when their parents had been killed. Empty-nest syndrome was a bitch.

"I want you to make me a promise," Stacy said.

"What is it?"

"You have to promise first."

"I can't promise until I know what it is I'm promising to do." Roxie hardened her chin. Around her everyone was picking up their luggage and heading toward the terminal, but she barely noticed.

"Promise me if an opportunity for a vacation fling comes up, you'll grab it with both hands."

"Stace…"

"I mean it. Promise me."

"Okay, all right, on the off chance that an opportunity for mad monkey sex with a handsome stranger presents itself, I promise I'll swing through the jungle."

Stacy laughed. "You don't have to do anything that kinky, sis. Just relax and let yourself have a good time. Go with the flow. You deserve it. For ten years you've been the ultragood girl. It's okay to be a little bit bad once in a while."

"How did you get so wise?"

"I had a great teacher."

A soft, mushy sensation replaced the lost, lonely feeling in her heart. She was so proud of her baby sister. A hand settled on her shoulder. A firm, masculine hand.

"Roxie." Dougal's voice was in her ear, her name on his tongue and his scent in her nostrils.

"Who was that?" Stacy asked.

"Huh?" She played dumb.

"You're the last one left," Dougal said.

Roxie looked over at him.

He held her luggage in one hand, pointed at the tour bus waiting beyond the chain-link fence surrounding the terminal gate. "We have to go."

"It's a guy. I definitely heard a guy's voice calling your name. You sly woman, you've already met someone!"

"Listen, Stacy, I have to let you go, the tour bus is getting ready to leave and—"

"Go, Roxie, get your groove on." Stacy chanted in a silly singsong voice. "Go, Roxie, get—"

"Goodbye, little sister. Don't forget to study while I'm gone."

"You do some studying of your own. My assignment to you—get up close and personal with physical anatomy. I'm rooting for you to get lucky with your new boyfriend."

"I'm not getting lucky and he's not my boyfriend."

Stacy made clucking noises. "Chicken."

"I'll call you later." Roxie closed her cell phone to find Dougal studying her intently. Had he overhead her conversation with Stacy?

"Let's roll." He held out his arm.

An edgy, warm feeling, thrilling and unwanted, pushed through her. She wasn't going to have an affair with him just because he was good looking and she hadn't had sex in years.

"I can walk myself to the bus, thank you very much." She snatched her suitcase from his hand and scurried toward the bus. She was just about to climb on when Dougal called out to her. "Oh, Roxie."

What now? She spun on her heels, still feeling hot all over. "What is it?"

"You're getting on the wrong bus."

AFTER HE MADE SURE ROXIE got on the right bus, Dougal spoke quickly to the Eros mechanics and told them to scour the plane for problems before letting it take to the air again. Then he placed a call to Taylor, but her cell phone went to voice mail, so he left her a message.

"Taylor, Dougal," he said. "There was a glitch with the autopilot on the plane. I put your mechanics on it. Nick Peters thinks it's nothing, but I…" He paused, looked toward the waiting bus, saw Roxie in profile at a window seat near the back. In all honesty could he really say he suspected the autopilot had been tampered with? It seemed like a simple problem. If someone was making good on their threats, they'd done a lousy job of it. "I think we should wait to hear from the maintenance crew before we make any snap judgments. I'll call you later."

He closed his cell phone and slipped it into his pocket just as Roxie's eyes met his. Her gaze was steady, but he saw a flicker of something inside those cool depths.

What was it and why couldn't he shake the feeling she was up to something? She was the most unlikely of suspects.

She smiled at him then, tentative and sweet, and gave him a quick wave. And damn if he couldn't help smiling and waving back. He got a soft, achy sensation in the pit of his stomach.

Aw hell, this feeling wasn't good. Not good at all.

THE TOUR BUS TOOK THEM to the Eros resort just outside Stratford-upon-Avon. Stubborn gray clouds hung in the sky, and even inside the bus the air smelled of impending rain and city soot. The driver wore rain boots and had a black umbrella stashed under the dashboard. Dougal sat up front behind the driver and narrated the sights as they motored through the crowded streets of downtown London. Outside the window the landscape looked just like in the pictures and movies she'd seen. Imagine. She was here. England.

Roxie found herself sitting across from twin sisters, while the seat beside her remained empty. That was just fine with her.

She didn't need a traveling companion, but then she thought wistfully of Stacy and wished her sister could have joined her on this adventure.

Yeah, drag your sister along while you commit corporate espionage. What fun. Not exactly the actions of a stellar role model.

A fresh stab of conscience had Roxie worrying her bottom lip between her teeth. If Stacy's entire future didn't depend on her salary, she'd call off the whole thing.

"Hi," said the twin sitting on the outside seat. She extended her hand across the aisle to Roxie. "I'm Samantha, but everyone calls me Sam."

The other twin leaned over her sister to extend her own hand. "And I'm Jessica, but everyone calls me Jess."

She shook their hands. "Hi, Sam, hi, Jess. I'm Roxie."

"Nice to meet you, Roxie," Sam and Jess said in unison.

The twins were gorgeous, their elegant thinness a sharp contrast to Roxie's rounded curves. They possessed matching noses so perfect Roxie wondered if rhinoplasty was involved, and they had high, dramatic cheekbones enhanced by artful application of blush. They looked as if they'd stepped from the cover of a fashion magazine with their stylish bobbed blond hair and designer jeans. Beside them, she felt frumpy and out of place in her summery yellow sundress.

Sam leaned across the aisle and lowered her voice. "You are so lucky."

"Lucky?"

"You got to sit next to Shakespeare for the entire flight." Jess nodded toward Dougal.

Roxie hadn't felt lucky, she'd felt...what had she felt? *Unsettled* was the best adjective she could come up with. "I guess there's an upside to traveling alone. The tour guides take pity on you."

"So tell us," Sam breathed. "What's he like?"

Roxie shrugged. "He's just a guy."

Jess's eyes widened as if she'd said something blasphemous. "Oh, no, he's not just a guy. Look at the muscles on him. And those aren't pretty-boy, gym-induced muscles. This guy does something rugged. Rock climbing, I'm guessing."

They all three turned to look at Dougal. He was busy pointing out Big Ben.

Yes, okay, the guy was gorgeous, but jeez, people. It wasn't as if they could take him home and handcuff him to their bed or anything.

Although Jess and Sam looked as if they wouldn't mind giving it a try.

"Skiing," Sam said. "You got a guess, Roxie? Or do you already know our hunky tour guide's sport of choice?"

Roxie cocked her head and studied him—the pugilistic set to his shoulders, the broadness of his chest, and she'd already seen the scars on his knuckles. "Boxing?"

"Ooh." Jess giggled. "Astute observation. I'll bet you're right."

At that moment, Dougal turned his head and stared straight at Roxie. Awareness buzzed through her body. His eyes burned black, hot. Unable to bear the scrutiny, she fumbled his gaze.

"*Mmm, mmm.*" Jess made a noise of appreciation. "That man is sweet."

"How come you're traveling alone?" Jess asked Roxie, after she and her sister were finished ogling Dougal. "Did a friend stand you up?"

Roxie shook her head. "I needed a private getaway."

"Ah." Sam nodded. "Busted romance."

Roxie started to correct her, but then decided to let Sam believe what she wanted to believe. She simply gave her a smile that said, "I'm putting up a brave front."

"You poor thing," Jess said. "I went through a breakup six

months ago. It's hard, but you know what? Honestly, it's the best thing that ever happened to me."

"It is." Sam nodded. "After Jess caught her fiancé doing the bedroom rumba with another woman just days before the wedding, she became a lot more assertive, and as a result of her changing attitude she got a big promotion at work."

"I stopped looking for love and just started having fun," Jess said. "Freed me up like you wouldn't believe."

"I'm envious of the easy way you approach romance." Roxie shifted her weight, did her best not to look in Dougal's direction.

"Oh, believe me," Jess said, "this is not about romance. This is about nothing but hot, hot sex."

The self-satisfied note in Jess's voice plucked a twinge of envy inside Roxie. In all honesty, she'd never been overly impressed with sex. Maybe she'd just never done it correctly.

"You've never had a casual fling?" Jess asked.

Roxie shook her head.

"Seriously, woman. It's the most liberating thing in the world. Discovering your sexual power, knowing it doesn't have to lead to anything more than it is. Glorious. Freeing."

"Really?"

"As long as you keep your heart out of the fray, and you're with the right guy, it can be mind-blowing."

"How do you keep your heart out of the fray?"

"That is a good question and it's important to prepare for it."

"I'm listening."

"First off, don't swap too many personal details about each other. No sharing intimate secrets. If you learn a lot of little details about each other, the next thing you know you start caring about them. That's not so good for a healthy casual fling," Jess advised.

"Thanks for the advice."

Sam reached over to touch Roxie on the shoulder. "Hey,

since you're all by yourself would you like to hang out with Jess and me? We'd love to have you."

The invitation shouldn't have pleased her as much as it did, and she should have thought of a graceful way to bow out. She didn't need to pal around with anyone on the tour. The more inconspicuous she made herself, the better. But she was flattered. More than that, she wanted to hang out with Jess and Sam. They seemed like a lot of fun.

"We understand if you say no," Jess hurried to add. "Since you've caught the attention of our tour guide. He hasn't stopped looking at you this entire ride. You might want to spend your time hanging out with him."

Roxie didn't dare turn her head to meet his stare. "I'm not interested in a romance."

"Who said anything about a romance?" Jess made a purring noise. "I'd just love to have a fling with him. If you're really not interested that is."

Roxie couldn't bring herself to say that she wasn't interested. There was that damned jealousy again. Illogical and annoying.

"Anyway," Sam said, "we'll save a place for you at dinner, unless Mr. Handsome Man over there sweeps you off your feet."

All in all, Roxie didn't have many friends. Of course Stacy was her best friend. There was Magda at work, and Mrs. Kingsly who lived across the street, and Susan, the checker at the supermarket. But they were all over thirty-five and married with children. She didn't really have anyone her own age she could relate to.

You can't hang out with them. You're here under false pretenses. Tell them you appreciate the offer, but you have other plans. Tell them you're hoping for a romance and you're worried guys will be less likely to approach women in a group than on their own.

Tell them…

She opened her mouth to use one of her excuses, but instead she spoke from her heart. "Sure, I'd love to hang out with you guys. Thanks for asking."

4

THE EROS RESORT WAS a hedonist's wet dream.

From the outside the place was picturesque. The main building was a replica of a sixteenth-century castle perched on a sloping green hill overlooking the river Avon, complete with its own moat. Inside the castle grounds, snug little thatch cottages were lumped like gray-green turtles along a unifying cobblestone path. The moment Roxie stepped off the bus in the thickening drizzle, she was hit with the acute sensation that her world had just cracked wide-open and she'd stepped into a fairy tale.

She tried not to stare openmouthed, but it was a bit difficult when they were met at the door by a cadre of bellmen all dressed in the same romantic sixteenth-century style as Dougal and speaking in the tongue of that time. They flirted and winked. Clearly it was their intention to make the guests feel both lusty and welcome.

"Let me take that for you, milady." A dashing bellboy, looking for all the world like Romeo Montague from Shakespeare's most famous play, bowed and relieved Roxie of her suitcase.

Jess and Sam tittered as similarly outfitted bellmen took their luggage.

The five-star rated resort's lobby was a sight to behold. It looked both old world and elegant and deadly romantic with huge vases of fresh-cut roses, Stargazer lilies and gladiola resting on highly polished antique tables. The air was scented with their sweet fragrance. The sofas and chairs placed strategically throughout the cavernous lobby were upholstered in rich matching fabrics of cranberry and gold. In the middle of the lobby was a grand fireplace made of gray lintels carved with quatrefoils and spanned by a four-centered arch with molded decorations and a frieze topping the lintels. Over the mantel hung a stately coat of arms.

Stenciled on the walls in gilded script lettering outlined in black were famous quotes about love. Her gaze traveled around the room as she read the slogans.

Naughty, naughty. Roxie pressed her fingers against her mouth, suppressing a grin. Just then a pretty female assistant dressed in a gauzy floor-length gown and a crown of braided flowers wandered over to distribute small flutes of complimentary ice wine to the thirsty travelers queuing up at the registration desk.

Roxie sipped her drink. She was delighted to discover it tasted like golden honey, sweet and thick and pure. She didn't imbibe often, and just a couple of swallows produced a warm glow that drew her deeper into the magical atmosphere. Porter Langley had no idea what he was getting into if he set his cap at competing with Taylor Corben's lavish destination resorts.

While they were waiting their turn to check in, an older woman, dressed in the same Tudor style as the young assistant, passed out a form printed on white card stock. "Hi, my name is Lucy Kenyon and I'm the entertainment director. To help tailor this experience to meet your needs, I'd appreciate it if you'd fill out this questionnaire and leave it with me."

Roxie took the form and read through the short list of questions. Most of them were centered on her personal likes and dislikes. She answered as best she could, but paused when she got to the end.

"What are your hobbies, special skills or talents that you still love but haven't had time for lately?" Jess read the last line on her card out loud just as Roxie poised her pen to answer it.

The question hit home. It had been so long since she'd gotten to do the things she'd given up after her parents' tragic car accident. Becoming a surrogate parent at eighteen had caused her to grow up quickly. She felt a tug of emotion in her belly, a sadness mixed with yearning for everything she'd lost. She didn't regret giving up leisurely pursuits for Stacy, but she did miss them, and she hadn't really realized it until now.

"Oh gosh," Sam said. "I guess we're spoiled. We pretty much do everything we love."

"What about you, Roxie?" Jess asked. "What are you putting down?"

Roxie doodled on the edge of the form, remembering how she used to enjoy acting. She'd even toyed with the idea of majoring in drama when she went to college.

Except she'd never gotten to college.

"I used to enjoying acting," she admitted.

Sam nudged Jess. "You used to be able to whistle 'Battle Hymn of the Republic.' That's a special skill."

Jess rolled her eyes. "It's not one I want to revisit. Anything else you used to like to do, but don't get to do now, Roxie?"

"Fencing."

Sam blinked. "You like putting up fences?"

"No, dork," Jess told her twin. "You know, *en garde*." She illustrated with a badly executed fencing pose. "Like Zorro."

"Ah, that kind of fencing." Sam nodded.

"My father qualified for the Olympic fencing team when he was twenty," Roxie shared with her new friends. "But my mother had just found out she was pregnant with me and he chose not to go."

"That's so sweet and romantic," Sam said.

"Fencing was one activity we did together, just he and I."

And she hadn't picked up a foil since his death. Roxie blinked, swallowed past the lump in her throat and wrote down acting and fencing in answer to the final question.

"Oh, I know," Jess said. "We used to go with Dad on stake-outs. Let's put down sleuthing."

"Your father was a cop?" Roxie asked.

"P.I.," Sam explained and frowned at her twin. "Sleuthing isn't going to come in handy around here."

"How do you know they're not going to have one of those mystery theater events? We'd kick ass."

"I'll take those, thanks." Lucy Kenyon smiled and plucked the forms from Roxie, Jess and Sam. "And when you're finished with registration, please feel free to visit the costume room. Many of our guests enjoy dressing up for the events."

"You have a costume room?" Roxie asked. She loved role-playing.

"We do." Lucy indicated an area at the back of the lobby before she turned to greet new arrivals.

"Wow." Jess craned her neck upward. "Get a load of that ceiling."

Roxie glanced up and gulped. While the lobby was pure class, the ceiling was pure erotica, albeit tastefully executed. Near-naked men and women frolicked overhead in what could be best described as an orgy about to happen. Lots of succulent fruit was involved in the suggestive tableau—hard yellow-green bananas, plump plums, curvy pears, ripe red strawberries, brilliantly orange kumquats. She could almost taste the sinful fruit salad.

Embarrassed, she jerked her gaze away from the sight and stepped back only to crash into someone behind her.

A masculine hand went to her elbow. "Steady."

She spun around, found herself face-to-face with Dougal, her cheeks scalding hot. "Um…I…er…"

Immediately her gaze was drawn to his enigmatic eyes. Did the man have any idea how compellingly sexy he looked in the white loose-sleeved silk shirt that floated over his broad masculine shoulders and those snug-fitting leather breeches that enhanced even more fascinating parts of his anatomy? Roxie shook her head, determined to empty her mind of such inappropriate thoughts.

He took a step closer and she caught a whiff of his scent—leather, sandalwood soap and man. She couldn't help noticing the softness of his windblown hair. She suppressed the disconcerting urge to reach out and tame the unruly strands with her fingers just to see if it was as soft as it looked.

"It is a bit overwhelming at first glance." His eyes twinkled.

"Huh?"

"The castle, the lobby, the ceiling."

"Um, yeah," she mumbled, not knowing what else to say, not sure she could or should say anything more. For one vivid flash of her imagination she'd pictured herself and Dougal joining the madcap couples on the ceiling, and that thought escalated the blistering of her cheeks. The fantasy overloaded her senses. Her muscles tensed. Her heart beat faster. It was in that moment she realized the stereo system was very quietly, almost subliminally, playing a seductive sound track of twin heartbeats beneath the lyrical flute music.

Looking into Dougal's eyes, hearing the steady strum-strum-strumming sound, smelling flowers, tasting fruit and ice wine, feeling his fingers at her elbow sent her emotions into tumult.

The primal music became an exclamation mark, underscoring her befuddlement, igniting her feminine passion. Her desire tasted of hot musk. The drumming altered with the changes inside her, growing deeper, more intricate and multifaceted. She felt this sudden and unexpected need everywhere—in her toes, in the pads of her fingertips, in the muscles of her buttocks. She'd never experienced anything like it and the air left her lungs on one expanded sigh.

He was standing way too near her, but she didn't know how to tell him to back off. If he were to dip his head down to say something to her, his lips would be kissably close. She retreated a step, her thoughts a chaotic tumble of craziness.

"Next," called the clerk behind the check-in desk.

"You're up."

Dazed, Roxie blinked at him. "What?"

Dougal nodded toward the desk. "You're next."

"Oh, right."

The spell was shattered. Dougal smiled and then turned and walked away.

AN HOUR LATER, DOUGAL entered the ballroom for the eight o'clock dinner seating. It bothered him that he hadn't been able to stop thinking about Roxie. What was it about her that had so slipped underneath his skin? He thought about her scent, delicate and sweet. Some kind of flower. Honeysuckle? Or maybe those white flowers that grew on those thick waxy-leaved trees in the South.

The way she looked at him in the lobby, wide-eyed and blushing, caused his gut to clench and his cock to harden. This was crazy. He was crazy. He was on assignment. He had to get his head in the game.

You're just falling victim to the Eros experience—the subliminal music, the suggestive paintings, the flowers, the candlelit sconces lining the hallways. Snap out of it.

As a tour guide, Dougal was expected to mingle with the guests, and he found himself seated at a table with two busty women who sat on either side of him and kept stroking his forearms. He felt like a piece of hamburger, but he endured it for the job, his gaze going around the room, looking for anything or anyone suspicious.

And then his eyes lighted on Roxie. She was seated at a table with the twin sisters she'd sat next to on the bus, looking up at one of the waiters, a man dressed in a troubadour costume. She was asking questions about the menu. The man leaned over, his shoulder brushing against Roxie's, his stare traveling straight down the cleavage of her dress.

Dougal suppressed an overwhelming urge to vault over the table and snap the man's neck like a twig. The impulse was so strong that he sucked in a whistle of air. *Whoa!* What was this all about?

Roxie smiled and handed her menu to the waiter, who went on to the next guest.

Dougal unclenched his jaw, said something to the woman on his right while the woman on his left ran her fingers up his arm. This kind of attention made him uncomfortable. He glanced at Roxie again.

She looked like dessert in that flowing period-piece costume and she had her sleek black hair pinned up off her shoulders, making her look even younger and sweeter. No woman her age could be that innocent. Her ingenuousness heightened his mistrust, at the same time his gut told him, *She's a keeper.*

This feeling unnerved him and that was reason enough to raise his guard, but it was more than that. It was the damned sexual attraction that scared him most. There was something so disarmingly appealing about this woman and being disarmed was not a position he ever wanted to be in again.

Their eyes met—*wham.*

He smiled, nodded.

She smiled back.

They held each other's gazes for too long, and then they both veered away at the same moment like two back alley drag racers with not enough bravado to see their game of chicken play out to a conclusion.

A fresh surge of blood rushed his groin. Something inside Dougal stirred and it wasn't just his dick. Something he really didn't want to identify. He took a swig from the mug of beer in front of him.

A hand on his shoulder caused him to jump. He yanked his head around and saw the recreational events director, Lucy Kenyon, standing beside him. Lucy was a lithe brunette in her early forties. He'd checked her credentials as he had all of Taylor's employees. She was recently divorced, her kids grown, and she was finally experiencing her lifelong dream of living in England. Like the rest of the staff, she was dressed in a costume representative of the Tudor era. "We're ready to start the entertainment portion of the evening, Dougal."

He put down his napkin, scooted back his chair and followed Lucy to the stage, feeling like a condemned man on his way to the gallows. This was the part of the assignment he dreaded. Dougal was loath to admit it, even to himself, but he was nervous. They'd practiced the skit, but this was the first time he'd performed in front of a live audience and his childhood issues with stage fright rumbled to life. Suddenly he was eight years old again, playing an onion in a play about the four food groups.

The ugly memory came rushing back as he climbed the steps of the stage behind the red velvet curtain. Eight years old and he'd barely been able to see through the eyeholes in the rotund, papier-mâché onion. It had smelled like paste and plaster and body odor from the previous kid who'd worn it.

Before the play, Dougal's mother had given him ginger ale to calm his stomach. The bubbly taste was sparkly sharp on his tongue, but he hadn't been the least bit calmed. Inside the dank, mushroomlike costume, he could barely hear what the narrator at the microphone had been telling the audience, but he could hear their laughter. His palms had been sweaty, his heart knotted tight in his chest, his knees wobbled as the spotlight had fallen on him and he'd looked out into the sea of faces.

They were all laughing and staring at him, just waiting for him to mess up.

And mess up he had.

When it was his turn to extol the benefits of five servings of fruits and vegetables a day, he'd opened his mouth and puked all over his sneakers. He'd had an aversion to onions ever since.

Ah, good times. Good times.

Why had he agreed to Taylor's insane plans?

For the money.

Oh yeah, there was that. Starting a private air marshal enterprise took a lot of time and money. A client like Taylor would cinch his reputation. It was time to face the horror of his oniony past and put it to rest once and for all.

"Find one person to focus on," Lucy whispered, somehow sensing his stage fright. Was he that transparent? "Perform only for that one person and it will calm the butterflies."

Right. Gotcha. He'd give it a try.

The sketch they were set to perform was a riff on the legend that Shakespeare left his second-best bed to his wife, Anne Hathaway. Anne had been eight years older than her famous husband. For entertainment purposes, Lucy was laughingly playing Anne as a sixteenth-century cougar. Dougal had the part of the Bard. The skit wasn't remotely historically correct, but rather it was designed as a bit of raunchy humor to kick off the Romance of Britannia two-week tour and set the tone for the adventure the guests were embarking upon.

At the microphone stood the emcee, a lean, long-haired young man dressed like a court jester. He welcomed the guests and then began setting up the scenario for the spoof.

Dougal took a deep breath. *Come on, you've been in charge of guarding fighter jets. You can handle this goofy piece of fluff with your eyes closed.* Closing his eyes? Was that an option? Right now dental surgery sounded like a more appealing alternative.

The curtain parted. The audience applauded. His stomach pitched.

In the center of the stage sat a four-poster king-size bed decked out with a baroque crimson comforter and matching pillows. It looked like whorehouse bedding. Lucy recited her line, and then she shot a glance at Dougal.

His brain froze. He couldn't think. He opened his mouth but no words came out.

Find one person to focus on.

He didn't plan it. How could he plan it when he couldn't think? His gaze swung through the audience and lighted on Roxie.

Perform only for her.

Roxie held Dougal's stare. To his surprise, the words that had been locked inside his head suddenly fell glibly from his lips. "Forsooth, madam, pray what shall I leave thee when I die? Perhaps my second-best bed?"

Lucy's advice had worked. Who knew it would be so simple?

"And which of these trollops shall inherit this, your finest bed?" Lucy waved at the bed and sneered. Then she comically narrowed her eyes and glanced out over the crowd as if they were her rivals for Shakespeare's affections.

"It shall be your choice," Dougal replied, his attention still locked on Roxie. "Select the lass with whom I will be sharing my bed."

"Three in a bed seems a bit crowded, husband," Lucy replied saucily. "Perhaps she and I will kick you out."

That line caused a titter to run through the crowd.

"Or perhaps," Lucy went on, "I shall select a lad to join us."

"Only a lass will do, woman." Dougal recited his lines.

"Pick her and pick her quick or I won't even leave you my second-best bed."

"As you wish." Lucy started down the steps to select someone from the audience to bring up onstage and a dozen hands shot up to volunteer.

"Pick me, pick me," someone called out.

"I'd love to spend time in Shakespeare's bed," said someone else.

"I'll whisper dirty limericks in his ear," hollered the audacious redhead who'd made yummm-o noises at Dougal on the airplane.

Lucy threaded her way through the tables, ignoring all the women who were straining to volunteer. She continued to speak her lines as she and Dougal bantered back and forth.

She stopped at Roxie's table.

And that's when Dougal realized Lucy was going to bring her up onstage.

5

"HI," ANNE HATHAWAY SAID.

Roxie recognized her as Lucy Kenyon, the woman who'd passed out the questionnaires in the lobby when they'd first arrived. She gulped and realized everyone at the table was watching her. Who was she kidding? Everyone in the *room* was watching her, even Dougal. For crying out loud, there was a spotlight on her. "Um…hi."

Lucy leaned in closer. "I saw on our survey that you enjoy acting."

"Yes," she replied, not knowing what else to say.

"Would you like to have some fun?"

They were magic words. Roxie knew that she should say no, but in that moment, all the joy of being onstage rushed through her. She recalled the fun she used to have performing at her parents' dinner theater, and remembered her role as the lead in her high school's production of *Romeo and Juliet.* In the school's history, no freshman had ever been given the lead role before her.

Roxie couldn't help smiling even as she said, "I don't know the lines."

"That's what we want, off-the-cuff improv. Come on," Lucy coaxed. "It'll be fun."

"Go on." Sam nudged her.

"You get to be onstage with Shakespeare," Jess pointed out. "Go for it, woman."

Roxie hesitated, but only for a moment. The ham in her took over and she nodded.

"Wonderful." Lucy held out her hand to Roxie and led her to the stage.

Her heart was pounding, but the minute she was facing the audience, exuberance embraced her. It had been so long since she'd done something solely for herself and she felt liberated.

"Lie down on this bed, fair maiden," Anne instructed, patting the mattress with a naughty gleam in her eyes. "And pray tell us your impression of my husband's best bed."

Giddily Roxie slid onto the bed and lay back against the pillows. The silky material of the pink, flower-print Renaissance frock she'd picked out from the costume room rubbed erotically against her skin. The tight bodice pulled across her nipples, causing them to bead beneath her camisole. Belatedly she realized she should have worn a bra instead.

"Wife," Shakespeare aka Dougal said, "you have chosen a comely lass."

"I did so for the benefit of my eyes, sir, not thine own." Anne gave Roxie a seductive look.

"However, wife, I am enjoying your feast." Dougal was looking at Roxie as if she were dipped in chocolate. He angled his head, licked his lips.

The crowd chuckled.

"So, maiden—" Anne swept across the stage "—what is thy opinion of the master's bed?"

Relishing her role, Roxie bounced up and down. The bedsprings creaked loudly. "'Tis a bit loud, milady. Might it wake the children?"

"Ah," said Dougal. "Shouldn't children learn that squeaky bedsprings are simply a part of grown-up life?"

"It's a bit too hard, as well," Roxie observed, flopping about on the mattress for effect.

"I told him it was too hard." Anne looked pointedly at Shakespeare's crotch, inducing catcalls from the audience.

Shakespeare and Anne bickered back and forth over the prone Roxie, each line of dialogue filled with ribald statements and sexy innuendo. Roxie rolled her eyes and heaved exaggerated sighs over their squabbling. "Married couples," she said as an aside to the audience.

The more she hammed it up, the louder the laughter grew. She was aware of—and exalting in—the fact that she was stealing the show.

Anne Hathaway said something to Shakespeare, but he didn't answer. A momentary silence fell over the crowd. Roxie turned her head to see Dougal staring at her as if they were the only two people in the room.

The expression on his face stole her breath. Her pulse skittered, and she felt twin dots of heat rise to her cheeks. She pursed her lips and crossed her arms chastely over her chest. It was as if he'd stripped her stark naked with his inscrutable gaze.

Lucy repeated her line, nudging him in the side with her elbow.

"Um…er…" Dougal sputtered.

"I can see the fetching vixen has stolen your tongue, husband," Anne said.

"No vixen, she," Dougal said, finally finding his voice. "But she is the very muse that moves my soul."

As Dougal stared into her eyes, Roxie felt as if the words were suddenly, oddly, illogically true. Her body grew heavy with sexual awareness and she felt herself go slick between her thighs. She gulped, disoriented.

Shake it off. What are you doing?

A corporate spy should fly under the radar. Getting up onstage was not the way to keep a low profile. But while her professional side berated her for this dumb move, her personal side was secretly reveling, having fun, doing the unexpected.

That is, until Dougal walked across the stage and plunked down on the bed, never breaking eye contact with her. He was beside her again as if he belonged there, turning her on.

She'd had daydreams like this, midnight reveries. Imaging herself a throwback to the Renaissance era. Such a romantic epoch filled with great art and music and the concept of chivalry. Dougal was the embodiment of her sexual fantasies.

Oh, dear. She couldn't tear her gaze off him. What to do? What to do? And here she'd thought falling into his lap on the plane had been erotic. But *this* was a hundred times more intense. They were side by side.

On a mattress.

Lying mere inches apart.

With a roomful of people watching their every move.

She could feel the power of his muscular body underneath his costume. She appreciated the natural mahogany highlights in his neatly trimmed beard. Surely no man in history had ever looked so manly in snug, black leather pants, a billowy white poet's shirt and knee-length black boots.

Eat your heart out, William Shakespeare.

The shadow falling over his face lent his expression a darkly dangerous air that was so damned sexy the hairs on her forearm lifted in response. One close-up glance at his angular mouth and all she could think about was kissing him. Her breathing quickened and her heart tripped over itself.

The collective laughed in response to something Anne Hathaway had said as she tromped in mock fury away from the bed, reminding Roxie where she was. Why had she agreed to come up onstage? Ego? The opportunity to live out her childhood fantasy of becoming an actress? To recapture her past? A chance to be near Dougal again?

Roxie feared the third option was the most accurate. What

was it about the man that made her want to live out a very X-rated *adult* fantasy?

"Forsooth," Anne called out to the audience, hand clasped to her bosom. "You are all my witnesses. Look upon my husband and see how he stares at the temptress. Has she not cast such a spell on him that he is left both speechless and brainless?"

Dougal looked stunned, as if he, too, had forgotten where he was and what he was supposed to be doing. Immediately he leaped from the bed, hair tousled and shirt askew. He placed a hand at the nape of his neck and stared down at Roxie, then quickly shifted his attention to Lucy.

"You are right, wife, I have been bewitched," he exclaimed.

"Trollop." Anne pointed an accusing finger at Roxie. "You have stolen the bed that should have been rightfully mine."

Okay. This wasn't fair. Roxie didn't have any lines and she had no way to know what was expected of her.

Improvise.

"Perhaps, milady," Roxie dared, going up on her knees in the middle of the bed, "if you had but satisfied your husband in this very bed, then he would not seek solace within my arms."

Both Shakespeare and his wife turned to stare at her, while the audience hooted with glee.

Roxie grinned at Dougal.

He grinned back, clearly enjoy her improvisational skills. "She has a point, good wife."

Anne looked a bit confused as what to say next. Roxie's input had knocked the skit off its trajectory. "All I want," Anne said at last, "is what's rightfully mine."

"Your husband?" Dougal said, stepping across the stage toward Anne with his arms outstretched.

"My bed," Anne cried, made a comical face and hopped onto the mattress beside Roxie.

The crowd dissolved into guffaws.

Dougal shrugged, raised his palms to the audience as if to say, "Easy come, easy go," and then held his hand out to Roxie. "Take the bed, wife, and I will take my muse."

Roxie didn't take his hand.

Dougal repeated his line, wriggled his eyebrows at her and added, "Come along, Muse."

Swept away by the thrill of performance, feeling decidedly impish, Roxie collapsed against the pillows. "My lord," she said. "This mattress is too desirable to leave."

"I thought it was too hard."

"Perhaps I was hasty in my judgment. For now it feels just right."

"Muse!" he bellowed and strode toward the bed, hand still outstretched. "Come here at once."

Excitement welled up, pushed against Roxie's chest, sent tingles shooting out through her nerve endings.

"Go get her, Shakespeare," a woman in the crowd yelled out.

"Shoot for the ménage à trois, Willie," countered a man.

Anne flashed a suggestive look at the audience that said she was intrigued by the prospect.

Shakespeare stopped, pivoted on his heel and peered out at the gathered guests. "Some men are foolish enough to think they can handle more than one woman at a time. I, however, am smart enough to know it's best to be a one-muse man."

"What about me?" Anne lamented.

"You, milady, have not been so much muse as nag," Shakespeare answered.

That brought fresh laughter.

Shakespeare turned his attention back to Roxie. "Now, Muse, come along, I have a sonnet in want of being written."

"What?" Roxie crossed her arms over her chest. "I do all the work and you get all the credit? The deal does not sound so fetching to me. How about this? I write my own sonnet."

"He gets bossy like this," Anne interjected. "Is his best bed really worth putting up with his high-handedness?"

"I need you, Muse." Dougal's words sounded so heartfelt that Roxie's pulse quickened. He extended his hand. "Pray, do not abandon me."

"He'll abandon *you,*" Anne warned, studying her nails with a nonchalant expression. "Next thing you know, it'll be a younger, prettier muse booting you out of bed."

"Don't listen to her," he said. "She's jealous."

Just like that, Roxie's improvisational skills evaporated. She whipped her head around to look at Anne, searching for a clue as to what to say next. Anne shrugged. Her expression said, *You're on your own.* Roxie was suddenly aware that every eye in the ballroom was on her, waiting to see what she'd do next. The urge to flee smacked her hard.

"Come." Dougal reached out; his hand barely grazed her knuckles and yet she felt blindsided.

Helpless to deny him, she rested her palm in his hand and he tugged her to her feet. His eyes hooked on hers, and she could not look away no matter how much she might desire to do so. Then, in his spine-tingling, baritone voice, Dougal began to recite a Shakespearean sonnet.

She knew the verse. She'd been forced to memorize it as part of a high school English assignment. Sonnet number twenty-one: "So is it not with me as with that Muse."

Kismet.

Dougal said a line, and then Roxie jumped in with the next one. His eyes lit up. They went back and forth with perfect timing as if they'd practiced this duet for weeks. He was holding her hands and they were staring deeply into each other's eyes and it was pure magic. This shared verbal inter-mingling was simply the most erotic thing she'd ever done with her clothes on.

The audience went wild for it.

"Woot!" she heard Jess holler. "Rock on, Roxie."

"Shake it, Willie!" Sam shouted.

Roxie recited the last line in a throaty whisper.

Dougal's jaw tightened. His chest muscles—readily visible through the deep V of the undone buttons on his shirt—flexed. The pulse at the hollow of his throat strengthened, slowed. He drew in a deep breath and slowly exhaled it as if by controlling his breathing he could control other responses.

Her body reacted to his physical clues. A warm gush of awareness oozed through her skin already heated by the overhead spotlights. She hadn't realized it until now, but the entire time they'd been reciting the sonnet, they'd been inching closer and closer to each other. Mostly unconscious of what she was doing, Roxie ran her tongue over her lips, tasting the poetic beauty of the sonnet.

His fingers were interlaced with hers. When had that happened? The tips of his leather boots were touching her sandals. Barely an inch of space existed between them. Their hip bones were almost touching, his chest so close she fancied she could hear his beating heart, and then realized it was her own heart she heard pounding with alarming power.

He glanced down. Her gaze followed his and she saw the tightness across the front fly of his pants.

This was insanity. They were total strangers. Not to mention that they were onstage in front of dozens of people with spotlights trained on them. Yet all Roxie could think about was throwing her arms around Dougal's neck to see if his mouth tasted as good as it looked.

Before she had a chance to do something rash, though, he took the reins. He slid an arm around her waist and pulled her tightly against him. She saw his eyes darken with desire, and she wondered if her own were undergoing the same changes.

The next thing she knew, they were kissing.

DOUGAL HAD FOUND HIMSELF lost in a fairy tale—the audience disappeared, Anne vanished, the spotlight no longer existed, the stage faded away. The only thing left in his world was *her.*

It was hard to say who made the first move. It was simultaneous really. When Roxie pulled his head down to meet her lips, Dougal breathed in the taste of her and tightened his grip around her waist. He'd been aching to kiss her from the moment he'd seen her in the plane, and damn if he didn't just let it happen.

She tasted as good as she looked. Better even. Her flavor was fresh and lemony and sensational. Initially, kissing her made him think of his mother's kitchen—warm and safe and comfortable. But underneath that soft comfort roused a stronger, more primal instinct.

Lust. Hot and heavy and intense.

And in spite of the wide-eyed innocent image she projected, what she was doing to him with her mouth was anything but innocent. He could get seriously addicted to this.

Dougal swallowed back a groan of pleasure at the feel of her thigh against his. She curled her fingers into his scalp, pressed her body into him, crushing her soft breasts against the silky Shakespeare shirt. His entire body caught fire. Without meaning to do so, he raised his hand to cup her buttocks.

She gasped.

It was only then he realized he'd closed his eyes, gotten washed away on a dream. Startled by the thought, his eyes flew open. Roxie's eyes were open, as well, and she was looking at him with a mixture of curiosity, amazement, excitement and mortification.

Dougal pulled his lips away.

She stared at him with those incredible blue eyes, her pupils dark and wide. She touched the tip of her tongue to her upper lip as if still thirsty for his taste.

He felt it, too, this thirst.

The audience members were on their feet, clapping wildly. "Bravo!"

"Encore."

"Make use of that bed!"

Roxie blushed, and Dougal recognized that everyone thought the kiss was part of the skit. She turned toward the crowd and took a bow.

Suddenly Dougal was confused. Had she been playing a part? Had Roxie been a plant in the audience? She'd been so quick on her feet with the ad libs. Perhaps it hadn't been improv after all. What was going on? Was Lucy in on this?

"You were great," he said.

She beamed. "Thank you. Not too shabby yourself."

He couldn't tear his gaze off her, and then overhead, he heard an ominous creaking noise.

"Look out!" someone in the audience shouted.

Dougal glanced up just in time to see that a spotlight had come loose from its mounting. It dangled precariously by an electrical cord, swaying directly over their heads.

The crowd gasped.

Dougal reacted out of pure instinct, pushing Roxie aside just as the heavy spotlight came crashing to the stage.

6

ROXIE LAY SPRAWLED on the floor, Dougal's big body pressed down on hers, his chest squashing her breasts, his warm breath heating her cheek. His pelvis was flush against hers, and he'd brought his arms up around her head to protect her.

Her heart thundered—from danger, from fear, from this man's proximity. Her ears rang. Her head spun. Her womb tightened reflexively. Disoriented both by lack of oxygen and his compelling, masculine scent, she simply stared up into his mesmerizing dark eyes.

What had just happened?

Why had Dougal knocked her to the stage?

She was vaguely aware of people converging on them, talking, letting out exclamations of surprise and asking questions, but all her focus was on him.

"Roxie," he whispered huskily, "are you okay?"

Lines of concern etched his forehead, pulled his angular mouth downward. Bits of broken glass glinted in his hair, clung to his beard. She frowned, still trying to piece together what had happened, still trying to make sense of the raging sexual awareness heightening her senses.

He rolled off her then, and air rushed into her lungs. He reached down to help her up. Once on her feet, Roxie's gaze shifted from Dougal to the twisted metal and shattered glass that was once the overhead spotlight. Reality hit her all at once.

"We could have been…ki-killed," she stammered.

"We weren't."

"You saved my life."

"Saved mine, too." He grinned humbly and shook his head to dislodge the glass. The simple action shouldn't have been sensual, but the way he raked his fingers through the chocolaty strands, mussing it with his thick fingers, captivated her.

And the way his shirt gaped open, revealing his honed chest muscles and a sprinkling of dark chest hairs, sent a sharp spike of pure physical longing jettisoning straight to her sex.

Roxie blinked. What was wrong with her? She'd almost been obliterated by a falling spotlight and all she could think about was how utterly delicious Dougal looked. She didn't have much time to consider her question because security and maintenance personnel appeared to assess the situation, while Lucy Kenyon and other staff members rounded up the guests and ushered them out of the dining room.

"You're trembling," Dougal said.

"Am I?" Surprised, Roxie realized her hands were quivering.

"Shock," he said. "Spent adrenaline."

Ah, maybe that could explain her inappropriately sexual thoughts. Chemistry, a hormonal response to stress.

"Come on," he said. "I'll walk you back to your cottage."

The moonlit walk across the cobblestone path deepened the odd spell she seemed to be under. The air was damp but sweet with the smell of springtime flowers, and a tinkling of flute music flowed through speakers placed strategically about the grounds. Dougal held her hand the entire way, only letting go when they reached the bungalow where she was staying.

"Here we are," he said.

"Here we are," she echoed.

"That was fun tonight," he said. "The skit I mean, not almost getting beaned by the spotlight."

"That was pretty amazing, how we got a rhythm going."

"Like great sex."

Why had he said that? Now all she could think was sex, sex, sex. Inhaling sharply, she met his gaze and got totally sucked in by those fascinating brown orbs. As she watched, his mercurial eyes changed from sweet milk chocolate to pure smoldering cocoa, the color a tantalizing complement to his ebony lashes and rich, dark brows.

His full lips quirked up at the corners as he shot her what she was quickly starting to recognize as a "come sin" grin. He might appear cool and controlled, but beneath that detached exterior she detected a current of something hot and taut and wild. The man was pure energy, raw and alive.

She was seriously screwed. With a sinking sensation she realized just how much she wanted him to kiss her.

He stood there, his hand at her waist, wearing the sexiest damn smile she had ever seen. How easy it would be to drag him into her cottage and make love to him. How easy and yet how utterly scary. She shouldn't. She couldn't. She wouldn't.

Kiss me, kiss me, kiss me.

Dougal moistened his mouth.

Roxie flicked out the tip of her tongue to wet her own lips.

He lowered his head.

Her heart jumped into her throat. His face was so close she could almost feel the brush of his beard against her cheek. *Kiss me, kiss me, kiss me.*

He pressed his mouth to her ear. She closed her eyes and leaned into him. Her body tensed…waiting, wanting, willing.

Dougal sucked in an audible breath. She tipped up her head. The look on his face was so feral, so hungry, as if it was all he could do to control his sexual urges. Her hands started quivering all over again. Did she really hold that much sexual power over him?

"Shakespeare," she whispered.

"Muse," he said, playing into her fantasy.

She wrapped her arms around his neck, and he pulled her close, nestling her into the curve of his body. She felt the determined poke of his penis through his leather breeches, but he made no move to take things further. He was long, thick and hard, no secrets on that score. She thought of them both naked, imagined him inside her, filling her up. They stood on the stoop, swaying together in the breeze.

She tried to deny the desire pushing up through her, closed her eyes and forced herself to concentrate on something other than the need knotting her entire body, but it was impossible.

They breathed in tandem, but Dougal did not make a move on her.

What in the hell was wrong with the man? How was he staying so controlled? And the more restraint he showed, the more desperately she wanted him.

She thought about all she'd missed out on in life. Fun, a good time, casual dating, casual sex. Suddenly she wanted to experience it all. Now. With Dougal. She was in England, at a hot, sexy, romantic resort. There was nothing stopping her from just enjoying good sex for good sex's sake.

Do it. Sleep with this man. You know you want to. It doesn't have to mean happily ever after, just happily right now.

She felt a racy sense of exuberance, of glorious feminine power. Like a moth on the wind, carried by the swell of pheromones, she let herself be swept away and did something she'd never done before.

She pulled out her best acting skills, pretending to be a saucy serving wench from the sixteenth century.

Roxie kissed him.

DOUGAL SHOULD HAVE BROKEN the kiss, pushed her away, fought his Neanderthal impulses, which were urging him to kick down the door and drag her into the cottage and have his way with her. He'd come here to make sure she was okay and he was trying to sort out in his mind whether the falling spotlight had been accidental or intentional.

But the fact that she—little Miss Innocence—had kissed him destroyed his capacity to think straight.

He took the kiss to a whole new level, dragged her tight against him, plundering her mouth with his, drinking her in. His head spun, his heart pounded. Some security expert he was turning out to be. He didn't even remember where he was, much less why he was here. All he knew was that he had to have more of Roxie.

His hand had a mind of its own, slipping down to cup her tight, round bottom. His cock strained against his fly. Flexing, he curled his fingers into the soft, willing flesh of her buttocks. He heard her quick intake of breath, and he couldn't believe what he was doing, squeezing her so possessively.

You're out of line.

But he couldn't stop kissing her or touching her. She was even tastier than in his fantasies. Her mouth was hot and moist and so was his. He kneaded her bottom and she trembled against him.

The air vibrated between them. The erotic promise buried in their kiss made him shudder. The push of her rose-petal lips disoriented him. His tongue traced the form and curve of her mouth. Supped from the delightful swell of her lower lip, the sculpted bow of the upper, explored the textured velvet of her mouth.

His need for her went beyond all reason. He'd never felt anything like this. He should escape while he could, but then she pulled her lips from his and whispered, "Would thee like to come inside, Shakespeare?"

No, no, say no.

But his stupid tongue did not obey. She was pulling him

headlong into her fantasy. What he said was, "Forsooth, there is nothing I would enjoy more, Mistress Muse."

She unlocked the door, flicked on the light, drew him inside the room with her. The door snapped closed behind them.

Blood pumped through his veins at a crazy rhythm. She tipped her head coyly, smiled at him. The shy girl was back, all sweet and demure. Which one was the real Roxie? The exciting temptress who'd just kissed him, or this reticent young woman who looked as if she'd scared herself with her bold moves.

"You can change your mind," he said. "I should back out. This isn't the smartest thing I've ever done—"

"Shh," she interrupted, "stay in character, don't ruin the spell." Then she captured his mouth with hers again.

That was all it took. Testosterone surged through his body. His muscles tightened. His hands roved over the lush curve of her body, and he dipped his head to kiss her again. If she was in the mood for acting, then he was eager to comply. Whatever turned her on.

Wait, stop, you can't do this. Remember the morality clause you signed.

The words battered at the back of his hormone-laced brain, but they sounded very far away, like a cell phone call from a tunnel—his sensible side snuffed out by instinct and molten desire.

This was so unlike him, losing control, losing his head. And yet he couldn't deny the power of this attraction. It was nonsensical and scary as hell, but it was too real to deny. His muscles ached. His skin burned. His cock throbbed.

If he didn't get her into bed, he felt as if he just might die from the wanting, the craving, the hunger.

She gently bit his bottom lip and he almost groaned. Not because she'd hurt him, but because her boldness and his stark need blindsided him. Had he ever in his life been this turned on?

Beyond all reason, he had to have her.

WALKING INTO THE COTTAGE was like stepping back in time over four hundred years into a medieval love nest designed to stoke the senses.

Gorgeous velvet and damask tapestries, replicas of the Renaissance era, adorned the walls. The heavy mahogany sofa and chairs were padded and upholstered in rich, dark leather. The colors were equally strong and luxurious—crimson, gold, indigo, salmon. The gas-powered fireplace, complete with a sixteenth-century-style inglenook, had been lit. Apparently it was part of the turning-down service because a basket of goodies wrapped in red cellophane lay on the trestle table in the kitchenette.

Not that Roxie really noticed. She was too hung up on the raw sexual energy rolling off Shakespeare and zapping into her.

She wasn't sure why she was doing what she was doing. She'd never had a one-night stand or even a weekend fling, but this felt too right to be wrong. She only knew she had to have him. For once in her life, she was going with the flow and would float wherever the current carried her.

Of course, the current rolling off Dougal was more like a tidal wave, but instead of feeling scared as she normally would have, she felt wildly intrigued and uncharacteristically daring.

His hands were all over her body, but more than that, she was all over him. Kisses landed in various places, lips, noses, foreheads, chins. They pulled at each other's clothing, eager to get naked. She plucked at the buttons of his shirt; his fingers searched for the zipper of her frock. In a clumsy tango of entangled limbs, they stumbled from the sitting room into the bedroom.

They tumbled onto the solid oak, ornately carved four-poster bed sporting an elaborate canopy draped with more opulent fabrics. The linens had been turned down, and foil-wrapped chocolates rested on the pillows along with packets of condoms. Clearly they didn't call the resort Eros for nothing.

She was on her back, her skirt hiked up to her waist. Her sex was already slick for him.

The subtle sconce lighting cast his face in shadows. He looked savage, primitive. His cheekbones appeared razor sharp, his lips full and foreboding and his chin firm beneath the perfectly trimmed beard. This man was a stranger, but instead of being frightened, she was highly aroused. Her nipples pebbled, womb contracted, every nerve ending taking note of this very masculine male.

He didn't move, just stood there looking down at her until she suddenly felt self-conscious. She reached up to pull her skirt down over her thighs, but he restrained her.

"No, do not hide, milady." Dougal shook his head. "Your beauty outshines the sun. My eyes long to feast upon you."

Roxie's cheeks heated. She'd never felt particularly attractive. She had a crooked front tooth and her forehead was too short and her skin was too pale, and those extra five pounds she lugged around and couldn't seem to lose converged into a round little pooch at her belly.

But the look in his eyes made her feel beautiful, and the way he was speaking—as if he actually were Shakespeare—shoved her libido into overdrive.

"There is none so lovely as you," he murmured, and ran his palm up her calf to her knee.

She pressed her knees together, wanting him desperately, but suddenly afraid she was going to disappoint him.

He paused, held her gaze. "Your hair is the color of ink, so dark and mysterious against your creamy skin. And the way you move—soft as a sigh." His hand slipped higher, a coaxing finger circling her kneecap.

Every muscle in her body tensed, and she had to bite the inside of her cheek to keep from moaning.

His fingers kept tickling, exploring, teasing. She let her

knees drop outward, giving him easier access. He made a noise of satisfaction and massaged the back of her knee.

He must have hit some kind of trigger point because a sizzling red-hot wire of glorious sensation shot from her knee straight up into her clenched womb. Reflexively her hips arched up off the mattress.

What a feeling!

A desperate, keening cry slipped past her lips. Tossed like an airplane on a sudden updraft, she fisted her hands, gathering up handfuls of the brocade bedspread. His hand trailed farther up her right leg, his fingers gliding over her left.

He took her by the waist and moved her into the middle of the bed and then he was there beside her, spreading her legs apart, dipping his head, touching her with his lips, his tongue a torturous taskmaster. He inched his mouth from her ankles to her calf to her kneecap, commanding her to moan and squirm and beg.

This was the sexiest thing that had ever happened to her. She had no idea her toes and feet and legs were so sensitive, so desperate for attention. She was electrified.

He finished slipping off her costume, leaving her wearing only her panties and camisole and slowly stroked her bare midriff. His fingers brushed against her navel, enlivening things even more. He went back to kiss her leg, moving up her thigh. One hand was teasing her navel, the other hand rubbing the back of her kneecap.

Roxie was in turmoil. Helplessly she quivered in his arms. "My lord, this is not fair to thee."

"To what does my lady refer?"

"You are still cloaked while I am laid bare." She surprised herself by saying, "'Tis time for me to see your naked skin."

"These damnable boots," he muttered, and went to work on getting them unlaced. He stood up, kicked them off, and the boots were quickly followed by his pants.

They were left in their underwear, aware of nothing but each other, the sounds of their hungry gasps raspy in the darkened room.

Roxie hadn't seen very many naked men in real life. Her two boyfriends and that was it. And neither John nor Marcus could compare with the man in front of her. In a word, Dougal Lockhart was beefcake. Big and thick and well, just...*amazing.*

Looking at him made her want to do things she'd never done before. Bold things. Exciting things. Wild and adventuresome things. A dozen different emotions pelted her at once—titillation, eagerness, curiosity, giddiness, hope. Sensory input overwhelmed her—the sound of Dougal's ragged breathing, the heat of his flesh against hers, the scrape of his beard as he claimed her mouth in another kiss.

A maelstrom of wicked delight swept her away; a rushing river of passion surging high, increasing the sexual drive that had been building since their encounter on the plane. He tasted rich and tangy like some spicy, exotic dish. She hungered for more. The tender slide of his palms underneath her breasts as he made her camisole disappear became an urgent quest to increase her pleasure.

Roxie's nipples were rock hard, her breasts swollen and achy. She was dripping for him, juicy and ready.

Compelled by the burning urge to stroke him, to travel the tempting terrain of his body, she ran her fingertips over his belly. She exalted in the way his taut stomach muscles quivered at her touch.

His low groan of pleasure lit her up inside. She tracked her hand lower, finding her way through the coarse curls to glide her palm up the long, hard length of him.

Dougal's fiery gaze roved over her; his hands sent ribbons of pleasure unfurling throughout her body. "Woman, do you have any idea just how damned sexy you are?"

"Shakespeare." She breathed, tossed by her tumultuous thoughts. Longing overwhelmed her. She couldn't resist. He was so damned handsome with that shock of dark brown hair and his tanned skin.

When she reached up, threaded her arms around his neck and went in for another kiss, he smiled and languidly dipped his tongue into her mouth.

She strummed her tongue against his, making herself an active participant. If she was going to go through with this, then she was going to take full responsibility for what happened. Afterward she could tell herself she'd known exactly what she was doing. This time there would be no regrets. Roxie didn't stop him when his hand drifted to her panties.

"Lift up your hips, Muse," he commanded.

She obeyed, levering her lower back off the bed as his big hand made short work of the slight material.

He made a guttural sound low in his throat. This was it. No begging off now. He rolled to one side and stripped off his boxer briefs in a motion so practiced she had to wonder how many bedrooms he'd performed it in, how many other women he'd slept with. His erection burgeoned, thick and heavily veined, the velvety head purpled and pulsating.

"Oh, my." She inhaled audibly.

It was his turn to blush, which did a strange thing to her heart. He was shy with her, this big, commanding man.

She sat up and reached for him, but he grabbed her wrist to stop her. "No," he rasped. "If you touch me now I shall be ruined."

Lowering his head, he pressed his lips to her bare belly and kissed his way to her breasts, heavy and aching. She shivered.

"Pray tell me thy pleasure. It is my honor to do your bidding."

"Yes," was all she could manage to say.

He flicked his tongue over one nipple and lightly bit down.

Razor-thin shards of pleasure spread throughout her breast. She moaned.

"Does this please thee?" he asked.

"No."

"No?" He pulled back, looked confused.

"It exalts me."

He grinned and kept going, his mouth sucking, his tongue teasing, fingers tickling. Brilliant. Absolutely brilliant. He left her nipples and traveled downward, moving his tongue in a counterclockwise motion. The maneuver produced crazy, erotic ripples in her belly that undulated all the way down into her heated sex.

When his lips reached her throbbing clit, he stopped just short of touching her with his tongue. His breath was hot against her tender flesh, igniting her beyond reason. She arched her hips again, trying to bring his mouth and her clit into contact, but he moved with her, keeping his mouth just out of her reach.

"My lord does see fit to torture me," she said through gritted teeth.

He chuckled.

"You are unkind."

"Patience, Muse, patience."

She didn't want to hang on. She wanted him to love her with his mouth right this second. Her brain was glazed with lust, her body worked up to a fevered pitch.

Gently he spread her thighs wider and moved his body around so that he knelt between her legs. "Beautiful," he crooned.

The head of his penis pulsed against her knee as he leaned forward. Roxie's excitement escalated. She couldn't stand it. She'd never felt such desperate pressure.

His big fingers gently caressed her clit as his tongue probed her inner folds. Her eyes slid closed as she savored what he was doing to her.

"Please," she whimpered. "Please don't stop."

He captured her clit with his mouth. Never in all her life had she been pleasured this way. It was ecstasy. He seemed to know exactly what she wanted and needed, even before she did.

While he suckled her clit, he slipped a finger into her slick wetness. The walls of her sex sucked at his finger, gripping and kneading him in rhythmic waves, pulling him deeper and deeper into her.

Sound was altered and she existed in a delicious void, simply floating, aware of every physical sensation. "Mmm," he intoned. "You taste of nectar, hot and sweet."

She rode his tongue, got lost in it. She hovered on the brink of orgasm, but he would not let her fall over. A steady strumming vibration began deep in her throat and emerged as a wild moan.

"Please," she begged. "Please."

"Please what, Muse? You must request what you need."

"Please, please make me come."

He let loose then, gave her his all. His tongue danced, his fingers manipulated. She let go of all control and just allowed him to take over. It seemed he was everywhere—over her, around her, in her, outside of her. He was magic. He was amazing. And she was his instrument, tuned and ready to be played.

"More." She thrashed her head. "Harder."

He gave it to her just the way she asked for it, pumping his thick finger into her, while his tongue pressed the button of her release. "Come, Muse, come," he cajoled.

She came. Exploding in great, writhing pleasure. She gave a long, low cry. It flowed from her, the release she'd needed for years.

Shakespeare pulled her to him, cradling her to his chest as her ragged breathing returned to normal. Roxie couldn't stop a spontaneous grin from spreading across her face.

"Why are you smiling, Muse?" he asked, leaning over to

brush her lips with his. Lying here with her calmed him in a way he'd never quite felt before. Roxie was as soothing as a soak in a hot tub, and playing this little Shakespeare game with her had been incredibly erotic.

"Oh, now you're angling for compliments," she teased.

"I just wanted to share in the joke."

"Believe me, big man, that was no joke."

He reached up to push aside a strand of hair that had fallen over her forehead. "You enjoyed it?" he felt compelled to ask, and then immediately regretted it. He didn't want her to think she needed to bolster his self-esteem on that score, but the truth was, it had been a very long time since he'd been with a woman and he was a little unsure of himself.

She looked up at him with those wide, vulnerable blue eyes that yanked on his heartstrings. What was it about her that got to him on such a primal level? "That's the first time…um… er…no one's ever…"

"Made love to you with their mouth?" he finished for her.

Even in the dimmed lighting, he could see her blush. "Yeah, that."

A thrill shot through him. Okay, maybe it was a bit chauvinistic, but he liked that he was the first to give her oral sex. "So what do you think? How was it?"

"If it wasn't for the fact that *you* got nothing out of the deal, I'd say chuck the whole intercourse thing and stick with oral sex."

"There are two things about that statement that bother me," he said. "One, nothing is better than good, old-fashioned sex, that is if you're doing it right, and two, I got plenty out of it. Knowing that I'm making you feel good charges me up."

"The male pride thing, huh?"

"Exactly, and besides, we're just getting started." He kissed her softly. "By the time this evening is over—"

The sound of his cell phone trilling the specialized ring tone he'd programmed to play when the resort's security staff called interrupted him. Much as he wanted to ignore it, he couldn't.

"Excuse me a minute," he said, slipping out from under her.

Roxie gave a soft noise of disappointment.

"I'll be right back." Dougal leaned over to kiss the tip of her nose. "Don't go anywhere."

He found his pants on the floor and fished his cell phone from the back pocket. "Hello?"

"Mr. Lockhart, this is Gerry McCracken."

Dougal had met Gerry and the other members of resort security after he'd arrived, and he'd held a small conference meeting, telling them to be hypervigilant concerning anything suspicious, but he'd stopped short of relating the details about a possible saboteur. Even though Taylor put her employees through a rigorous background check, Dougal was by nature a suspicious man. It took a lot for him to trust people, even those he'd known a long time.

And yet, within hours after meeting her, you've bedded Roxanne Stanley.

"What's up?" he asked Gerry, waving to Roxie as he padded out of the bedroom, cell phone pressed to his ear.

She waved back.

"I smell rotten fish in Denmark," Gerry said.

Dougal stepped into the sitting area, shutting the bedroom door behind him. His gut clenched, knowing from the sound of Gerry's voice that he was going to confirm what Dougal suspected. "What did you find out?"

"I was investigatin' why the spotlight fell, and I noticed all the nuts were missin' from the mountin' bolts. I thought you might wanna come see for yourself."

Alarm raced up Dougal's spine. "I'll be right there."

"I'M SORRY," DOUGAL SAID as he wrestled into his clothes. "I have to go."

"What's wrong?" Roxie sat up in bed, her legs curled underneath her, the sheet drawn up to cover her nakedness. She felt suddenly shy in spite of what he'd just done to her with his wicked mouth and tongue.

"Um…tour-guide emergency." An odd look passed over his face and as soon as he said it, she knew he was lying.

"What kind of emergency does a tour guide have in the middle of the night?" she asked, insecurity grabbing hold of her.

"You know…disgruntled guests." He sat on the edge of the bed, jammed his feet into his boots and began lacing them up.

"Can't the concierge handle it?" Why was she pushing this? If the man wanted to leave, she should let him leave. That was the logical conclusion to a one night stand. If she was going to play the game, she had to accept the rules. Except she'd gotten off and he hadn't. What guy left before he'd claimed his orgasm?

"I'm afraid not." He got up. "I don't want you to think I'm running out on you."

"But you are."

"Yeah, but it's got nothing to do with you. Duty calls."

Right. She ducked her head. She shouldn't have any expectations from this man. Easy come, easy go. Pun intended.

He leaned over the bed, cupped his palm under her chin, and tilted her face up to meet his gaze. "Hey."

"Yes?"

"You and I need to talk."

"There's nothing to talk about. I'm fine." She waved, tried to ignore the gentle pressure on her chin and how good it felt to be touched by him. "Go, do your thing."

"I wouldn't be leaving if this wasn't important."

"It's okay."

"It's not okay. Listen…" He inhaled, met her gaze. "I don't

want you to think I go around doing this sort of thing. I don't. I'm not a casual guy. Not about my work, not about my relationships, certainly not about sex."

"You don't have to explain yourself to me."

"I want to explain myself to you, dammit," he snapped.

"Sorry, I didn't mean to irritate."

"You didn't irritate me. I just wanted you to understand." His voice and expression softened. "I'm not a casual guy. I don't get swept away by my passion."

"And yet you did."

"And yet I did," he echoed.

Roxie raised her palms as a strange emotion she couldn't identify slithered through her. "Whoa."

"Yeah," he whispered. "Whoa."

"Listen," they said in unison and then laughed.

"You first." He nodded.

"I came on this trip to let loose, let go, explore my…um…" Roxie hesitated. She wasn't completely lying. Sure her boss had sent her to spy on Eros, but she had her own agenda, as well. She wanted to make up for lost time, let her hair down, have some fun, find out what she'd been missing.

"Sexuality."

"Yeah, that. I've been sheltered and I figured it was time I saw what the world has to offer."

He nodded. "That's the reason everyone comes to an Eros resort."

They stared in each other's eyes.

"What we just did," he went on, "well, I violated all the rules. There's no excuse for it. I crossed the line. But here's the funny thing—I'm a big stickler for the rules. I don't break them and yet one kiss from you and my brain short-circuited."

"What rules?" she whispered, thrilling to his words. She'd

never driven a man to break the rules before and it was a heady rush.

"It's in my contract. A morality clause. No fraternizing with the guests."

"We just fraternized," she pointed out.

"Big-time."

"So what does this mean?"

"I can't, I shouldn't…this needs to…"

"Stop?" She arched an eyebrow.

"Yeah."

Disappointment arrowed through her. She'd known being with Dougal was too good to be true. So much for her wild vacation fling.

"But I don't want it to stop," he murmured.

"What are you saying?" She lowered her voice, both intrigued and titillated.

"We shouldn't take this any further."

"No." She nodded as if she meant yes.

Dougal's hand was still on her chin, his eyes locked on hers. "But this chemistry between us…" He shook his head. "Wow."

"Wow," she echoed.

"If it was another time, another place, we'd owe it to ourselves to fully explore it."

"We would."

"It might even have been the best sex of our lives."

"I have no doubt." The way he looked at her sent blood pumping hot and thick straight to her groin.

"I really do have to go now," he said. "Tomorrow on the tour—"

"Got it. Act like nothing happened."

7

DOUGAL COULDN'T BELIEVE what he'd just done. This was so unlike him. He wasn't a rebel, no rule breaker, and yet the thought of an illicit affair with Roxie excited him as nothing ever had.

What was it about her that turned him inside out? It was more than just that rich ebony hair and those impossibly blue eyes. More than just her porcelain skin and lush, curvy body. It was in the way she looked at him, full of trust and admiration. She made him feel strong and honorable and heroic, and he had an overwhelming urge to live up to all of her expectations.

How had this happened? What did it mean? Startled, he stepped back from the bed. "Sleep well," he mumbled.

"Until tomorrow," she whispered.

Dougal left the cottage, rushed up the cobblestone walkway and into the castle, his heart thumping fast and hard.

Gerry McCracken was in the dining room with a few members of the cleaning staff when Dougal arrived, mentally muddled and emotionally sheepish. The minute Gerry spied him, he stalked over, hands on his hips, his shock of carrot-colored hair mussed as if he'd been repeatedly running his fingers through it. He sized up Dougal with a sidelong look. "Did I interrupt you in the middle of something?"

"Um…no," Dougal lied. "Why would you ask that?"

"Your shirt's buttoned up wrong." The Scotsman, who

was almost as tall as Dougal, smirked. "Sorry to be spoilin' your evenin'."

"Let's take a look at the stage lights." Dougal hastily unbuttoned his shirt and buttoned it up again and followed Gerry to the metal staircase leading to the overhead scaffolding.

They both had to lower their heads as they made their way up, and then crouch and duckwalk as the space grew narrower where the lights were mounted.

"See here," Gerry said, pointing out the studs in the bracket that had once held the spotlight that had crashed onto the stage. "Studs are intact."

"Meaning they didn't break off." Dougal stroked his beard with his thumb and index finger. He moved over to take a look at the remaining spotlights. They all had washers with self-locking nuts. No way could the nuts on the one that had fallen come off by themselves.

"I'm thinkin' someone loosened all the nuts until they were held on by just one thread, so it held for a while until the pressure from the weight of the spotlight popped them off."

"If that's the case, the nuts will be around here somewhere. Let's go back down and check the stage."

Ten minutes later, they'd found all eight nuts, and Dougal wore gloves to collect them in a plastic bag to keep from obliterating any fingerprints that might be on them. This was clearly no accident.

Gerry looked at the wing nuts, shook his head. "There's no doubt about it, Dougal. This was sabotage."

Dougal had to agree and that meant calling Taylor. He excused himself and headed outside to make the call. He couldn't stop his gaze from straying to Roxie's cottage. The lights were out. Random thoughts roamed through his mind. Was she naked under the covers? Was she thinking of him?

Thinking of him and touching herself the way he wanted to think of her and touch himself?

Stop it! Don't get sidetracked.

Purposely he shook off his unprofessional fantasies and punched in Taylor's number. When she answered, he told her what had happened with the spotlight. "This definitely looks deliberate."

Taylor made a noise of concern. "I heard back from the mechanics about the autopilot on the plane."

"And?"

"The results were inconclusive."

"Meaning it may or may not have been an accident."

"Yes."

Dougal cleared his throat. "Taylor," he said, "I've been thinking and I'm not sure I'm the right person for this job."

"What do you mean? You're the perfect person for the job."

"There's someone on the tour…." What was he going to say? That something about Roxie raised his suspicions at the very same time his gut was telling him she couldn't possibly be a saboteur? He had no proof to go on, and honestly, if she was the culprit, why would she risk standing under the spotlight she'd loosened?

"That's got all your senses on alert?" Taylor supplied.

That was certainly true. "Yes."

"You suspect this person?"

Dougal drew in a deep breath. How did you tell your boss that you'd already broken the morality clause you'd signed and you'd broken it with your prime suspect. "I don't know."

"Is it a woman?"

"Yes," he said.

"And you're attracted to her?"

"I am," he said.

"You don't seem like the kind of guy who would renege on an agreement," Taylor said.

"I'm not reneging. I just don't think I can be objective about this person."

"What makes you say that?"

"She was a volunteer in the Shakespeare skit and she, um…kissed me."

"And you felt things."

He didn't deny it. "So you see why I need to excuse myself from the case."

"Don't be ridiculous," Taylor said.

"What do you mean?" Dougal frowned and paced the cobblestone walkway.

"If she is the saboteur and she's attracted to you, this gives you the perfect opportunity to get close to her, get her to let down her guard and confess her sins to you."

You have no idea how close I've already gotten to her.

"Just don't act on the attraction. If word got out that members of my staff were sleeping with the guests…well, let's just say it would be a PR nightmare. But I do encourage you to string her along, keep her wanting more."

This is the time. Tell her you've already acted on it.

But for some reason, Dougal simply couldn't force himself to say the words. Part of his silence was a misguided attempt at chivalry. Part of it was because he felt ashamed for losing control so easily. He also didn't want to disappoint Taylor.

"Don't let this attraction throw you. You're a strong man both physically and mentally," Taylor said. "You can get close to her and determine if she could be our suspect without letting your feelings take over. You learned your lesson in Germany, did you not?"

"I did."

That, Dougal realized, was the real reason he didn't tell

Taylor the whole truth about what he'd just done to Roxie in her bedroom. When it came down to it, this assignment was all about proving that he had learned from his mistakes.

"Dougal," Taylor said, "just find who is undermining my resorts by any means possible."

ROXIE COULDN'T SLEEP. If it wasn't so late, she'd go knock on Sam and Jess's door and ask for advice on how to keep casual sex casual.

But it was almost three o'clock in the morning, and Dougal had been gone for hours. Already she missed him.

This wasn't good. Not good at all.

And she was wallowing in a hole in the bed from all her tossing and turning. She might as well get up and take a moonlit walk in the gardens. Maybe the fresh air would clear her feverish head.

She got dressed, slipped on a light sweater and stepped out to stroll the cobblestones. She kept thinking about Dougal. Emotions overwhelmed her. She felt thunderstruck, inquisitive, voracious, jubilant, empowered and amorous all at once. Good feelings, euphoric feelings, but very scary. She wanted to hop up and down and clap her hands like a six-year-old at her birthday party.

At last.

The thought hung in her mind. She didn't know what it meant; she simply felt it in every part of her body.

At last.

At last what? That she was finally exploring the sexuality she'd hidden down deep inside her while she'd raised Stacy? At last she'd found a guy who didn't mind role-playing with her? At last…

She didn't really want to follow that thought to all the places it could lead because she knew she was vulnerable. Knew

Dougal was the kind of guy she could fall in love with. Especially since she had no experience with keeping things casual. She trailed through the garden, the air heavy with the scent of flowers and dew collecting on her slippers.

So what was she to do? Forget about all the delicious promise inherent in a fling, or take the plunge and risk getting her heart broken? She plunked down on a cement bench at the back of the garden and pondered the question under the glow of the moon.

Maybe you don't have to get your heart broken, whispered the quiet voice at the back of her mind. *If you just keep playacting, maybe you can have your sex and keep your heart intact.*

If she pretended to be someone else and donned a new persona every time she was with Dougal, she wouldn't be the one falling for him. It would be the muse falling for Shakespeare or Lady Chatterley falling for the stableman or Elizabeth Bennet falling for Mr. Darcy.

What an appealing idea.

Roxie made up her mind and arose from the park bench with fresh waves of excitement washing over her. That's exactly what she was going to do. Meanwhile, she had a job to do for Porter Langley and since she couldn't get to sleep, now was a perfect time to do a little snooping.

THE NEXT MORNING, Roxie climbed onboard the tour bus headed for an excursion throughout the English countryside. Today she was Lady Chatterley and Dougal was Oliver.

"Hello, good morning, welcome aboard." Dougal greeted her just as he'd greeted every other guest boarding the bus.

Roxie did not linger near him, although she longed to do so. She caught a whiff of his cologne and the spicy, masculine smell immediately filled her mind with images of the previous night. Ducking her head to hide the pink flush burning her cheeks, she headed for the long bench seat at back of the bus, figuring it was safest to put as much distance between Lady Chatterley and Oliver as possible.

She'd just sat down when Jess and Sam plunked into the seat beside her, chattering nonstop. "So what happened last night?" Jess asked.

"Happened?" Roxie fiddled with the strap of her purse.

"You know, with Mr. Handsome, after the spotlight fell," Sam added.

"Um…nothing happened."

"That wasn't what we were reading from his body language," Jess said. "That man is seriously into you."

Be cool. Don't give yourself away.

"Is he?" she said mildly. "I hadn't noticed."

"Woman, you need to make an appointment with an ophthalmologist because you're going blind. When you two are near each other, the rest of us can practically see the smoke rising off you," Sam said.

From his place at the front of the bus, Dougal was regaling the group with saucy tales of legendary lovers throughout British history. His eyes landed on her. Quickly Roxie jerked her gaze away.

"See," Jess crowed. "That right there." She made a hissing noise like the sound of bacon hitting a hot griddle. "Sizzle."

"I think we're making her uncomfortable," Sam said at Roxie's fidgeting.

"Oh, sorry," Jess apologized. "I was just teasing."

Roxie quickly changed the subject.

For their first stop of the day, the tour visited an estate in Derbyshire. Reportedly it was the site of D. H. Lawrence's fictional tale of *Lady Chatterley's Lover.* Dougal herded the group through the house, and then thirty minutes later, he led them to the stables.

"Anyone who's read the book knows this is the setting of some of the most erotic scenes in classic literature," he said.

Roxie lifted her head to find him staring straight at her. Feeling decidedly unsettled, she flicked out the tip of her tongue to whisk away a tiny pearl of perspiration that had suddenly beaded on her upper lip.

"I haven't read the book," Sam said. "Can you fill us in?"

"Let's just say there's a reason haylofts have come to signify passion in the countryside," Dougal explained.

This brought suggestive comments from the crowd.

The air inside the barn smelled earthy, musty, lusty. Dust motes danced on a shaft of sunlight. Saddles and horse blankets and leather riding crops hung on the walls. Cameras clicked as everyone vied for the best shot. Jess and Sam mugged it up in comically sexy poses with some guys they'd met on the tour.

Unbidden, Roxie imagined that it was she and Dougal making good use of the hayloft and its intriguing accoutrements. She gulped at the fantasy of his long, tanned fingers caressing her body.

"Ultimately," he said, his tone of voice stroking something deep inside Roxie, "Lawrence's book is about Connie's realization that she cannot live by her mind alone, that she must be sexually active to remain vital. As Oliver and Connie's relationship develops, she learns that sex is nothing to be ashamed of, while he learns about the spiritual challenges that come from sexual love."

Roxie knew it was a canned speech, but Dougal's eyes smoldered. All she could think about was getting him into bed again. The events from last night kept circling her brain, tossing her thoughts around like a tumultuous tornado.

For the remainder of the tour, she avoided meeting his eyes, but she couldn't shake the scent of him from her nostrils. By the time the tour was over, Roxie's skin ached hot and raw; her imagination was a fertile and dangerous erotic playground. In the ladies' room, she dampened a paper towel and pressed it against the nape of her neck.

"Are you okay?" Sam asked.

Roxie forced a smile. "I'm fine."

"Are you sure?" Jess piped up. "Your cheeks are flushed."

"And your eyes are shiny," Sam added. "Do you have a fever?" She made a move as if she was going to put her hand to Roxie's forehead to check.

Roxie stepped back. "No, no, I just got a bit—" she paused, searching for the right word "—overheated in the hayloft."

"Didn't we all?" Jess fanned herself with a hand. "Dougal sure made *Lady Chatterley's Lover* come alive."

Jealousy bit into her. She knew most of the women on the tour were lusting after him, but she didn't want to hear about it.

"But Dougal only has eyes for Roxie," Sam said.

Roxie washed her hands. She dashed out into the hall and almost ran smack-dab into Dougal's hard, muscled chest.

"Whoa," he said, reaching out a hand to slow her forward momentum. "Where's the gold rush?"

Flustered, she sidled away from him. "Sorry."

"No need to apologize."

She didn't look at him, but she could feel his eyes on her.

Once everyone had rejoined the group, Dougal said, "Let's head back to the bus. Next stop is lunch at Tom Jones Tavern."

Forty minutes later they arrived at a quaint little pub on the outskirts of a picturesque village. Just before he signaled for the driver to let them off the bus, Dougal sauntered down the aisle passing out orange plastic tags with numbers printed on them. "We're mixing things up for this meal," he said. "The numbers on the tags correspond with a seating chart inside the restaurant. A stimulating vacation pushes you out of your comfort zone and that's what's happening today. So go find your seats and enjoy meeting new friends."

A murmur ran through the crowd at this turn of events.

The bus doors whispered open and by the time the front of the bus emptied, Dougal had made it to the back. He passed the last two tags out to Jess and Sam.

"We'll see you inside." Sam waved to Roxie and then turned to follow her twin sister off the bus.

"Will you look at that," Dougal said, holding out his open palms. "I've run out of tags. Looks like you'll just have to sit with me."

"You did that on purpose," she said.

"It's the only way to have lunch with you without calling attention to our having lunch together." He leveled a seductive smile at her. She thought about last night and a shiver raced down her spine.

"Are you sure it's wise to risk it?"

"Wise?" He arched an eyebrow. "Probably not."

"But you're going to do it anyway?"

"I can't seem to stay away from you."

Roxie was flattered. She'd never had a guy flirt with her like this. Then again, she usually did her best to avoid male attention. Normally it made her uncomfortable. The fact that she was enjoying this banter with Dougal was quite telling indeed. The Gordian knot in her stomach tightened.

Once inside the pub, they took the last remaining booth tucked into a darkened corner away from the majority of the diners. On the flat-screen television above the bar, the eating scene from the movie *Tom Jones* played out its lusty message of culinary excess. Menus lay on the table. She picked one up and studied it.

Dougal folded his hands and sat watching her. After a moment, she glanced up from the menu and forced herself to meet his gaze. "I have a yearning for a nice, juicy turkey leg. What are you getting?"

"I'm tempted to say oysters." His gaze flicked to the on-screen movie snippet where the actors were in the midst of seducing each other with raw oysters. "But that would be too obvious." His own lusty smile heated her from the inside out. "I think I'll join you and have the turkey leg, as well."

His eyes snagged her gaze and held it over the flicking candles secured with wax into the necks of empty ale bottles. The walls were constructed of knotty pine, the floors of centuries-old planks. Food was served in trenchers instead of on plates, the drinks in pewter mugs. The rustic decor, along with the scent of roasting meat, had the intended effect—basic, raw, sexy.

The waitress, decked out in a serving wench costume, appeared at their table. "What'll you two be 'avin'?" she asked, hamming up the Cockney accent.

"Two turkey-leg lunches." Dougal ordered for them both. "With all the trimmings. I'll have a lager and she'll have…" He paused, raised his eyebrow at her.

"I'll have a lager, too," she said. Why not? She was on vacation.

After the waitress left, Roxie leaned forward to whisper, "Are you sure we should be doing this so out in the open?"

"Is there a better way to conduct a secret affair? No one suspects if you're open about it."

"Are we having a secret affair?"

"You tell me."

"Aren't you afraid of losing your job?"

"I'm more afraid of losing the chance to get to know you better."

That surprised and embarrassed her a bit. She'd never had a man come on so strong. And she liked it. Was that bad? "Really?"

His eyes were warm. "Really."

"Still, I'd feel guilty." She glanced around the room, but no one seemed to be paying them any attention. That helped her to relax a little. She sank against the back of the booth. "If you got into trouble…"

"Let me worry about that."

Roxie didn't know what to say. Her body yearned for his touch and getting to know him was a smart thing in regard to her reason for being here. Surely he possessed insider information she could pass along to her boss, but the thought of using him left a bad taste in her mouth.

Dougal leaned back, mirroring her movements. "So," he said, "tell me more about Roxanne Stanley."

"I'm pretty boring, actually," she confessed. "You already know I love emocore, chicken Marsala and walnut brownies and that I'm an executive assistant. I'm originally from Albany, but I moved to Brooklyn when I got a job in the city. That pretty well covers me."

"What about your parents, your siblings?"

Roxie drew in a deep breath. Even though it had been ten years, she still hurt to think about her parents. "My folks were killed in a car crash when I was eighteen and my little sister, Stacy, was eight."

He looked genuinely sympathetic. "I'm sorry to hear that. I apologize for prying. I didn't mean to stir up bad memories. You don't have to tell me anything else."

"It's okay." She told him about Stacy, how she'd raised her alone. "I couldn't bear the thought of sending her to live with distant relatives or worse, having her end up in foster care. We're really close."

"That must have been really hard on you."

"You'd think so, but honestly we didn't notice. We had each other and we had a lot of fun together. Because I was so young myself, I let her do things like have ice cream for breakfast once a week and on Saturdays we'd spend the day in our pajamas."

"A girlie version of Neverland?"

"Something like that. Plus we had friends and neighbors that helped us. The experience taught me people are basically very good at heart. Of course, growing up with parents who ran a dinner theater had already given me a cheery, soft-focus view of the world. We were always playing or singing or watching upbeat movies together."

"So that's where you got your acting talent. It sounds like a nice way to grow up," he said.

"It was. The biggest adjustment for me was moving to the city and figuring out not everyone was as kind and welcoming as the people I'd grown up around. Even so, I've met more nice people than rude ones, but I've been accused of wearing rose-colored glasses. The criticism doesn't bother me. I believe people and places live up to your expectations. How about you?" she asked. "Where are you from?"

He made a face. "I don't like to talk about my childhood."

"Hey, that's not fair. You can't leave me hanging. I opened up to you. For this to be a real conversation you have to reciprocate."

"You're right." He shifted in his seat, then paused a moment before saying, "I was born in Detroit, on the wrong side of the tracks."

"I've heard Detroit is a tough town."

"It can be."

"Do your parents still live there?"

His eyes darkened. "My father took off when I was eight. I haven't seen him since."

She saw the long-ago pain of being abandoned by his father flicker in his eyes, but it quickly disappeared. "What about your mom?"

"After my dad left, she was a wreck. She took up with the

first guy who came along. He turned out to be a con man who took her life savings." Dougal clenched his teeth. The muscle at his jaw jumped.

Roxie reached out to touch his hand. "You felt responsible, like you should have protected her."

"Yeah," he admitted, then offered her a fleeting smile. "I blamed myself. I wondered what I'd done to chase my father off."

"You were just a kid. Kids blame themselves for things beyond their control."

"I know."

"But it still haunts you."

"You're too perceptive for my own good, Roxanne Stanley."

"So how's your mom now?"

"Good. She moved to Florida to take care of my grandmother when I joined the Air Force and signed up for officer's training. After my grandmother died, she started her own business, a transportation company that chauffeurs the elderly and disabled to where they need to go."

"You must be proud of her."

"I am. She's a strong woman."

"Through the Air Force you got to see the world."

"I did."

"I'm jealous. Until I moved to Brooklyn, I'd never been out of Albany."

"Have you traveled much since then?"

"I went to Atlantic City once and the Catskills."

"That's it?"

"I'm here now."

"So this is Roxie's big adventure." His gaze was heated.

The waitress returned with their food and drink order. Roxie took a big swallow of lager and cast about for something to say to get her mind off the hot, tingling firing along her nerve endings.

Dougal picked up a piece of thick black bread and began buttering it. “Although I’m not sure how smart it is to take off across the Atlantic on your own.”

“I’m not on my own. I’m with a tour group.”

“But we’re all strangers to you.”

“Anyone can betray you—strangers, acquaintances, friends. You can’t live your life being afraid of getting deceived. I know we’ve just met, but I get the feeling you’re a pretty suspicious guy,” she said, but then she reminded herself he had every right to be suspicious, especially where she was concerned. Like it or not, she was a spy. She kept forgetting that. While she wasn’t doing anything illegal, she was certain that Taylor Corben would consider her conduct unethical. Plus, spying went against Roxie’s own moral code and she wished she wasn’t in a position to have to do it. She bit down on her bottom lip thinking of the photos she’d snapped of the resort during the middle of the night and had e-mailed to her boss. She hadn’t exposed anything yet, but she knew he’d pressure her for more.

“You’re right.”

“You’ve been betrayed?”

“Haven’t we all?”

“If you ever want to talk about it…” She shrugged. Why was she trying to get close to him? She should take Jess’s advice and keep the personal information to a minimum. With his eagle-eyed gaze and leery nature, he stood a good chance of figuring out what she was really doing here. “I’ve been told I’m a good listener.”

“Thanks for the offer,” he murmured, but his eyes said, *There’s no way in hell I’m taking you up on it.*

And Roxie couldn’t help wondering why she suddenly felt so sad for him.

8

AFTER LUNCH, THE TOUR headed to some ancient Roman ruins. The sky had grown overcast and the air hung damp and gloomy. They drove for over an hour and then passed a small village. The bus took a corner near a pub and souvenir shop, then ambled along the road curving up a rolling hillside. From out of nowhere, imposing rock ruins rose out of the bucolic English countryside.

Tiny blue butterflies basked on colorful flowers sprouting amidst the stone walls. Yellowhammers and greenfinches darted among the hedgerows. A magical place straight out of the storybooks layered with detailed history.

Dougal regaled them with stories about the Roman invasion of Britain in 43 AD, and Roxie's imagination stirred. He led them through the ruins to find a small stone church on the other side. "The church is believed to have been built in the twelfth century, over six hundred years after the Romans abandoned this location for reasons unknown. It was erected over a Roman temple using the original stones."

They moved away from the church, down a grassy green slope toward a small stream babbling over rocks. There lay an ancient cemetery, dark tombstones sticking up in the gathering fog.

"There's also a romantic legend attached to this cemetery." Dougal pointed out a gravestone. "It centers on a brave knight, Sir Gareth, who fell in love at first sight with lovely Sarah Mead, the daughter of the local lord. But alas, she was betrothed to another. To be together, they were forced to meet in secret in the bell tower of the church. There on the eve of Sarah's wedding to another man, they consummated their love."

It was fascinating stuff, but not as fascinating as the man doing the talking. His incredible body was too distracting for words. Roxie kept imagining she and Dougal were those star-crossed lovers. He was a stalwart knight and she was a maiden in a fix, doing the forbidden by following her heart. Desire held her tightly in its grip, and she couldn't shake the thought of making love to Dougal in that bell tower just as the young lovers had done centuries before.

"The lord's men caught them in the act, and he had the knight beheaded and his daughter banished to a nunnery. Distraught over losing her one true love, the grief-stricken Sarah took her own life," he continued.

Emotion hit low in Roxie's stomach. History was filled with such cruel stories about couples who'd gambled it all on love and lost not only each other, but their lives.

Romantic sentiment overwhelmed her as she thought of the past. She wanted to feel passion like that. Her gaze strayed to Dougal.

His eyes were on her.

Her pulse raced and in that moment she *was* Lady Sarah and he was Sir Gareth.

Dougal moistened his lips with the tip of his tongue.

Excitement she'd never felt before blazed through her. She had to do something about this neediness inside her or go mad. *The bell-tower church,* she thought. It was the perfect place to be alone and fantasize that she and Dougal were those doomed lovers.

Or better yet, entice him into making love to her right here.

DOUGAL WAS DOING HIS BEST to keep his mind on the task at hand and off Roxie, but he wasn't having much luck. As he talked, his gaze traveled over the bodice of Roxie's dress. She leaned over to study a headstone, enhancing his view of her cleavage. He took in the rounded swell of her breasts, her luminous skin.

She cast him a sideways glance and that's when he realized she was purposely letting him see straight down the opening of her top. She was teasing him, the little minx. The realization shot hot lust clean though his bones.

He couldn't make himself look away. Not even when he fumbled over the story. He'd been wound up tight as a coil ever since last night when he'd tasted her womanly sweetness. It was a flavor he craved again and again.

She lowered her lashes and stepped away from the group. He tracked her steps, struggling not to be obvious about watching her. Where was she going?

For a whisper of a second, she stopped, cast a look at him over her shoulder, then she moved toward the church. Almost instantly the fog swallowed her up.

He had to know where she was headed, what she was up to. Quickly he finished the tale of the mournful lovers. "Feel free to explore on your own," he said. "There are supplies for gravestone rubbings inside the bus if anyone is interested, or if you feel like walking, you can take tea at the pub we passed on the way in and browse the souvenir shop. It's a quarter of a mile to the end of the road and you have an hour before the bus leaves."

Without another word, he left the group standing where they were and went off after Roxie. It was stupid and he knew it, but he was compelled by a force he could neither control nor explain. He caught a glimpse of her dress as she disappeared behind a large headstone and the very air seemed to quiver with her spirited sexuality, beckoning him to follow.

He wove through the graveyard in hot pursuit. He was breathless but not from exertion—he was an athlete after all.

Rather it was excitement that stole the oxygen from his lungs. Stark physical need was a solid hand, reaching out to grab him.

Where was she? Which way had she gone?

There. Around the back of the old church. He spied a flash of her blue dress. She'd gone inside.

The fist of excitement tightened.

He continued to trace her steps and inhaled the now-familiar scent of her honeysuckle perfume. Stepping over the threshold into the crumbling shelter, he was just in time to see her disappear through the archway leading to the main part of the church. Did she know he was following her?

The thought that she was luring him inside for a delicious and unexpected seduction sent a shock of lust to his groin. With a grin of anticipation spreading across his face, he rushed after her.

ROXIE HEARD DOUGAL'S footsteps behind her. Her heart jackhammered at the hollow of her throat. She pressed her body flat against the stone wall of the chapel, just inside the archway. The pews stretched out ahead of her, leading to the altar. A hot, heavy feeling pushed through her lower abdomen, suffusing her sex with a persistent throb.

Hiding from him turned her on in a way she had not expected.

Dougal came barreling through the door so fast he didn't see her standing just to the side of the entrance. He took several long-legged strides away from her, heading for the exit behind the altar.

Pulse pounding, Roxie spun away from the wall and headed back out the archway he'd just come through, her shoes echoing loudly against the stone. She had no doubt that he'd heard her. Thrilled yet oddly terrified, she ran for the spiral staircase leading to an upper level. She had no plans, no idea what she was intending. Primal instinct drove her, the feminine urge to tease and seduce.

Immediately his footsteps changed directions; he was in pursuit of her again. Her mouth went dry as adrenaline surged, sending a metallic taste spilling into her mouth.

The game was on.

Feeling wild and free and crazy, she took the steps two at a time. She had never done anything like this and she gloried in the feelings vibrating through her. She had the distinct impression that Dougal, too, was enjoying the chase.

Exhilaration burned her cheeks. A tangle of images filled her mind, all of them erotic and involving unorthodox uses of a church. She reached the top of the stairs and entered the bell tower, blood whooshing loudly in her ears.

The tower was a big open room, the bell long gone. There was nowhere to hide. That's when she realized that the footsteps behind her had stopped.

Had Dougal given up, or had some members of the tour appeared in the church and halted the game?

She turned, walked back to the head of the stairs and cautiously peered down.

Dougal lounged on the staircase with his shoulder propped against the wall, arms folded over his chest, his eyes half-closed, an insouciant grin on his face.

She sprang back from the opening. The scrape of his shoes on the staircase sent gooseflesh up her arm. He was coming after her again and there was nowhere to run.

You started it.

Yeah, but she hadn't given much thought to finishing it.

She stood motionless, her skin smoldering, her body a five-alarm blaze. What was he going to do to her when he got up here?

Was he as excited as she? Did he have an erection? Was chasing her driving him as crazy as hiding from him was driving her? Her breasts grew heavy with longing.

His dark head crested the top of the stairs, followed by the rest of him. The sleeves of his shirt were rolled up to reveal his tanned arms roped with muscles. The foggy mist had curled his hair into ringlets at the back of his neck. He looked provocative in his costume of white shirt and black leather pants—basic, masculine, romantic. A whiff of his scent wafted over to her.

They did not speak. Roxie stood in the middle of the room, trembling with anticipation, her mind racing to guess what was going to happen next.

Then, with a noise of intense masculine desire, he crossed the room in a few strides. Roxie turned to flee, but found herself backed into a corner. She spun around to face him.

She was watching him and he was watching her. They sucked in rough, tandem gulps of oxygen.

The wrenching tug of jitters pulled her toward him at the same time it scared her deeply. She'd never felt this level of sexual arousal, this variety of achy sensitivity. Her body demanded release and he held the key.

Dougal gathered her into his arms and kissed her as if it was the last kiss he would ever receive.

The idea that they could be caught at any minute, that one of the other Eros guests could wander into the church and up the bell tower, escalated their cravings.

"We have to be quick about it," he rasped.

"Yes, yes, quick and hard," she agreed, barely recognizing herself but loving this new, brazen Roxie.

Dougal grasped her by the waist, turned her around. "Hands on the wall," he commanded.

Heart thudding, she obeyed, splaying her palms against the cool stone wall, her muscles tensing in shivery expectation. Reverentially, Dougal's hands skimmed over her body as if he loved the feel of her beneath him, as if she was a special gift he couldn't wait to unwrap.

He squashed his chest against her back, pressed his mouth to her ears and murmured sweet nothings as his hand dipped down to the hem of her skirt and his fingers slid up her quivering thigh.

Arching her back into him, she moaned softly against his tender stroking. He kissed the nape of her neck and breathed her name on a sigh.

"Doth my stalwart knight wear protection?" she whispered.

He groaned. "No."

Disappointment arrowed through her.

"Worry not, Lady Sarah," he said, role-playing with her as he'd done the evening before. "Your pleasure is my command."

Huh?

He tightened his grip around her waist and ground her bottom against his crotch. "My lady," he whispered, "there is none as captivating as you."

Roxie whimpered.

Dougal used his knee to spread her legs wider. He flipped the hem of her skirt up over her ass and with one swift move, pulled down her panties. He held her steady with one hand, while his other hand rubbed her cheeks, then he inched his hand lower and slipped inquisitive fingers between her legs. Playfully he swatted her fanny.

She hissed in air.

"Does that please my lady?"

She nodded, unable to speak.

Lightly he swatted her once more, the smack of his palm against her butt creating a very sexy sound in the cavernous room. The torturous pressure inside her womb twisted. How she wanted him inside her!

"Beautiful." His fingers caressed her bare skin and there was such reverence in his touch that Roxie's heart careened against her rib cage.

Slowly he eased one finger inside of her and her juice flowed warm and wet. He stroked the tip of his pinkie finger over her throbbing nib with just the barest hint of pressure and then gently slid back.

The velvety chafing, the considerate vigor, the excruciating rupture of awareness as his finger strummed her clit had Roxie's head spinning dizzily. She could not take it all. Her palms, splayed against the wall, were damp with sweet stress.

He stroked her harder, faster. Again and again. His focus was amazing, the way he was touching her made her feel cherished and cared for.

And that thought worried her almost as much as it pleased her.

Each firm but gentle stroke edged her closer to insanity. Then he placed a thumb at the entrance to her bottom, lightly rimmed the outside of her ass.

What was he doing?

"Do you like for me to touch you this way, my lady?"

Roxie nodded, held her breath. Her bottom was so achy, the feel of his thumb so exquisite.

"Tell me."

"I like it," she whispered.

He slid a third finger inside her feminine core, filling her up. His pinkie slid over her clit, his thumb rhythmically stroking outside her eager opening.

Sir Gareth increased the tempo. The fact that at any moment her father's henchmen could come up those stones steps and see him pressing his body against Lady Sarah's naked ass made her hornier than ever.

"More," she murmured. "More, more, more."

Through the material of his pants, she could feel his rock-hard penis. Realizing how much he wanted her made her want him all the more.

His hand played her. Fingers, thumbs, faster and faster.

Inside the sexy haze, in the electricity that was her own

skin, Lady Sarah squeezed her eyes closed and listened to the thumping piston that was her heart sending her blood rolling hot and thick through her veins.

His mischievous thumb edged into her. Pushing her to places she'd never been, giving her new roles to play, novel dreams to dream, fresh wings to fly.

Delight flooded her brain, pleasure blinded her, wanting lit up every cell in her body. She was lost, and she could not see or smell or hear or taste or touch.

But Sir Gareth offered the way out, his fingers giving her a joy beyond measure.

This sweet invasion was more than she could comprehend. The sensations were completely out of the realm of anything she had ever experienced. Lady Sarah was transported. Her pleasure was that intense, her passion that great.

She was gasping and crying and begging for more. She was tumbling, soaring, shuddering.

Who knew, who knew, who knew it could feel like this?

The muscles of her womb spasmed, squeezing tight, and Roxie experienced a release that transcended everything. The feeling sent her soaring, past time and place, through galaxies and universes. In great, writhing echoes of pleasure, she came and came and came.

ON THE WAY BACK TO THE RESORT, Dougal brooded. What the hell was wrong with him? He'd abandoned the tour group and just followed right after Roxie as if he didn't have a brain. What would have happened if someone had caught them?

The idea appalled him, but it was the very thing that had made their illicit hookup exciting.

Pervert.

He needed to get his head back on his job, remember the reason he was here and stop thinking about Roxie. But how could he do that when just the sight of her clouded his mind and narrowed his focus to his cock?

What had happened to his control? How had he let this thing between them turn into a full-blown sexcapade? He dared to dart a gaze to the back of the bus.

Roxie sat beside Jess and Sam, talking and laughing. Absent-mindedly she reached up to tuck a strand of hair behind her ear.

Damn, how he wished she was stroking him.

He had never intended on following Roxie inside the old church, and his unmanageable impulses had him questioning his principles. He'd signed a morality clause. He was breaking all the rules. Yes, he hadn't completely crossed the line. They hadn't made love all the way yet, but damn nearly had. The lines had blurred, and he was losing all sense of right and wrong. If he kept going with this affair, he was risking losing himself, and that scared Dougal more than he cared to admit.

All the way back to the resort, his tangled mind gnawed on the dilemma. What should he do about Roxie? He didn't find any answers, and in fact, as she got off the bus and he caught a whiff of her sensual scent, he felt his control unraveling all over again.

Gerry met him as he walked into the lobby. "Canna speak with you a moment?"

"What's up?" Dougal asked, fearing that somehow Gerry had guessed his secret.

"Step into my office." Gerry led him down the corridor and when the door was closed behind them, he perched on the corner of his desk and said, "Somethin' else 'as occurred."

"What happened?"

"Someone beheaded the water sprinklers inna back garden," Gerry explained.

Okay, Dougal thought. Maybe this wasn't connected. Cutting off sprinkler heads wasn't in the same league as tampering with a plane or rigging a spotlight to fall. "When?"

"I don't know for certain. The sprinklers were workin' last night, but the gardeners discovered the problem this mornin' after you'd already left with the tour group. I thought about callin' or textin' ya, but it didn't seem that big an issue. We've already bought new sprinkler heads and they're bein' replaced. Do ya think it could be the same person who tampered with the spotlight?"

Dougal shook his head. "I don't know."

"It seems more like petty vandalism than sabotage. Maybe there's no connection."

And maybe there is.

"What about the security cameras?" Dougal asked.

"There's no camera inna back garden," Gerry said, "but I've footage of the side gardens and the back patio area."

"Have you reviewed them?"

"Ya."

"Anything alert your interest?"

"Not really. But a guest was out strollin' the gardens at 3 a.m."

"Can you cue up the tape for me?"

"Sure." Gerry went to his computer, typed on the keyboard and in a few moments camera surveillance of the side gardens popped into view. The gardens looked beautiful in the moonlight. After a couple of seconds a woman stepped from one of the cottages. She was too far away to make out her features, but then she came closer, moving over the cobblestone walkway through the flowers. She had her head down, sweater wrapped tightly around her.

Then she looked up and the camera caught her face.

Dougal's stomach tightened.

It was Roxie.

ROXIE'S BODY STILL BURNED from the encounter she'd had with Dougal in the bell tower. The achy throb between her legs a sweet reminder of what they'd done. She was wild with wanting and couldn't wait to have more delicious sexual adventures with him.

And from now on, she wasn't going anywhere without a condom.

She dug through the gift basket left in her cottage, pulling out all the prophylactics and stuffing them in her purse. There was a sucker in the basket in the shape of a penis. Feeling giddy at the erotic whimsy, she laughed and opened the sucker and stuck it in her mouth.

Mmm, cherry.

She was humming to herself and licking her lollipop when the doorbell rang. When she looked through the peephole and saw it was Dougal, she tossed her sucker in the trash and flung open the door.

"Hi," she greeted him.

"Hello," he said, his voice subdued, his eyes somber. "Can we talk?"

"Sure, sure." She stood aside and waved him in. "Would you like something to drink? Water? Soda? Wine? Or I could make a pot of coffee."

"Water's fine."

She took bottles of water from the well-stocked fridge and held one out to him. He sauntered closer, his masculinity assaulting her senses. Her breath caught and her chest rose, gently pulling against the nubby texture of her robe. His dark, enigmatic eyes snared hers and she felt time simultaneously contract and expand, creating a surreal sensation as if she'd stepped into the pages of a fairy-tale storybook.

Their fingers touched in the transfer of the water bottle. It was barely discernible, the gentle brushing of his skin against hers and yet she felt it shoot straight to the center of her stomach.

"Thanks." He smiled, revealing white teeth that contrasted

sexily with his tanned skin and the reddish highlights in his dark, well-trimmed beard, but his smile didn't reach his eyes.

"Let's sit down," he said.

"Okay."

He plunked down on the couch in the sitting area; Roxie perched on the chair opposite him.

"Um, so what was it you wanted to discuss?" she ventured.

He sat with his legs spread apart, his elbows resting on his knees, his hands—clasping the water bottle—dangling between his legs. He canted his head, met her gaze. "Is there anything that you want to tell me?"

A ripple of apprehension ran over her. "Um…no. Why do you ask?"

His eyes darkened. "Why did you really come on this tour alone?"

"Didn't I tell you? My date backed out on me at the last minute," she lied, and immediately wondered why she'd done so. Normally she was a very honest person. Had spying on Eros for her boss already started her sliding down a slippery slope of sin?

"You didn't consider canceling your trip?"

She raised her jaw. "Why should I?"

"A lot of other women would have."

"I'm not like a lot of other women."

"I can see that."

"I needed an adventure." That much was true. She hadn't had a good adventure since, well…*never.*

"So that was the only reason you came to England alone? No secret agenda?"

His question caused her pulse to race. Why was he asking her that? Could he suspect what she was really doing here? Had she somehow inadvertently given herself away? Darn it, she'd told her boss she was wrong for this job.

Dougal leaned in closer. Was it her imagination or was that a glint of something very sensual in his eyes? Was he—like she—thinking about what had happened in that bell tower?

He did not look away. She wanted to drop her gaze, but she was afraid that he'd read something into it if she did—like guilt. *Cool it. You're going to give yourself away.* "No other reason."

Damn! Her voice sounded too high, too reedy, too jumpy.

"Just looking for adventure, huh?" He leaned back against the couch.

"Yes." What was he hinting at? "What's this all about?"

"About today…" He paused, futzing with the label on his water bottle and not meeting her eye.

Omigosh, he was regretting it. Her cheeks flamed. Roxie gulped. "Yes?"

"I don't want you to take this the wrong way. You're great. Better than great. You're a really special woman. It's just that I—"

"I get it," she interrupted, struggling to tamp down the dismay rising inside her and the feeling that she'd been a silly fool. "I've given men the brush-off before. The old 'it's not you, it's me' routine. Seriously, Dougal, don't give it a second thought. I had fun, you had fun…" She shrugged like it was no big deal.

"It's that it's so intense and moving so fast…"

"It's bound to burn out just as quickly," she finished for him.

"So you feel the same way?" He looked so relieved she wanted to reach out and smack him.

"Hey," she said, feigning nonchalance, "I was up for a casual thing, but I understand your job prohibits it."

"I'm sorry," he apologized. "I shouldn't have done what I did. It was wrong. I led you on."

She crossed her arms over her chest. "You did."

"But this thing between you and me." He toggled his finger back and forth. "It simply can't go any further."

She gulped, nodded, even though she longed to ask, "Why not?"

"Will you accept my apology?"

What could she say? She forced a smile. "Of course, but there's no reason for you to apologize."

"Thank you, Roxie. You're one class act."

Yeah? Well, what was she supposed to do about this unpleasant feeling mucking around inside her?

"There's one other thing."

"Yes?"

"Maybe you should skip the tour for the next couple of days. Stay in Stratford, do some local sightseeing. Get a massage on the house. Hang out at the pool."

"You're kicking me off the tour?" Something inside her shriveled.

"No, no, it's just that if we gave this thing a couple of days to cool down, maybe it wouldn't be so difficult for either of us to resist temptation."

"Okay, sure, fine," she rushed to assure him. She didn't want Dougal Lockhart thinking she cared.

He stood up and held out his hand, the same hand that had done very intimate things to her just hours before. "Friends?"

She took his hand, shook it and lied. "Friends."

LEAVING HER COTTAGE feeling worse than when he'd arrived, Dougal went to his own living quarters. His plan had backfired. He'd gone to coax a confession out of Roxie, and instead he'd felt such overwhelming chemistry it had been all he could do to get out of there without ripping her clothes off and doing her on the rug, carpet burns be damned.

He'd sat and looked at her and realized there was no way

she could have decapitated those sprinkler heads or tampered with the spotlights or messed with the autopilot on the airplane. At least that's what his gut was telling him.

But his mind—his cautious, distrustful mind—was telling him he could not completely ignore the fact that Roxie had been in the gardens around the time the sprinklers had been vandalized. Plus, who was she really? She could have the technological know-how to sabotage the autopilot. Or she could be working with a skilled accomplice. It was flimsy evidence at best, and the only concrete thing he had to link her to any of the problems at the resort. By focusing on her, he was closing himself off to other possible suspects.

His head wasn't in the game. His brain was lust-glazed, his body consumed. He'd had to break the spell she'd woven over him and telling her that they could not take their relationship any further was a step in that direction. And he'd lied about being friends. There was no way he could just be friends with her.

It had been a painful moment, but he'd made the right call. Besides, if she stayed behind at the resort for the next few days and something else happened, his doubts about her innocence would be solidified. Conversely, if nothing happened, it would go a long way in proving that his gut was right, that she wasn't involved in any kind of subterfuge.

Unless, whispered the doubting voice at the back of his head, *she's smart enough not to make a move when most of the other guests are away from the resort.*

Roxie's not like that, argued his stubborn gut. She was honest and genuine and open-minded. She didn't seem furtive at all.

Except Dougal no longer knew if this was his gut that was talking. It could easily be his penis.

Or even worse...*his heart.*

9

FOR THE NEXT FOUR DAYS, Roxie stayed at the resort. In between the spying and researching she did for Porter Langley, collecting a lot of information about the inner workings of Eros, taking photos, talking to employees and e-mailing updates to her boss, she did as Dougal suggested. She visited the Eros spa, got a manicure and a pedicure, a facial and a two-hour massage. She had to admit that after years of self-sacrifice and denial, it felt luxuriously decadent to pamper herself. But even as she did so, she couldn't help feeling guilty for what she was doing. Not because it was illegal, but because it went against her moral code. She felt as if she was betraying Dougal—having a good time at his resort and essentially stabbing him in the back at the same time.

She tried to forget everything by renting an inner tube and spending one whole day just floating around in the heated moat. Another day she walked into Stratford and took a self-guided tour of the town. Then on Friday, she went shopping, buying souvenirs for Stacy and her friends. That same afternoon, she'd explored the grounds of the castle and she discovered a replica of a medieval torture chamber in the dungeon that she found both exciting and disturbing. But no matter what she was doing or what she found to occupy herself, Dougal was never far from her mind.

Constant fantasies bombarded her and more than once, she

took respite in the bathtub, filling it with hot water and scented bath beads, leaning back against the cool porcelain and rubbing herself in all the right places with a nubby washrag. It had given her some physical relief, but her mental torture kept building. Why on earth couldn't she stop thinking about that man?

It's because he never finished what he started, she rationalized.

On Saturday, Eros was throwing a Lord Byron-themed Regency ball. The slogan was Mad, Bad and Dangerous to Know, the reigning color scheme lavender and gold. Guests were encouraged to dress in the garb of their favorite Regency-era character and wear provocative masks. Roxie was excited about attending and seeing Dougal again. It would be interesting to learn if time apart had dampened their enthusiasm for each other or whetted it.

Roxie dressed in a floor-length gown, which according to the lady at the checkout kiosk of the costume room was exactly like something Jane Austen would have worn to a party of this caliber. "You'll be the spitting image of Elizabeth Bennet," the woman had assured her. Roxie had also picked out a purple sequined mask that matched the violet wood sorrels on the print of her dress. When she put it on, she had to admit she felt utterly bewitched.

Guests packed the ballroom dressed as Jane Austen, Beau Brummell, the first Duke of Wellington, Lady Caroline Lamb, Princess Lieven, Walter Scott, William Wordsworth and many other colorful historical figures. There were also dozens of Elizabeth Bennets and Mr. Darcys, but that was to be expected.

Roxie made note of the attention to detail Taylor Corben lavished on the event. From the romantic decor to the lyrical music to the lavish buffet, everything was impeccable. The romantic atmosphere swept everyone back in time to that manners-driven era sandwiched between the Georgian and Victorian periods. Darn if she didn't feel as though she'd stepped into an 1813 drawing room.

She arrived at the party at the same time Sam and Jess did, but immediately after entering the grand ballroom, her gaze skimmed over the gathering. After several minutes, she thought she spied Dougal in the corner with his back to her talking to one of the staff members, but then he turned, and the man was beardless. Still, how many men possessed shoulders like his?

He looked up and from behind his exotic black mask, his eyes met hers and she had no more doubts. It was Dougal after all, looking for all the world like Mr. Darcy himself in his period attire.

Her heart tripped.

She missed the skintight leather *Shakespeare in Love* pants, but he did look just as fine in riding breeches and his clean-shaven jaw. The sight of his unadorned face took her breath away. His chin was firmer, larger than she'd imagined. The difference in his appearance heightened her awareness.

And her arousal.

He stalked across the ballroom toward her.

Fear and longing did a tandem tango through Roxie's body, pounding her heart, bubbling her blood, setting little firestorms up and down her nerve endings. Her muscles tensed and her knees weakened.

"Hi," he said, drawing near.

"Hi," she answered, sounding all girlish and breathy.

Even in the Regency finery, everything about him was rugged, all male. He had the kind of masculinity that couldn't be defined by clothing or facial hair. His nails were clipped short, but not manicured. His palms were calloused. Old scars crisscrossed the back of his knuckles as if he'd had to punch his way out of more than a few arguments. He had a flinty-eyed, old-fashioned-movie-lawman aura about him beneath the Mr. Darcy facade.

She didn't know what to say to him after not having spoken

to him for four days, so she just gave him a coy smile and ducked her head.

"Would you like to dance?" he asked.

"Wouldn't that be breaking the rules?"

"It's a party. I'm expected to mingle with the guests."

"Ah, so that's it."

"You're going to make me beg, aren't you?" He smiled.

"You did dump me."

"Alas, to my regret."

"Are you admitting it was a mistake?" She could not stop a thrill of excitement from zipping through her.

"I am." He bowed, held out his hand. "Pray, Miss Bennet, a dance?"

Oh, he'd already figured out her weakness. The bastard.

"I do not know this dance."

"I shall teach you."

"Pray, dear sir, do you honestly wish to suffer trampled toes?"

"My toes are my own concern, dear lady. I suspect your hesitation has less to do with your dancing skills and more to do with your fear of my proximity."

"You are goading me, sir."

"A challenge perhaps, but goading, no."

"Since you have issued a challenge, it appears I am not in a position to deny you this dance."

"Indeed." He raised a rakish eyebrow that jutted up high above his mask and proffered his hand.

How could she resist? Roxie smiled and placed her hand in his.

She was a little nervous about dancing, but the minute he winked reassuringly, she felt more at ease. Have fun. Live in the moment. Tonight would make up for all the things she'd missed—senior prom and the homecoming game, the senior class trip, her graduation ceremony, having a boyfriend in high school.

Dougal, it seemed, was fully in command of the dance floor.

She simply followed his lead, letting him take charge. Oddly enough there was something highly erotic about the simple contact of their hands in the midst of the communal line dance. The music was bouncy and lively, and she quickly found herself laughing breathlessly with the rest of the group.

Who knew dancing could be so much fun? More accurately, who knew dancing with Dougal could be this much fun? She was enjoying herself more than she ever had, but she didn't feel the least bit guilty about it.

The song ended and they broke apart. A sheen of perspiration dampened her brow, and she wiped it away with the back of her hand. "Mr. Darcy," she said. "You have certainly proven your dancing skills. You may extend my compliments to your mother for insisting you learn the proper way to propel a young lady across the dance floor."

"My mother will be quite pleased to hear of your compliment," he said. "And might I add I appreciate that you did not once trample upon my toes."

"You are most welcome, Mr. Darcy."

"May I offer you some refreshment after our exertion? Some water perhaps? Or would a stronger beverage be to your liking?"

"Water is in order." She fanned herself with a hand. "Thank you kindly for your offer."

It wasn't so much the dancing that overheated her but staring at Dougal, who didn't seem the least bit winded. The man was amazing—virile, strong, loaded with stamina. Most of the guys she'd gone out with were cerebral, long on college degrees, short on actual real-world experiences. They loved to pontificate and get into intellectual discussions, but when it came to putting theory into action they moved with the speed of a stone pony. Sudden insight dawned. Was dating professor types her way of rubbing elbows with the education she'd never received?

She pondered this realization and it made her look at Dougal in a whole new light. He wasn't her usual type and yet he made her feel more alive than any man she'd ever been with. Was he the perfect antidote she needed to shake her from this habit of choosing men who seemed to make up for what she lacked? Being with him jolted her system. He was a worldly man, who'd really lived. Not a pontificating professor who'd spent his life wrapped up in books.

He escorted her to the bar, where he requested two glasses of water, then headed for an empty table in the corner. She followed, trailing awkwardness behind her. Once they were off the dance floor, she had time to realize that hanging out with him was counterproductive to her mission as a corporate spy, but she couldn't seem to help herself.

All the more reason to tell him good-night.

He set down their drinks and then pulled out a chair for her. His mother had clearly raised a gentleman. Roxie sat and he stopped to unbutton the jacket of his costume.

"It is growing quite warm in the confines of the building," he explained.

You can say that again. She felt a trickle of sweat slide between her breasts.

"Would you find me too forward if I removed my outer garment?"

"By all means, Mr. Darcy. Your comfort is my utmost concern."

"I appreciate your permission to cool myself." He stripped the jacket off his shoulders and draped it over the back of his chair. Roxie couldn't stop herself from watching his small striptease.

Looking more obscenely impressive than Lord Byron himself, Dougal scooted his chair as close to hers as he could get and sat. She shut her eyes and bit down on her bottom lip, willing herself not to be so aware of him, but it was futile.

He was so near she could smell him. His scent, a pleasing,

masculine aroma—part soap, part perspiration, part spray-starch, part leather—crept over her. If it was a color it would be verdant Kelly green, live, rich and fertile.

Dougal shifted in his seat; his thigh briefly brushed against hers. Accidental or intentional? His eyes behind that dark mask were enigmatic.

Did it matter? The touch immediately caused her thigh to tingle. Nervously she drummed her fingernails against the tabletop.

Dougal closed his hand over hers, stopping her restless tapping. She waited for him to say something, but he did not. He just held her hand.

Roxie forgot to breathe, and she didn't dare raise her gaze to meet his. She didn't know what else to do so she simply sat there, sipping her water, staring at the dancers, aware of nothing but the pressure of his hand on hers.

"Would you like to discuss what is troubling you?" he asked after a very long moment.

"I have no need to offer conversation," she said, her words tumbling out on a whoosh of pent-up air. She was in over her head with this guy, like an inexperienced swimmer who'd wandered away from the kiddie pool and found herself in deep water with no life preserver in sight. Time apart served to sharpen her awareness of him, not thwart it as she'd hoped.

"You seem quite agitated, my dear Miss Bennet."

Roxie blew out her breath on a flippant puff of denial. "No, not I, sir. Agitated is not a state of mind with which I am familiar."

"Pray tell, then, why does your knee bob up and down so vigorously?"

Was she doing that? Lovely, she was. She placed her free hand on her knee to stop her fidgeting. "I fear I have developed an annoying habit," she explained.

"Might a case of nerves be the reason behind this nervous habit of yours?" he asked.

"Absolutely not, sir. I have no call to be nervous about anything."

"No?" There went that eyebrow again, launching higher on his forehead.

"No." That was her story and she was sticking to it. She raised her hand to nibble on her thumbnail but stopped herself with her hand halfway to her mouth, grimacing at her action.

"Ah." He cracked a smile but his tone said he wasn't buying her explanation, not for a second. "I thought maybe I'd flustered you."

"Not at all." Okay, where did she sign up for the liar's hall of shame? She was a shoo-in.

He held fast to her hand.

Roxie ached to snatch her hand away, but she couldn't because then it would confirm she was a great big fibber and he *had* flustered her. "You know," she said, "everyone has nervous habits."

Dougal said nothing, but stared at her through half-lowered lids, the look in his eyes weighted with hidden meaning.

She reached out to trace her fingertips over his clean-shaven jaw. She felt the muscle tense beneath her touch even as she saw he was steeling himself not to flinch. What was she doing?

"Now who's flustered?" she whispered, amazed at how she'd managed to turn the tables on him and thrilled at her brazenness.

He interlaced his fingers through hers, holding her hand anchored to the table. No escape. It was as if he was waiting for her to tell him the truth, spill her guts about why she was really here.

She thought of the first time she'd seen the movie *Bambi* when she was six years old. The most vivid scene for her had been the one where two quails were hunkered down in the grass, trying to be quiet to avoid a gun-toting hunter stalking closer and closer and closer. Watching it, she'd known that if the quails just didn't make a move, if they would just stay cool, their lives would be spared. But the tension tightened with each encroaching footstep. Then the hunter had suddenly stopped oh so near those crouching birds. Roxie remembered holding her breath at that point in the movie, her stomach twisted into knots, her fist clenched. Finally one of the quails screamed, "I can't take it anymore," flew into the air, revealing herself to the hunter, and he shot her dead.

Right now she felt exactly like that panicky quail, and Dougal was shooting her dead with his glittery dark eyes. He tightened his fingers around hers.

Stay quiet. Reveal nothing. Don't lose it and expose yourself.

His eyes burned into hers, his gaze stealing all the oxygen from the room.

"I do have a sinful secret," she whispered.

Don't be a quail.

Dougal's mouth opened slightly. His lips were full and sensuous, the skin of his chin smooth where he'd shaved. His chest jerked up and then inward with each compelling breath. His scent, that devastating scent of his, assailed her nostrils.

"What is it?" he murmured. He was positioned between her and the door. Getting away from him wasn't a viable option. She had to deal with this to the end. What would Mata Hari do?

For years, Roxie had suppressed her impulses, placing Stacy's needs above her own. She'd done it for so long, second-guessing herself was default mode. But the panicky sensation that quail had experienced swept over her and she simply reacted.

She got up, crooked a finger at him. "Come with me, Mr. Darcy."

HE SHOULDN'T FOLLOW HER. Dougal knew it, and yet when it came to Roxie, he possessed zero self-control. Add to that the fact that he hadn't seen her in four days and he was off-the-charts horny.

Where was she leading him?

It didn't really matter for it seemed he would go with her to the ends of the earth if that's where she took him.

Four days without her had been pure torture, and when there had been no further incidents of sabotage in that time, his gut told him she was innocent, even as his mind told him he was a fool for letting down his guard.

She moved through the crowd of masked partygoers and out the side exit, his attention fixed on her swaying hips. God, how he loved her curvy feminine figure. He was just itching to cup her round, full bottom in the palms of his hands.

"Where are we going?" he asked.

She didn't answer him, just kept walking, and her silence only served to escalate his desire. She wandered down the corridors, her shoes echoing against the stone. He was getting so hard he was having trouble walking.

She descended a long flight of stairs. Down, down, down they went.

At the bottom of the stairs was a stone door. She stopped, turned her head and glanced at him over her shoulder. Her blue eyes looked deliciously cool beneath her purple sequined mask. She put out her sweet pink tongue and swept it across her lips. His heart galloped.

Still, she did not speak. She pushed open the heavy door. It swung inward with a groan revealing a dark, narrow foyer lit only by flickering wall sconces. Excitement pressed tight against his chest.

She stepped over the threshold and he followed.

Once inside, the door automatically creaked closed behind them. They were in a dungeon.

"I have a feeling we're no longer Elizabeth Bennet and Mr. Darcy." He chuckled nervously.

She reached for something on the wall. He didn't see what it was, but he heard the unmistakable crack of a whip. Instantly his balls drew up tight against his body. "Into the chamber with you, heretic," she roared.

Trepidation raised the hairs on his arms, and Dougal realized he'd never in his life been so turned on.

Another door creaked—metal, this time, from the sound of it—and another faint glow of flickering orange light. A cool draft blew across his face. It smelled musky and damp like sex. She cracked the whip again. "Inside!"

He went.

She slammed the door behind them and turned a big black skeleton key in the lock.

The stone walls had iron manacles mounted on them. Dougal gulped. Oh shit, he thought and his cock got so hard he feared he might shoot his wad then and there.

"Stand here." She flicked the whip at the spot on the floor beneath the manacles.

Compelled by a force he could not explain or manage, he obeyed.

Her role-playing was exciting. She could slip under the skin of anyone and fully become that character. She was everything he was not. She was expressive, unrestrained, eager. She was real and true with her sexuality, and he admired her for it.

"Arms up."

He raised his arms over his head.

She had to reach up to clamp the manacles around his wrists and when she did, her breasts grazed his chest, and he groaned at the contact. The woman was driving him insane.

Roxie slid to her knees in front of him, and then coyly canted her head up. A wild glow of excitement sparked in those eyes behind that mask. The contour of her lips changed, her posture was looser. Her fingers worked frantically, undoing his pants. She tugged his trousers and underwear to his ankles, revealing his jutting, rock-hard cock.

He flinched at the first touch of her mouth on him, but her lips felt so hot and wet around his shaft that Dougal couldn't help groaning. The sensation was achingly sweet and so powerful he was grateful for the manacles that kept him from toppling over.

He was a lucky, lucky bastard. No doubt about it. He looked down at her and his heart stuttered. He swayed.

She spread her hands over his buttocks to help steady him, her fingers splaying into him. And when her mouth latched on to him with a strong suction, Dougal's eyes rolled back in his head. She was lapping and suckling as if she could never get enough of him. He knew he couldn't get enough of her.

She tickled the small of his back with one hand, cupped his balls with the other. Dougal almost yelped. It felt damned incredible.

Systematically she set about dismantling him with her mouth.

He felt embarrassed then, and in spite of his body's intense ache, he wanted to break free from the manacles, reach down to pull her to her feet, but he was ensnared in a chaotic whirlwind of sensation. He was afraid. He wanted his control back. He wanted to feel balanced again. This powerful sexual attraction caused him an inner discord that went against his nature.

Dougal moaned as the heat escalated inside him. Her rhythm picked up. Her hands slid all over his body. Indescribable, this intimacy. His chest expanded, tightened. It was unlike anything he'd ever experienced. This took the meaning of sex to a whole new level.

"Yes," he hissed as she moved back and forth. "Yes, yes, yes."

Roxie worked her magic with her fingers, her tongue leading him into uncharted territory. He was on sensory overload as she gently guided him to a paradise he'd only dreamed of.

But this wasn't a dream. The warm wetness of her mouth on his cock, the heavenly smell of her femininity, the greedy sound of her tongue swirled through him. This new awareness of her was breaking up his brittle outer shell.

She was beyond beauty to him. She was pure life, pure joy. She and her sensual impulses merged together against all the rules of proper conduct. Her mouth moved over him without caution or fear. She pushed him past his knowledge of himself. He had never before been so physically possessed. The dungeon walls seemed to ripple. Could this be an earthquake?

No. The ground did not tremble, only his body. Dougal was nervous and exalted and awed. He accepted the inevitable.

"Yes," she murmured. "That's right. Let go. Give up everything."

How had she discerned the mental shift in him? The letting go?

Relentlessly, Roxie pushed him forward. He was aching, gushing, throbbing, beating. He threw back his head and cried out, pleading for release from this magnificent torture, from the ecstasy he could almost touch.

Soon. Please, please let it be soon. It had better be or he was going to drop dead from need.

And then, just like that, it was upon him.

Dougal tumbled. Jerking and trembling into the abyss, the world cracked open, enveloped him.

He peered down, blinked. He could barely see. Roxie was sitting at his feet, smiling coyly, her lips glistening creamy and wet. She winked at him and then sweetly swallowed his essence.

If he hadn't been manacled, Dougal would have pitched

forward onto his knees. Instead, he hung there sweating, shuddering, panting for breath.

He was used up, spent. His cock emptied as he struggled to wrap his mind around what had just happened.

10

ON SUNDAY MORNING, the bus took them for a day trip to Cambridge. The schedule was unstructured, allowing guests to choose from a variety of activities. There was shopping in Market Square and King's Parade, tours of the local colleges and museums, helicopter tours for hire or punting on the Cambridge River. A punt was a flat-bottomed boat with a square bow, used to navigate shallow bodies of water. Roxie, Jess and Sam elected to try their hand at maneuvering these unwieldy watercrafts.

"What are you doing for the day?" Jess quizzed Dougal as they got off the bus.

"I'm going to hang out at the commons." He didn't look at Roxie nor she at him. Not for one second had he been able to stop thinking about what had happened in the dungeon last night.

"Have you ever punted before?" Sam asked.

"I have," Dougal admitted.

"Where did you learn how to punt?" Roxie asked.

"I was in the Air Force, remember?" Dougal smiled. "I was stationed at Lakenheath, which is only twenty-five miles from here. My friends and I frequently came down to punt the Cam when we were on leave."

"Then come hang out with us," Sam said. "We're going to buy a picnic lunch and take the river to Grantchester. I've even brought a blanket for picnicking." She held up the thin cotton blanket she had tucked under her arm.

"That's a long way. Perhaps you should just punt The Backs. It's only takes thirty minutes. Grantchester and back is a four-hour round-trip."

"We've got friends who went to college here and they said everyone does The Backs," Jess said, referring to the waterway that ran behind the row of colleges. "We want something lazier, less crowded and more relaxed."

"Have you ever punted before?" Dougal asked.

"No." Jess grinned. "Why do you think we're inviting you along?"

"You could hire a chauffeured punt," he pointed out.

"But we like you."

"You want me to take you to Grantchester?" Dougal slid Roxie a quick glance. She shrugged. She had no idea Jess was going to ask him along for the ride.

"Pretty please?" Jess clasped her hands together as if she was saying a prayer.

"That wouldn't be fair to the other guests," Roxie said, giving him an out. "I'm sure they'd all like Dougal to punt them on the Cam."

"Yes," Jess said, "but I asked, and they didn't."

Dougal laughed.

"We tip big," Sam added.

Dougal looked straight at Roxie. "How can I say no with such beautiful enticements?"

"Oh, goodie." Jesse danced a little jig. "Let's go."

Thirty minutes later, they were on their way in the small, flat-bottomed boat. It was long and thin and rectangular in shape with just enough room to seat two people next to each other. This particular punt was designed to carry five—two couples inside the boat, the punter out on the platform at the stern. Jess and Sam wedged in together, a big picnic basket at their feet.

Roxie sat alone, closest to the platform where Dougal stood, holding a long, thick pole.

They scooted under a bridge, headed away from the majority of the punters angling for The Backs. The weather was gorgeous—blue skies with soft puffs of clouds, mild temperature, a soft caressing breeze. And the view from the river! The architecture of the old buildings stirred the imagination as did the beautiful gardens. Ducks floated by looking for handouts from the boaters.

In the distance, church bells rang, announcing the 10 a.m. hour. It didn't take long until they'd left most of the buildings behind and found themselves surrounded by lush green fields on both sides of the river.

Jess and Sam chattered all the way to Grantchester. Roxie tried to pay attention, but Dougal's proximity derailed her focus. He handled the punt like a pro, and she couldn't stop herself from watching him. His movements were smooth, muscles rippling underneath the sleeves of his shirt. Because he wasn't guiding a tour today, he wasn't in costume and wore blue jeans and a blue polo shirt with a collar, and he'd traded his boots for sneakers.

Dressed in street clothes, he looked like a different person, and she found herself loving this new image of him. It was a cleaner look, simple and direct. Was this the real Dougal? she wondered.

They were halfway to Grantchester when a punt passed by them, headed toward Cambridge with two young men aboard. "Jess? Sam? Is that you?" one of them asked.

"David! Mike!" Jess and Sam squealed simultaneously and waved at their friends.

It turned out that Jess and Sam had gone to college with David and Mike, who were backpacking their way through Europe. The punts stopped side by side for some conversation. David and Mike were leaving Cambridge later that day, and they bemoaned the fact they wouldn't get to see more of Jess and Sam.

"We could go back with you," Sam said, shifting her gaze to Dougal. "If that's okay with you and Roxie."

Dougal shrugged. "It's your vacation. Just remember the bus back to Stratford leaves at six."

"What about the picnic?" Roxie asked.

"We'll feed you girls," David spoke up. "A late lunch at Whims?"

"That's the best restaurant in Cambridge," Jess exclaimed. "I'm in."

"You and Dougal can keep the picnic basket," Sam added.

Then Jess and Sam carefully transferred over into David and Mike's punt and the group poled away.

"What are you grinning about?" Dougal asked Roxie when their friends had disappeared from sight.

"We're all alone."

His eyes twinkled. "That we are. Would you like to learn how to punt?"

"Another adventure," she said. "Sure."

He laughed.

"What?"

"You're like a kid. So bright-eyed and eager."

"Hey, I spent a long time not having adventures. I'm not going to pass up a single one."

"Then come up here and take hold of the pole. But first let's review the golden rule of punting."

"Which is?"

"Stay with the punt, not the pole."

He got down from the platform and held out his hand to help her up, then he passed her the pole. She eyed the platform suspiciously. It looked scary, slippery and not very big. Tentatively she took her position and the ridiculously long ten-foot pole, acutely aware of her wavering balance.

Nervously she glanced over at Dougal who'd sat down in the boat. "What do I do now?"

"Hold the pole upright and over the right-hand side of the punt, drop the pole into the water and position it slightly behind where you're standing. If the pole is too far away from the punt, it will go in circles when you push. If you put the pole in the water level to or ahead of you, the punt will go backward," he explained.

She did as he suggested and felt the pole land solidly on the bottom.

"Now push down on the pole. The harder you push, the faster you'll go."

Roxie pushed and the punt glided forward, but the pole wouldn't budge from the mud. "What do I do?"

"Let go of the pole!" Dougal said, but his warning came too late. The punt was out from under her and she was holding on to the pole in the middle of the water.

"Help!" she managed just as the pole starting leaning over against her weight. She was going in, no two ways about it.

But then suddenly, there was Dougal, paddle in hand, angling the punt right back to her and she was able to get one foot back on the platform and right herself with only one leg getting wet.

"You saved my fanny," she said.

"You forgot the golden rule." Dougal chuckled. "Don't worry. Everyone does their first time."

"I think maybe I've had enough of punting." She giggled. "You make it look so easy."

"No, go on, give it another go."

She took another stab at it, and this time she managed to propel the boat down the river without mishap. After a few more rounds of drop and push, she started to get the feel for it. The activity was more strenuous than she'd counted on.

"I'm getting tired," she said after several more minutes. "Could you take over?"

"How about we stop for lunch?"

"We're not at Grantchester."

"No law saying we have to go all the way. We can stop here." He waved at an inviting field. "Let's have lunch, and then punt on back to Cambridge."

"I'm for that," she agreed.

Dougal took over and angled them toward the riverbank. He tied up the punt, and then helped her ashore.

Roxie spread Jess's blanket beside a large weeping willow, making a nest among the brightly colored wildflowers sprinkled across the lush green grass. Out here in nature, with no one else around, it felt as though they were the only two people on their planet.

Dougal flopped down on the blanket beside her as she opened the white wicker picnic basket, his fingertips stroking her forearm so softly that at first she thought she was imagining it. Then she felt the tickle of his lips, hot and sexy, kissing a path up her arm. She glanced over at him, his eyes were half-closed, a lazy smile curled at the corners of his mouth. She loved the feel of his hard body beside hers.

"You look so relaxed," she said.

"Punting the Cam agrees with me."

"Me, too."

"What's in the basket?" He propped himself on his elbows.

"Let's see." Roxie lifted the blue gingham napkins and poked around inside. "Ah, a bottle of French wine. Sauvignon blanc. Two glasses and a corkscrew."

"Good start."

Roxie dug around in the basket. "Gourmet sandwiches. Hmm, let's see." She lifted the corner of the bread. "Yum, looks like roasted turkey and white cheddar with some kind of fancy fruit chutney on a baguette and a side dish of pearl couscous salad, plus apples and a variety of cheeses and oh my...*look.*" She held up dessert for him to see.

Dougal broke into a grin. "Walnut brownies."

They ate in companionable silence, enjoying the beauty of the moment, savoring the delicious food, reveling in the company. Roxie's mind traveled, as it always did, to another time and place. They were indeed Adam and Eve, munching sinfully on apples and happily touching each other.

"Who are we now?" Dougal asked.

"What do you mean?"

"I know you enjoy playacting," he said. "The first day we were Shakespeare and his Muse. Then in the church we were star-crossed Sir Gareth and Lady Sarah. Last night we were Mr. Darcy and Elizabeth Bennet, before we turned into the dungeon dominatrix and torture victim." He grinned and her heart pumped with excitement as she remembered last night's sexual adventure. "Who are we today?"

"Adam and Eve," she admitted.

He looked around at the pastoral setting, and then his gaze tracked hotly over her body. "I can get into that."

Roxie's pulse quickened. She had never role-played with any of her other boyfriends and she was loving this.

"Let's see," he said. "You've just tempted me with your apple and as a matter of course, we must now sin." He took the apple core from her hand, tossed it aside.

She studied his face.

He looked at her as if he'd just tumbled out of bed, his hair wild and whorled, his eyes heavy-lidded and filled with the vestiges of a fantastic wet dream. She appreciated his body, dressed casually in that blue shirt and jeans. He looked rock-solid, substantial, an athlete with muscular legs and a strong back. And when he turned his head, she could see his muscles in one long ripple underneath his shirt.

Her hands tingled, yearning for his touch. Between her legs, she ached for him. The scent of fertile rich soil was potent and loamy, the smell kicking her arousal up a notch.

Dougal's eyes held hers and she knew he smelled it, too, their lust, brewing. She tasted him before their lips touched completely.

He reached out and took her hand and pulled her close, running his fingers along the curve of her back. He kissed her in the verdant green field dotted with beautiful wildflowers. The sweet smell of bluebells and forget-me-nots and musk mallow and meadow cranesbill mingled with the musky aroma of the water. Dougal was like that river. Strong and steady and reliable and Roxie couldn't resist. There was no point in even trying.

Dougal Lockhart was her downfall.

He lay on his back, and she stretched out on top of him, staring down at him, her thighs on either side of his waist.

He kissed her tenderly, tentative and questioning, as though he feared she might disappear if he was too bold. But how could he fear that after last night?

The breeze gusted and the willow tree branches rustled, blowing a wave of fluttering caresses over their skin. She touched her forehead to his, looking deep into his eyes, and her pulse shifted from a saunter to a trot.

Silence stretched heated and heavy. Something new was being created between them. Vistas as yet unexplored. She realized that her hands were trembling.

The blue vein at his temple throbbed. The tempo of its beat matched perfectly the aching in her sex.

Dougal kissed her again, deeper. He groaned and she felt the vibration of it rumble from his chest and the almost painful tightening of his hands around her waist.

She wanted him desperately. She had to get his clothes off him. Right this minute. She snatched at his shirt and he helped her wrestle it over his head. His skin was molten.

"Wait, wait, time-out," she said, suddenly realizing she didn't want to be in the same predicament she'd found herself in before, and pulled a condom from her bag.

He reached for the buttons of her dress and slowly began undoing them. With each button he loosened, her breathing sped up. After he undid the last button, he ran his hands under her camisole, pushing it aside so he could stroke her bare breasts.

Goose bumps spread over her skin, engulfing her in shivers. She was exposed, astride him in a pasture in broad daylight. It was a dulcet, decadent sensation. Roxie could feel exactly how hard he was for her.

"You are so beautiful," he said huskily. "The way the sun glints off your ebony hair. You take my breath away."

Dougal smelled like cotton and leather. He made her feel safe and taken care of when she hadn't really felt that way since her parents had been killed. It was a startling, disconcerting feeling. Roxie was used to being the protector, not the one being protected.

She closed her eyes, but she could still see the ocean of wildflowers waving merrily all around them. He was pinching her nipples gently but firmly, sending little rockets of pleasure flying across her nerve endings.

He sat up with her legs still positioned on either side of him and laved his tongue over one of her nipples while his hand stole down and slipped between her legs.

He was doing all the right things, touching her in all the right ways, giving her all the right looks. Misery crawled through her. She couldn't go through with it. Making love—really making love—with him wasn't fair to either one of them. Not when she was hiding her true identity.

"Dougal." It was a plea. "We need to talk."

"No talking. Not now. Just feel, Roxie."

How easy it was to just give in to the sensations sweeping through her. To relinquish all control as he eased her legs farther apart and planted a kiss on her knee.

Arching her spine, she rocked back a little on his pelvis, giving him freer entry. His hand slid down her belly, past the waistband of her panties. His fingertips found her clit and she gasped at the heat of his touch.

And then he started rocking against her, rhythmic and pleasing.

Her legs shook and she could feel the pressure of his body underneath her buttocks, pressing stiffly against her. He was panting, and she was panting until she didn't think she could bear one more minute of this torture.

In the distance they heard voices out on the river, another punt gliding along.

Someone was going to see them!

Frantically she tried to break away, to pull her dress closed around her nakedness, but Dougal wrapped one hand tight around her waist while at the same time pushing a finger deep inside of her. Sucking in her breath, she let out a cry of happy surprise as a hot wave of bliss passed over her.

He sat all the way up, pushing her down on her back. Her nose filled anew with the fertile smell of wildflowers and Dougal. He smiled down at her, his eyes mischievous. She could hear the people on the river laughing and joking.

"They're not going to stop," he said. "And neither am I."

Her heart clutched. She loved this dangerous game he was playing.

The sound of the people in the punt came closer, escalating her excitement. She moved, shifting away from him and went for his zipper, wanting his cock more than she'd ever wanted anything in her life.

Soon they were both completely naked, relishing in the glory of each other's bodies on the banks of the river Cambridge, far away from reality. They were Adam and Eve. New lovers, excited, giggling and exploring.

They stared into each other's eyes and smiled, embarrassed suddenly but in a good way. Roxie reached out to touch his face and he let her caress his clean-shaven chin, his mouth, his chest, but he closed his eyes. Did not look at her again.

Was he nervous? Or was he savoring this moment as much as she was?

"Have you ever done anything you deeply regretted?" he asked hoarsely.

"Haven't we all?" she whispered.

"Tell me, Roxie, what do you regret?"

"I regret not meeting you sooner," she said. "Look at all the fun I've been missing. What about you? Are you regretting this?"

"No." He squeezed her tightly. "Never."

"Not even putting your job on the line?"

"I wish I didn't have a morality clause in my contract because I'm not the kind of guy who goes back on his word, but when I'm around you I can't help myself. I have zero control." He kissed her again. "You do strange things to me, woman. You make me do things I wouldn't normally do."

"Right back at you, big man."

"Is that a bad thing or good?"

"You tell me," she whispered.

He finally opened his eyes and looked deeply into hers. "These last few days with you…"

"Yes?" She held her breath.

"They've been special." She could tell by his serious expression he did not say such things lightly. "You're special."

"I think you're special, too."

"But you scare me," he admitted. He looked so vulnerable in that moment, so utterly breakable.

"How so?"

"You have this wide-eyed innocence about you as if you've been sheltered most of your life, and yet you've also got this sensible, grounded side, as well. You're a bit of a paradox."

"Yeah, well, you're all rough and tough and manly and yet you're squiring tourists around Europe. Not that there's anything wrong with that, it's just not very..." She searched for the right word to describe him. "Urgent. You seem like the kind of guy who needs something urgent to do."

He looked at her with quizzical eyes and something else, an emotion she couldn't label. It was almost a sad expression, but not quite. It was more rueful. Or could it be disappointment?

Had she disappointed him in some way or did he fear that she would? "You've been hurt before."

"I have."

She fingered his lips. "You're not a man who easily gives his heart."

"I'm not," he whispered.

Now she was feeling as vulnerable as he looked. "If you're not ready, it's okay. This doesn't have to mean anything, Dougal. I'm not expecting anything from you." At least that's what she kept telling herself. "And I don't think you should expect anything from me other than what we've got in this moment, right now. Sex is enough."

"Roxie." He said her name on a sigh. "I want you, need you. Now."

She slipped her fingers through his hair, held his head still and kissed him with all the fervent intensity she had inside her. She was slick for him and he was hard for her.

His penis was so big, so awesome. She licked her lips. "Condom," she gasped. "Where's the condom?"

He found it.

In her desperation to have him, she snatched the condom

from his hand, ripped it open with her teeth and with trembling fingers, pushed him back just long enough to roll it on.

He pushed inside of her on a rush of heat. Her muscles tensed around him, drawing him in deeper.

"You are so tight." He groaned.

She couldn't answer. Emotion constricted her throat. She'd always dreamed of sex like this—wild and hungry and brilliantly good—but this was so much more than she'd ever bargained for. With each fevered thrust she wanted more. Wanted him deeper.

Dougal twisted his hips, rocking deeper and deeper into her softness. Her mind was mush. Colors, sounds, sensations flashed in her head. Nothing had ever felt like this before.

This was unique. This was Dougal. This felt like the missing piece of the puzzle.

Her body tingled from the top of her head to the tips of her toes. She bucked her hips up to meet his thrusts, ran her hands over his sweat-slicked skin, dug her fingernails into his muscles.

He expanded inside her, growing larger and harder until he occupied all of her. She was his. Owned, claimed, possessed.

Yes.

Every other thought left her head. There was only room for him.

She wrapped her legs around his waist pulling him in deeper still. His fierce, insistent thrusts pushed her to the limits of her endurance.

They were perfectly in tune. Coupled. It was as if they'd known each other centuries instead of for just a few short days. As if she'd been waiting for this man her entire life and her life until now had been nothing but a dress rehearsal.

Unerringly he seemed to know her body. Where she ached to be stroked, how she liked to be kissed, what areas begged for pressure, which ones hungered for a soft touch.

Every stroke took her higher and higher toward her ultimate

goal. It was fierce, basic, extreme, elemental. She cried his name over and over until tears rolled down her cheeks.

It was too much. Too wonderful. She didn't deserve this kind of pleasure—not when she was lying to him about who she was.

"You're crying," Dougal whispered and stopped moving. "Roxie, what's wrong? Am I hurting you?"

"No, no." She smiled at him. Emotion clogged her chest, made it hard for her to draw in air. "You're making me very happy."

"These are good tears?" He looked confused.

"The best kind," she sniffled.

He made a noise low in his throat and kissed tears from her cheeks as he began moving inside her again with soft, determined strokes.

"Ah," she murmured. "That feels so good."

He quickened his pace. They were all slippery mouths and sweaty bodies, high-speed lust.

Then he pulled his mouth from hers and flung his head back, groaning as he let out a cry of raw animal pleasure. The power of his climax took her so completely that Roxie's immediately followed.

She was tumbling, tripping, rolling into the orgasm as if it had always been her fate. She heard his groan and knew he was following her into the abyss, rocking and pumping and thrusting.

"Roxie," he called out, and the sound of her name on his lips changed her forever.

11

ALL THE WAY BACK to the Eros resort, Roxie floated on a cloud of postcoital bliss. The rays of the sun glowed brighter; the air smelled sweeter; the birds' song sounded more melodic. She had no idea sex could feel so joyful.

She sat at the back of the bus, lazily watching Dougal while Jess and Sam chatted gaily about their afternoon with their friends. She didn't hear a word they said. All she could think about was Dougal.

And then a small fissure of worry settled into the center of her chest.

This feeling was too good. Too perfect. Soon she would be leaving England, going back to her job at Getaway Airlines, never to see Dougal Lockhart again.

She found the notion far more disturbing than she should. He was nothing more than a fling. She knew that. And yet, she couldn't stop herself from wanting more. The man had gotten under her skin, and the thought of quitting him made her feel panicky. Now that she'd found him—learned what great sex was really all about—she was just supposed to give him up?

Roxie whimpered inwardly. She didn't want to, but what kind of future could she have with this man when their entire relationship was built on a lie? He didn't even know who she really was. Everything between them had been an act. A role she'd been playing. Was that what had made the sex so good?

The fact that she'd stepped outside of herself and donned a wild-woman persona?

She reached up to trace a finger over the comedy-tragedy necklace at her throat.

Who was she behind the emotional mask? Mild-mannered Roxie from Brooklyn? Or the sort of bold, brazen woman who made love in a field of wildflowers with a man she barely knew?

Although she'd only known Dougal a week, this chemistry between them ran deeper than physical desire. She'd never felt this kind of connection with anyone; it was as if he really saw her for who she was. He knew who she was at her essence and she knew him just as well. She couldn't explain it. She simply accepted that it was true.

Dougal possessed a cautious and guarded nature, but in spite of all that, she'd been able to slip past his defenses and he'd slipped past hers.

He caught her gaze as she got off the bus with the rest of the guests and her heart swooned. He winked.

Be cool. Don't show what you're feeling. You don't want to get him in trouble.

But she couldn't help herself. She winked back, sharing their little secret.

Roxie didn't know what was going to happen between them once the trip was over. Most likely nothing. But she wasn't going to let it stop her from enjoying the game right now.

Her sense of fun was shattered, however, when she returned to her room and checked the voice mail on her cell phone. Porter Langley had called. Three times. She pushed the button to review the letters in her mailbox.

"Roxie? Why do you have your cell phone turned off? Call me."

"Roxie, it's Porter again. Where are you? We need to talk."

"I really need to talk to you today. Call me back as soon as you get this message."

Sighing, she kicked off her shoes, plunked down on the big four-poster Tudor bed and punched in her boss's number.

"Where have you been?" Porter asked the minute he picked up the phone.

"Hello, Mr. Langley."

"I've been trying to call you all day."

"I've been out on an excursion."

"I'm not paying you to have a good time. Take your cell phone with you and keep it turned on."

"Now how dumb would that be?" she asked. "I wouldn't be incognito if I had to stop and answer a call from my boss every five minutes. What's so urgent?"

"Okay, okay, you're right. Listen, you know I'm in the process of courting Limerick Air."

"Yes."

"Well, they were all gung-ho last week. We were this close to inking a deal, and suddenly they're acting coy, not returning my calls, being evasive when I do talk to them. My gut tells me they've got another suitor and I'm pretty sure it's Taylor Corben," he said.

"So what do you want from me?"

"Find out for sure. If I know what's going on, it will give me more leverage."

"How am I supposed to do that?"

"Talk to the staff at Eros. Snoop around. See what you can dig up. You have my full permission to do whatever it takes. Even if that means bending a few rules or even breaking a few laws."

Roxie blew out her breath. "I'm really not comfortable with this. I'm having second thoughts about this whole thing. I hate lying and spying and—"

"It's too late for regrets," her boss snapped. "You're in this up to your neck. Find out if Taylor Corben is in negotiations with Limerick Air or you can kiss that PR position goodbye."

That's fine, tell him you quit. You're a good assistant. You can get a job anywhere. Don't let him intimidate you. You've already compromised your values. Stop before it's too late to come back.

But as much as she might want to do that, she knew she couldn't. Stacy was depending on her. She swallowed hard. "I'll do my best."

ROXIE FIGURED THE INFORMATION she needed could be found in the resort's main computer room. The investigating she'd done to date told her that the staff who worked inside the room went home at five. It would remain empty until the following morning, although getting into the room would require a little breaking and entering.

The thought of crossing the line from spy to burglar made her stomach hurt. *You're not really a burglar,* she tried to convince herself. *You're just breaking in, you're not stealing anything.*

Who was she kidding? She was stealing information. It might not be physically tangible, but it was theft all the same.

She wrestled with her conscience, torn between calling up her boss and telling him to go to hell, and the very real fact that if she lost her job, Stacy would be forced to drop out of college.

It's almost over, whispered her practical voice that had gotten her through many tough times. *Just grit your teeth and get Porter the information he wants. You'll be on your way home in a few days and then you can put this whole thing behind you.*

Of course the biggest question weighing on her mind was how to get by the locking mechanism on the door, which was like the ones used on the bungalows. They opened with an electronic key card. She'd need one to gain entry. The housekeeping staff wore their master keys on lanyards around their necks. Somehow, she was going to have to steal one.

Fresh anxiety deepened the pains shooting through her stomach and she pressed her palm against her belly. Her mind spun and she felt guilty, guilty, guilty.

If Dougal knew what she was up to... She hitched in a breath. He'd be so disappointed in her. She was disappointed in herself.

Just do it, get it over with.

Squaring her shoulders, she left her bungalow under cover of darkness and crept into the main building, her mind working out the details of how she was going to get her hands on one of the master key cards that would give her entry to the computer room.

It turned out that luck was with her. She found a housekeeping cart parked outside the computer room and the door propped open with a mop. She wouldn't have to steal a key card after all. She could slip in while the housekeeping staff was inside and find a place to hide until they left.

Still, her pulse was pounding as she eased past the mop and into the room crowded with computers and other office equipment. She heard someone cough in the room beyond the main one she'd just stepped into.

Quick, find a place to hide.

Frantically, she cast her gaze around the room and spied what appeared to be a free-standing metal supply closet with double doors. On tiptoes, she darted toward it and then twisted one of the handles. A hinge creaked. Heart pounding, she thrust herself inside with the copy paper, toner, paper clips and staples and pulled the door closed behind her. She held her breath, waiting, her heartbeat thumping loudly in her ears.

After a few seconds she slowly let out her breath, gathered up her courage and pressed one eye to the thin crack between the two doors. A minute passed, then another. Just when she thought she couldn't stand the suspense a second longer, she saw a man in a housekeeping uniform toddling around emptying the trash cans. What seemed like an eternity later, he finished up his duties, picked up his mop, clicked off the light.

Roxie stayed put for a bit longer, making sure he was truly gone. Then she eased from the closet. Her breathing had slowed, but her legs were shaking. She went to the nearest desk, clicked on a light and quickly scanned the papers stacked there. Nothing of interest. She moved to the next desk and then the next. She didn't have a system and she wasn't really certain what she was looking for or where to find it. At this rate, she'd be here all night.

Sighing, she plopped down in a chair at the last remaining desk and played the flashlight over the papers there. A green file marked Confidential caught her eye. She picked it up. The file was sealed. Did she dare open it?

Put it down, move on, directed her conscience.

But what if the very thing she needed was inside the file folder?

Knowing she really had no choice, she reached for the letter opener sticking from the container full of pens and pencils by the side of the computer monitor. With trembling fingers, she slid the letter opener underneath the sealed flap and sliced it open. She pulled the document from the file.

It took a second for her to realize what she was reading, but when she did, she understood she was facing another big dilemma.

The documents were copies of confidential financial reports about Taylor's company intended for the director of IT. These were proprietary details that would cause her boss to salivate. Should she tell him or not? That was the loaded question. She could keep her mouth shut and he would never know she found it. On the other hand, delivering this kind of information would guarantee her that promotion.

Pushing back the guilt chewing her up inside, Roxie stuffed the documents in the file folder, then stood up, lifted her blouse and shoved the folder into the waistband of her jeans. She pulled her blouse back down. Her palms were sweaty and her heart was thumping faster than ever. She needed to get out of here before she was caught.

Just as she was about to shut off the light, she noticed a calendar on the wall with something scrawled across the bottom of it. Squinting, she stepped closer to read: Taylor arrives May 22 for a stopover on her way to Dublin.

Bingo. Here was proof that Taylor was heading for Ireland.

Roxie had found out far more than she'd bargained for.

DOUGAL WALKED THE CORRIDOR of the Eros resort, his nostrils filled with the sexy smell of burning incense, his ears teased by mood music, his mind wrapped tightly around Roxie. He'd come back from the trip to Cambridge in a daze, his body achy in all the right places, and he couldn't seem to stop smiling. It was almost 11 p.m., and most of the guests had retreated to their cottages for the evening.

After getting back from the day trip, he'd had a meeting with Gerry McCracken. There'd been no further incidents of sabotage, and Gerry was of the mind that the incidents weren't related, but Dougal wasn't so sure. Still, there was no evidence that tied the autopilot problems on the plane to the tampered spotlight or the beheaded water sprinklers. And by now he was completely convinced that if someone was behind the incidents, it wasn't Roxie.

That feeling of certainty stirred other feelings inside him, tender feelings that urged him to take another risk on love. With Roxie, he was finally willing to let go of the foolishness he'd felt after Ava's betrayal and take a chance on the chemistry that sizzled between him and Roxie. The trick was taking that first step and admitting to her that he wanted more.

He'd taken his dinner with the guests, and after the meal was over he made his rounds of the resort, on the lookout for anything suspicious. He found nothing out of the ordinary, and he was debating whether or not to show up at Roxie's cottage when he heard a door open, saw a swath of light fall onto the marble floor.

Not just any door, but the door leading to the nerve center of the resort—the main room that housed the computer systems, which should have been locked at this time of night. Was someone working late? Or could it be the cleaning staff?

Then a shadow crossed the doorway and the light clicked off.

The hairs on Dougal's neck lifted and his gut squeezed. Something wasn't right. He stepped back into an alcove where he could watch the room without being seen. He held his breath, waited. Someone emerged.

Dougal narrowed his eyes. It was a woman—medium height, curvy, jet-black hair. She pulled the door closed behind her, looked furtively up and down the corridor and then turned for the exit.

He stepped from the alcove and called her name. "Roxie."

AT THE SOUND OF HER NAME, Roxie froze.

Footsteps hurried toward her.

Okay, don't panic. Act cool and calm. She coached herself, slipped into the role and turned to face Dougal.

"Hi!" She smiled brightly. Did she sound too cheerful? Was she trying too hard?

"Hey," he said softly, but his eyes looked troubled. "What are you doing here?"

"Um…I was just out for a walk."

"Did you need something?" He glanced toward the door of the office she'd just exited.

"Er…no…um…I was walking by and saw that the office door was open," she lied, cradling her arms across her chest so he couldn't see the outline of the file beneath the blouse.

"No one was inside," she went on, "so I just turned out the light and closed the door."

He looked as though he did not believe her.

"So," she said, anxious to distract him. "Where are you off to?"

"I was coming to see you."

"You were?"

He smiled. "I was hoping you were free for the evening."

"Um..." Her body yearned to be with Dougal again, but she was feeling far too guilty. Plus, she wanted to get this information to Mr. Langley straightaway and tell him that she'd more than delivered on her promise and now she wanted out of the spying business. "It's pretty late, maybe tomorrow night."

His eyes darkened with a meaning she could not read. "Okay."

"I had a good time today," she said.

"As did I."

If that was the case, why did he look so stiff and why did she feel so leaden? They stood looking at each other. The moment was awkward and tense. She wasn't sure what she should do or say next.

"So, good night," he finally said.

"Good night."

Was he going to kiss her? She held her breath.

But he did not. He simply touched her shoulder, gave her a wistful smile and walked away in the opposite direction.

DOUGAL LAY ON THE BED in his room in the staff quarters at the back of the castle, his mind troubled over his encounter with Roxie. Why had she been in that office? Could it be true? Had she really found the door open and just shut it to be thoughtful? He wanted to believe her.

But his certainty of her innocence had been shattered.

From the first moment he'd seen her, he'd known she was different. That she wasn't who she seemed to be. He cursed his heightened instincts that allowed him to see trouble ahead of other people. It was an important skill in the security business, but sometimes it made you see and feel and understand things you didn't want to see and feel and understand.

Roxie Stanley was up to something and he was going to do what he should have done days ago—run a thorough background check on her.

He flipped onto his other side and thought of their day punting on the Cam. It had been simply one of the best days of his life. Sadness twined through him.

When had it happened? When had he started falling for the wrong woman? When and why? He'd known better and yet he'd let it happen. No two ways about it. He was going to get hurt. Again.

Stupid, stupid.

The phone at his bedside rang. He sat up in surprise, glanced at the clock. It was two in the morning. Who was calling?

He picked it up as a bad feeling curled through him. "Hello?"

"Dougal, it's Gerry."

"What's wrong?"

"The computers have all gone down, nothing's working. We can't take reservations. It's chaos."

"At all the Eros resorts or just this one?"

"Just this one so far."

"What caused it?" he asked, trepidation creeping up his spine. "Do you think it's a virus?"

"I doubt it," Gerry said. "All the backup batteries have been shut off, as well. The whole system has crashed. It looks like we've lost everything."

FOR THE NEXT TWO DAYS, the staff worked to fix the problems caused by the crash while Dougal and Gerry talked with an expert in computer forensics to find the source of the sabotage. Their research led them to determine that someone at the resort had let a Trojan loose on the Eros system, and it had happened around the same time Dougal had discovered Roxie in the offices. But of course the Trojan horse could have been released remotely so that didn't necessarily mean someone on site had caused it.

He didn't want to believe her capable of such a thing, but the evidence was damning, although he wanted to be absolutely certain before he confronted her. Instead, he had to go on the remaining tours and pretend nothing had changed between them. He kept Taylor apprised of the developments, but stopped short of implicating Roxie, since he had no real proof it was her.

Saturday was the big finale of the scheduled events of the tour. A Renaissance Festival to end all Renaissance Festivals, and the event was open to the public. He used prepping for the event as his excuse to avoid going to Roxie's cottage every time she invited him in. Finally she stopped asking.

But he hadn't stopped wanting to go to her.

Saturday's schedule was chock-full of events from the opening parade featuring actors hired to play King Henry the Eighth and Jane Seymour. The slate included jousting, crafts, animal herding and other live dioramas depicting life in the sixteenth century—fortune-tellers, falconry, games of chance and weaponry demonstrations, including knife throwing and fencing. The minute Dougal saw Roxie dressed as a saucy serving wench, his heart flipped.

He was in big trouble. If she was the saboteur, she'd been leading him down the primrose path and he'd stupidly followed his dick where she'd led.

Roxie met his glance and quickly looked away. Dougal's pulse leaped. It was all he could do not to make his way through the crowd to her. And if Lucy Kenyon hadn't brushed past him with a worried expression on her face, he probably would have.

"Lucy," he called to her, "what's wrong?"

"It's nothing, no big deal, and you've got enough on your slate without hearing my tales of woe."

Had something else happened? He touched Lucy's arm. "Talk to me. Maybe I can help."

"The men we had coming to do the fencing clinic called in sick with food poisoning. I've been on the phone trying to find replacements, but on such short notice I'm not getting anywhere. I'm probably going to have to shut down the demonstration."

"I know how to fence," Dougal said. "I could step in."

Lucy's jaw dropped. "Seriously?"

"Seriously. So now you only need to find one replacement."

"You know what? One of the guests put down on her profile that she fences. Of course, she might not be willing to participate, but let me go ask her." Lucy hugged Dougal around the neck. "Oh, you are a lifesaver."

"When do you need me?"

"The first demonstration starts in an hour… Oh look, there she is." Lucy rushed up to Roxie.

He blinked. The guest who knew how to fence was his Roxie? *She's not* your *Roxie.*

"Dougal." Lucy waved him over. "Come here."

Heart thundering, he went.

"Roxie's agreed." Lucy beamed.

Roxie's gaze seared into Dougal's.

"Well," Lucy said. "I'll just leave you two alone to talk strategy and get changed into your fencing outfits. So much to do."

She fluttered off, leaving Roxie and Dougal standing together in the thick of the crowd pouring over the moat bridge onto the castle grounds.

"So," he said, "you know how to fence."

"You sound surprised."

"It's not a skill many young women possess."

"Right back at you. I've never dated a guy who fenced. I mean…um…" she stammered. "That's not what I meant. I didn't mean to imply we have any kind of relationship… I—"

"We have a relationship."

"Yes, sure, of course, but I didn't want to assume anything. This is a vacation for me, a fantasy. We might be totally different in the real world." She slapped a palm over her mouth. "I'm babbling."

He grinned. He couldn't help it. She was just so adorable. How could a woman so cute and open and vulnerable be a saboteur?

"Why don't we go get changed and pick out our equipment and do a few practice moves before the demonstration?" he suggested. "We can meet out behind the jousting area. It's isolated and we won't be interrupted."

"Yes, good, great." She still seemed a bit off balance at the prospect of fencing with him. To be honest, he was a bit nervous himself.

"It's okay," he said. "Just relax. You'll be fine."

"Thanks for calming me down. I haven't fenced in years."

"Neither have I."

"My dad was a fencer," she said as they walked toward the equipment tent. "He was all set to go to the Olympics, but my mom got pregnant with me and he decided to forgo it."

"That's impressive."

"What? That he was a potential Olympian or that he chose my mother and me over his passion for fencing?"

"Both," Dougal said.

"Dad started teaching me to fence when I was five years old. He had dreams of me following in his footsteps, but I was never that good. So, what about you? How did you get into fencing? You don't really seem the type."

"What does that mean?"

"There's something poetic about it. Romantic." She cocked

her head at him. “You don’t strike me as either particularly romantic or poetic.”

He splayed a hand over his heart, feigned a hurt expression. “I’m wounded, truly wounded.”

“Yeah, you look utterly shattered.” She laughed.

“Actually, my football coach suggested it. Said it would help my balance and coordination. It was either fencing or ballet. *That* was a no-brainer.”

“Ah, football, now it all makes sense.”

“I see,” he teased. “So you’re saying instead of romantic and poetic I’m more the cave-dwelling, Neanderthal type?”

“You said it, I didn’t.”

“Well, the fencing worked to refine this caveman. The year I learned to fence, our football team went to the district play-offs.”

“What position did you play?”

“Wide receiver.”

“Well, at least you weren’t quarterback.”

“What’s wrong with quarterback?”

“Too much of a cliché. You’re good-looking, rugged, confident. If you’d been quarterback, as well…”

“Nope, I wasn’t quarterback.”

“Class president?”

“Not that smart.”

“Prom king?”

He hung his head. “Guilty as charged.”

“I knew it,” she crowed.

“From the way you’re scoffing, I take it you weren’t head cheerleader, class president or prom queen,” he said.

“Not even close.”

“You hung out in the library.”

“And proud of it.” She lifted her chin.

“Really? Because from where I’m standing, you should have owned that high school.”

"A lot of things can change in ten years. In high school I had braces and I was horribly shy. The two places I felt like my true self was when I was on stage pretending to be someone else or when I had an épée in my hand."

He narrowed his eyes and leaned in so close he could smell the scent of her soap. "You're quite the mystery, Roxanne Stanley."

"No more so than you, Dougal Lockhart."

"Touché."

"Pun intended?"

"An insider fencing pun," he confirmed.

They weaved through the crowd. At just after nine in the morning, the place was already packed; excitement rippled through the air. On the way to the equipment tent, they passed the fencing area. A banner overhead proclaimed, Classical Fencing: The Martial Art of Incurable Romantics.

That made Dougal smile. He'd told Roxie he'd taken fencing at his football coach's suggestion and that was true, but he'd had a secondary reason for taking up the sport. The martial art component appealed to him. Not that he was an incurable romantic by any means. Rather he'd been interested in the weaponry. Fencing was just another fighting technique in his arsenal. During high school, before he'd switched to football, he'd taken up boxing and been a Golden Gloves contender. He'd become proficient at Krav Maga, and he'd been a wickedly good marksman long before he'd entered the military.

The thing was, Dougal had been dedicated to taking care of his mother, especially after her loser boyfriend had cleaned out their bank account and skipped town. He flashed back to the memory of the ten-year-old kid he'd been, helplessly patting his mother on the shoulder, trying to comfort her as she sobbed her heart out.

It had been a pivotal moment. He'd already been trying to fill his father's shoes after the old man had abandoned them two years earlier, but seeing his normally strong, practical mother dissolve into tears made Dougal realize what a poor job he'd been doing. Mowing the lawn, taking out the trash, helping her cook dinner wasn't enough. He had to step up to the plate and learn how to protect her.

The next day he'd asked her to enroll him in boxing classes and she'd agreed. And he'd spent the rest of his life trying to be a good and honorable man.

"I'm worried," Roxie whispered, leaning against his shoulder.

He shifted toward her. "What about?"

"It's been so long since I've fenced, and I'm not exactly in peak physical condition."

Dougal drew a languid gaze over her body. "I wouldn't say that," he drawled.

She swatted his arm. "You know what I mean. You're Mr. Bulked Up, and the most exercise I get is walking from the subway to the office. Granted it's ten blocks, and I often take the stairs to the sixth floor, but still…it probably won't take much to wind me."

"You did fine at ballroom dancing the other night."

She pondered that. "I guess I did."

"You're probably in better shape than you think you are."

They stepped into the equipment tent, and Dougal explained to the property clerk they were taking over the fencing demonstration. The guy led them over to the weaponry section.

"Which shall we spar with?" she asked, running her hands over the hilt of the weapons lined up in a wooden rack. "Foil, épée or saber?"

"I never learned to use the foil."

She stared at him as if he'd said something blasphemous. "You've got to be kidding. Everyone starts with the foil."

"Not at my high school. Our coaches decided right off the bat which weapon suited you because they needed to train fencers quickly for interscholastic competition. Besides, the foil just didn't suit me. I'm too large."

"Ah, I get it. You're one of those guys who believe the foil is for girls."

"I don't." He did, but he wasn't going to tell her that when she was standing there with a saber in her hand.

"You were misinformed," she said.

"There are too many rules with the foil. It's unrealistic. You couldn't use foil rules in a real fight. You'd be killed."

She made a *tsk, tsk* noise with her tongue. "You miss the point entirely."

"Pun intended?"

"It's going to be one of those days, isn't it? Don't try to charm your way out of a lecture. You know you're wrong."

He chuckled, beguiled by her inflexibility on the topic. "I'm wrong, huh?"

"Here's the secret of the foil," she said. "Pay attention because this is the key to fencing with all weaponry. The foil teaches you *personal control.* Control yourself and you control your opponent. The rules teach you how to think logically in combat. Having been in the military you should understand that. The rules are based on truth. You attack when you have a clear opportunity and you defend when threatened."

"Your girl is right." The clerk nodded. "Dead-on."

"That's a matter of opinion," Dougal countered. What he wanted to say, but didn't was, "Who asked you, buddy?" See? That showed personal control.

The clerk shrugged. "I'm guessing you two will be going with the saber?"

"Obviously." Roxie rolled her eyes. "Since it's the only thing he knows how to handle."

"Hey, if you can handle a saber, you don't need anything else."

Why was he feeling so defensive? Was it because in his heart he knew she was right? That he hadn't learned personal control?

"Everything is not about brute force, as I'll soon school you," she said.

They collected their gear—fencing jacket, a mask, a glove, the underarm and chest protectors and shoes—and went into the changing room. They emerged a few minutes later. Then, with sabers in hand, went to the quiet spot behind the wooden bleachers set up for the big joust scheduled for later that day.

Grinning at each other, they squared off on the soft ground.

"En garde," Roxie said, using the fencing equivalent of "On your mark."

They lowered their masks and struck their positions, sword outstretched, one leg forward.

"Prêt," she said, meaning "Get set."

Dougal's muscles tensed.

"Allez." Roxie lunged, taking him off guard with her ferocity. It was saber play, so naturally attacks were fast and furious, but after her speech about personal control, he did not expect such immediate flurry.

Dougal parried in defense, moving his weapon to push aside her attacking blade. He immediately followed with a riposte, and it was Roxie's turn to parry.

The sound of their clashing blades rent the air, clacking and clanging.

She stamped her front foot on the ground, producing a sound known as an appel. The intention was to startle him. He anticipated the lunge, raised his saber to meet hers, gliding it down her blade, keeping her in constant contact.

They went at it in a free-for-all. The sound of their meeting weapons filled the air.

She looked so mysterious, dressed in the white outfit, the mask hiding her features and he loved the way the material of her fencing pants clung to her curvaceous thighs. A sexual thrill jolted through him, but he had no time to enjoy it. Relentlessly she came at him.

Dougal defended.

Roxie lunged.

He parried. Enough of this. He was taking control. Dougal countered, lunging hard, sending her back.

Or so he thought.

But it was a feint tactic and he hadn't seen it coming. She caught him unaware with the feint-deceive, doubling back to hit him with the completion of her lunge.

"Touché." She'd earned a point.

He'd gone for the full-on aggressive speed and power. She'd finessed him by moving around on the tactical wheel, not following the conventional moves. The woman was amazing.

"Foil fencing is for girls, huh?" Roxie came at him with a fluidity that stole his breath.

And just like that he was back on the defensive.

"I think you're lying," he said, in a flurry of blade activity. His goal was to knock her off guard with a provocative statement. Everyone was lying about something.

His ploy worked. She fumbled, letting down her guard for a split second and the edge of his saber clipped her shoulder, giving him the right-of-way and a point.

"One-one," he said.

Her breasts rose as she chuffed out a breath of air, just before she attacked again. He felt the tension in her blade; something had changed. She'd lost focus.

"Give up the deception, Roxie. Admit the truth." He scored another hit and she let out a cry of frustration. "I know your secret."

"Huh?" She hesitated.

He scored another point. "Touché."

"Dammit," she mumbled.

"About that secret..." Their sabers clashed.

"I don't have any secrets." Her voice sounded reedy, breathless.

"I know you're lying," he said, attempting to rattle her into telling him the truth right here, right now.

"Okay," she chuffed. "You've got me."

He held his breath. *Was she going to confess?*

"I *have* fenced since high school."

"I knew it," Dougal went on, in spite of the disappointment knotting his chest.

She recovered from her slipups, returning full force, dazzling him with fancy footwork, her mental strategy, her lightness of action, her point control.

And just like that, she scored again.

They dueled in a smooth, loose rhythm as if they'd been fencing together for decades. Thrust and parry. Lunge and defend. Feint and deceive. It was like great sex with all their clothes on.

By the end of their allotted time, they were flagging and breathing heavily. Roxie seemed to be losing steam—her saber wasn't held as high as previously. He had her if he wanted to take her.

Did he want to do her in? His killer instincts said yes.

Unless this was another deception.

They rounded on each other. She was weakening. His competitive instincts, his familiarity with the saber, his desire to prove her wrong about the foil drove him in for the final point of the match.

He lunged with the brute force, take-your-opponent-down-as-soon-as-possible strategy he'd been taught.

Roxie parried, sank back.

Dougal came on strong, prepared for her riposte. It didn't come. Aha, he had her for sure. He made one final lunge.

And suddenly the tip of her saber was centered squarely at his breastplate.

He stared down in disbelief, the pressure of her weapon pressing against his chest. How had that happened?

"The true art of fencing," Roxie gloated, triumphantly ripping off her mask, her face flushed, her black hair spilling over her shoulders, her blue eyes snapping with delight, "is to make the other guy run into your point."

12

"GREAT JOB," DOUGAL TOLD HER after their last demonstration of the day as they were returning their supplies to the equipment tent. "You put me through my paces."

"Thank you." She smiled. "I really enjoyed it."

He looked at her and he just knew she simply could not be involved in the stuff he feared she was involved in. His gut and his heart were urging him onward, even if his mind was telling him to be cautious. No matter why she'd been in that office, he was sure she had a good reason. A reason unrelated to the computer sabotage. He couldn't deny his need for her. It overrode everything else. He had to have her. Had to speak with her. They needed a long, intimate talk to clear the air.

"You know," he said, "this is our last real evening together. The flight leaves at 6 a.m. on Monday."

"I know."

"I was hoping we'd get to spend it together." Damn if he didn't feel as nervous as a schoolboy. She looked into his eyes, and Dougal's gut sent him that same message it had that first day on the plane: *She's the one you've been waiting for.*

"I'd like that. We can order room service."

He reached out to touch her arm. "I was wondering…" He trailed off, not knowing how to broach the subject.

"Yes?"

"If it could just be you and me."

"Of course."

"No," he said. "Just you and me making love. No props, no costumes, no role-playing. Just Roxie and Dougal unplugged. Honest, open. No secrets. No hidden agendas."

She looked decidedly nervous, although he was determined not to read anything into it. "But…but I thought you liked our role-playing."

"I do," he said. It was just that they'd been donning so many masks he wasn't sure who the real Roxie was, and before he made up his mind to extend this relationship outside the realm of Eros, he wanted her to be herself with him. No roles, no guises, nothing to hide behind. "But for tonight I'd like it to just be us."

"Um…okay."

"Sevenish?"

"That sounds great."

ROXIE COULDN'T BELIEVE how nervous she felt. The thought of making love with Dougal without the armor of costumes scared the dickens out of her. She'd be fully opening herself up to him. What if plain old Roxie couldn't please him the way Muse or Lady Sarah or Dungeon Dominatrix or Elizabeth Bennet or apple-eating Eve could?

To help calm her nerves, she took a hot bath with lavender soap and sipped a cup of chamomile tea.

She'd just dried off and gotten dressed then when the doorbell rang. She ran a hand through her hair to smooth it and scurried to wrench open the door. It was Dougal with the room-service cart.

"Hey." Dougal wriggled two fingers at her.

"Hi," she smiled.

"You smell good."

"So do you."

He set up their meal in front of the window with a view of

the gardens. She giggled when he took the lid off the platters, revealing chicken Marsala, tossed salad, bruschetta and walnut brownies for dessert. To wash it all down, they shared a bottle of rosé. They sat nibbling off each other's plates like longtime lovers.

"I hate that our time together is coming to an end," he said.

"So do I." She dabbed her mouth with her napkin. "But I had no expectations beyond this."

"Really?" He looked as if he didn't believe her.

"I had a great time with you, and I think you had a great time with me. We can just leave it at that. You don't have to make me any promises."

"What if I don't want to leave it at that?"

She inhaled sharply. *Don't toy with me,* she wanted to say, but instead she just said, "Oh?"

He reached across the table and took her hands in his. "I…it's been a long time since I've had such fun with anyone."

His gaze sizzled straight through her, melting any resolve she had about keeping things casual. When had she started hungering for more? This wasn't good. The sexy environment of Eros's resort had put romantic notions into her head. Notions that had no place in her real life. When Dougal found out the truth about her… Roxie gulped. How had she ended up in this fix?

Suddenly he let go of her, pushed his hand through his hair. "You…you don't feel the same way. Aw, hell, I'm an idiot."

"No, no, I had a wonderful time. It's just that you're an Eros employee. I'm on vacation. It's—"

"A bad idea. You're right." He looked as if she'd drop-kicked him.

She felt as though she'd drop-kicked herself. If she wasn't here under such sneaky pretenses then she might have had the romance of her life. As it was, fantastic sex was the very best she could hope for. But when she looked at him she couldn't stop herself from longing for more, wishing she could have a real relationship with him. God, she'd messed things up so badly.

"This is hard for me," he said.

"And you think it's a cakewalk for me?"

"No, I don't, but I think we owe it to ourselves to fully explore the potential here."

"Dougal, I…"

But she got no further. Dougal pulled her to her feet and clamped his mouth over hers, and she was lost. Roxie's body awakened like Sleeping Beauty's to Prince Charming's kiss. No wait, scratch that. She'd promised no role-playing. She was Roxie awakening to Dougal's kiss.

Suddenly she was aware of everything, all her senses attuned. Dougal tightened the embrace, crushing her soft breasts against his muscled chest. There was no missing the hardness of his erection.

This was wrong. This was crazy. There was no cause to compound the problem. Why was she kneading her fingers along his spine? Why was she throwing back her head, exposing her throat to his hungry mouth? This could only end badly. She tried to wriggle away, but it was a tepid effort. She'd waited years for someone like him to come along, and she didn't want to fight it.

His teeth nipped lightly at the tender skin underneath her chin. Like an arrow to a bull's-eye, he'd found her secret erogenous zone. She sucked in a breath. How could this be wrong when he seemed to know exactly what to do to turn her inside out?

Just when he had her writhing mindlessly in his arms, Dougal pulled back and stared down into her face, his eyes black with a lusty sheen. "You're so beautiful."

She felt her cheeks heat. She'd always thought her skin was too pale, her nose too small, her cheeks too round to be classically beautiful, but the way he looked at her made her feel like the most attractive woman on earth.

In that moment she forgot about why this was wrong. All she could think about was how much she wanted him. Roxie ached to feel his hands skimming over her bare skin, longed to hear him call out her name in the throes of ecstasy.

He was everything she'd ever dreamed of. She could live the adventures she'd had to put on hold to raise Stacy. Her secret desires, right here, right now—it was all within her grasp. But no matter how she might wish otherwise, this relationship couldn't end well.

"I want you so badly I can't breathe," Dougal whispered. "I want to make love to you tonight, slow, soft and easy. I can't stop thinking about you, Roxie."

"Dougal…" She should say no, but when it came to him she was so weak.

"Please," he cajoled, and then he kissed her again and she knew the time for total honesty had passed. Her body swirled with need. Stunned, she realized she didn't care about the consequences. All she wanted was to have him here, now, and not think about tomorrow.

Still kissing her, Dougal guided her down the hallway and waltzed her to the bed. He eased her onto the duvet, his mouth never leaving hers. His fingers undid the buttons of her blouse. He slipped it off her shoulders, then skimmed his palms over her back to coax open the clasp of her bra.

While he was undressing her, she was frantically clawing at his shirt.

"Hey, hey," he said, finally tugging his lips from hers. "Slow down. Soft and easy, remember." The gentle expression in his eyes lit her up inside. "I want to savor this."

She pulled her bottom lip up between her teeth and whimpered.

He chuckled. "Never fear, sweetheart. We'll get there. Just give me time to pull out all my best moves."

She reached for the snap of his jeans just when his mouth

found hers again and branded her with fresh, sizzling kisses. He shucked off his pants and boxer briefs, and it wasn't until then that she realized somewhere along the way he'd kicked off his shoes. He stood on the floor; she sat on the edge of the bed, her heels hooked over the bed rail.

"What happened," she whispered, tracing the puckered scar at the top of his right thigh. She'd seen it before, but had never asked him about it because it seemed too personal a question, but if they were on the verge of taking things to the next level, she wanted to know.

"Huh?" He blinked groggily and saw where she was staring.

She reached out a hand to touch the silvered wound, but he flinched, stepped back. "Don't."

"You were shot?" She looked up to meet his eyes.

"Yes."

She wanted to ask him what had happened, but the look on his face warned her off. She dropped her gaze and instead took in the sight of his jutting, erect penis. It was a glory to behold.

Here in the soft glow from the bedroom light, she could appreciate just how gorgeous he was. Lowering her head, she lightly touched her tongue to his tip.

Dougal hissed out a long breath as if he'd been scalded. "Oh, yeah, that feels so sweet."

She took him in her mouth.

"As good as that feels, sweetheart, if you keep that up I won't last a minute."

Roxie drew back, looked up at him, at his scarred leg, his flat abdomen, his naked chest, his broad shoulders and then up to his dark eyes. He was so masculine. So strong.

Lower and lower she kissed, headed for dangerous territory.

He threaded his fingers through her hair. "No, no," he protested weakly.

"Yes…" She kissed him. "Yes."

Another kiss.

Then her hand was on him, stroking his throbbing head.

Roxie dipped her head and she tasted his flesh. Instantly wet heat gushed through her body. The muscles deep within her pelvis tightened. Her heart beat faster, and she surprised herself by how quickly she grew slick.

She slid down the length of his body, savoring the salty taste of his hot skin—tasting, licking, exploring the mysteries of his body.

He moaned when her lips closed over his shaft. He tasted so good! She felt an electrical current run through her as she licked him and reveled in her feminine power.

She loved him with her mouth, caressed him with her tongue, coaxing him to the edge of ecstasy. His body was as tense as stone.

"Not yet," he whispered. "Not yet. I want to be inside you."

"Come here," she said.

He didn't protest when she took his hand and pulled him down on the bed beside her. His eyes were dark with lust, and she spied goose bumps tracking up his arm. She grinned wickedly.

Now where had she put that condom? A quick search and she discovered it had slid onto the other side of the duvet while she'd been undressing him. She tore open the packet with her teeth, and palmed the round rubber ring.

She stood up only to discover her legs quivered like running water. She quickly turned and straddled his knees, her own knees digging into the covers.

He'd braced himself on his elbows and was watching her intently. He was the most beautiful specimen of manhood she'd ever seen, and she could hardly believe he was here with her.

His eyes met hers and his gaze was so raw, so primal, she had to look away and calm herself before she could proceed.

Trying to look casual, as if she did this all the time, Roxie ran her hand up his thigh.

He groaned and the sound served to resurrect her hunger.

Tentatively she reached out and stroked one finger down his chest, while the other hand—the one with the palmed condom—went up to touch the head of his cock.

He felt heavy and large in her hand. She thrilled to his bigness. Dougal's penis was at once velvet soft and hard as steel, an erotic combination of texture and heat. She could feel the blood pulsating through his shaft.

He groaned again, and she felt more than saw him fall back against the pillows. She took her time. Touching, kneading, stroking. He moved his hips. She could feel the muscles of his buttocks tighten. He wanted to thrust.

Teasing, she lowered her mouth to his tip.

"Don't..." he warned. "I want to be inside you and if you put your mouth around me, I'll blow it."

"Just a little taste," she said and swirled her tongue around the head of his penis.

He sucked air into his lungs in an audible gasp. She could feel him struggling to hold on to his restraint. "Roxie..."

The taste of him was both savory and sweet. A unique flavor, all Dougal. She licked him like an ice-cream cone, seeking to arouse but not to set off an inferno.

She stroked his balls while she licked, and his body stiffened. "Do you like that?"

His answer was nothing more than a hard grunt and a short, rough nod. She played with him a bit longer, feeling his penis grow to an impossible length.

When his balls pulled up tightly against his shaft she knew it was time to pull back, let his heart rate settle down.

"Roxie..." He breathed her name, pure awe in his voice. "You're a vicious goddess."

She rocked back on her heels, grinned at him.

"Come here." He pulled her into his arms.

"Wait." She moved back just enough to roll the condom down over his erection.

"Now," he said. It was a command, not a request. "Get on top of me."

Her knees were anchored on either side of his waist and she was dripping wet for him. He wrapped his hand around her neck, tugged her head down to plant a hot kiss on her mouth.

Roxie melted into him. He tasted like her, and she tasted like him. It was a sexy combination that fired her up all over again.

He settled his hands on her hips and guided her down on top of him. They both hissed out air in unison as he filled her up and she engulfed him.

She set the pace, slow and deliberate, driving him mad.

"Hurry," he urged.

"Nope," she murmured. "Payback's a bitch."

"You've got a cruel side, babe."

"It'll be worth the wait," she promised.

"Two can play this game," he said, and roguishly reached up to pinch her nipples between this thumbs and index fingers.

Fire shot down her nerve endings from her breasts to her feminine core. "Devil," she dared.

"Don't forget it." He laughed.

He moved beneath her, arching his hips, thrusting her high. His hands roved over her waist, her back, her belly and back to her breasts. At some point it felt as if he had a dozen maddening hands.

She tried to hold him off, to make him wait as long as possible, but then the clever man slipped his fingers between her legs and found her pleasure spot.

"No fair," she cried weakly, but all she got in response was a wicked chuckle.

He wriggled his finger and she couldn't hold off any longer. She rode him as if her life depended on it.

Then just before she was about to have her mind-blowing orgasm, he placed both palms around the sides of her head and pulled her down to stare deeply into her eyes.

They gazed straight into each other's souls.

At the same moment, he thrust as hard into her as he could, and the earth shifted and Roxie spiraled out of control.

His face contorted, but he never stopped looking at her, never stopped thrusting her over the edge until they both exploded in simultaneous bliss.

Her body spasmed. Jerked.

He clutched her to him. He was shaking all over.

Roxie collapsed against his chest, heard the thunderous pounding of his heart.

He squeezed her tight, kissed her all over, her eyelids, her nose, her cheeks, her chin. Then finally he found her mouth and kissed her with a joy that forever captured her heart.

SOMETIME LATER, SHE AWAKENED clutched tight in the circle of Dougal's arms.

"You awake?" he asked.

"Uh-huh."

"I've been lying here listening to you sleep. I love the way you breathe when you're sleeping. It's a soft little purring kind of noise."

"Are you saying I snore?" she teased.

"Not at all. It's just the nicest sound. Like you're completely relaxed, totally trusting."

"Hmm," she murmured.

He reached over and threaded his fingers through hers. "There's something I want to tell you."

"Does it have anything to do with the bullet wound on your thigh?" she asked.

"Yes," he said. "It does."

"Oh."

"I haven't been with a woman since—" he swallowed audibly "—since I got shot."

"How long ago?"

"Eighteen months."

"It's been a long time for me, as well," she said. "Much longer than eighteen months."

"The last time I felt this way…the way I'm feeling about you. Well…let's just say my feelings were unreliable."

"You're scared the same thing is happening with me that happened to you with this other woman?"

He hesitated, shifted. She could tell this wasn't easy for him. He wasn't the kind of guy who readily talked about his feelings.

"I'm listening," she coaxed.

A long moment ensued, and finally he ventured, "Before I went to work for Eros, I was a captain in the Air Force, specializing in aviation security."

"Uh-huh." She nodded encouragingly.

"I was stationed in Germany, and I was in charge of guarding the Air Force fleet."

"Sounds like a lot of responsibility."

"It was." He paused again, wiped a hand across his mouth before continuing. She squeezed the hand that still held hers. He gave her a wan smile. "I met a woman there. Her name was Ava, and I fell for her like an avalanche."

Jealousy, hot and unexpected, poured over her.

"By nature I'm not a particularly trusting guy. I tend to see the darker side of people, but with Ava, I was blind. I ignored my gut, which told me she wasn't all she seemed."

Roxie could tell that this was headed in a bad direction. She made a noise of sympathy at the back of her throat.

You should tell him. Tell him right now. About Langley, about Stacy, about spying for Getaway Airlines. Roxie opened her mouth, but she couldn't force out the words that she knew would ruin everything.

"We slept together, and I thought I was in love." Dougal shook his head. "One day I caught her going through my office. She pretended that she'd come there to set up a romantic scenario, but that was when the first suspicions started to creep in. I didn't want to believe she was up to something. I ignored my instincts."

"She was using you."

Dougal nodded. "I had her investigated and I discovered she was working for a terrorist cell. She'd stolen classified information from my locked files. I still don't know how she managed to get access to them, but I managed to stop her cohorts as they were rigging up a bomb in one of the planes that was due to carry military brass back to the Pentagon. Ava showed up while I was in the middle of arresting them, and she shot me in the thigh."

Roxie splayed a palm over her mouth.

"I felt like such a fool." Dougal's voice turned hard. "When my tour of duty was over, I left the Air Force. I couldn't do my job effectively. Not when I could allow my heart to rule my head. I'm telling you this because it's been very hard for me to trust a woman ever since then. But I trust you, Roxie, and that's a huge thing for me to admit."

You have to tell him the truth. You have to tell him now!

His sincere dark eyes sliced right through her. If she told him, though, she'd lose her job and then Stacy would drop out of school.

"But you, Roxie." His whisper was husky. "*You* make me want to try again."

His honesty, the vulnerability all over his face clawed at her. She was a horrible person for deceiving him, and he didn't deserve to be treated this way. "Dougal, there's some—"

But before she could work up the courage to tell him her dark secret, his lips were on hers. He slipped his arms around her, lifted her up, kissed her tenderly as if she was the most precious thing on earth.

Lust swamped her. She had to have him again. Had to have him or she would surely die. She ran her tongue around his lips, and he made a masculine noise of enjoyment.

She moaned, loving yet hating the sweet torture. She wriggled into him, her breasts pressed flush against his muscled chest.

Tell him.

He ran his fingers up and down her shoulders. She threw back her head, and he trailed his kisses to the underside of her neck, nuzzling and nibbling.

Experimentally he rubbed his thumbs over her nipples and they beaded so tight that they ached.

"Ah," he said. "So you like that?"

"It feels awesome."

A hazy hotness draped over her, thick with sexual urgency. She wanted him so badly that her need was a solid, unyielding mass in her throat.

"What about this?" His tongue laved the underside of her jaw.

She shuddered against him.

"And this?" Lightly he tickled the skin on the inside of her upper arm.

"Wild man." She gasped.

"Exactly." He grinned.

When his mouth found its way back to hers again, Roxie could hear nothing except for the tyranny of her beating heart. The force of his desire caused her to tremble and sweat. Her knees quivered. Her heart pounded.

He tunneled his fingers through her hair. She felt his presence in every cell of her body, in every breath she took, in every strum of the blood pumping through her veins.

This new sensation drove her into a frenzy. Her muscles flexed. Blinding flashes of light. The rushing sound of ocean waves in her head. Uncontrollable spasms rattled her body.

Her world quaked.

Madly, frantically, they grappled with each other. His hands were broad and warm. His mouth an instrument of exquisite torture. Time spun, morphed, as elusive as space.

The entire time he was buried inside of her, he stared deeply into her eyes, as if he was lost in her gaze and could not find his way out. Did not even want to find his way out.

They were one. Mated. Trembling and clinging to each other.

His cock filled her up, pushing deep inside of her until he could go no farther.

Then he pulled back. In and out, he moved in a smooth rhythm that rocked her soul. He rode her and she rode him until they both came in a searing white blinding light.

And all she could think of was that she could never have him for her own.

13

DOUGAL HEARD ROXIE padding quietly against the tile floor before he saw her.

He stood at the stove whipping up a big breakfast. Eros had fully stocked the kitchenette with everything a romantic chef would need. When he was growing up, his mother had insisted he learn how to cook, so Dougal could flip a mean Denver omelet.

After last night, he and Roxie needed sustenance. They must have burned a thousand calories. He was going to feed her and then he was going to make love to her all over again. He'd made her come four times the night before—a personal best for him—and he was eager to shoot for number five.

Cooking for her spurred his urge to nourish Roxie in every way possible.

Hearing her approach above the noisy sizzle of the bacon and hissing steam from the espresso machine, he knew she was going to wrap her arms around his waist before he even felt her petite palms slide across his belly.

Dougal set the spatula on the granite countertop and turned into her embrace, pulling her close to him for a kiss. She tasted pepperminty and wore silky pink pajamas without a bra.

"Good morning," he murmured against her lips.

He could feel her nipples bead up against his chest. He cupped Roxie's butt. No panty lines. She was totally naked underneath that silk.

Instantly his cock hardened.

Don't burn the bacon. They'd been in bed for over twelve hours. They needed to eat so they could hit the sack for another twelve. While he thanked heavens it was Sunday, that meant tomorrow was Monday and they'd be flying home. It was over.

"Well." She chuckled and pressed herself tighter against his erection. "Good morning to you, too."

"I can't help it," he said. "See what you do to me?"

She blushed prettily, which was amazing since they'd just done some very intimate things together. She really was quite bashful.

"Breakfast is ready. I hope you're hungry."

"Starved," she said. "Although it looks like you made enough food to feed the entire tour group."

"No way, babe. Today it's just you and me. Have a seat."

She pulled out a chair at the quaint little bistro table in front of the picture window. "Whatever it is you're cooking, it smells heavenly."

"Not as heavenly as you."

She lowered her lashes and sent him a coy half smile—sassy but demure, Snow White through and through. Something hitched his chest. An emotion he couldn't identify. The feeling was at once hot and sweet and uncomfortable.

He realized he wanted much more than sex from Roxie, and at the same time, he knew that circumstances were such that he could never have it. The sudden loneliness that stabbed through him was as sharp as it was unexpected.

Dougal set their plates, loaded up with omelets, bacon and biscuits on the table. Roxie angled her head and her dark hair swung fetchingly over her shoulders like a shimmery black curtain. Grinning, she rubbed her palms together. "It's been ages since anyone has cooked for me. I feel pampered. Thank you."

"No problem. I like to cook."

"You are an enigma, Dougal Lockhart. A guy's guy who knows his way around a kitchen. Tell me again why you're not married?"

"Never found the right girl." He produced two forks from the silverware drawer, napkins from the pantry and butter from the fridge. Steam rose from the coffee cups he parked beside the plates. He plunked down across from her, happy to notice she was digging into the omelet with gusto.

"Mmm." She made a sexy noise of pure pleasure. "Seriously, if you ever decide to give up the tour-guide business, you could have an amazing career in food service."

"Good to know I have options," he said, feeling pleased that he'd pleased her.

"I get the impression that you're skilled at a lot of things." She cut a pat of butter from the stick and slipped it between the folds of her biscuit. "Are these homemade?"

He nodded. "My mother's recipe."

She sat looking at him with her intense blue eyes, and he just came unraveled. He reached for her at the same moment she dropped her fork to her plate with a clatter and leaned across the table toward him.

"Dougal." She breathed in.

He exhaled. "Roxie."

His brain fogged. The smell of her tangled in his nose and drove him wild. He acted purely on instinct. His dick was as hard as the granite countertop. In fact, he was going to take her on that countertop. Spread her legs and do her right there.

The next thing he knew they were naked and he was sheathed in a condom, bending her over the counter, and entering her from behind. She was slick and ready for him.

"You're so wet." He groaned and sank in deeper.

Trembling, he wrapped his arms around her waist, dropped his forehead to her shoulder blade and closed his eyes to savor her tightness. Dougal could hardly think. His mind was obliterated by the feel of her around him. His emotions blistered hot, intense and unexpected.

Frantically he pumped into her. There was no smooth landing, no easy glide. Dougal was on a jet plane headed straight to the ground, spinning out into the clear blue sky. His whole body shook, and sweat slicked his back. He was helplessly out of control. It scared him while at the same time he felt utterly blissful. What in the hell was happening to him? He'd never ever been this rough, this rushed.

Then from out of nowhere, he felt her fingertips caress his balls and boom!

One tickle and he came. Just a simple light scratch from her soft hand and he detonated. He stiffened against her, his hips arching, grinding so hard against her, the fluid poured out of him, his cock so hot and drained he thought he'd disintegrate.

Blindly he clung to Roxie, squeezing her tightly as if she was the only thing keeping him from falling apart.

He cursed himself. "I'm sorry, I'm sorry," he apologized. "I've never gone off like that."

"Shh," she whispered, separating them, turning in his arms to cradle his head between her hands and kiss his lips. "It's okay."

"It's not. I'm a rude, selfish bastard and I—"

"I like it that I can make you lose control." She ran her fingers over his face. "It makes me feel feminine and powerful."

Maybe that's what scared him so much. He'd always been in control with women. He'd never lost it like this. Why was it happening? What did it mean?

He was still rock hard. He cupped her buttocks and lifted her up on the counter, entered her from the front and rocked against her. Dishes clattered to the floor. Silverware flew under the table. They didn't notice. She moaned and tossed back her head. She sank her fingers into his hair, directed his head to her breasts.

"Suck my nipples," she commanded.

He did as Roxie asked, taking first one pink, straining nipple into his mouth, then the other, lightly nibbling each one until she moaned again.

He wouldn't have thought it possible, but he grew even harder inside of her.

Her muscles tightened around him. Groaning, he fisted a hand through her hair and pulled her head back, plied his teeth and lips and tongue along the silky column of her long, slender throat.

Dougal's nerve endings tingled. His heart thumped. His lungs chuffed. His belly burned with damaging need. Forget control. Trying to gather it was a lost cause. *He* was a lost cause. He was going to blow again and he still hadn't made her come.

No way was he going to let that happen.

With a supreme effort of will, he eased back and slipped his hand down to where she was stretched tight around him. His fingers tangled in the soft damp hairs at her feminine entrance. He found her clitoris, and she hissed in her breath as he lightly brushed the pad of his index finger over the swollen nub.

He captured her mouth with his at the same time as he increased the pressure, swallowed up her startled gasp. A hot wire of excitement flashed down his spine straight to his groin. He pushed inside her warm box again, all the while still stroking her twitching hood.

Pinning her to the counter with his body, his tongue deep in her mouth, he thrust into her hard and fast.

And felt the rising rumble overtake him at the same time as she let out a thin, strangled sound.

Lost. They were lost together in this beautiful, splendid world.

Grinding and aching, clutching and shaking, they shot into orbit together.

Something inside Dougal broke loose, cracked open, shattered. He was raw, primal, exposed.

Ah, hell, he thought.

All the energy left his body in one exhausted release, leaving him spent.

Roxie was nothing—*nothing*—like any other woman he'd ever experienced. She was something else entirely.

Dougal's eyes misted and his nose burned. He clenched his jaw tight, blinking back the onslaught of emotions. He pressed his face into her hair, heaved in a shuddering breath, closed his eyes and held her close while his heart rate slowed.

"Thank you," Roxie gasped. "That was exactly what I needed. Straight-up wild sex with absolutely no strings attached."

No strings.

She was letting him off the hook, setting him free. That should be great news. He should be happy.

But he wasn't.

"You're the best I've ever had," she whispered, pressing her mouth against his ear. "Not that I've had a lot of experience, but you're definitely an A plus."

Something every man longed to hear, but it sounded so hollow. All he could think was *no strings attached.*

He wanted to find the sturdiest ball of twine he could get his hands on and bind her to him forever.

That's when Dougal knew he was in serious trouble.

WHY HAD SHE SAID WHAT she'd said about no strings attached? She wanted strings and lots of them. She wanted a whole yarn barn full of strings.

But she couldn't have them. She'd made love to him under false pretenses, hiding the reason she was really on this tour. Spying and betraying Dougal's confidence to Porter Langley, a man she was rapidly losing respect for.

Dougal looked at her with eyes so sad she feared he could read her thoughts. Misery moved into her heart, set up house.

She dropped her gaze, grabbed up her pajamas and scrambled into them. She was a horrible person, and she should just come clean right now and take her punishment.

Dougal pulled on his pants, zipped them up. "Roxie?"

"Yes?" She plunked down in the chair to slip on her socks.

Dougal took the chair next to her, rested his palm on her forearm. "Look at me."

Reluctantly she lifted her head.

"I've got something I need to tell you." His tone was serious. "I haven't been completely honest with you."

A lump the size of Alaska chunked up in her throat. "You've got a girlfriend," she quipped. *Please don't let him have a girlfriend.*

"I don't have a girlfriend."

"Whew, that's good. I didn't want some chick chasing me down to yank my hair out for fooling around with her man."

"I would never do that. When I'm with a woman, I'm with her." His hand was still on her forearm.

"Oh," she said, not knowing what else to say. *Be with me.* That's what she wanted to say, but of course, she couldn't.

"I'm going to have to ask you to keep what I'm about to tell you in strictest confidence. Can you promise me that, Roxie?" His intense gaze pinned her to the spot.

She couldn't promise him that, not when her job and Stacy's future might depend on sharing the information with her boss. "Dougal, I..."

"I can trust you." He interlaced his fingers with hers, squeezed her hand.

Compelled by the vulnerable expression on his face, Roxie nodded mutely. She couldn't help feeling flattered that he trusted her, especially after what had happened to him with that other woman.

"I'm not really a tour guide."

She laughed nervously. "What do you mean?"

He leaned forward, shoulders tense, his eyes never leaving hers. "I'm a private duty air marshal undercover as a tour guide. I own my own security firm. Taylor Corben hired me because she's received some threats against her airline and the resorts. She wants to make sure her guests are kept safe."

Fear plunged a dagger in her heart.

He knows!

This wasn't about him trusting her. He suspected she was a spy and he was testing her. That's was probably why he'd come to her suite last night, but things had heated up between them and he'd gotten distracted.

And she'd allowed it to happen.

The fear escalated into panic. What was she going to say? She was a terrible liar. He'd caught her. She might as well surrender, confess and get it over with.

"Roxie," Dougal's voice broke through her rampant, runaway thoughts.

"Yes?" She trembled.

"You can't tell anyone about this."

She nodded. Everything was ruined. The early euphoria she'd felt fled like sunshine at nightfall. She couldn't have him. There was no hope for salvaging anything between them. She'd betrayed him, and she had to tell Dougal the truth. Never mind that Porter Langley would be disappointed. Never mind that she wouldn't get her promotion or that she'd be out of a job. She could find some other way to get the money for Stacy's college. She could cash in her 401(k). There wasn't much in it, but it might just be enough to pay for her sister's next semester. She could take a second job, a third if necessary, but she couldn't keep lying to Dougal.

In all honesty, she should have already told him. What she'd been doing was wrong and she had to set things right because she was falling in love with him.

Love.

The realization clubbed her. She hadn't been looking for it. Hadn't expected it, but there it was. She was in love with Dougal Lockhart. Her pulse quickened and her gut squeezed miserably.

She was in love with him, and she was about to hurt him as swiftly and as surely as that other woman who'd betrayed his trust and broken his heart.

"Dougal," she said, "there's something very important that I have to tell you, as well."

He went suddenly still. Something in her tone of voice had given her away. "What is it?"

She dragged in a deep breath. "It's a confession really."

He inhaled audibly, and his gaze drilled a hole straight through her. "A confession?"

"I…" Nervously she ran her palms over the tops of her thighs. "I have an ulterior motive for being here."

"And what's that?" he asked.

She swallowed. This was the most difficult news she'd ever had to break to anyone, beyond telling Stacy their parents were never coming home. One sentence and he was never going to look at her the same away again. He'd just spoken of how much he trusted her, and in one breath she was going to take it all away. "This is hard to say."

"Just open your mouth and spit it out."

"I'm not who you think I am."

Dougal looked completely and utterly *crushed.*

"I can explain everything," Roxie said, but Dougal wasn't responding.

"Dougal?" Her voice trembled.

He stared at her as if she was a stranger, his face expressionless. Dougal fisted his hands, a muscle jumped in his jaw, a frown dug deep into his brow. "You're the saboteur." He ground out the words.

Roxie blinked. What was he talking about? "Saboteur?"

He staggered to his feet.

"You." He spat out the word. "You sabotaged the autopilot on the plane."

"What?" She raised a hand to her mouth. Her stomach roiled. *Please don't be sick.* "How would I know how to do something like that?"

"Maybe you had an accomplice. Or maybe the autopilot wasn't part of the sabotage, and it was just a malfunction."

"Huh?"

"You loosened the screws in the stage-light rigging. Anyone could have done it. You wouldn't have to have specialized knowledge."

She gaped at him, unable to believe what he was accusing her of. Speechless, she shook her head.

"You're the one who decapitated the sprinklers. That's a simple matter, as well."

"What?" she repeated dumbly.

"And somehow you infected the computer system with a Trojan."

"I didn't," she whimpered.

His face was pure fury now as he came toward her.

Fear mingled with remorse. She'd never seen him looking so angry. Roxie took three quick steps backward, her retreat halted only by the wall. Her knees locked like rusty hinges.

"Don't lie to me," he said.

"I could never do any of those things," she cried. "I can't believe you think that of me. Dougal, I'm not a saboteur. I swear."

"Then what are you?"

"I'm..." She drew in a heavy breath. "I'm a corporate spy."

He leaned in close, his big body crowding hers. "Who are you working for?"

"Getaway Airlines," she admitted.

"Porter Langley sent you here?"

She nodded. "I wasn't doing it for myself, I was doing it to—"

"You used me."

Roxie stepped toward him, hand outstretched. "It wasn't like that. It was…"

She stopped because what he said was true. Not that she'd slept with him to find out about Eros. By the time they'd made love, she'd forgotten all about the assignment. At that point she'd just been having fun, enjoying her adventure and…*relating everything he told you about Eros right back to Mr. Langley.*

Oh God, it had been exactly like that. Briefly she closed her eyes, knotted her fists. There was no way out of this.

"We have to talk," she said, "and get this straightened out."

"There's nothing to straighten out."

She understood the pain she'd caused him, and it rushed at her dark and hot. There was a hole in her heart, black and empty and guilty, so guilty. Roxie winced, cringed. "I did it for my sister. To get a promotion that would help keep her in college."

"I don't need to hear your excuses. The bottom line is I trusted you." His eyes were hard and dark. He was trying to cloak his feelings, but she could see the hurt simmering in those murky depths. "I told you everything and you didn't come clean with me. You betrayed my trust, Roxie."

Anger shot through her. Yes, she was wrong, but there were two people in this room. She raised her chin defiantly. "I wasn't the only one who was lying. You're not really a tour guide."

"I was undercover. It was my job."

"And I was only doing my job. It's okay for you to deceive me, but it's not okay for me?" She sank her hands on her hips. "That's a double standard if I ever heard one. You just wait for people to slip up so you can crow, 'Oh, I knew I couldn't trust them all along.' You go around with suspicion sitting on your shoulder like Poe's raven, just waiting for someone to make a mistake. But look at your own behavior, Mr. Lockhart. How trustworthy have you been? Sounds like to me that you've got to learn to trust yourself, Dougal. I was wrong, yes, but I did it for the right reasons."

"I guess that's what you have to tell yourself in order to live with what you're doing."

Her anger fled. She was just so sorry things had ended up this way. She'd never wanted to be a spy in the first place. Roxie swallowed. "Dougal, I…please forgive me. I made a big mistake. You've got to forgive me because—"

"I won't be played for a fool, Roxie. I thought we had something special, but now I see we don't."

Then he turned and walked out the door, leaving Roxie to sink down the length of the wall, plant her bottom on the carpet, draw her knees to her chest and sob her heart out.

DOUGAL HARDENED HIS HEART and stalked across the cobblestones, even as some small part of him whispered, *Forgive.*

Roxie was right after all. He was holding her to a different standard than he held himself. Why was it okay for him to deceive under the guise of his job, but it wasn't okay for her to do the same thing?

He was in the right, dammit! He was protecting Taylor's interests.

His inability to trust had led him here, just as she'd accused. He hadn't really let down his guard with her, he'd only pretended. He'd held part of himself in reserve, waiting for the other shoe to drop and when it had, he'd felt vindicated.

But he sure as hell didn't feel good.

She might be a corporate spy. She might have lied and done some unethical things, but her motives were honest. She was a good person at heart.

Forgive.

His old bullet wound ached. Absentmindedly Dougal rubbed his thigh. Then he hardened his chin and put Roxie out of his mind. He couldn't worry about this now. If she wasn't the saboteur, he had to determine who was.

His cell phone rang. He pulled it from his pocket and checked the caller ID. It was Taylor. "Hello?"

"Dougal," Taylor snapped. "We've got a big problem. Get to a computer. We need to have a video conference call. Now."

AFTER DOUGAL SLAMMED THE DOOR behind him, Roxie admitted the last time she'd felt this lonely, this utterly wretched, was the day she'd learned her parents had been killed. If they could see her now, they'd be so disappointed. The thought ate at her soul.

From the minute she'd agreed to her boss's scheme, she'd known something bad was going to happen. She'd violated her principles, and in doing so, she'd betrayed herself as surely as she'd betrayed Dougal. How could she expect him to forgive her? She couldn't forgive herself. She had knowingly done wrong, even if her motives had been noble.

What was that saying? The road to hell was paved with good intentions.

So what are you going to do about it?

She had to make amends. To herself. To Eros Airlines. To Dougal.

But how?

She needed someone to talk to about what had happened between her and Dougal. She couldn't burden Stacy, but if she just had somebody objective she could tell, it might help her see things more clearly.

Jess and Sam. Yes. That was it. The twins were friendly and upbeat and they weren't personally invested in the outcome. Roxie was certain they could bring a fresh perspective to her dilemma.

Happy to have something to do, somewhere to go and someone to confide in, Roxie picked herself up off the floor and went in search of the twins.

14

"WHAT'S UP?" DOUGAL ASKED Taylor when they had the video conference call connected. She looked royally pissed off, but she'd refused to tell him what had her so upset. She said she wanted him to see for himself.

"I want you to go to this blog," Taylor said and gave him the Internet address.

Dougal tapped it in, and a second later up popped a blog with the headline: Our Eros Vacation. On the right side was a photograph of Jess and Sam.

"What am I looking for?' Dougal asked as he started reading the blog.

"Scroll down."

He did and more photographs popped into view, photographs not of the twin sisters, but of him and Roxie. There was one of them kissing in the punt. It looked as if it had been snapped from above, as if Sam and Jess had lain in wait on one of the bridges on the Cam to catch them at exactly the wrong moment. There was a picture of them climbing down the bell-tower steps together, holding hands. Another photograph depicted Dougal and Roxie onstage when they'd recited the sonnet together, their lips mere inches apart. But it was the last photograph that killed his soul. It was a shot of him and Roxie leaving the dungeon together, their clothes askew, their faces flushed, and he was looking at Roxie with such love on his face that a blind man could have seen his feelings for her.

Beside the photographs were snarky little captions all designed to draw attention to the fact that an Eros tour guide was behaving inappropriately with a guest of the resort.

"I'm so sorry, Taylor."

"Who is this woman?"

"She's a spy for Porter Langley," Dougal said.

"Is she the same person who has been sabotaging my resorts?"

"No."

"Well I gotta tell you, Dougal." Taylor ran a hand through her hair. "This feels just the same as sabotage."

"I'm truly sorry, Taylor. Of course I will give you back your fee," he said. "I not only didn't do my job, but I exhibited unprofessional behavior."

"That's not necessary. I just wanted to know if you were okay. After what happened in Germany, this must be a blow to discover the woman you're in love with is a corporate spy who was just using you."

The pain in his chest stabbed fresh and sharp. "I'm not in love with her," he denied.

"Oh, Dougal, you don't have to lie to me."

His shoulders slumped, his heart slid to his feet. "It's that obvious?"

"If I could, I'd reach out and give you a big hug."

He snorted. "It was my own stupidity."

"Are you sure she doesn't feel anything for you?"

He shook his head. "I'm not sure of anything anymore, Taylor."

"May I give you a piece of advice from someone who denied love for too long?"

He shrugged. "If you think it will help."

"Go to her, tell her how you feel. Even if she doesn't feel the same way, it's better to know where you stand than to keep forever guessing."

"AND THAT'S THE WHOLE sordid story," Roxie said to Jess and Sam after she'd related everything that had happened.

They were all submerged in a bubbly hot tub just off the lobby of the resort, underneath a pergola.

"Wow," Sam said, "that's some tale."

"I would never have taken you for a spy," Jess added.

Roxie thought confessing her sins to the twins would make her feel better, but it had not. On the contrary, she was more miserable than ever and no closer to a solution.

Sam lifted a glass of wine to her lips. "I think—" She broke off and her eyes widened.

"Um, oh," Jess said, staring in the same direction as her sister.

Roxie swiveled her head to see what had captured the twins' attention.

It was Dougal. Stalking straight toward them and glowering darkly.

Thrill at the sight of him and fear at the fierce displeasure in his eyes squeezed Roxie's heart. What had she done now?

Jess and Sam were suddenly scrambling out of the hot tub, grabbing for their bathrobes and towels. They looked supremely guilty.

What was going on?

"Hey," Dougal said, breaking into a trot. "Stop right there, you two."

"Um..." Jess raised a hand, sent him a dazzling smile. "Hi, Dougal."

"Don't give me that," Dougal barked, his long legs taking him to the edge of the hot tub. He never even glanced in Roxie's direction. "I know what you've been up to."

Confused by the turn of events, Roxie slogged from the water. Feeling extremely exposed, she reached for her own robe, pulled it over her one-piece bathing suit and belted it at the waist. She glanced from Dougal to the twins and back again.

"You ambushed me and Roxie. Took compromising pictures of us and posted them on the Internet," he accused.

Jess and Sam looked sheepish.

Befuddled, Roxie pushed her damp hair off her face and tried to understand what he was saying.

"Who hired you to sabotage Eros?" Dougal demanded.

Jess and Sam were the saboteurs? Roxie's mouth dropped open.

"You did something to disrupt the autopilot on the Eros jet," Dougal continued. "You loosened the stage lighting so it would fall. You destroyed the sprinklers—"

"Whoa, hey." Sam held up her palms. "Wait just a darn minute. We're not involved in anything like that."

Dougal's scowl deepened. "Then what are you involved in?"

Jess darted a nervous glance toward Roxie and wet her lips. "Um, could we have this discussion in private?"

For the first time since he'd arrived, Dougal looked at Roxie. His expression was unreadable, but she was getting weird vibes from both him and the twins. "What is going on?" she demanded.

"We might as well just tell her," Sam said to her sister. "She's going to find out."

"Tell me what?" Roxie's bare feet chilled against the redwood decking, but it wasn't so much from the cool springtime air as from the discussion.

Jess shifted her weight but didn't meet Roxie's eyes. "Because," she told Dougal, "we were playing matchmaker."

"Matchmaker?" Dougal and Roxie said in unison.

"We got you to take us on the punt, and then we arranged for Mike and David to show up so we could force you and Dougal to be alone together," Sam said.

"In a romantic venue," Jess added. "And under titillating circumstances."

"But why would you do that?" Roxie asked.

Jess slid her twin a look. Sam nodded, giving her the go-ahead. "Porter Langley hired us to make sure Roxie had an affair with one of the Eros staff members."

"And it worked," Sam pointed out.

"What?" Stunned by what they'd just admitted, Roxie could only stare.

"You had an affair with him." Jess jerked her head toward Dougal.

"I don't get it." Roxie felt lost. "Porter sent me here to gather insider information on Eros."

"That's just what he told you," Sam said. "In actuality, he was using you as a pawn."

"Wait." Dougal sank his hands on his hips. "Now I'm confused. What exactly is Porter Langley up to?"

"Here's how he explained it to us," Jess put in. "He wanted to create a scandal for Eros. His plan was to send Roxie on the Romance of Britannia tour as a corporate spy. His real play was to capitalize on her inexperience in romantic relationships and use it to bring down Taylor Corben."

"To that end—" Sam picked up the story "—he hired us. We're private investigators, specializing in tempting cheating husbands to make passes at us so their wives have grounds for divorce."

"That's entrapment," Dougal growled.

Jess shrugged. "We make a very good living."

"Actually," Sam said, "that's how we met Porter. He tried to pick us up for a threesome."

Roxie couldn't believe what she was hearing. "But why would you do this to me?"

"To get proof that Eros employees are having sex with the guests."

Roxie's breath fled her lungs. "What? And how were you going to prove this?"

"We're very good at our jobs," Jess said. "You should be

careful what you do in semipublic places." She shook her head. "And telephoto lenses are quite the modern miracle."

Roxie felt as if she'd been kicked in the gut. "You…you have pictures?"

"Yes, and we already posted them to our Web site," Sam confirmed.

Roxie's head swirled. Her boss had used her, and these women who she'd thought were her friends had betrayed her. The enormity of what had happened washed over Roxie. Not only had her stupidity got her into trouble, but she'd put Dougal's job in jeopardy, as well. "But I trusted you."

"That was your first mistake." Sam held up her palms.

"You should be ashamed of yourselves," Dougal snarled and fisted his hands.

"No," Jess countered, "you should be ashamed of yourself. Having sex with a guest." She clicked her tongue. "You broke the rules, Dougal, and now you're going to have to deal with the consequences."

NO WORDS COULD DESCRIBE the savage despair churning inside him.

He was angry, yes. Worried, most assuredly. But even though those emotions were strong, they weren't primary. No, the main sensation raging inside him was the urge to protect Roxie at all costs.

One look at her face told him the whole story. She was hurt beyond measure. Questioning herself, doubting her ability to read people. He knew what she was feeling, because he'd been there. He'd felt her pain.

"Roxie." He called her name without knowing what else he was going to say. He reached for her, but she was in no state of mind to turn to him. With jerky movements she stepped back, arms raised.

"Roxie," he called.

"Leave me alone. Please, just leave me alone." She ducked her head and ran away, her bare feet pattering against the tiles.

Glaring, he turned to Jess and Sam. "Are you proud of yourselves? You've hurt one of the finest women I've ever known."

"Hey," Jess said, "we were only doing a job. It was nothing personal."

"Destroying someone is always personal," he growled. "Her career will be ruined, her reputation in shambles."

Sam defiantly lifted her chin. "In that case, you should accept responsibility for your role in Roxie's downfall."

Her words sliced him clean through the bone. She was right. If he'd been a stronger man, more in control of his desires, this never would have happened. He'd failed Roxie and he'd failed himself.

FEELING HUMILIATED OVER the knowledge that her tryst had been caught on camera and that her boss had hired Jess and Sam to manufacture a romance between her and Dougal to bring scandal to Eros, Roxie fled to her room. She got out of her bathing suit and put on some clothes.

You'll get through this, she tried to reassure herself, but she felt so lost and alone. And all she could think about was Dougal. How she'd violated her own moral code by agreeing to spy on Eros for her boss, and in the process, she'd inadvertently betrayed Dougal.

But he'd betrayed her, too. He'd thought she was a saboteur. He'd been nice to her, romanced her, when in reality he'd been trying to get her to trip up. Roxie didn't believe that he'd made love to her to get her to confess. On that score she truly did believe he'd simply been as swept away by their chemistry as she'd been. She curled her hands into fists, her fingernails biting into her palms.

What she needed was something to stop her mind from whirling. A distraction. A physical outlet. A run, a swim… That's when she realized she'd paused outside the resort's gymnasium. Apparently her subconscious had brought her here. She read the activities offered on the menu outside the door. Aerobics classes, Pilates, free weights, a fencing area.

Fencing.

Yes, yes. A good fencing workout was exactly what she needed, but the posted hours said the gym was closed after noon on Sundays. Dammit.

In frustration, she grabbed the door handle, intending on shaking it just to let off some steam, but to her surprise the door opened. Someone had forgotten to lock up.

The lights were out in the gym, but the big picture window provided more than enough light. Furtively she glanced around. The corridor was empty. Smiling, she stepped into the gym as the door whispered closed behind her.

"GO TO HER, TELL HER HOW you feel. Even if she doesn't feel the same way, it's better to know where you stand than to keep forever guessing."

Taylor's words rang in his ears.

How could he be in love with Roxie? He'd only known her two short weeks. And yet his heart ached in an odd way it had never ached before. He had to tell her…what?

He had no idea what he was going to say. He just knew he had to talk to her.

He went to her room, banged on the door, but she didn't answer. Finally he flashed his badge and asked a maid to let him into her room.

It was empty.

The twinge in his heart tightened. Where was she?

Dougal searched the resort. She wasn't in the any of the restaurants or bars, nor was she hidden away in an alcove. No Roxie in the lobby or the swimming pool area or the business office. He interviewed the valets, who swore that no one matching her description had left the resort. He almost skipped over the gym because it was closed on Sunday afternoons, but as he passed the door he heard the unmistakable sound of adept footwork, accompanied by the noise of a dueling sword slicing through the air.

Gotcha.

Grinning, he pushed open the door.

Roxie's back was to him, and she was in the middle of battling an imaginary opponent with her foil. She wore no fencing gear. Immediately his eyes were drawn to the flexing movements of her sweet little fanny encased in a pair of formfitting slacks.

"*En garde,*" he murmured.

She whirled around, her weapon at the ready. Although she didn't wear a fencing mask, her expression was unreadable. Her eyes lit on his as she struck the basic advance pose. "*En garde.*"

He glanced to the rack where the dueling weapons lay. He stalked over, picked out a foil, unsheathed it and turned to square off with her.

Without a word, she stamped her front foot to the ground, producing a sound known as an appel. The intention was to startle him. He anticipated the lunge, raised his foil to meet hers, gliding it down her blade, keeping her in constant contact.

Dougal had never fenced without gear. For a man who was always braced for trouble, it felt strange being so unprepared for battle, but oddly calming.

"Are you okay?" he asked.

She executed an interesting little maneuver called a balles-tra lunge that was a lunge, feint, lunge combo that almost made him lose his footing. "Don't worry about me."

"I can't help it," he said, regaining his balance and coming at her before she could mount a fresh attack. "I know what it's like to be on the receiving end of a betrayal."

"Have you ever considered," she asked, "that you set yourself up for betrayal?"

"Excuse me?"

"You expect people to let you down and so they usually do. I've discovered that when you treat people as if they are trustworthy, they generally are." Their blades clanged loudly in the high ceiling gym.

"Oh yeah, just like Jess and Sam and your boss were trustworthy."

"Yes, they betrayed me. Yes, I was gullible and naive and too trusting. But you know what? That's my own fault."

"For placing your trust in others." Dougal nodded.

"No," Roxie said, her face deadly earnest as she rounded on him with a new lunge. "For not getting out there and experiencing things before now. I used raising Stacy as an excuse to hide from life. I was afraid of being hurt, so I never let myself love anyone other than my little sister."

Her swordplay was aggressive, her expression fierce. They went back and forth, thrust, parry, thrust, parry.

"You on the other hand…"

"Yeah?"

"You distrust people as a way to avoid pain."

"Excuse me?"

"Distrust is your modus operandi. Your fallback position."

"Is that so?"

"If you assume people can't be trusted, then you can't ever be truly disappointed."

He lunged, causing her to retreat down the fencing strip. "And where did you get your degree in psychology?"

"Ooh, sarcasm. Another defense mechanism for the disillusioned," she retorted.

She was right but he was loath to admit it. "You do understand the real problem, don't you?"

"I'm positive you're about to enlighten me."

"It wasn't until I found out about Jess and Sam working for Porter Langley that I got it."

Okay, fine, she'd piqued his curiosity. "Got what?"

"You don't trust other people because you don't fully trust yourself."

"I'm missing the connection," he said.

"I trusted too much. I thought other people would be like me. Open, honest, caring. So that made me think that you're distrustful because you expect people to be like you."

"Huh?"

"It's a paradox, I know. But until you allow yourself to be open and vulnerable, then you'll never be able to fully trust your instincts or other people." Her blade tipped lightly against his shoulder. It was only when he felt the air against his skin that he realized she'd cut through the sleeve of his flannel shirt.

"Touché," Dougal croaked.

"Like it or not, I get you."

He did like it, and *that's* what he didn't like.

Her swordplay sent him backward. She scored another point on his other sleeve, and then did a crazy little ripple with her foil. Suddenly she'd cut off his shirt. The garment fluttered to the ground in shredded pieces, revealing his bare chest.

Their gazes locked. Lust shot through him sharp as her sword. How he wanted her!

Roxie came at him again. Dougal was on the defensive and he was unlikely to recover. She was a much better fencer than he, with far superior control and understanding of the finer points of engagement. She took him off the fencing strip and into a corner. He would already have lost in match play. His back was literally to the wall. He had nowhere to go.

If he had any hope of walking away unscathed from his encounter with her, it was now or never. Dougal lunged toward her at maximum thrust, desperately seeking to regain control, but Roxie smoothly sidestepped, simultaneously wielding her foil in a swift maneuver and disarmed him.

His sword clattered to the floor.

He was doomed.

Roxie's smile was wicked, and it filled him with a kind of happiness he'd never felt before. It was the kind of feeling that altered a man in every way possible.

"I see you for who you are, Dougal Lockhart," she murmured. "I know what's got you twisted up inside."

He stood there, fully exposed, vulnerable, his chest rising and falling rapidly as he sucked air into his lungs.

She raised her blade.

Dougal gulped, lifted his arms over his head in the universal gesture of surrender.

Then with a blindly swift motion, she sliced open the leg of his jeans right at the level of his scar. With the gentlest of a feather-soft caress, she touched her blade to his ravaged skin and whispered, "Do you trust me?"

DOUGAL NEVER TOOK HIS GAZE off her face. "I trust you," he said, and she could tell he meant every word.

Roxie dropped the foil.

He wrapped his arms around her, squeezed her as if he was never going to let her go. Then his lips were on hers and everything that had driven her to this moment made perfect sense.

Roxie twined her arms around his neck, and for the longest time they just kissed. She couldn't get enough of his touch, his taste, his smell. He was in her blood, in her heart, and she knew she could never get him out.

Finally they had to come up for air.

"I'm not sure what this thing is, sweetheart—" he began.

"We don't have to define it."

He placed a finger to her lips. "Listen to me for a minute."

She quieted, watching his face.

"You're right about me. Deep down, I don't trust myself. I'm always afraid I'm going to make a mistake and someone is going to suffer because of me. But with you, because of you…" He took a deep breath. "Roxie, I think we could have something really great."

She gulped, overcome by emotion. "I do, too."

"It's probably too soon to say the word *love*…but you're right. I've got to allow myself to be vulnerable or I'll never be able to trust myself. I'm scared as hell, I'm going out on a limb here and I'm saying it. Roxanne Stanley, I think I'm falling in love with you."

"Oh, Dougal," she sighed, filled with so much joy and happiness she could hardly speak. "I think I'm falling in love with you, too."

Epilogue

"YOU HAVE THE JOB IF YOU want it," Taylor Corben said. "But only under one condition."

Roxie drew herself up to her full five-foot-six height. She desperately needed this job after telling off Porter Langley and walking away from Getaway Airlines, but there were a few things she just wouldn't do.

"What's the condition?" she asked.

Taylor jerked a thumb to Dougal, who was leaning insouciantly against the wall on one shoulder, his arms crossed over his chest. "Keep doing whatever it is you've been doing to this guy. I've never seen him so happy."

Roxie thought of everything they'd been doing during the two weeks they'd been back in the States—making love, picnicking in Central Park, making love, walking hand in hand through the Museum of Art, making love, taking in a few Broadway plays, making love, meeting each other's friends and families, making love. "That's not a hard promise to keep."

"Pun intended I hope," Taylor teased. "But seriously, Roxie, I'm glad to have you aboard."

"I'm just so happy you gave me a chance after I spied on your operation for Getaway."

"Are you kidding? Good executive assistants are worth

their weight in gold. And even though you told him to get stuffed, Porter Langley gave you a glowing recommendation."

"His conscience must have got the best of him." Roxie smiled.

"And don't worry, I won't ask you to do anything that goes against your moral code."

"Thank you."

"About your starting salary…" Taylor said, and named a figure that was one and a half times what Langley had been paying her. "You'll be getting a raise at the end of your three-month probationary period, of course. I hope that's satisfactory."

"Very satisfactory." Roxie couldn't help shooting a look of triumph over at Dougal. He looked so handsome. Her man.

Her man.

The words warmed her up inside.

"Wonderful." Taylor leaned across the desk to shake Roxie's hand. "Welcome to Eros Airlines."

"Thank you."

Taylor turned her attention to Dougal. "So no word on the saboteur?"

He shook his head. "We were unable to conclusively tie any of the occurrences on the Romance of Britannia tour together. My men report there've been no problems at any of the other resorts. I'm beginning to think those threatening letters are just that—empty threats."

Taylor nodded but she didn't look placated. Just then her cell phone rang. She raised a finger for Dougal and Roxie to excuse her as she took the call. They got up to leave, but Taylor suddenly motioned them to stay. She listened to the caller, and then said, "Do it."

She hung up the phone and looked at Dougal, her face noticeably pale.

"What is it?" Dougal asked.

Taylor swallowed "They found a bomb in the lobby of our Japanese resort. Looks like those threats aren't so empty after all."

* * * * *

A BARGAIN WITH THE BOSS

BARBARA DUNLOP

Thanks to Kieran Slobodin for the title.
And thanks to Shona Mostyn and
Brittany Pearson for the shoes!

One

Saturday night ended early for Lawrence "Tuck" Tucker. His date had not gone well.

Her name was Felicity. She had a bright smile, sunshine-blond hair, a body that could stop traffic and the IQ of a basset hound. But she also had a shrill, long-winded conversational style, and she was stridently against subsidized day care and team sports for children. Plus, she hated the Bulls. What self-respecting Chicagoan hated the Bulls? That was just disloyal.

By the time they'd finished dessert, Tuck was tired of being lectured in high C. He decided life was too short, so he'd dropped her off at her apartment with a fleeting good-night kiss.

Now he let himself into the expansive foyer of the Tucker family mansion, shifting his thoughts ahead to Sunday morning. He was meeting his friend Shane Colborn for, somewhat ironically, a pickup basketball game.

"That's just *reckless*." The angry voice of his father, Jamison Tucker, rang clearly from the library.

"I'm not saying it'll be easy," said Tuck's older brother, Dixon, his own voice tight with frustration.

Together the two men ran the family's multinational conglomerate, Tucker Transportation, and it was highly unusual for them to argue.

"Now, *that's* an understatement," said Jamison. "Who could possibly step in? I'm tied up. And we're not sending some junior executive to Antwerp."

"The operations director is not a junior executive."

"We need a vice president to represent the company. We need you."

"Then, send Tuck."

"Tuck?" Jamison scoffed.

The derision in his father's voice shouldn't have bothered Tuck. But it did. Even after all these years, he still felt the sting in his father's lack of faith and respect.

"He's a vice president," said Dixon.

"In name only. And barely that."

"Dad—"

"Don't you *Dad* me. You know your brother's shortcomings as well as I do. You want to take an extended vacation? *Now?*"

"I didn't choose the timing."

Jamison's voice moderated. "She did you wrong, son. Everybody knows that."

"My wife of ten years betrayed every promise we ever made to each other. Do you have any idea how that feels?"

Tuck's sympathies went out to Dixon. It had been a terrible few months since Dixon had caught Kassandra in bed with another man. The final divorce papers had arrived earlier this week. Dixon hadn't said much about them. In fact, he'd been unusually tight-lipped.

"And you're angry. And that's fine. But you bested her in the divorce. We held up the prenup and she's walking away with next to nothing."

All emotion left Dixon's voice. "It's all about the money to you, isn't it?"

"It was to her," said Jamison.

There was a break in the conversation, and Tuck realized they could easily emerge from the library and catch him eavesdropping. He took a silent step back toward the front door.

"Tuck deserves a chance," said Dixon.

Tuck froze again to listen.

"Tuck had a chance," said Jamison, his words stinging once again.

When? Tuck wanted to shout. When had he had a chance to do anything but sit in his executive floor office and feel like an unwanted guest?

But as quickly as the emotion formed, he reminded himself that he didn't care. His only defense against his father was not to care about respect or recognition or making any meaningful contribution to the family business. Most people would kill for Tuck's lifestyle. He needed to shut up and enjoy it.

"I knew this was a bad idea," said Dixon.

"It was a terrible idea," said Jamison.

Tuck reached behind himself and opened the front door. Then he shut it hard, making a show of tromping his feet over the hardwood floor.

"Hello?" he called out as he walked toward the library, giving them ample time to pretend they'd been talking about something else.

"Hi, Tuck." His brother greeted him as he entered the dark-hued, masculine room.

"I didn't see your car out front," Tuck told him.

"I parked it in the garage."

"So you're staying over?"

Dixon had a penthouse downtown, where he'd lived with Kassandra, but he occasionally spent a day or two at the family home.

"I'm staying over," said Dixon. "I sold the penthouse today."

From the expression on his father's face, Tuck could tell this was news to him, as well.

"So you'll be here for a while?" Tuck asked easily. He loosened his tie and pulled it off. "What are you drinking?"

"Glen Garron," Jamison answered.

"Sounds good." Tuck shrugged out of his jacket and tossed it onto one of the deep red leather wingback chairs.

With a perimeter of ceiling-high shelves, a stone fireplace, oversize leather chairs and ornately carved walnut tables, the library hadn't changed in seventy years. It had been built by Tuck's grandfather, Randal, as a gentleman's retreat, back in the days when gentlemen thought they had something to retreat from.

Tuck didn't fill the silence, but instead waited to see where his father and brother would take the conversation.

"How was your date?" his father asked.

"It was fine."

Jamison looked pointedly at his heavy platinum watch.

"She wasn't exactly a rocket scientist," Tuck said, answering the unspoken question.

"You've dated a rocket scientist?" asked Jamison.

Tuck frowned at his father's mocking tone.

The two men locked gazes for a moment before Jamison spoke. "I merely wondered how you had a basis for comparison."

"First date?" Dixon queried, his tone much less judgmental.

Tuck crossed to the wet bar and flipped up a cut crystal glass. "Last date."

Dixon gave a chopped laugh.

Tuck poured a measure of scotch. "Interested in the game with Shane tomorrow?" he asked his brother.

"Can't," said Dixon.

"Work?" asked Tuck.

"Tying up loose ends."

Tuck turned to face the other men. "With the penthouse?"

Dixon's expression was inscrutable. "And a few other things."

Tuck got the distinct feeling Dixon was holding something back. But then the two brothers rarely spoke frankly in front of their father. Tuck would catch up with Dixon at some point tomorrow and ask him what was going on. Was he really looking at taking a lengthy vacation? Tuck would be impressed if he was.

Then again, their father was right. Tucker Transportation needed Dixon to keep the corporation running at full speed. And Tuck wasn't any kind of a substitute on that front.

Amber Bowen looked straight into the eyes of the president of Tucker Transportation and lied.

"No," she said to Jamison Tucker. "Dixon didn't mention anything to me."

Her loyalty was to her boss, Dixon Tucker. Five years ago, he'd given her a chance when nobody else would. She'd been straight out of high school, with no college education and no office experience. He'd put his faith in her then, and she wasn't going to let him down now.

"When was the last time you spoke to him?"

Jamison Tucker was an imposing figure behind his big desk in the corner office on the thirty-second floor of the Tucker Transportation building. His gray hair was neat, freshly cut every three weeks. His suit was custom-made to cover his barrel chest. He wasn't as tall as his two sons, but he more than made up for it in sturdiness. He was thick necked, like a bulldog. His brow was heavy and his face was square.

"Yesterday morning," said Amber. This time she was telling the truth.

His eyes narrowed with what looked like suspicion. "You didn't see him last night, sometime after the office closed?"

The question took her aback. "I... Why?"

"It's a yes-or-no answer, Amber."

"No."

Why would Jamison ask that question, and why in such a suspicious tone?

"Are you sure?" Jamison asked her, skepticism in his pale blue eyes.

She hesitated before answering. "Do you have some reason to believe I saw him last night?"

"*Did* you see him last night?" There was a note of triumph in his voice.

She hadn't. But she did know where Dixon had been last night. He was at the airport, boarding a private jet for Arizona. She knew he'd left Chicago, and she knew he wouldn't be back for a very long time.

He'd told her he'd left a note for his family so they wouldn't worry. And he'd made her promise not to give anyone more information. And she was keeping that promise.

Dixon's family took shameless advantage of his good nature

and his strong work ethic. The result was that he was overworked and exhausted. He'd been doing an increasing share of the senior management duties at Tucker Transportation over the past couple of years. And now his divorce had taken a huge toll on his mental and emotional state. If he didn't get some help soon, he was headed for a breakdown.

She knew he'd tried to explain it to his family. She also knew they refused to listen. He'd had no choice but to simply disappear. His father and his lazy, good-for-nothing younger brother, Tuck, were simply going to have to step up.

She squared her shoulders. "Are you implying that I have a personal relationship with Dixon?"

Jamison leaned slightly forward. "I don't imply."

"Yes, you do. You did." She knew she was skating on thin ice, but she was angry on her behalf and Dixon's. It was Dixon's wife who had cheated, not Dixon.

Jamison's tone went lower. "How dare you?"

"How dare you, sir. Have some faith in your own son."

Then Jamison's eyes seemed to bulge. His complexion turned ruddy. "Why, you—"

Amber braced herself, gripping the arm of the chair, afraid she would be fired on the spot. She could only hope Dixon would hire her back when he returned.

But Jamison gasped instead and his hand went to his chest. His body stiffened in the big chair and he sucked in three short breaths.

Amber shot to her feet. "Mr. Tucker?"

There was genuine terror in his expression.

She grabbed the desk phone, calling out to his assistant as she dialed 911.

Jamison's assistant, Margaret Smithers, was through the door in a flash.

While Amber gave instructions to the emergency operator, Margaret called the company nurse.

Within minutes, the nurse had Jamison on his back on the floor of his office and was administering CPR.

Amber watched the scene in horror. Had his heart truly stopped? Was he going to die right here in the office?

She knew she should get word to his family. His wife needed to know what had happened. Then again, Mrs. Tucker probably shouldn't be alone when she heard. She probably shouldn't hear news like this from a company secretary.

"I need to call Tuck," Amber said to Margaret.

All the blood had drained from Margaret's face. She dropped to her knees beside Jamison.

"Margaret?" Amber prompted. "Tuck?"

"On my desk," Margaret whispered, as if it was painful for her to talk. "There's a phone list. His cell number is there."

Amber left for Margaret's desk in the outer office.

While she punched Tuck's cell number, the paramedics rushed past with a stretcher. The commotion inside Jamison's office turned into a blur.

"Hello?" Tuck answered.

She cleared her throat, fighting to keep from looking through the office door, afraid of what she might see. She thought she could hear a defibrillator hum to life. Then the paramedics called, "Clear."

"This is Amber Bowen," she said into the phone, struggling to keep her voice from shaking.

There was silence, and she realized Tuck didn't recognize her name. It figured. But this wasn't the time to dwell on his lack of interest in the company that supported his playboy lifestyle.

"I'm Dixon's assistant," she said.

"Oh, Amber. Right." Tuck sounded distracted.

"You need to come to the office." She stopped herself.

What Tuck really needed to do was to go to the hospital and meet the ambulance there. She searched for a way to phrase those words.

"Why?" he asked.

"It's your father."

"My *father* wants me to come to the *office*?" His drawling tone dripped sarcasm.

"We had to call an ambulance."

Tuck's voice became more alert. "Did he fall?"

"He, well, seems to have collapsed."

"*What?* Why?"

"I don't know." She was thinking it had to be a heart attack, but she didn't want to speculate.

"What do you mean you don't know?"

"The paramedics are putting him on a stretcher. I didn't want to call Mrs. Tucker and frighten her."

"Right. Good decision."

"You should probably meet them at Central Hospital."

"Is he conscious?"

Amber looked at Jamison's closed eyes and pale skin. "I don't think so."

"I'm on my way."

"Good."

The line went silent and she set down the phone.

The paramedics wheeled Jamison past. He was propped up on the stretcher, an oxygen mask over his face and an IV in his arm.

Amber sank down onto Margaret's chair, her knees wobbly and her legs weak.

Margaret and the nurse emerged from Jamison's office.

Margaret's eyes were red, tears marring her cheeks.

Amber rose to meet her. "It's going to be all right. He's getting the best of care."

"How?" Margaret asked into the air. "How could this happen?"

The nurse excused herself to follow the paramedics.

"Do you think he has heart problems?" Amber asked quietly.

Margaret shook her head. "He doesn't. Just last night..." Another tear ran down her cheek.

"Did something happen yesterday?" Amber assumed Margaret had meant yesterday, maybe late in the afternoon.

"He was in such a good mood. We had some wine."

"You had wine in the office?"

Margaret stilled. Panic and guilt suddenly flooded her expression, and she took a quick step back, glancing away.

"It was nothing," she said, focusing on some papers in her in-basket, straightening them into a pile.

Amber was stunned.

Jamison and Margaret had been together last night? Had they been *together*, together? It sure looked like it.

Margaret moved briskly around the end of her desk. "I should… That is…" She sank down in her chair.

"Yes," Amber agreed, not sure what she was agreeing to, but quite certain she should end the conversation and get back to her own desk.

She started for the hallway, but then she paused, her sense of duty asserting itself. "I'll call the senior managers and give them the news. Did Jamison tell you about Dixon?"

Margaret looked up. "What about Dixon?"

Amber decided the news of Dixon leaving could wait a couple of hours. "Nothing. We can talk later."

Margaret's head went back down and she plunked a few keys on her keyboard. "Jamison had a lunch today and a three o'clock with the board."

Amber left Margaret to her work, her mind racing with all that would need to be handled.

Dixon was gone. Jamison was ill. And that left no one in charge. Tuck was out there somewhere. But she couldn't even imagine what would happen if Tuck took the reins. He wasn't a real vice president. He was just some partier who dropped by the office now and again, evidently giving heart palpitations to half the female staff.

A week later, Tuck realized he had to accept reality. His father was going to be weeks, if not months, in recovery from his heart attack, and Dixon was nowhere to be found. Somebody had to run Tucker Transportation. And that somebody had to be him.

The senior executives seated around the boardroom table looked decidedly troubled at seeing him in the president's chair. He didn't blame them one bit.

"What I don't understand," said Harvey Miller, the finance director, "is why you're not even talking to Dixon."

Tuck hadn't yet decided how much to reveal about his brother's disappearance. He'd tried calling, text messaging and emailing Dixon. He'd had no response. And there was nothing to go on except the cryptic letter his brother had left for their father, saying he'd be gone a month, maybe even longer.

"Dixon's on vacation," said Tuck.

"Now?" asked Harvey, incredulity ringing through his tone.

Mary Silas's head came up in obvious surprise and chagrin. "I didn't hear about that."

She was in charge of human resources and Tuck knew she prided herself on being in the know.

"Get him back," said Harvey.

Instead of responding to either of them, Tuck scanned the expressions of the five executives. "I'd like a status report from each of you tomorrow morning. Amber will book a one-on-one meeting for each of you."

"What about the New York trade show?" asked Zachary Ingles, the marketing director.

Tuck's understanding of the annual trade show, a marquee event, was sketchy at best. He'd attended a couple of times, so he knew Tucker Transportation created and staffed a large pavilion on the trade-show floor. But in the past he'd been more focused on the booth babes and the evening receptions than on the sales efforts.

"Bring me the information tomorrow," he said.

"I need decisions," said Zachary, his tone impatient.

"Then, I'll make them," Tuck replied.

He might not have a clue what he was doing, but he knew enough to hide his uncertainty.

"Can we at least conference Dixon into the meetings?" asked Harvey.

"He's not available," said Tuck.

"Where is he?"

Tuck set his jaw and glared at the man.

"Do you want a full quarterly report or a summary?" asked Lucas Steele. He was the youngest of the executives, the operations director.

Where the others wore custom-made suits, Lucas was dressed in blue jeans and a dark blazer. His steel-blue shirt was crisp, but he hadn't bothered with a tie. He moved between two worlds—the accountants and lawyers who set strategic direction, and the transport managers around the world who actually got things from A to B.

"A summary is enough for now." Tuck appreciated Lucas's pragmatic approach to the situation.

Lucas raised his brows, silently asking the other men if there was anything else.

Tuck decided to jump on the opportunity and end the meeting.

"Thank you." He rose from his chair.

They followed suit and filed out, leaving him alone with Dixon's assistant, Amber.

He hadn't paid much attention to her before this week, but now she struck him as a model of fortitude and efficiency. Where his father's assistant, Margaret, seemed to be falling apart, Amber was calm and collected.

If she'd wandered out of central casting, she couldn't have looked more perfect for the part of trustworthy assistant. Her brunette hair was pulled back in a tidy French braid. Her makeup was minimal. She wore a gray skirt and blazer with a buttoned white blouse.

Only two things about her tweaked his interest as a man—the fine wisps of hair that had obviously escaped the confining braid, and the spiky black high-heeled sandals that flashed gold soles when she walked. The loose wisps of hair were endearing, while the shoes were intriguing. Both could have the power to turn him on if he was inclined to let them.

He wasn't.

"We need to get Dixon back," he told her, setting his mind firmly on business. His brother was priority number one.

"I don't think we should bother him," she replied.

The answer struck Tuck as ridiculous. "He's got a corporation to run."

Her blue eyes flashed with unexpected annoyance. "*You've* got a corporation to run."

For some reason, he hadn't been prepared for any display of emotion from her, let alone something bordering on hostility. It was yet another thing he found intriguing. It was also something else he was going to ignore.

"We both know that's not going to happen," he stated flatly.

"We both know no such thing."

Tuck wasn't a stickler for hierarchy, but her attitude struck him as inappropriately confrontational. "Do you talk to Dixon this way?"

The question seemed to surprise her, but she recovered quickly. "What way?"

He wasn't buying it. "You know exactly what I mean."

"Dixon needs some time to himself. The divorce was very hard on him."

Tuck knew full well that the divorce had been hard on his brother. "He's better off without her."

"No kidding." There was knowledge in her tone.

"He talked to you about his wife?" Tuck was surprised by that.

Amber didn't reply right away, and it was obvious to him that she was carefully formulating her answer.

He couldn't help wondering how close Dixon had become to his assistant. Was she his confidante? Something more?

"I saw them together," she finally said. "I overheard some of their private conversations."

"You mean you eavesdropped?" Not exactly an admirable trait. Then again, not that he was one to judge.

"I mean, she shouted pretty loud."

"You couldn't leave and give them some privacy?"

"Not always. I have a job that requires me to be at my desk. And that desk is outside Dixon's office."

Tuck couldn't help but wonder exactly how far-reaching her duties had become when Dixon's marriage went bad. He took in her tailored clothes and her neat hair. She might be buttoned down, but she was definitely attractive.

"I see..." He thought maybe he did.

"Stop that," she snapped.

"Stop what?"

"Stop insinuating something without spitting it out. If you've got something to ask me, then *ask* me."

Fine with Tuck. "What were you to my brother?"

She enunciated carefully. "I was his confidential assistant."

He found himself easing forward. "And which of your duties were confidential?"

"All of them."

"You know what I'm asking."

"Then, ask it."

Despite her attitude, he liked her. There was something about her straightforward manner that he admired very much. "Were you sleeping with my brother?"

As he looked into her simmering blue eyes, he suddenly and unexpectedly cared about the answer. He didn't want her to be Dixon's mistress.

"No."

He was relieved. "You're sure?"

"That wouldn't be something I'd forget. My car keys, maybe. To pick up cat food, yes. But, oops, having sex with my boss just slipped my mind?" Her tone went flat. "Yes, Tuck. I'm sure."

He wanted to kiss her. He was suddenly seized by an overwhelming desire to pull her close and taste those sassy lips.

"You have a cat?" he asked instead.

"Focus, Tuck. Dixon's not coming back. At least not for a while. I know you've had a cushy run here, but that's over and done with. You've got work to do now, and I am not letting you duck and weave."

Now he really wanted to kiss her. "How're you going to do that?"

"Persuasion, persistence and coercion."

"You think you can coerce me?"

"What I think is that somewhere deep down inside you must be a man who wants to succeed, a man who actually wants to impress his father."

She was wrong, but he was curious.

"Why do you think that?" he asked.

"You strike me as the type."

"I never imagined I was a type."

Truth was he didn't want to impress his father. But he did want to impress Amber, more than he'd wanted to impress a woman in a very long time.

Unfortunately for him, she wasn't about to observe him in the part of suave, worldly, wealthy Tuck Tucker. She was about to watch him fumbling around the helm of a multimillion corporation. He couldn't have dreamed of a less flattering circumstance.

Two

Amber was torn between annoyance and sympathy.

For the past week, Tuck had arrived at the office promptly at eight. He seemed a little groggy for the first hour, and she'd fallen into the habit of having a large coffee on his desk waiting for him. She could only guess that he hadn't yet modified his playboy nights to fit his workday schedule.

She'd moved from her desk near Dixon's office to the desk outside Tuck's office. Tuck didn't have his own assistant, since he was so rarely there, but now he was taking on Dixon's work. He was also taking on Jamison's. Margaret had been out sick most days since Jamison's heart attack, so Amber was keeping in communication with directors and managers and all of their assistants, trying to be sure nothing fell through the cracks.

This morning, voices were raised behind Tuck's closed door. He was meeting with Zachary Ingles, the marketing director. They were two weeks from the New York trade show and deadlines were rapidly piling up.

"*You* were tasked with approving the final branding," Zachary was shouting. "I sent three options. It's all in the email."

"I have two thousand emails in my in-basket," Tuck returned.

"*Your* disorganization is not *my* problem. We've missed the print deadline on everything—signs, banners and all the swag."

"You need to tell me when there's a critical deadline."

"I did tell you."

"In an email that I didn't read."

"Here's a tip," said Zachary. But then he went silent.

Amber found herself picturing Tuck's glare. Tuck might be out of his depth, but he wasn't stupid, and he wasn't a pushover.

A minute later, Tuck's office door was thrown open and Zachary stormed past her desk, tossing a glare her way. "Tell your boss he can pay rush penalties on every damn item for all I care."

Amber didn't bother to respond. She'd never warmed up to Zachary. He was demanding and entitled, always running roughshod over his staff and anyone else below him in the corporate hierarchy. Dixon put up with him because he was favored by Jamison, and because he did seem to have a knack for knowing how to appeal to big clients with expensive shipping needs.

Tuck appeared in the office doorway.

"Lucas will be here at ten," she told him. "But your schedule is clear for the next half hour."

"Maybe I can read a few hundred emails."

"Good idea."

He drew a breath, looking like he wanted to bolt for the exit. "What am I doing wrong?"

"Nothing."

"I'm behind by two thousand emails."

"Dixon was very organized."

Surely Tuck didn't expect to rival his brother after only a single week. It had taken Dixon years to become such an effective vice president.

Tuck frowned at her. "So everyone tells me."

"He worked very long and hard to get there."

Yes, Tuck was arriving on time. And really, that was more than she'd expected. But Dixon had taken on far more than his fair share of early mornings and late nights working out systems and processes for covering the volume of work. Tuck seemed to expect to become a boy wonder overnight.

Tuck's tone hardened. "I'm asking for some friendly advice. Can we not turn it into a lecture about my sainted brother?"

"You can't expect to simply walk through the door and be perfect."

"I'm not expecting anything of the sort. Believe me, I know that Dixon is remarkable. I've heard about it my entire life."

Amber felt a twinge of guilt.

Tuck did seem to be trying. Not that he had any choice in the matter. And it didn't change the fact that he'd barely bothered to show up at the office until he was backed into a corner. Still, he was here now. She'd give him that.

"Zachary should have given you a heads-up on the branding," she said. "He should have pointed out the deadline."

"I shouldn't have missed it," said Tuck.

"But you did. And you're going to miss other things." She saw no point in pretending.

"Your confidence in me is inspiring."

She found herself annoyed on Tuck's behalf, and the frustration came through in her voice.

"Tell him," she said. "Tell them all. Tell them that it's *their* job to keep you appraised of critical deadlines, and not just in an email. Make it a part of your regular meetings. And make the meetings more frequent if you have to, even daily. I mean, if you can stand to see Zachary every day, that is."

Tuck cracked a smile.

It was a joke. But Amber shouldn't have made it. "I know that was an inappropriate thing to say."

He took a couple of steps toward her desk. "I don't have a problem with inappropriate. It's a good idea. I'll send them an email."

"You don't have to send them an email." Her sense of professionalism won out over her annoyance at his past laziness. "I'll send them an email. And I can triage your in-basket if you'd like."

His expression brightened and he moved closer still. "You'd read them for me?"

"Yes. I'll get rid of the unimportant ones."

"How will you do that?"

"I have a delete key."

He leaned his hands down on the desk, lowering his voice. "You can do that? I mean, and not have the company fall down around my ears?"

Amber found herself fighting a grin. "With some of them, sure. With others, I'll take care of them myself, or I'll delegate the work to one of the unit heads. And I'll flag the important ones for you."

"I swear, I could kiss you for that."

It was obviously a quip. But for some reason his words resonated all the way to her abdomen.

Her gaze went to his lips, triggering the image of a kiss in her imagination.

She caught the look in his eyes and the air seemed to crackle between them.

"Not necessary," she quickly said into the silence.

"I suppose the paycheck is enough."

"It's enough."

He straightened, and a twinkle came into his silver-gray eyes. "Still, the offer's open."

She considered his handsome, unapologetic face and his taut, sexy frame. "You're not like him at all, are you?"

"Dixon?"

She nodded.

"Not a bit."

"He doesn't joke around."

"He should."

Her loyalty reasserted itself. "Are you criticizing Dixon's performance on the job?"

"I'm criticizing his performance in life."

"He's been through a lot."

She didn't know how close Tuck was to his brother, but she had seen firsthand the toll Kassandra's infidelity had taken on Dixon. Dixon had been devoted to his wife. He'd thought they were trying to start a family while she had secretly been taking birth control pills and sleeping with another man.

"I know he has," said Tuck.

"He was blindsided by her lies."

Tuck seemed to consider the statement. "There were signs."

"Now you're criticizing Dixon for loyalty?"

"I'm wondering why you're so blindly defending him."

"When you're an honest person—" as Amber knew Dixon was "—you don't look for deceit in others."

Tuck's gaze was astute. "But you saw it, too."

Amber wasn't going to lie. "That Kassandra had a scheming streak?"

"Aha." There was a distinct ring of triumph in Tuck's tone.

"I saw it, too," she admitted.

He sobered. "I don't know what that says about you and I."

"Maybe that we should be careful around each other?"

"Are you out to get me, Amber?"

"No." She wasn't.

She didn't find him particularly admirable. An admirable man would have shown up to help long before now. But now that he was here, she'd admit he wasn't all bad.

"Are you going to lie to me?"

"No."

"Will you help me succeed?"

She hesitated over that one. "Maybe. If you seem to deserve it."

"How am I doing so far?"

"You're no Dixon."

"I'm never going to be Dixon."

"But you seem to have Zachary's number. I can respect that."

It was a moment before Tuck responded. "How'd he get away with that crap with my dad?"

"He didn't pull that crap with your dad."

"He's testing me."

"We all are."

"Including you?"

"Especially me."

But Tuck was faring better than she'd expected. And she seemed worryingly susceptible to his playboy charm. She was definitely going to have to watch herself around him.

At home in the mansion, Tuck found himself retreating to the second floor, spreading work out in the compact sitting room down the hall from his own bedroom. Stylistically, it was different from the rest of the house, with earth tones, rattan and stoneware accents. He found it restful.

The big house had been built in the early 1900s, with hardwood floors, soaring relief ceilings, elaborate light fixtures and archways twenty feet in height. It was far from the most welcoming place in the world, full of uncomfortable antique chairs and somber paintings. And right now it echoed with emptiness.

Last week, they'd moved his father to a specialized care facility in Boston. His mother had gone with him to stay with her sister. His mother had asked her trusted staff members to come along for what looked to be an extended stay.

Tuck could have replaced the staff. But he was one man, and he had no plans to do any entertaining. Well, maybe a date or two, since he didn't plan to let his responsibilities at Tucker Transportation keep him celibate. But the house still had two cooks, two housekeepers and a groundskeeper. He couldn't imagine needing any more assistance than that.

For now, he headed down the grand staircase to meet his college friend, Jackson Rush, happy with both the opportunity for conversation and the break from office work. While Tuck had studied business at the University of Chicago, Jackson had studied criminology. Jackson now ran an investigations firm that had expanded around the country.

"I hope you have good news," said Tuck as Jackson removed his worn leather jacket and handed it to the housekeeper.

"Dixon took a private jet from Executive Airport to New York City," said Jackson.

"But not a Tucker Transportation jet." Tuck had already checked all the company records.

"Signal Air," said Jackson.

"Because he didn't want my dad to know where he went."

"That seems like a solid theory."

The two men made their way into the sunroom. It was dark outside, not the perfect time to enjoy the view through the floor-to-ceiling windows, but the sunroom was less ostentatious than the library.

"So he's in New York." As far as Tuck was concerned, that was good news. He'd worried his brother had taken off to Europe or Australia.

"From there, it looks like he took a train to Charlotte."

"A train?" Tuck turned his head to frown at Jackson. "Why on earth would he take a train? And what's in Charlotte?"

"Secrecy, I'm guessing." Jackson eased onto a forest-green sofa. "He wouldn't need ID to buy a train ticket. You said your dad tried to stop him from leaving?"

Tuck took a padded Adirondack chair next to a leafy potted ficus. "Dad was terrified at the thought of me actually working at Tucker Transportation."

"Then, I guess things didn't work out so well for him, did they?"

"Are you making a joke about his heart attack?"

"I didn't mean that the way it sounded. From Charlotte, our best guess is Dixon went on to either Miami or New Orleans. Anything you know of for him in either of those cities?"

Tuck racked his brain.

"A woman?" asked Jackson.

"He's barely divorced from Kassandra."

Jackson shot Tuck a look of incredulity.

"She was the one who cheated, not him. I doubt his head was anywhere near to dating again."

"Well, we're checking both cities, but so far he's not using his credit cards or hitting any bank machines. And there's no activity on his cell phone."

Tuck sat back. "Does this strike you as bafflingly elaborate?"

"Your brother does not want to be found. The question is, why?"

"He doesn't know about my dad," said Tuck. "He doesn't know he's abandoned Tucker Transportation to me alone. If he did, he'd be here in a heartbeat."

"Anything else going on in his life? Any chance he's got an enemy, committed a crime, embezzled from the company?"

Tuck laughed at that. "Embezzle from himself? He's got access to all the money he could ever want and then some."

"An enemy, then. Anybody who might want to harm him? Maybe the guy who slept with Kassandra?"

"Dixon's not afraid of Irwin Borba."

"What, then?" asked Jackson.

"He said he needed a vacation."

Tuck wanted to believe that was the simple answer. Because if Dixon was at a beach bar somewhere drinking rum punch and watching women in bikinis, he'd be back home soon. It had already been two weeks. Maybe Tuck just had to hang on a few more days without sinking any ships—either figuratively or literally—and he'd be off the hook. He sure hoped so.

"There's a major trade show coming up in New York," he told Jackson. "And we're launching two new container ships in Antwerp next week. Surely he'll return for that."

"He's expecting your dad will be there." Jackson restlessly tapped his blunt fingers against his denim-covered knee.

That was true. Dixon would assume Jamison would represent the company in Antwerp.

"Have you checked his computer?" asked Jackson. "Maybe he's got a personal email account you don't know about."

"Maybe." Tuck wasn't crazy about the idea of snooping into Dixon's business, but things were getting desperate.

"Check his office computer," said Jackson. "And check his laptop, his tablet, anything he didn't take with him. It looks to me as though he's traveling light."

Tuck had to agree with that. "What's he up to, switching transportation in two different cities?"

"He's up to not being found. And he's doing a damn good job of it. Any chance he's got a secret life?"

"A secret life?"

"Doing things that he can't tell anyone about. He does travel a lot. And he runs in some pretty influential circles."

"Are you asking if my brother is a spy?"

Jackson's shrug said it was possible.

"If there's one thing I've learned in the past week, it's that Dixon couldn't have had time for anything but Tucker Transportation. You wouldn't believe the amount of work that crosses his desk."

"Don't forget you're doing your dad's job, as well," Jackson pointed out.

"Even accounting for that. I'm starting to wonder..."

Tuck wasn't crazy about saying it out loud. But he had to wonder why they hadn't asked for his help before now. Was he truly that inept?

"You're a smart guy, too." Jackson seemed to have guessed the direction of Tuck's thoughts.

"I don't know about that."

"Well, I do. Your dad and Dixon, they probably got into a rhythm together early on. And you never seemed that interested in working at the company."

"I tried." Tuck couldn't keep the defensiveness from his voice. "In the beginning, I tried. But I always seemed to be in the way. Dad definitely didn't want me around. Dixon was his golden boy. After a while you get tired of always barging your way in."

"So you're in it now."

"I am. And it's scaring me half to death."

Jackson grinned. "I've been in the thick of it with you before. I can't picture you being afraid of anything."

"This isn't the same as a physical threat."

"I'm not just talking about a barroom brawl. Remember, I'm running a company of my own."

"That's right." Tuck perked up at the thought of getting some free advice. "You are. How big is it now?"

"Four offices, here in Chicago, New York, Boston and Philly."

"How many employees?"

"About two hundred."

"So you could give me a few tips?"

"Tucker Transportation is on a whole different scale than I am. You're better off talking to your friend Shane Colborn."

"I'm better off finding Dixon."

"I'll fly to Charlotte in the morning."

"You need a jet?"

Jackson cracked a grin. "I'm not going to say no to that offer. Sure, hook me up with a jet. In the meantime, check out his computer."

"I'll get Amber to help."

"Amber?"

"Dixon's trusty assistant."

An image of Amber's pretty face came up in his mind. He wasn't normally a fan of tailored clothes and no-nonsense hairstyles. But she seemed to look good in anything.

And then there were those shoes. She wore a different pair every day, each one sexier than the last. Something was definitely going on beneath the surface there. And the more time he spent with her, the more he wanted to figure out what really made her tick.

When Tuck strode into the office Monday morning, Amber's hormones jumped to attention. He was dressed in a pair of faded jeans, a green cotton shirt and a navy blazer. His dark brown hair had a rakish swoop across the top, and his face had a sexy, cavalier day's growth of beard.

He definitely wasn't Dixon. Dixon's confidence was never

cocky. And Dixon had never made her heart pump faster and heat rise up her neck.

"I need your help," he stated without preamble.

Amber immediately came to her feet. "Is something wrong?"

"Come with me." His walk was decisive and his voice definitive.

She experienced a new and completely inappropriate shiver of reaction.

This was a place of business, she told herself. He wasn't thinking about her as a woman. He sure wasn't thinking the same things she was thinking—that his commanding voice meant he might haul her into his office, pin her up against a wall and kiss her senseless.

What was wrong with her?

Tuck headed into Dixon's office and she forcibly shook off her silly fantasy.

"Do you know his password?" Tuck asked, crossing the big room and rounding the mahogany desk.

"His password to what?" she asked.

"To log on to the system." Tuck leaned down and moved the mouse to bring the screen to life.

She didn't answer. Dixon had given her his password a couple of months back on a day when he was in Europe and needed her to send him some files. She still remembered it, but she knew he'd never intended for her to use it again. What she technically knew, and what she ought to use, were two different things.

Tuck glanced up sharply. "Tell me the password, Amber."

"I..."

"If you don't, I'll only have the systems group reset it."

He made a valid point. As the acting head of Tucker Transportation, he could do whatever he wanted with the company computer system.

"Fine. It's ClownSchool, capital C and S, dollar sign, one, eight, zero."

Tuck typed. "You might want to think about whose side you're on here."

"I'm not taking sides." Though she was committed to keeping her promise to Dixon. "I'm trying to be professional."

"And I'm trying to save Tucker Transportation."

"Save it from what?" Had something happened?

"From ruin without my father or Dixon here to run it."

"What are you looking for?" she asked, realizing that he was exaggerating for effect and deciding to move past the hyperbole.

Tucker Transportation was a solid company with a team of long-term, capable executives running the departments. Even from the top, there was a limited amount of damage anyone could do in a month.

"Clues to where he went," said Tuck.

Then Tuck seemed to have an inspiration. He lifted the desk phone and dialed.

A moment later, a ring chimed inside Dixon's top drawer.

Tuck drew it open and removed Dixon's cell phone, holding it while it rang.

"How does it still have battery power?" he asked, more to himself than anything.

"I've been charging it," said Amber.

His attention switched to her, his face crinkling in obvious annoyance. "You didn't think to *tell me* his cell phone was in his desk drawer?"

Amber wasn't sure how to answer that.

"And how did you know it was there anyway? Were you snooping through his drawers?"

"No." She quickly shook her head. She was intensely respectful of Dixon's privacy. "He told me he was leaving it behind."

Tuck's piercing gray eyes narrowed, his brows slanting together in a way that wrinkled his forehead. "So he told you he was leaving? Before he left, you *knew* he was going?"

Amber realized she'd spoken too fast. But now she had no choice but to give a reluctant nod.

Tuck straightened and came to the end of the desk, his voice gravelly and ominous. "Before you answer this, remember I'm the acting president of this company. This is a direct order, and I don't look kindly on insubordination. Did he tell you where he was going?"

Dixon had given her an emergency number. And she'd recognized the area code. But he hadn't flat-out told her where he was going.

"No," she said, promising herself it wasn't technically a lie. "He needs the time, Tuck. He's been overworked for months, and Kassandra's betrayal hit him hard."

"That's not for you to decide."

She knew that was true. But it wasn't for Tuck to decide, either.

"He doesn't even know about our father," said Tuck.

"If he knew, he'd come home."

Tuck's voice rose. "Of *course* he'd come home."

"And then he'd be back to square one, worse off than he was before. I know it must be hard for you without him."

"You *know*? You don't know anything."

"I've worked here for five years." It was on the tip of her tongue to say that it was a whole lot longer than Tuck had worked here, but she checked herself in time.

"As an *assistant*."

"Yes."

"You don't have the full picture. You don't know the risks, the critical decisions."

"I know Dixon."

Tuck's tone turned incredulous. "You're saying I don't?"

Amber's voice rose. "I'm saying I've been here. I watched how hard he's worked. I saw how much your father slowed down these past months. I watched what Kassandra's infidelity did to him. He was losing it, Tuck. He took a break because he had no other choice."

Tuck gripped the side of the desk, his jaw going tight.

Amber mentally braced herself for an onslaught.

But his voice stayed steady, his words measured. “My father was slowing down?”

“Yes. A lot. Margaret was funneling more and more work to Dixon. Dixon was scrambling. He was staying late, coming in early, traveling all over the world.”

“He likes traveling.”

“You can’t constantly travel and still run a company. And then Kassandra.”

“Her behavior was despicable.”

“It hurt him, Tuck. Yes, he was disgusted and angry. But he was also very badly hurt.”

Tuck rocked back on his heels, his expression going pensive. “He didn’t let on.”

Amber hesitated but decided to share some more information. If it would help Tuck understand the gravity of the situation, it would do more good than harm.

“There were times when I heard more than I should,” she said. “I know Dixon was ready to be a father. He thought they were trying to get pregnant. Instead, she was taking birth control pills and sleeping with another man.”

It was clear from Tuck’s expression that Dixon hadn’t shared that information with him. He sat down, and his gaze went to the computer screen. “He still needs to know about our father.”

She knew it wasn’t her place to stop Tuck. “Do what you need to do.”

He glanced up. “But you’re not going to help me?”

“There’s nothing more I can do to help you find Dixon. But I’ll help you run Tucker Transportation.”

“Finding Dixon is the best thing we can do to run Tucker Transportation.”

“I disagree,” she said.

“Bully for you.”

"The best thing you can do to run Tucker Transportation is to *run* Tucker Transportation."

Tuck was silent while he moved the mouse and typed a few keys. "You should have told me."

"Told you what?" She found herself moving around the desk, curious to see what he would find on the computer.

"What he was planning," said Tuck as he scrolled through Dixon's email. "That he was secretly leaving."

She recognized the headers on the email messages, since they automatically copied to her account. "I'm Dixon's confidential assistant. I don't share his personal information with anyone else."

"There's nothing here but corporate business," said Tuck.

Amber knew that would be the case. Dixon was always careful to keep his personal email out of the corporate system. And he'd been doubly careful with the details of his secret vacation.

Tuck swiveled the chair to face her. "What would you do if you were mine?"

The question caught her off guard while her brain zipped off on a disorienting, romantic tangent. To be Tuck's. In his arms. In his life. In his bed.

He rose in front of her. "Amber?"

"Sorry?" She scrambled to bring her thoughts back to the real world.

His voice was rich and deep, laced with an intimacy she knew she had to be imagining. "If you were *my* confidential assistant, what would you do?"

"I'm not." She wasn't his anything, and she had to remember that.

"But if you were?"

If she was Tuck's assistant, she'd be in the middle of making one colossal mistake. Because that would mean she was sexually attracted to her boss. She'd want to kiss her boss. Eventually, she *would* kiss her boss. She was thinking about it right now. And if the dusky smoke in his eyes was anything to go by, he was thinking about it, too.

She plunged right in with the truth. "I would probably make a huge and horrible mistake."

The lift of his brows told her he understood her meaning. And he slowly raised his hand to brush his fingertips across her cheek. "Would it be so horrible?"

"We can't," she managed to respond.

He gave a very small smile. "We won't."

But he was easing closer, leaning in.

"Tuck," she warned.

He used his other hand to take hold of hers, twining their fingers together. "Professionally. On a professional level, given the current circumstances, what would you do if your loyalty was to me?"

She called on every single ounce of her fortitude to focus. "I'd tell you to go to the New York trade show. It's the smart thing to do and the best thing to do for the company."

"Okay."

His easy answer took her aback.

She wasn't sure she'd understood correctly. "You'll go?"

"We'll both go. I'm still going to find Dixon. But until I do, I'm the only owner this company has got. You're right to tell me to step up."

Amber moved a pace back and he released her hand.

New York? Together? With Tuck?

She struggled for a way to state her position. "I don't want you to get the wrong idea. I'm definitely not going to—"

"Sleep with me?" he said, finishing her thought.

"Well. Okay. Yes. That's what I meant." She hadn't planned on being that blunt, but that was it.

"That's disappointing. But it's not the reason I want you in New York. And I promise, there'll be no pressure on that front." He smoothly closed the space between them and leaned down.

She waited, her senses on alert for the kiss that seemed inevitable.

But he stopped, his lips inches away from hers, his voice a whisper. “I really like your shoes.”

She reflexively glanced to her feet, seeing the jazzy, swirling gold-and-red pattern of her high-heel pumps.

“They’ll look good in New York.” He backed off, his voice returning to normal as he took his place in front of the computer screen. “Let’s stay at the Neapolitan. Book us on a flight.”

Once again, she fought to regain her emotional equilibrium. She swallowed. “Do you want an airline ticket or should I book a company plane?”

“What would Dixon do?”

“Dixon never flies commercial.”

Tuck grinned. “Then, book us a company plane. If I’m going to take Dixon’s place, I might as well enjoy all his perks.”

Amber wanted to ask if he considered her one of Dixon’s perks. But the question was as inappropriate as it was dangerous. Her relationship with Dixon was comfortably professional. By contrast, her relationship with Tuck grew more unsettling by the day.

Three

Tuck knew he had no right to be cheerful. Dixon was still missing and Zachary Ingles was unforgivably late arriving at the JWQ Convention Center in midtown Manhattan. Add to that, thirty Tucker Transportation employees were working with the convention center staff to assemble the components of the company's pavilion, with less organization than he would have expected.

Still he couldn't help but smile as he gazed across the chaos of lights, signs, scale models and scaffolding. Amber was at the opposite end of their allotted space, watching a forklift raise the main corporate sign into position. Her brunette hair was in a jaunty ponytail. She wore pink-and-black checkerboard sneakers, a pair of dark blue jeans and a dusky-blue pullover. It was as casual as he'd ever seen her.

"Mr. Tucker?" A woman in a navy blazer with a convention center name tag on the lapel approached him through the jumble. "I'm Nancy Raines, assistant manager with catering and logistics."

Tuck offered his hand. "Nice to meet you, Nancy. Please call me Tuck."

"Thank you, sir." She referred to the tablet in her hand. "We have the east-side ballroom booked for Friday night, a customized appetizers and hors d'oeuvres menu with an open bar for six hundred."

"That sounds right," said Tuck.

He'd read through the company's final schedule on the plane and he understood the general outline of each event. Out of the corner of his eye, he saw Amber coming their way.

"We understand that there was a last-minute booking of a

jazz trio, Three-Dimensional Moon," said Nancy. "Are they by any chance an acoustic band?"

"An acoustic band for six hundred people?" Tuck found the question rather absurd. How would anyone ever hear the music above the conversation?

"The reason I ask," said Nancy, "is we have no arrangement in place for a sound system."

"There's no sound system?"

That was clearly a mistake. Aside from the music, there were three speeches on the event schedule and a ten-minute corporate video.

Amber arrived. "Can I help with something?"

"This is Nancy. She says there's no sound system for the reception."

"There should be a sound system," said Amber. "And three projection screens."

But Nancy was shaking her head. "There was no tech ordered at all."

"Someone from the marketing department should have handled that. Have you heard anything from Zachary?" Tuck asked Amber. He needed to get to the bottom of this right away.

"I've texted, emailed and left a voice mail, but he's not returning."

Tuck withdrew his phone from his pocket. "We'll need the tech setup," he said to Nancy. "Can you take care of it?"

She made a few taps on her tablet. "I can try. It will have to be rush, and that'll mean a significant surcharge." She looked to Amber. "Do you have the specs?"

"I'll get them to you," said Amber, pulling out her own phone. "I'll track someone down."

Nancy handed her a business card. "You can send them to my email. I'll call a couple of local companies."

"Thanks," said Amber.

Tuck pressed the speed dial for Zachary.

Once again, it rang through to his voice mail.

"Maybe his flight was delayed," Tuck mused.

Amber held up her index finger. “Melanie? It’s Amber. We need specs for a sound system for Three-Dimensional Moon. Can you find their web page and contact their manager?” She paused. “In the next ten minutes if you can.”

Tuck checked his text messages, and then he moved to his email interface.

“I’ve got a new message from Zachary.” He tapped the header.

He read for a minute and felt his jaw go lax.

“What?” Amber asked.

“It’s a letter of resignation.”

“No way.” She moved to where she could see his small screen.

“It says he turned in his keys to security and asked them to change his password.”

Tuck had no idea what to make of the message. Zachary had been with the company for a decade, rising through the ranks to his current, very well-paid position.

“Why would he do that?”

Excellent question.

Tuck’s phone rang. He saw that it was Lucas Steele.

Tuck took the call, speaking without preamble. “Do you know what’s going on?”

“Zachary walked,” said Lucas.

“I just got his email. Do you know why?”

“Harvey went with him,” said Lucas.

“Harvey, too? What on earth *happened*?” Tuck couldn’t keep the astonishment from his voice. Two long-term directors had quit at the same time?

Amber’s eyes widened while she listened to his side of the conversation.

“Peak Overland made them an offer,” said Lucas.

“Both of them?”

“Yes.”

The situation came clear in Tuck’s mind. “Without Dixon, we look vulnerable.”

"Yes, we look vulnerable. Nobody knows anything concrete, so there are theories all over the place. I'm hearing everything from he's been thrown in jail in a foreign country to he was killed skydiving."

"He's in New Orleans," said Tuck. "Or maybe Miami."

There was a silence.

"You don't know where he is." Lucas's voice was flat.

"He's on vacation. He needs some time alone."

"The divorce?" asked Lucas.

"That's my best guess."

"Okay," said Lucas, his tone growing crisp again. "You need me to come out there?"

"Yes. But I also need you in Chicago. And I need you in Antwerp."

What Tuck really needed was Dixon and there was absolutely no time to waste. His next call would be to Jackson.

Lucas gave a chopped chuckle. "Where do you want me?"

"Can you hold the fort in Chicago?"

"I can."

"Talk to security. Change the locks, change the system passwords. Make sure they can't do any damage."

"Will do."

"Is there an heir apparent to either Zachary or Harvey?"

"Nobody comes instantly to mind. But I'll think about it. And I'll ask around."

"Thanks. Talk to you in a few hours."

Tuck's lack of knowledge and experience with the family company suddenly felt like an anvil. He needed his brother more urgently than ever before.

"I'd choose Hope Quigley," said Amber.

"Who?"

"She's a manager in the marketing department. She's been on the social media file for a couple of years, but she's incredibly organized."

"You want me to promote a blogger to marketing director?"

Amber frowned. "It's a lot more than just blogging."

"That's a huge jump in responsibility."

Her hand went to her hip. "And you'd know this, how?"

Tuck did not want to have to make this decision on his own. "I'm calling Jackson. No more messing around. We're turning over every possible rock to find Dixon."

Something shifted in Amber's expression. "You don't need Dixon back."

What an absurd statement. "I absolutely need Dixon back."

"You can promote Hope. And there are others who can step in."

"The company needs a strong president. Look around you. We've got two days to pull this thing together. The reception is already in trouble, and there are thirty private meetings set up with the *marketing director*."

"You take the meetings."

"Yeah, right." As if he was going to speak knowledgably about Baltic Exchange indices and intermodal freight transport.

"Take Hope with you. Give her a new title. She's got two days before the meetings. She can come up to speed on the specific client accounts."

"I've never ever met the woman."

"Then, take Lucas with you."

"Lucas has to keep our current freight moving across the ocean."

"You're right." Amber pursed her red lips, folding her hands primly in front of her. "It's all hopeless. We should just give up and go home."

He didn't have a comeback for her obvious sarcasm. He knew what she was doing, and he didn't appreciate it.

"Are you this insubordinate with Dixon?" How had she kept from being fired?

Tuck dialed Jackson.

"I don't need to be insubordinate with Dixon. He knows what he's doing."

"Well, I…" But there was no retort for that. Tuck didn't know what he was doing. And that was the problem.

Jackson answered his phone. "Hi, Tuck."

"You need to pull out the stops," said Tuck. "Do whatever it takes."

"But—" Amber began.

Tuck silenced her with a glare. "I just lost my marketing director and my finance director."

"Did you fire them?" asked Jackson.

"They quit. Rumor has it they got an offer from a rival, and with Dixon out of the picture—"

"People are getting nervous." Jackson filled in the thought.

"It seems I'm not seen as a strong leader."

"You've barely gotten started."

Tuck knew that was no excuse. Maybe he should have barreled past his father's objections years ago. They might have been able to stop him from having any power at Tucker Transportation. But they couldn't have stopped him from learning. This was his fault, and he had to fix it.

"Find him," he said to Jackson.

"I'm in New Orleans."

"Do you think he's there?"

"I don't know that he's not. There's no evidence that he left."

"Is there evidence he arrived?"

"Maybe. It could be nothing. Can I get back to you?"

"Don't take too long." Tuck's gaze met Amber's.

She gave a slight shake of her head.

He knew she wanted him to leave Dixon alone and do it all himself. But there was too much at stake. He didn't dare try.

Tuck looked fantastic in a tuxedo. But then Amber had known that all along. She'd been seeing pictures of him in the tabloids for years, mostly at posh events or out on the town with some gorgeous woman. His ability to work a party had never been in question.

The Tucker Transportation reception was ending, and the

last few guests trickled out of the ballroom. Amber made her way to the main doors, grateful to have the evening at an end. Her feet were killing her, though that was her own fault. She'd knowingly worn two-hour shoes to a five-hour party.

But she hadn't been able to resist. This was by far the fanciest party she'd ever attended. And she'd never even taken the silver lace peep-toe pumps out of the box. They had a crimson stiletto heel and she'd done her toenails to match. Her feet looked fabulous, setting off her rather simple black dress.

The dress had cap sleeves and a slim silhouette. Its one jazzy feature was the scattering of silver sequins at the midthigh hemline. She'd worn it at least a dozen times, but it was tried and true, appropriate to the occasion.

Tuck appeared beside her, lightly touching her waist. "You promised me a dance."

"Your dance card seemed full," she answered him.

"Women kept asking, and I didn't want to be rude."

Amber kept walking toward the elevator. "You forget the point of hosting such a lavish reception was for you to make business contacts, not to collect phone numbers."

"You sound jealous."

She wasn't jealous. She refused to be jealous. She was merely feeling critical of his wasted opportunities.

"That was a business observation, not a personal one."

"No?" he asked.

"No."

Though, at the moment, it felt intensely personal. His hand was still resting at her waist. The heat from his body called out to her. And his deep voice seemed to seep through to her bones.

"Dance with me now."

She steeled herself against the attraction. "The band is packing up."

The only music was the elevator kind emanating from the small hotel speakers on the ceiling.

"We can go somewhere else."

"It's late. My feet are killing me. And I don't know why I'm giving you excuses. No. I don't want to go somewhere else and dance with you. I want to go to bed."

He let a beat go by in silence. Then there was a lilt in his voice. "Okay. Sure. That works for me."

They came to the elevators. "Tell me you didn't mean that how it sounded."

He pressed the call button. "That depends. How did it sound?"

"You can't flirt with me, Tuck."

"Am I doing it wrong?"

"That's not what I—"

"It was a great party, Amber. Against all odds, we got our pavilion up and running in time. The crowds have been super. And the party came off without a hitch. We even had a good sound system. Thank you for that, by the way. Can we not let our guard down and enjoy the achievement for just a few minutes?"

"I work for you."

She needed to nip his playboy behavior in the bud. It didn't matter that he was a charming flirt. And it didn't matter that he was sharp and funny and killer handsome. This wasn't a date. It was a corporate function, and she wasn't going to let either of them forget it.

"So what?" His question seemed sincere.

"So you can't hit on me."

"Is that a rule?"

"Yes, it's a rule. It's a law. It's called sexual harassment."

"I'm not seriously asking you to sleep with me. I mean, I wouldn't say no to an offer, obviously. But I'm not making the suggestion myself. Except, well, you know, in the most oblique and joking way possible."

Amber was stupefied. She had no idea what to say.

The elevator door opened, but neither of them moved.

"You're my boss," she tried.

"Dixon is your boss."

"You know what I mean."

"Are you saying I can't even ask you on a date? That's ridiculous. People date their bosses all the time. Some of them marry their bosses, for goodness' sake."

The door slid closed again.

She couldn't seem to stop herself from joking. "Are we getting married, Tuck?"

He didn't miss a beat. "I don't know. We haven't even had our first date."

She blew out a sigh of frustration. "What I'm saying, what the law says, is that you can't in any way, shape or form hint that my agreement or lack of agreement to something sexual or romantic will impact my job."

"I'm not doing that. I'd never do that. How do I prove it? Is there something I can sign?"

She pressed the call button again. "Tuck, you have got to spend more time in the real world."

"I spend all my time in the real world."

The door slid back open and they walked inside the elevator.

She turned to face the front. "If you did, you'd know what I was talking about."

"I do know what you're talking about. All I wanted to do was dance."

The door slid shut and they were alone in the car.

He was right. She didn't know how the conversation had gotten so far off track.

"We don't have time to dance," she told him. "You need to focus on tomorrow's meetings. You have the list, right? Did you study the files?"

"I looked at them."

"What does that mean?"

"I scanned them. I know the basics. Besides, you agreed to be there with me."

"You can't defer to your assistant when you're meeting with owners and executives of billion-dollar companies."

"I've been busy. I had to work some things out with Lucas. And then I took your advice and interviewed Hope."

"You did?" Amber was glad to hear that.

"Yes. I liked her. I'm going to give her more responsibility."

"That's good."

"So forgive me if I didn't find time to memorize the details of thirty client files."

Amber was tired, but she shook her brain back to life. Thank goodness she'd said no to the second glass of champagne.

"We'll go over them tonight," she told him.

He glanced at his watch.

"Unless you want to get up at 4:00 a.m. and go over them in the morning."

"Four a.m. is a late night, not an early morning."

"You're starting with a breakfast meeting."

"I know. Who set that up? Breakfast meetings are evil. They should be banned."

The elevator came to a stop on the top floor.

"Let's get this over with," Amber said with resignation.

Together, they walked the length of the hall to Tuck's suite. She'd been in it yesterday, so she knew it wasn't a typically intimate hotel room.

The main floor was a living area, powder room and kitchenette. You had to climb a spiral staircase to even get to the bedroom. According to the floor plan sketched on the door, there was a whirlpool tub on the bedroom terrace, but she had no intention of finding out in person.

As she set her clutch purse down on a glass-topped table and slipped off her shoes, her phone chimed. Curious as to who would text her at such a late hour, she checked the screen.

She was surprised to see it was her sister.

Jade lived on the West Coast and only contacted Amber if she needed money or was having an emotional crisis. It was uncharitable, and maybe unfair, but Amber's first thought was that Jade might be in jail.

"Are you thirsty?" Tuck asked, crossing to the bar.

Amber sat down on a peach-colored sofa. It was arranged in a grouping with two cream-colored armchairs in front of a marble fireplace.

"Some water would be nice," said Amber, opening the text message.

"Water? That's it?"

"I'd take some fruit juice."

I just hit town, Jade's text said.

"You're a wild woman," said Tuck.

"I'm keeping my wits about me."

Which town? Amber answered her sister.

"In case I make a pass at you?" asked Tuck.

"You swore you wouldn't."

"I don't recall signing anything."

Chicago.

What's wrong? Amber typed to her sister.

Nothing all good. Well, dumped boyfriend. Jerk anyway.

"Amber?" Tuck prompted.

"Hmm?"

"I said I didn't sign anything."

She glanced up. "Anything for what?"

He nodded to her phone. "Who's that?"

"My sister."

"You checked out there. I thought it might be your boyfriend."

"I don't have a boyfriend." She absently wondered what she'd ever said or done to make Tuck believe she had a boyfriend.

I'm in New York City, Amber typed to Jade.

"Good," said Tuck in a soft tone.

A shimmer tightened her chest.

I was hoping to crash with you for a couple of days, Jade responded.

Amber's fingers froze and she stared at the screen.

"What does she say?" asked Tuck, moving closer.

"She wants to stay with me."

"Is that bad?"

"She's not particularly…trustworthy."

Jade was constantly in and out of low-paying jobs, and in and out of bad relationships. The last time she'd stayed with Amber her sister had prompted a noise complaint from a neighbor, drunk all of Amber's wine and left abruptly without a goodbye, taking two pairs of Amber's jeans and several of her blouses along for good measure.

I'll call you when I get back, Amber typed.

"Oh?" Tuck took a seat on the other end of the sofa.

Thing is, Jade returned, I kind of need a place now, tonight.

Amber swore under her breath. It was coming up on midnight in Chicago, and her little sister had nowhere to go. She didn't delude herself that Jade would have money for a hotel.

"What is it?" asked Tuck.

"She needs a place now."

"Right now?" He glanced at his watch.

"I'm guessing she just got in from LA." Amber wouldn't be surprised if Jade had hitchhiked.

Hotel? Amber wrote.

Can't afford it. Jerk took all the money.

Of course the jerk boyfriend took Jade's money. They always did.

"I take it cash flow is an issue," said Tuck.

"That's a polite way to put it."

"Send her to the nearest Aquamarine location."

Amber raised her brow in Tuck's direction. The Aquamarine was a quality, four-star hotel chain.

"Tucker Transportation has a corporate account," said Tuck.

"I know Tucker Transportation has a corporate account."

"You can tell her to use it."

"I can't misuse the company account for my sister."

"You can't," he agreed. "But I can."

"I won't—"

"I need your attention," said Tuck. "I need you off your cell phone and I need you not worrying about your sister. The way I see it, this is the cheapest way forward."

"That's a stretch."

Tuck's tone turned serious. "Tell her. Let me make that an order."

Amber wanted to argue. But then she didn't particularly want to send Jade to her town house, nor did she want to rouse a neighbor at this hour to give her a key.

"I know you respect orders," said Tuck. "You are the consummate professional."

"You're messing in my personal life." Amber knew she shouldn't take him up on it, but she was sorely tempted.

"Yeah," he said. "I am. Now send her to the Aquamarine."

Amber heaved a sigh.

Before she could send the message, Tuck scooped the phone out of her hand, typing into it.

"Hey!"

"You know it's the best answer."

She did know it was the best answer. And she'd been about to do it herself. Further protests seemed pointless.

"She says great," said Tuck.

"I'll bet she does."

He set the phone down on the coffee table. "You're a good sister."

"In this instance, I think you're the good sister."

"Never been called that before."

"Neither have I."

Tuck chuckled, obviously assuming she was making a joke.

She wasn't.

Four

Tuck was pretty good at handling late nights, but even he was starting to fade by the time he and Amber shut down the last client file. She looked exhausted, her cheeks flushed, makeup smudged under her eyes and her hair escaping in wisps from the updo.

"That's as ready as we can be," she said.

They were side by side on the overstuffed sofa, a lamp glowing on an end table, the lights of the city streaming through open curtains on the picture window across the room.

Tuck had long since shrugged out of his suit jacket and loosened his tie. His shirtsleeves were rolled up, but he was still too warm. The thermostat might be set too high. More likely, it was his attraction to Amber.

She was intensely sexy, every single thing about her, from her deep blue eyes to her rich brunette hair, to the delicious, sleek curves revealed by her fitted dress.

"Do you feel confident?" she asked, tipping her head to look at him.

He realized he'd been silently staring at her.

And he was still staring at her. He was overwhelmed by the urge to kiss her, kiss her deeply and thoroughly, taste those soft, dark red lips that had been teasing his senses all night long. He knew he shouldn't. Her earlier reluctance was reasonable and well founded. Anything romantic between them was bound to be complicated, today, tomorrow and into the future.

"Tuck?" she persisted, clearly confused.

He lifted his hand, brushed the stray hairs back from her cheek.

She sucked in a quick breath and her eyes closed in a long

blink. When they opened, they were opaque, misty blue with indecision.

It wasn't a no, he told himself. She wasn't ordering him to back off. She was tempted, just like him.

He knew there had to be a whole lot of reasons not to do this, but he couldn't seem to come up with them at the moment. So he leaned forward instead, slowly and steadily.

She could stop him, run away from him, pull back from him at least. Whatever she decided, he'd accept. But he had to at least try.

She didn't do any of those things, and their lips came together, his bold and purposeful, hers heated, smooth and delicious. He altered the angle and his arms went around her. He kissed her once, twice, three times, desire pulsing through his mind and electrifying his body.

She kissed him back, tentatively at first. But then her tongue touched his, tangled with his. Her body went malleable against his, her softness forming to his planes. He eased her back on the sofa, covering her from chest to thighs, tasting her mouth, inhaling her scent, feeling her back arch intimately and her heartbeat rise against his chest.

He wanted her bad.

He kissed his way down her neck, pushing the cap sleeve of her dress out of the way, leaving damp circles on her bare shoulder. He thought about her zipper, imagined pulling it down her back, the dress falling away, revealing a lacy bra, or her bare breasts, that creamy smooth skin that was silken to his touch.

"Tuck?" Her voice was breathless.

"Yes?"

"We…"

He stilled. He knew what came next, though every fiber of his being rebelled against it.

"Can't," she said, finishing the thought.

He wanted to argue. They could. They really could, and the world wouldn't come to a crashing halt.

But he'd never coerced a woman into his bed before and he wasn't about to start with Amber.

"You sure?" he asked.

He could feel her nod.

"I'm sorry," she said.

He eased back. "No, I'm the one who's sorry. I shouldn't have kissed you."

"I should have said no."

"I'm glad you didn't."

"I'm… Oh, this is not good." She struggled to sit up.

He moved out of the way, offering his hand to help her up.

Neither of them seemed to know what to say.

Tuck broke the silence. "I guess we're ready for the meeting."

"Tuck, I—"

"You don't have to explain."

A woman was entitled to say no for any reason she wanted. And he did understand her hesitation. She worked for him, at least temporarily. She was smart not to let it get complicated.

She rose to her feet. "You're an attractive guy. But you know that."

He stood.

"I'm sure most women would—"

"I don't like where this is going." He didn't.

"I know you don't often get turned down."

"Now, how would you know that?"

"I read the papers."

His annoyance grew. "You believe the tabloids?"

"They have pictures." Frustration crept into her tone. "You can't deny you have gorgeous girl after gorgeous girl on your arm."

"Is that what you think of me? I didn't kiss you because you're beautiful, Amber."

"I *know* that. I'm not comparing myself to them."

"Comparing yourself?" He didn't understand her point.

"I'm not suggesting I'm one of your bombshells."

"Good."

She was so much more than that. He might not have known her long, but he knew there was more depth to her than a dozen of his Saturday-night dates combined.

Her shoulders dropped. "I'll just say good night."

"You didn't do anything wrong."

He didn't want her to leave. He wanted to keep talking, even if they were arguing. He liked the sound of her voice. But he also wanted to kiss her again and carry her off to his bed. He couldn't do that.

"It's late," she said. "We're both tired. Let's not say or do anything we're going to regret."

"I don't regret a thing."

"I do."

The words were like a blow to his chest. "I'm sorry to hear that."

"I'm your employee, Tuck."

"You're Dixon's employee."

"Tucker Transportation's employee. And you're a vice president."

"In name only." He found himself parroting his father's words.

"You need to change that, Tuck. You really do."

"Are you lecturing me on my corporate responsibility?"

"Somebody has to."

He was about to retort that they already had. But then he realized it wasn't true. Neither his father nor Dixon had lectured him. They'd never pushed him to become more involved in the company. They'd barely suggested he show up. But he wasn't about to admit that to Amber.

He had to stop himself from taking her hands in his. "How did we get here?"

Her eyes narrowed in puzzlement. "We were prepping for the client meetings."

"I meant in the conversation. We were talking about us, and suddenly we're on to Tucker Transportation."

"There is no us."

"There was almost an us."

It was barely there, but he could tell she stifled a smile. It warmed his heart.

"I'm leaving now," she said.

He reflexively grasped her hands. "You don't have to go."

"I do have to go."

"Stay." He gave himself a mental shake, backing off. "I'm sorry. I never do that. I never try to convince a woman to sleep with me."

She arched a brow. "They normally throw themselves into your bed?"

They did. But he knew how that sounded.

"I like you, Amber."

"I'm not going to sleep with you, Tuck."

"That's not what I'm asking."

"It's exactly what you're asking. It's 2:00 a.m., and I'm in your hotel room." She hesitated. "That was my mistake, wasn't it? What was I thinking?"

"You didn't make a mistake."

She tugged her hands from his. "I didn't think this through. I just assumed you wouldn't misunderstand."

"I didn't misunderstand. I didn't plan this, Amber." He'd taken her behavior at face value. He knew she was only trying to help him get ready for the meetings.

She held up her palms and took a couple of backward paces. "Time for me to say good night. Don't forget the breakfast meeting." She took her purse from the table. "Don't be late."

"I'm never late."

"True," she allowed as she retrieved her shoes and strode toward the door. "But I always expect you to be late."

"Why?"

"I'll see you tomorrow." And then she was gone.

He wanted to call her back. He *wished* he could call her back. But he'd made enough mistakes for one night. He realized that if he wanted Amber to let him get anywhere close to her, he had to back off until she was ready.

Back in Chicago two days later, Amber dreaded meeting up with Jade. She was happy her sister had dumped whatever loser boyfriend she'd hooked up with this time, but she also held out no hope for the next one, or the one after that. Bad boyfriends and heartache had been Jade's pattern since she'd dropped out of high school.

Amber tried to harden her heart. Jade was an adult and responsible for her own behavior. But Amber couldn't help remembering her sister as a lost little girl, younger, who had struggled even more than Amber with their mother's addiction to alcohol.

She made her way from her car up the stone pathway to the lobby of the Riverside Aquamarine. Jade was going to meet her in the coffee shop. But since it was shortly after noon, Amber wasn't going to be surprised to find her in the lobby lounge. It was sadly ironic that Jade had turned to alcohol to combat a childhood ruined by alcohol.

The hotel lobby was bright and airy, decorated by white armchairs and leafy plants. The lobby lounge was central, but Amber didn't see Jade at any of the tables. She moved on to the coffee shop that overlooked the pool and quickly spotted Jade at a booth.

As Amber approached, Jade slid from the bench and came to her feet.

Amber's jaw nearly dropped to the floor.

Jade was pregnant. She was very, very pregnant.

"What on earth?" Amber paced forward, coming to a stop in front of her sister.

"Seven months," said Jade, giving a wry smile as she answered the obvious question.

"But…when? How?"

Jade's expression sobered. "Seven months ago. And the usual way. Can we sit down?"

"Oh, Jade." Amber couldn't keep the disappointment and worry from her tone. Jade was in no position to be a good mother.

"Don't 'oh, Jade' me. I'm happy."

"How can you be happy?"

"I'm going to be a mother." Jade slid back into the booth.

As she took the seat across from her, Amber noted she was eating a salad and drinking a glass of iced tea. "You're not drinking, are you?"

"It's iced tea," said Jade.

"I don't mean now. I mean *at all*. You can't drink while you're pregnant, Jade."

"Do you think I'm stupid?"

Stupid, no. But Jade's judgment had always been a big question mark.

"That's not an answer," Amber pointed out.

"No, I'm not drinking."

"Good. That's good. You've seen a doctor?"

"Yes, I saw a doctor in LA. And I'll find a clinic here in Chicago, too."

A waitress appeared and Amber ordered a soda.

She stared at her sister, noting the worn cotton smock and the wrinkled slacks. Jade's cheeks looked hollow and her arms looked thin. Amber hated to think her sister might not be getting enough to eat.

All the way here, she'd been hoping Jade's stay in Chicago would be brief. She'd dreaded the idea of having her move into the town house for days or weeks. Now she realized that was exactly what had to happen. Jade needed stability, a warm bed, good food.

"Have you been taking care of yourself?" Amber asked.

Jade gave a shrug. "It's been okay. Kirk was getting more and more obnoxious about the baby. He said he didn't mind, but then he started talking about putting it up for adoption."

Amber's opinion of this Kirk person went up a notch. "*Have* you thought about adoption?"

Jade's expression twisted in anger. "I am *not* giving away this baby."

"To a good home," said Amber. "There are fantastic prospective parents out there. Loving, well educated, houses in the suburbs—they could give a baby a great life."

Jade's lips pressed together and her arms crossed protectively over her stomach. "Forget it."

"Okay," said Amber, letting the subject drop for now. "It's your choice."

"Damn right it's my choice."

"Yours and the father's."

"There is no father."

"You just said Kirk wanted to give the baby up for adoption."

"Kirk's not the father. That's why he wanted to give the baby away. It's not his."

The revelation took Amber aback. Kirk dropped back down in her esteem. "I don't understand."

"I was pregnant when I met Kirk. He said he didn't mind. He said he loved kids. But then…" Jade gave another shrug.

"Who's the father?" asked Amber. Maybe there was some hope for financial support. Heaven knew Jade was going to need it.

"It was a one-night thing."

"You didn't get his name." Amber shouldn't have been surprised.

"Only his first name. Pete."

Amber tried not to judge, but it was hard.

"He was a sailor."

"You mean in the navy?"

Jade nodded.

"Well, did you try to find him?"

"It was weeks before I knew I was pregnant."

"What about DNA? After the baby's born. The navy must have a database."

"He was Australian."

"Still, did you contact—"

"Amber, I am not going to track down some Australian sailor and ruin his life over a one-night stand."

"Why not? He ruined—"

"Don't you *dare* say he ruined mine. He seemed like a really nice guy. But I went into it with my eyes wide-open, and it was my choice to carry on with the pregnancy. I'm having a baby, my son or daughter, your nephew or niece, and I'm going to take care of it, and I'm not going to drag some poor man kicking and screaming into an obligation he didn't sign up for."

Jade's words and attitude were surprising but in some ways admirable. Amber wasn't used to her taking such personal responsibility.

"Okay," she told her sister. "You can come and stay with me."

Jade was silent for a moment. "Thank you."

"We'll figure this out together."

But Jade was shaking her head. "I'm not looking for you to take over my life."

Who'd said anything about taking over?

"It's only temporary," Jade continued. "I'm studying. I'm going to write my GED. Then I'm going to get a proper job."

Amber could barely believe what she was hearing. "You're working on your GED?"

"I've been working on it for months now."

The surprises just kept on coming. "Seriously?"

"Why would I joke about that?"

"That's fantastic." Amber was beyond impressed. "I'll help you. We can—"

"Whoa. You need to dial it down."

"I didn't mean to dial it up."

"Giving me a place to stay is great, *really* great. But that's all I need right now."

Amber forcibly curbed her excitement. But it was the first time Jade had shown an interest in anything but partying, and Amber's hopes were running away with her. A baby was an enormous responsibility. But other single mothers had pulled it off. If Jade could keep up this new attitude, she might have a fighting chance.

Amber couldn't help but smile at the possibilities, even as Jade came back with a warning frown.

"I thought we'd have him back by now," Tuck said to Jackson.

It was late-afternoon Tuesday, a week after the New York trip, and the rain was streaming in sheets down the picture window overlooking the river. The two men lounged in the armchair group in the corner of Tuck's office. Tuck's desk was piled with paper and his email in-box was approaching the breaking point. Most of it was bad news, and he was anxious for Dixon's return.

"I thought so, too," said Jackson. He had one ankle over the opposite knee, his legs clad in black jeans topped with a steel-gray T-shirt. "Your brother's wreaking havoc with my reputation."

"I know I'm losing faith in you," said Tuck. "And I'm beginning to consider the wild rumors."

"That he's a spy?"

"That there's at least something going on that I don't know about." Tuck didn't believe Dixon had a secret life. But he was all out of reasonable explanations. It had been nearly a month since his brother had disappeared.

"Is there anything we could have missed?" asked Jackson. "Some paper record, a secret email account, a different cell phone?"

"I've searched his office. I've looked through the mansion. I even called Kassandra."

"You *called* Kassandra?"

"You didn't?"

"Of course I did. But it's my job to chase down every lead."

"It's my company," said Tuck. "And it's going rapidly downhill without Dixon."

"What was your take on Kassandra?" asked Jackson.

"That's she's a selfish, spoiled princess who gambled and lost." Tuck couldn't help a grim smirk at the memory. Clearly, his former sister-in-law had expected a hefty financial settlement.

"She's holding a grudge," said Jackson. "Do you think she'd harm him?"

"She probably wants to. But that would require risk and effort. She's lazy."

"Yeah," Jackson agreed. "I'm starting to wonder if he was kidnapped."

Tuck frowned. He'd been picturing Dixon on a tropical beach somewhere. If his brother was in trouble, then Tuck's anger at him was completely misplaced.

"Maybe he was forced to write that letter to your dad," said Jackson.

"Tell me you're not serious."

"Who saw him last?"

Tuck nodded to his closed office door, his thoughts moving to Amber. She'd kept him carefully at arm's length since the night in New York, but he was practically obsessing over her.

"His assistant, Amber," he told Jackson. "He was in the office for a few hours the day he left."

"Can you call her in?"

"Sure." Tuck came to his feet. "But I've already pumped her for information. She's the one who gave me his password. He didn't tell her where he was going."

He crossed to the door and drew it open, walking into the outer office.

Amber was at her desk, profile to him as she typed on the keyboard.

"Can you join us?" he asked.

She stopped typing and glanced up, her blue gaze meeting his. There was a wariness there, which he chalked up to the kisses in New York. Could she tell he wanted to do it again?

He was dying to do it again. He feared it was written all over his expression every time he looked her way.

"Sure." She smoothed out her expression and pushed back her chair.

As usual, her outfit was straitlaced, a navy blazer over a matching pleated skirt and a white blouse. Her spike pumps were bright blue with a slash of white across the toe. They appeared simple by Amber-footwear standards, but they still struck him as sleekly sexy. Or maybe it was only his fevered imagination.

As she rose, he caught a glimpse of lace beneath the neckline of her blouse and his desire went into hyperdrive. He warned himself to bide his time until Dixon returned. When things were back to normal, he'd try approaching her again. Amber would no longer be working for him then.

"What do you need?" she asked as she passed by him.

"Jackson has a couple of questions." Tuck fell into step behind her.

"What kind of questions?"

"About Dixon."

She twisted her head, pausing just outside the office door. "What about Dixon?"

Did he detect guilt in her eyes? Was she nervous?

"The usual questions." He found himself scrutinizing her expression.

"What are the usual questions?"

"Shall we find out?"

"I've told you everything I know."

"You say that in a way that makes me wonder."

"Words strung into a sentence make you suspicious?"

"You're jumpy," he said.

"I'm annoyed."

"You have no reason to be annoyed."

"I've got work to do."

"So do I. And none of our work gets easier until Dixon is back."

Her eyes narrowed. "He shouldn't be your crutch."

"He's everybody's crutch. Do you know where he is?"

"No."

He gestured her forward. "Then, let's go talk to Jackson."

Amber squared her shoulders and moved into the office.

Jackson rose. "Nice to see you again, Amber."

"Why do I feel like this is an interrogation?" she asked.

"I have that effect on people," said Jackson.

"You should stop." She took one of the armchairs in the grouping.

"I'll keep that in mind."

For some reason, the exchange grated on Tuck. Jackson wasn't flirting with her. But he was joking with her and Tuck didn't like it.

"Your questions?" he asked Jackson.

Jackson caught his gaze and looked puzzled.

"Sure," said Jackson, obviously waiting for Tuck to sit down.

Tuck perched on the arm of a chair. He folded his arms over his chest.

It took Jackson a moment to move his attention back to Amber.

"I'm sure you'll agree," he said to her, "that Dixon has been gone longer than any of us expected."

"How long did we expect him to be gone?" she asked.

"Did he tell you how long he'd be gone?"

Amber glanced fleetingly at Tuck. "His letter said a month."

"It's been a month."

"Almost."

"No phone call? No postcard?"

"Who sends a postcard these days?"

"People who want you to know they're having a good time and wish you were there."

Amber's gaze hardened. "I doubt he's having a good time."

Tuck could almost hear Jackson's senses go on alert.

"Why?" Jackson asked.

"You know about his ex-wife." Amber wasn't asking a question.

"I do."

"Then you know he's recovering from her treachery."

"Treachery?"

"What would you call it?"

"Infidelity."

"Okay."

Jackson paused. "What was your relationship with Dixon?"

"Hey," Tuck protested. "Amber's not on trial."

Jackson shot him a look of astonishment. "Should I be doing this without you?"

"He was my boss," said Amber. "Full stop. And if one more person insinuates it was something inappropriate, I'm walking out the door."

"Who else insinuated that?"

"Back off," said Tuck. This was getting them nowhere. It was only annoying Amber, and rightly so. He didn't blame her for being ticked off.

"Who else?" asked Jackson.

"Tuck." She slid him an angry glance.

He held up his hands in surrender. He hadn't considered anything of the sort for quite some time now.

"And Jamison," said Amber.

Jackson's tone slipped up in obvious surprise. "Jamison thought you were having an affair with his son?"

"Only because Jamison was having an—" Amber snapped her mouth shut.

Jackson blinked.

Tuck rose to his feet.

Amber stiffened her spine.

"You're going to have to finish that sentence," said Tuck.

She shook her head.

"I insist."

"We all know what she was going to say," Jackson said.

"I didn't say it," said Amber.

"My father was having an affair?"

She glared at Tuck. "Let it go."

"With who?" he demanded. Tuck's first reaction was that it couldn't be true. Then again, it absolutely could be true. Lots of high-powered, self-gratifying people cheated. Why not his father?

"It's not for me to say," Amber responded. "I found out by accident. In fact, I don't even know for sure."

"Who do you suspect?"

Who it was might have no bearing on Dixon's situation. Then again, it might. Had Dixon known about the affair?

"That would be gossip," said Amber.

"My father is in the hospital. My brother is *missing*. Gossip already."

She glanced from Tuck to Jackson and back again. "Can I swear you two to secrecy?"

"Amber," Tuck all but shouted.

This wasn't a negotiation. There were no conditions. She was answering the question.

"Yes," said Jackson. He glared at Tuck. "We'll keep it to ourselves. As you say, it's speculation. It would be wrong for us to act on hearsay."

"Margaret," said Amber.

"His Margaret?" Tuck asked.

"Who is Margaret?" asked Jackson.

"His assistant," said Amber.

"But—" Tuck couldn't wrap his head around it. Margaret Smithers could best be described as matronly. She was middle-aged, slightly overweight, her hair was partly gray and her clothes were polyester.

"Expecting a blond supermodel?" asked Amber.

Tuck wasn't about to admit that was true. "I was expecting him to be faithful to my mother."

"Did Dixon know?" asked Jackson, his thoughts obviously moving along the same lines as Tuck's.

Dixon had just been a victim of infidelity. Finding out about their father might have angered him enough to leave. Tuck couldn't help but wonder if he planned to stay gone.

"No," said Amber.

"How can you be sure?" asked Tuck. It would at least have been some kind of explanation.

Amber had to think about it for a moment. "I'm as sure as I can be. I didn't figure it out until the heart attack. And Dixon never acted as if he knew."

"How did you figure it out?" asked Jackson.

"The way Margaret acted when Jamison collapsed," said Amber. "She mentioned they'd had wine together the night before. Then when she realized what she'd said, she panicked."

"You were with Jamison when it happened?" asked Jackson.

"I was in his office. He was upset, grilling me about Dixon. When I wouldn't tell him anything, he got really angry." She fell to silence, and her shoulders drooped. A cloud came over her eyes. "Maybe I should have told…"

Tuck looked to Jackson. Both men waited, but she didn't elaborate.

"Should have told what?" Jackson prompted in a soft voice.

Amber refocused on him. "Nothing."

"What was he asking?"

"Where Dixon went."

"But you didn't tell him."

"No."

"Tell us."

She drew back. "I don't know."

"You just admitted that you did," said Tuck.

She shook her head in vigorous denial.

"You said maybe you should have told him, but you didn't tell him."

"That's not what I—"

"No," said Tuck. He kept his tone carefully even, but inwardly he was furious. She'd been lying to him. She'd watched him struggle all these weeks. She'd pretended to help him, when all the while the solution had been at her fingertips.

"You can't walk it back," he said. "You know where Dixon went. Tell me. Tell me right this second."

She compressed her lips, staring at him, her expression a combination of guilt and defiance.

"That's an order," he said. "Tell me, or you're fired—"

"Tuck," Jackson cut in.

"No," said Tuck. "She's sat back and let Tucker Transportation fall down around my ears. She doesn't get to do that and keep her job."

"I can't," she protested.

"Then, you're fired."

Five

Tuck's final words echoed inside Amber's ears.

She put her compact car into Park outside her town house, set the brake and gripped the steering wheel. She was home an hour early, and it felt surreal. The sun was too high in the sky and kids were still playing in the park across the street, whooping it up on the slide and the jungle gym.

Fired. She'd been fired from Tucker Transportation. She had no job. She had no paycheck. Her savings might take her through the next month, but she had mortgage payments, utility payments, phone bills and food bills.

She cursed the new shoes on her feet. She'd worn them for the first time today and she couldn't take them back. Then again, they were gorgeous and they'd been on sale. And, really, how much would a refund help? It would barely fill up her gas tank.

She couldn't waste time worrying about might-have-beens. She had to get it together. She had to start job hunting right away.

The front door opened and Jade stood there, looking out, her rounded belly pressing against an oversize plaid shirt. Amber was reminded that she also had Jade and the baby to worry about. Not that it changed her plans.

She'd update her résumé tonight and get out job hunting first thing tomorrow. It would have been nice to have Dixon as a reference. She sure couldn't use Tuck.

She turned off the engine, trying unsuccessfully to banish his image from her mind. He'd been angry. That much was certainly clear. But he'd looked hurt, too, seeming disappointed that her loyalty was to Dixon. She wished she could have given Tuck what he wanted, but she couldn't serve them both.

She stepped out of the car and waved to Jade as she walked up the stepping-stones. The sage and asters were barely hanging on. The other blooms had faded away, and only the leaves remained. October was not exactly a cheerful month.

As she approached the door, she pasted a smile on her face. "How are you feeling?"

"Huge."

Amber widened her smile at the joke.

"I made an appointment at the community clinic," said Jade, as she stepped back from the doorway.

"That's good." Amber had been insistent that Jade get proper medical care. "When is the appointment?"

"I told them my due date and they got me in tomorrow."

Amber glanced at Jade's stomach. "I guess they know there's no time to waste."

"Being pregnant is not an illness."

"But you want a healthy baby."

"Oof." Jade's hand went to her stomach. "This one's healthy, all right. It's got a kick like a soccer player."

"I can drive you to the appointment," said Amber. She'd be happier if she heard firsthand what the doctor had to say.

"I can take the bus."

Amber dumped her purse and headed for the living room. "It's no trouble. I can afford to take a little time off."

"Are you sure?"

"Positive."

Amber would be taking more than just a little time off. But she didn't see any need to say so immediately. Hopefully, she'd have a new job lined up before she had to share the news about losing this one.

"Are you hungry?" she asked Jade.

"I made macaroni casserole."

Amber couldn't hide her surprise. "You cooked?"

Not that macaroni casserole was exactly gourmet, but Jade

had never been handy in the kitchen, nor particularly self-motivated when it came to household chores.

Jade grinned proudly as they walked to the kitchen. "It's all ready to pop into the oven."

"That sounds delicious. Thanks."

Jade turned on the oven while Amber set out plates and cutlery and let her optimism build. She had five solid years of work at Tucker Transportation. She'd built up her administrative skill set, and surely that would be transferable to any number of companies. Maybe she could gloss over her reasons for leaving. She might even be able to use Margaret as a reference.

She hoped Tuck wouldn't be vindictive and spread word around the company that she was fired. But she really had no idea how he'd handle it. He was pretty angry right now.

There was a sudden knock on the front door.

"Expecting someone?" asked Jade.

"Not me. You?"

"Nobody knows I'm here."

Amber went for the door, suspecting it was a neighbor, maybe Sally Duncan from next door. She was on the townhouse council and loved to complain. Perhaps old Mr. Purvis was barbecuing on his patio again.

Amber had voted to repeal the prohibition on barbecues at the last council meeting. Sure, the smoke was annoying. But who in their right mind would ban hot dogs and hamburgers?

She swung open the door, startled to find Tuck standing on her porch. He was frowning, eyes narrowed. Worry immediately clenched her stomach.

"What do you want?" she asked him.

"To talk."

"I have nothing else to say."

"After you left, Jackson pointed out the error of my ways."

She didn't want to hope. But she couldn't help herself. Was Tuck offering her job back?

"I came here to give you another chance," he said.

She waited.

"You being gone helps neither of us," he said.

She had to agree with that. But she doubted he cared about helping her.

"Another chance to what?" she prompted.

"What can you tell me about Dixon?"

"I've told you everything—"

"Well, hello there." Jade arrived, breaking in with a breezy tone. "Are you one of Amber's neighbors?"

Tuck's brow shot up as he took in the pregnant Jade.

"He's my boss," said Amber, instantly realizing it was no longer true. But before she could correct the statement, Jade was talking again.

"Really? Very nice to meet you. I'm Amber's sister, Jade." Jade stuck out her hand.

"Jade, this really isn't a good time."

"Tuck Tucker," said Tuck as he shook Jade's hand.

"Are you hungry?" asked Jade.

"No, he's not," Amber quickly responded.

"I need to borrow your sister for a few minutes," Tuck said to Jade.

"Does she need to go back to work?" asked Jade.

"No," Tuck and Amber answered simultaneously.

"I just need to speak with her," said Tuck.

"Oh," said Jade, glancing between them, obviously picking up on their discomfort. "Then, I'll leave you two alone."

As Jade withdrew, Amber moved onto the porch, pulling the door closed behind her. It was cold outside, but she wanted to get this over with.

"The job market's very tight out there," said Tuck.

"Are you trying to frighten me?"

"I'm asking you to be realistic. I need to talk to my brother."

"I promised him I wouldn't tell a soul. That included his family."

"So you admit you know where he is."

"I don't know with any certainty where he is."

"Why are you talking in riddles?"

She reached behind herself for the doorknob. "I've told you what I can."

"I can't imagine Dixon wants you to be fired."

"I can't imagine he does, either."

Dixon had always given her top-notch performance evaluations. He'd praised her work, often saying he didn't know how he'd live without her. She liked to think he wouldn't want her fired.

"Don't make me do it," said Tuck.

"I'm not *making* you do anything."

"Ignoring an order is gross insubordination."

"Betraying a confidence is worse."

He leaned in. "Circumstances have changed since you made that promise."

She knew they had. But she also knew Dixon's doctor had told him to get away from the pressures of Tucker Transportation.

"Amber." Tuck reached out, his hand encircling her upper arm. "I *need* this, please."

His touch brought a rush of memories—the strength of his embrace, the taste of his lips and the scent of his skin. Suddenly, she was off balance, and she felt herself sway toward him. Her hand moved to steady herself, her palm coming up against his chest.

He groaned deep in his throat. "I don't want to fight with you."

She jerked her hand away, but he was faster, engulfing it in his own, pressing it firmly back against his chest.

His tone was gravelly. "Don't make me fight with you."

She battled the desire rising in her body. She wanted nothing more and nothing less than to collapse into Tuck's arms and kiss him until every other thought was driven from her brain.

She met his gaze. "I've told you everything I can."

His expression turned mocking. "And you *still* claim there's nothing going on between you and Dixon."

"I'll claim it as many times as it takes. It's the truth."

"Yet you'll give up your job for him?"

"I'll give up my job for a principle."

He tugged her closer, voice going quiet. "You sure about that?"

She enunciated each syllable. "Positive."

He kissed her.

She was so surprised that she didn't fight it. Her lips were pliable under his—soft, welcoming—and, for a second, she kissed him back. Her brain screeched at her to stop. But his embrace was oddly comforting. His kiss was tender. And the warmth of his chest seemed to make its way into her heart.

Then reason asserted itself. She forced herself to push against him, staggering back and thudding against the closed door. They stared at each other. Her chest rose and fell with labored breaths.

"I had to be sure," he said.

"Sure of *what*?"

"That you're not in love with my brother."

"Go away." She scrunched her eyes shut to block him out. "Just go away, and stay gone. I think I might hate you."

He didn't make a sound.

After a moment, she opened one eye. His back was to her and he was halfway down the path, striding toward a sleek black sports car.

Thank goodness he was leaving. Thank goodness he was out of her life. She could get a new job. She *would* get a new job. The last place on earth she wanted to be was working for Tuck.

The door opened behind her.

"Amber?" Jade's voice was hesitant.

"Yes." Amber shook some sense into herself.

"Your boss is your boyfriend?"

Amber turned. "What? No."

"You just kissed him."

"That?" Amber waved it away. "That was nothing. He was being a jerk, is all. He fired me."

"He *what*?"

"We had a disagreement. No. More a difference of opinion. I'd call it a difference of principles and values. He's not a man I want to work for." Amber paused. "I'm fine with the way things turned out."

She was fine. At least she would be fine.

"What will you do?" There was worry in Jade's expression.

Amber linked her arm with her sister's and moved them both inside. "I'll get another job. This was a good job, but it's not the only job. I have skills and experience. Maybe I'll even make more money."

"You sound confident."

"I *am* confident."

Maybe her leaving Tucker Transportation was inevitable. Jamison had most certainly planned to fire her before his heart attack. If she looked at it like that, she'd actually been granted an extra month with Tuck at the helm. But it was doomed to end one way or the other.

Dixon would eventually come back and he'd probably take her side. But Jamison was the president of the company. Eventually, he'd recover fully and overrule Dixon. And with Tuck now on Jamison's side… Well, this was definitely the time for her to move on.

Tuck's workload had gotten completely out of control. Without Amber as the gatekeeper, he was inundated with problems, big and small. He had a temporary assistant, Sandy Heath, borrowed from the finance department, but she mostly just asked him a lot of questions, slowing him down instead of speeding him up.

Jackson had followed a new dead-end lead to Cancún, and another manager had resigned this morning. They were bleeding employees. His father's recovery was going more slowly than expected. Jamison might not return to work at all.

"Sandy?" Tuck called through the open door.

"Yes?"

He could hear her stand and move to the door.

"Is Lucas Steele on his way up?"

Sandy paused in the doorway. "I don't know."

Tuck took a beat. "Could you find out?"

"Sure."

Tuck glanced at his watch to confirm the time. "Did you tell him ten?"

"I believe so. I mean, I called when you asked me to. But I got his voice mail."

"Did you try his assistant?"

Sandy paused. "I'll do that now."

"Great." Just great. Tuck couldn't even get his operations director into his office when they only worked three floors apart.

He came to his feet. "Never mind."

She looked puzzled. "You don't want Lucas?"

"I'll go down."

"I can—"

"I'll find him."

"I'm sorry."

Tuck relaxed his expression. "Don't worry about it."

There was no point in being annoyed with Sandy because she wasn't Amber. Only Amber was Amber, and she was ridiculously good at her job.

He went to the elevator and rode down to twenty-nine. The hallway on that floor was linoleum rather than carpet. The offices were smaller than on the executive floor, and there was far more activity. It was the nerve center of the company, where every company conveyance was tracked on a series of wall-mounted screens, with information on every single shipment available with a few keystrokes. Tuck had come to like it here.

Lucas's office was at the far end of the hallway. It was large but utilitarian, its numerous tables cluttered with maps and reports, keyboards and screens. Tuck knew Lucas had a desk in there somewhere, but he wasn't sure the man ever sat down.

"Hey, boss," Lucas greeted from behind a table.

One of his female staff members was working beside him, clicking keys and watching a set of three monitors.

"The *Red Earth* is back on schedule," the woman said without looking up. "They'll make their 6:00 a.m. port time."

"Good," said Lucas. "Need me?" he asked Tuck.

"You didn't get Sandy's voice mail?"

Lucas glanced guiltily at his desk phone. "We've been slammed this morning."

"Not a problem," said Tuck. "Got a minute?"

"Absolutely. Gwen, can you make sure we get the fuel agreement signatures sent? We have until close of business in Berlin."

"Will do," said Gwen, again without looking up.

Lucas led the way out of his office, turning immediately into a small meeting room along the hall.

"What's up?" he asked Tuck, closing the door behind them.

"I feel as if we should sit down for this," said Tuck.

"Bad news?" Lucas crossed his arms over his chest. "Are you firing me?"

Tuck scoffed out a laugh at the absurdity of the statement. "I'm promoting you."

"Yeah, right." Lucas waited, alert.

"I'm serious," said Tuck.

"Serious about what?"

"I'm promoting you."

It took Lucas a beat to answer. "Why? To what? There's nothing above director."

"Nothing in operations," said Tuck.

"Right," said Lucas, as if he'd just proved his point.

"Vice president," said Tuck.

"Are you running a fever?"

"I need you upstairs."

"I'm no vice president." Lucas gave an exaggerated shudder.

"You think I am?"

"Yes."

Tuck pressed his lips together. "Only because they gave me the title."

"You're nuts."

"I'm serious."

"Okay." Lucas braced his feet slightly apart. "Vice president of *what*?"

"I don't know."

"I can see you've really thought this through."

"Executive vice president."

"That's *your* title."

"I'm acting president."

Lucas's arms moved to his sides. "I suppose you are."

"I'm drownin' up there. Dixon's completely dropped off the planet, and Dad's recovery is pushed back. I know it's not your first choice, but what am I supposed to do?"

"Hire someone."

"I'm hiring you."

"Hire someone else."

"I will. For your job."

"You don't need to hire anyone for my job. Gwen can do it. She can probably do it better than me."

Tuck didn't feel any need to respond to the statement. Lucas had just made the next argument for him.

"Yeah, yeah," said Lucas. "I know what you're thinking."

"What am I thinking?" Tuck asked.

"That you can pick me up and plunk me into some fancy office, and the operations department won't even notice I'm gone."

Tuck fought a smirk. "Your words, not mine."

"They're true."

"That's good."

"I wouldn't have the first idea of what to do upstairs," said Lucas.

"And you think *I* do?"

"You're a Tucker."

"You're the last one left," said Tuck.

"The last one of what?"

"The last director. The others quit."

"Not Oscar?"

"Yesterday. The rumor mill now has Dixon pegged as an

embezzler who will bring down the company, and the head-hunters are out in force."

Lucas frowned. "There's no chance he actually…?"

Tuck was astonished. *"You, too?"*

"No. Not really. What would be his motivation? Plus, you'd have noticed the missing millions by now and reported it. Law enforcement would be crawling all over this place."

Tuck couldn't help but admire Lucas's combination of faith and hard, cold analysis. "He has no motivation. And he didn't do anything illegal."

"I gotta agree," said Lucas.

"Doesn't mean I won't knock his block off."

Lucas pulled out a molded plastic chair and sat down at the rectangular meeting table.

Tuck took the seat across from him.

"You're serious," said Lucas.

"Completely. While Amber was here, it was doable, marginal but doable. Without her, I can't keep it going. We've lost three major accounts since Zachary left."

"You think he's poaching them."

"I know he's poaching them. What I don't know is how to make it stop. I mean, maybe I can make it stop, if I can find the time to make some calls and build up some relationships. But I don't even have time to breathe. I need Dixon, and I need him now."

"I thought Jackson was looking."

"He hit a dead end. It's dead end number eight, I think."

"Hire another investigative firm."

"There's nobody better than Jackson. If only—"

Tuck's thoughts went back to Amber. Usually, when he thought about her, it was about their kisses, particularly that last kiss. A woman didn't kiss like that, especially not in the middle of a fight, if she didn't have a thing for the man. Amber had to be attracted to him on some level, and the knowledge made his skin itch.

"If only what?" asked Lucas.

"She knows something. She can get Dixon back for me."

"Who?"

"Amber."

Lucas pulled back in his chair, a speculative expression coming over his face.

"Not like that," said Tuck. "Not at *all* like that. She was his confidential assistant and he confided in her."

"What did he tell her?"

"She's not talking. I ordered her. Then I fired her. But she's not talking."

"Bribe?" asked Lucas.

"She just gave up her job over integrity."

"Blackmail, then?"

"With what? She's as straight up as they come. The only thing outrageous about her is her shoes."

"Her shoes?"

"You've never noticed?"

Lucas shook his head. "Can't say that I have."

"I don't see how I blackmail her over red glitter stilettoes." Though Tuck would love to have pictures of them.

"Can't believe I missed that."

Tuck forced his mind back to the job. "Will you do it?"

Lucas curled his fingertips against the table. "Temporarily."

Tuck felt a rush of relief. "I hope that's all I'll need. Even together, we can't replace Dixon."

"No, we can't."

"I'm going to find him."

"You should definitely bribe her."

"She'll never go for it."

"You don't know that until you ask."

"Yes, I do."

If Amber was willing to trade ethics for money, she'd never have let him fire her.

Amber sat down at her kitchen table, taking up where she'd left off scrolling through an employment website. Jade was across from her, writing her way through a practice math exam. The coffeepot was between them and their breakfast dishes were piled in the sink.

Jade had offered to clean up later while Amber made the rounds of some more major companies in the city. Surprisingly, after three weeks in Chicago, Jade was still following her new life plan. She was rising every morning with her alarm, eating healthy and studying for the GED test she hoped to pass before the baby was born.

By contrast, Amber's new life plan was completely falling apart. She'd applied for dozens of jobs, had landed only three interviews and had so far been beaten by other candidates on two of them. Every morning, she told herself not to lose hope. But she'd already dipped into her savings to make the month's mortgage payment. Other bills were coming due, including Jade's appointments at the community clinic.

"You look nice today," said Jade. "Very professional." She nodded approvingly at Amber's blazer and skirt.

"Focus on the test," said Amber.

"I bet you get an offer."

"That would be nice." Amber wasn't going to let Jade see her worry.

"Ooh." Jade's hand went to her stomach. "That was a good one."

"I bet it's a boy," said Amber. She copied and pasted a promising-looking job ad into her open spreadsheet.

"Girl," said Jade. "But a soccer player."

"Boy," said Amber. "A placekicker for the Bears. Big money in that."

"You think we'll need Junior's money?"

Amber was beginning to think they'd need it before Junior even started preschool.

"I doubt we will," said Jade. "We're both going to get jobs—good jobs, high-powered jobs. We'll get promoted up the ladder and make fortunes."

Amber couldn't help but smile. She liked it when Jade was optimistic. "Dreamer."

"I am," said Jade. "For the first time in my— Ouch. I think that one went through the uprights."

The phone rang. Amber couldn't control the lurch of anticipation that hit her stomach. It could be another interview, or possibly a job offer from Pine Square Furniture. Please, let it be a job offer. Pine Square Furniture paid quite a bit less than what she'd made at Tucker Transportation, but she'd jump at anything right now.

As Amber started to rise, Jade leaned back and lifted the receiver.

"Hello?"

Amber held her breath.

"Oh, hi, Dr. Norris."

Amber's disappointment was acute. She turned to hide her expression from Jade, rising and pretending to check the printer for paper.

"Okay," Jade said into the phone.

Amber reminded herself these things took time. She could make it a few more weeks, even a couple of months. She hadn't really expected to find a job the next day, had she?

"Which test?" There was worry in Jade's tone.

Amber turned back.

"Is that a problem?" Jade's worried gaze met Amber's.

Amber quickly returned to the table, sitting down in the chair beside Jade.

"That sounds scary," said Jade.

"What is it?" Amber whispered.

Jade's eyes went glassy with the beginnings of tears.

"What?" Amber said louder. "What's wrong?"

Jade unexpectedly pushed the receiver at her, nearly dropping it between them.

Amber scrambled to get it to her ear. "Dr. Norris? This is Amber."

"Hello, Amber. Is Jade all right?"

"She's upset. She's okay. What did you tell her?"

"I have a concern with her blood pressure."

Amber had known that. "Yes."

They'd talked about Jade taking some medication to keep it down in the last few weeks of her pregnancy.

"I'm afraid the follow-up tests aren't encouraging."

Amber rubbed Jade's shoulder. "Is everything okay with the baby?"

"So far, yes. Jade has a condition called preeclampsia. It's serious. I'm recommending you bring her into the hospital."

The hospital? "How serious?"

Jade sniffed and reached for a tissue.

"I'd like to monitor Jade's health and the baby's health."

"Overnight? Until the medication kicks in?"

"Until the birth, I'm afraid. We can't take this condition lightly. There are risks to the placenta, organ damage for Jade, even stroke."

Amber squeezed Jade's hand. "How soon should I bring her in?"

"Is she still having headaches?"

Amber moved the phone from her mouth. "Headache?" she asked Jade.

"It's not bad," said Jade.

"Yes," Amber said to the doctor.

"Then, let's not wait. This morning if you can."

"We can," said Amber.

"My office will make the arrangements."

"Thank you." Amber ended the call.

"So I have to go back?" asked Jade.

"Yes. The doctor says they need to monitor you. She wants you in the hospital."

"The *hospital*?"

"She's worried about your blood pressure."

"But they said there was medicine."

"We can ask more questions when we get there." Amber couldn't help feeling a sense of urgency.

"How long will I have to stay?"

"It might be for a while. We don't want to take any chances. This is what's best for you, and what's best for the baby." Amber stood. "Let's go pack a few things."

Jade gestured to her books. "But I'm studying."

"I'll bet you can study in the hospital. In fact, it might be the perfect place to study. There'll be nothing else for you to do. They'll cook for you. They'll clean for you."

"Hospital food?"

"I'll smuggle you in a pizza."

Assuming Jade was allowed to eat pizza. Amber drew Jade to her feet.

"I can't do this," said Jade. "I can't just up and leave for the hospital at a moment's notice."

"Sometimes it works that way."

Jade glanced around the kitchen. "How can I, what can I— Oh, no." She grasped tightly onto Amber's arms.

Amber's heart leaped. "Is something wrong?"

"The money."

"What money?"

"The *money*, Amber. This is going to cost a fortune. Where will I get the money?"

"Don't worry about that."

"I have to worry about it."

"Worrying won't help anything. Not you, and definitely not the baby." Amber would have to do the worrying for them.

"But—"

"We'll borrow it. Then we'll pay it back." Amber struggled to put confidence in her voice.

"I'm so sorry."

"This isn't your fault. You're doing so well." Amber motioned to the books. "You've been studying. You've been eating right. You're here. You need to keep doing everything you can to give your baby the best possible chance."

"I'm scared." But Jade started to move.

"I know. I'm not saying it isn't unsettling. But it's going to be fine. Everything is going to be fine."

Amber would get Jade to the hospital, and then she'd talk to her bank. She had some equity in her town house and a decent credit rating. Once she found a job, she would qualify for a loan. So she'd find a job. She'd find one fast. She'd flip burgers if that was what it took.

Six

Tuck knew a losing hand when he was dealt one. But he also knew he couldn't walk away from this. For better or worse, and so far it was definitely worse, the company was his responsibility.

It was Saturday afternoon and he'd parked down the block from Amber's town house, waiting for her car to appear. The block was neat and bright, lawns trimmed, gardens tended, with kids playing in the park and people walking their dogs. The homes were compact, four to a building, with very little traffic passing on the street out front.

He figured he'd have the best chance if he tried to reason with her in person. It was too easy for her to hang up a phone. And he doubted she'd answer a text or email. Plus, her expression might help him, give him a signal as to which tactic might sway her and which was a nonstarter.

He knew it wasn't about self-interest for her. And he couldn't imagine she'd have one iota of sympathy for him. But maybe she'd care about the other employees. Maybe she would care that the demise of Tucker Transportation would be job losses and financial ruin for the families of her former coworkers. The way he saw it, that was his best hope.

He spotted her silver hatchback pull up in front of the town house, and he quickly exited his sports car. While she hopped from the driver's seat he approached from the side.

Dressed in a pair of navy slacks and a striped pullover with a matching blazer, she was lithe and graceful as she moved across the sidewalk. Her hair was in a neat braid, while her low-heeled boots were a sexy purple suede. She was compellingly beautiful in the cool sunshine, her profile perky, her skin smooth as silk.

She hadn't seen him yet, so she had a smile on her face. He supposed he'd change that soon enough.

It didn't take long. She caught a glimpse of him, squinted at him and then frowned.

"Hello, Amber," he said, covering the last few paces between them.

Her glance flicked behind him as if seeking context. "What are you doing here, Tuck?"

"Been out shopping?" he asked conversationally. It seemed like a reasonable guess for a Saturday afternoon.

"I've been visiting—" She stopped herself. "What do you want?"

"I need to talk to you."

"I don't have time to talk." She started for the walkway that led to her front door.

"It won't take long."

She turned. "Then, let me be more blunt. I have all the time in the world, but I don't care to spend any of it with you."

"You're still angry."

"What was your first clue?"

"I didn't want things to go this way."

"Goodbye, Tuck." She took a backward step.

"Dixon is still missing."

She shrugged.

"It's been over six weeks. I'm getting worried."

"He can take care of himself."

Under normal circumstances, Dixon could take excellent care of himself. But these weren't normal circumstances.

"Who takes a six-week vacation?"

"Lots of people."

"Not my brother."

Even if their father had been healthy and at the helm, Dixon would never have left for this long, especially not without contacting them. Tuck's focus had been on Tucker Transportation, but he was becoming genuinely worried about his brother.

"Maybe you don't know him as well as you think you do," said Amber.

"Clearly, I don't. Why don't you enlighten me?"

"Why should I know him any better than you?"

"You know him."

It was in her eyes.

"You knew why he left," said Tuck. "And you know where he went." Tuck believed there was no romance between her and Dixon. But there was something—a closeness, respect, confidence.

"He doesn't want to talk to you?"

"He's got nothing against me."

Tuck and Dixon might not be the closest brothers in the world. But they weren't estranged. They weren't fighting. There was no particular animosity between them.

Tuck stepped forward. "Things have gotten worse since you…left."

"You mean since I was fired."

"Yeah, that." He didn't know why he'd tried to soften the words. They both knew what had happened. "We're losing accounts. We're losing staff. We've gone from high profitability to a projected loss for next month."

There was no sympathy in her blue eyes. "You might want to do something about that."

"I'm worried about the employees," he said, ignoring her jab. "If this goes on much longer, people could lose their jobs."

"What does that have to do with me? Considering I already lost mine."

"I'm appealing to your basic sense of humanity."

"While I'm still standing on my basic sense of ethics and values."

He eased closer. "Where is he, Amber?"

"I don't know."

"What do you know?"

She raised her chin. "That he didn't want me to tell you anything."

"That was weeks ago."

"I haven't heard anything to contradict it."

"So you haven't heard from him?"

She drew back in obvious surprise. "No."

"Does he know how to contact you?"

"He'd probably try to call me at my desk."

"Touché."

"He knows how to contact you, too, Tuck. If he wanted to talk to you, he'd call." She turned to go.

"What about an emergency?" Tuck called out. He could taste failure, bitter in the back of his mouth. "Can you get a message to him? That's all I'm asking. Get a message to him. You can name your price."

She stopped. Then she pivoted, gaping at him in clear astonishment. "My *price*?"

"Anything you want." He could feel his last chance slipping away. "What do you want?"

To Tuck's immense relief, she actually looked intrigued.

"You'd pay me to get a message to Dixon."

"Yes."

She seemed to think about it. "What would you want me to say?"

"You'll do it?"

Had Lucas actually been right? Was money going to sway her?

"What would you want me to say?" she asked again.

"Tell him about my father's heart attack and tell him I'm destroying the company."

She looked a little surprised by the last statement. "You want to make certain he comes home."

"I want to make certain he knows the cost of staying away."

"I'm not going to lie for you."

"It's not a lie."

"It is. You're not destroying the company. You've hit a rough patch, sure, but—"

"You haven't been there."

It was every bit as bad as he was making it sound.

"You're exaggerating," she said.

They could have this debate all day long and get nowhere. He had a toehold on a yes here, and he didn't want to give her a chance to back out.

"What'll it cost me?" he asked.

"You're talking about a flat-out cash bribe?"

"If that's what works."

She looked skeptical. "And I'd only have to tell him about your father."

"And that I'm destroying the company."

"I'm not using the word *destroy*."

"Then, tell him I've projected a loss for next month." Tuck knew that would come as a colossal shock to Dixon. He'd be on the first plane home.

He could see the debate going on behind her eyes.

"How much?" he asked.

What would she ask for? Five figures, six? He'd pay whatever she wanted.

"My job back," she said.

He hadn't been prepared for that. And he was shocked she'd be willing. "You want to work for me again?"

"I want to work for Dixon again."

"Job's yours," he said. He'd be thrilled to have her back. In fact, he felt guilty that her request was so modest. He moved a little closer. "You have to know you've got me over a barrel?"

"Do you want me to ask for something more?"

He did. If nothing else, he was curious. "Yeah. Go wild."

She hesitated.

He raised a brow, waiting.

"All right." She withdrew a paper from her purse, unfolding it. "Since you insist."

"What's that?" He tried to look, but she pulled it toward her chest.

"You can give me a signing bonus."

"How much?"

"Twenty-eight thousand, two hundred and sixty-three dollars."

Now she really had him curious.

"Where did that number come from?"

"None of your business." She refolded the paper and stuffed it back in her purse.

"Seriously. What are you paying for?"

"Seriously. None of your business."

Tuck told himself to shut up and take the victory. "You'll call him."

"I will."

"I mean now."

"Right now?"

He gave a sharp nod.

"I suppose." She turned again for the front door.

He followed and she twisted her head to look at him.

"You don't trust me?"

"I do. I don't." No, that wasn't true. He couldn't imagine she'd lie about making the call. "I do trust you. But I want to see what happens."

She unlocked the front door, pushing it open. "I don't know for sure where he is. I didn't lie to you about that. But he did leave an emergency number."

Tuck wanted to ask exactly how bad things had to get before she decided it was an emergency. But he didn't want to start another argument.

He stayed silent, and she dropped her purse on a table in the small foyer and extracted her phone, dialing as she moved into the living room.

"Did he get a special cell phone?" Tuck asked. That made the most sense.

Amber shook her head, listening as the call obviously rang through.

She sat down on a cream-colored loveseat and crossed her legs. Tuck perched on an end of the sofa at a right angle to her. It faced a gas fireplace and a row of small watercolor seascapes.

"Hello," said Amber. "Can you connect me to Dixon Tucker's room?"

A hotel, obviously. Tuck wanted to know where. He wished he could see the area code.

"He's not?" asked Amber, her tone sharper.

Tuck focused on her expression.

She was frowning. "I don't understand. When did he do that?"

Tuck didn't want to be suspicious, but he couldn't help but wonder if she was playing him. Was she going to pretend she'd tried to get Dixon but failed?

"That's less than a week. Did he say where he was going?" She met Tuck's eyes, sitting up straight and bracing her feet on the carpet. Either something was actually wrong, or Amber had a great future in acting. "Yes. I understand."

"What?" he asked her.

"Thank you," she said into the phone. "Goodbye."

"What did they say? Who was that? Where's Dixon?"

Amber set the phone onto the sofa cushion beside her. "He left."

"Left *where*?"

"Scottsdale."

"Arizona?"

"It's called Highland Luminance."

It struck Tuck as an odd name. "A hotel?"

"A wellness retreat."

The words weren't making sense.

"What's that?" Tuck asked. "And what was he doing there?"

"Getting well. At least he was supposed to be getting well.

But he left." Concern furrowed her brow. "He left after only a few days. Why would he do that?"

"Why would he go there in the first place?"

Sure, Dixon's divorce had been ugly. But people went through ugly divorces all the time.

"For help," said Amber. "They have a spa, yoga, fresh air and peace, organic food, emotional and physical therapy."

"You're trying to tell me that my brother took off to Arizona for organic food and yoga."

"I'm not *trying* to tell you anything."

Tuck searched his brain for an explanation. "None of this makes sense."

"He was exhausted," said Amber. "Upset by—"

"Yeah, yeah. You've told me all that. But it's not credible. Dixon's a smart, solid, capable man."

Amber's voice rose. "You worked him into the ground."

"I didn't do a thing."

"Exactly," she said with finality.

He glared at her. "You're saying this is *my* fault?"

"Yes. Yours, your father's, Kassandra's, all of you."

He opened his mouth to defend himself, but no good argument formed inside his brain. Was it his fault? Why hadn't Dixon come to him? They could have talked. They could have worked things out. He'd have been happy to support his brother.

"Dixon is very private," Tuck explained to Amber.

"If I was you," she responded in a flat tone, "I'd stop worrying about why he went to Arizona. I'd worry about where he went from there."

She had a point. She had a very good point.

He pulled his phone from his shirt pocket and dialed Jackson.

"Hey" was Jackson's clipped answer.

"Dixon went to Arizona," said Tuck.

"You sure?"

"Scottsdale. A place called Highland Luminance. He

left there about five weeks ago, but we can pick up his trail. I'll meet you—" Tuck looked at Amber. "*We'll* meet you in Scottsdale."

Her eyes widened and she shook her head.

"I'm in LA," said Jackson. "I can be there in the morning."

"We'll be there tonight," said Tuck.

"No way," said Amber.

Tuck ended the call. "You obviously know my brother better than I do. You work for me again and I need you in Scottsdale."

"I really can't."

"Yes, you can." As far as Tuck was concerned, this was not negotiable.

Amber slipped quietly into Jade's hospital room, not wanting to disturb her if she was napping.

But she was sitting up in the bed reading a textbook, and she smiled. "Did you forget something?"

"No," Amber answered.

Jade wore a large yellow T-shirt and a pair of stretchy green pants visible though the open weave of her blanket.

"Is everything okay?" she asked.

"How are you feeling?"

"Good. I'm fine. But I'm feeling guilty just lying around here."

"You're studying." Amber rounded the bed, pulling a bright orange vinyl chair up closer.

"Not as hard as I should."

"That's okay. Your main job is to stay healthy and grow that baby for a few more weeks."

Jade's cheeks were rosy, her face puffier than usual, but her eyes looked clear and bright. She put a hand on her budging stomach. "The baby's getting bigger by the hour."

"That's what we want. I have some good news."

"I can go home?" Jade hesitated. "Well, to your home."

"No, you can't go home. Not yet. But I did get a job."

Jade started to smile, but for some reason she sobered, looking sad. “You’re so good. You’re amazing.”

Amber wondered if her sister’s hormones were messing with her mood. “It’s just a job, Jade.”

“No, it’s not just a job.” Jade looked like she might tear up.

“Hey.” Amber reached for her sister’s hand, worrying this might be a sign something was wrong. “What is it?”

Jade blinked. “It doesn’t matter what I do, how much trouble I cause. You always take such good care of things.”

“You’re not causing trouble. I’m your big sister. Of course I’m going to help you.”

Amber wished she didn’t have to leave town right now. She knew Jade was an adult, and she knew the hospital would take good care of her. But she still felt guilty.

“Do you remember Earl Dwyer?” asked Jade.

The name took Amber by surprise. “You mean Mom’s old boyfriend?”

Jade nodded, sniffing and dabbing at her nose with a tissue. She gazed for a moment at the reflection in the window. “I was thinking about him last night.”

A picture of the man came up in Amber’s mind and her neck prickled at the memory. “There’s no reason to think about him.”

“You remember how he yelled at us all the time?”

“You should be thinking happy thoughts for the baby.”

“Do you remember?”

“Yes, I remember. But I’m surprised you do. You couldn’t have been more than five when he moved out.” Amber remembered Earl’s snarling face, his booming voice and how she’d locked herself and Jade in their bedroom whenever an argument had started between him and their mother.

“I remember everything about him,” said Jade, her voice going small.

Amber moved to the bed, perching on the edge to rub Jade’s shoulder. “Well, stop. He’s long gone.”

“Do you remember the fire?” asked Jade.

"Yes." Amber couldn't figure out where Jade was going with this.

Was Jade worried about her own choices in men? Maybe she was worried about how her future boyfriends might impact her baby.

"Mom used to tell Earl not to smoke on the sofa," said Jade. "She yelled at him about it all the time. She said he was going to pass out, light the place on fire and kill us all."

"He nearly did." Amber shuddered at the memory of the acrid smell, the billowing smoke, the crackling flames rising from the sofa stuffing.

"That's how I knew it would work." Jade's eyes seemed unfocused.

"How what would work?"

"He passed out that night," said Jade, twisting her fingers through the blanket weave as she spoke. "Mom was in her bedroom. I remember Janis Joplin was playing on the radio." Jade sang a few bars. "You were asleep."

"So were you," said Amber.

But Jade shook her head. "I was awake. I went into the living room. I was so scared he'd wake up. I pictured it over and over, like an instant replay, those pale blue eyes opening, his stinky breath, his scabby hands grabbing me."

Amber went cold all over.

"But he didn't wake up," said Jade.

Amber let out a shuddering breath of relief.

"So I took his lit cigarette from the ashtray. I took the newspaper off the table. I crumpled a corner, just like I'd seen them do on that wilderness show. You remember? The one with the park ranger and the kids in Yellowstone?"

Amber couldn't answer.

"I tucked it all between the cushions, and I went back to bed."

"Oh, Jade," Amber rasped, her hand tightening on her sister's shoulder.

"I lit the fire, Amber." Tears formed in Jade's eyes. "I lit the fire and you put it out. It wasn't until years later that I realized I could have killed us all."

"You were five years old." Amber couldn't wrap her head around such a young child conceiving and executing that plan.

"Do you think I'm evil?"

"I think you were scared."

"I knew it would work," said Jade. "I knew if Earl set the sofa on fire that Mom would kick him out and we'd never have to see him again."

Amber drew Jade into her arms, remembering her as such a small child. "It was a fairly brilliant plan," she whispered against Jade's hair. "Another time, you might want to have a plan for putting the fire out."

"I was thinking last night," said Jade.

"You need to stop thinking about this. It's over."

"I was thinking that's how it's been my whole life. I've been starting fires, and you've been putting them out. And now I'm pregnant. And I'm sick."

"You're going to get better."

"But you have a new job. So my baby and I won't starve on the streets."

Amber's chest tightened painfully. "You're going to be just fine. We're *all* going to be just fine."

Jade's voice broke. "Thank you, Amber."

"You are so very welcome."

"I'm going to do better."

"You're already doing better."

"I'm going to get a job and I'm going to pay you back. And somehow, some way, I'm going to be the one helping you."

"Sure," said Amber. "But, for now, I have more good news."

Jade pulled away and looked up. "What more could there be?"

"I got a signing bonus. And it's enough to cover your hospital bill."

Jade blinked, her eyes clearing. "Are you kidding me?"

"I'm serious."

"Why? How? What's the job?"

Amber wasn't going to lie. "It's my old job."

It took Jade a moment to respond. "You're going back?"

"I'm going back."

Jade looked worried. "To Tuck? To the guy who kissed you?"

"To his brother. Dixon. Dixon will be back soon and I'll work for him again."

"He's the nice one, right?"

"He's the nice one." All Amber had to do was find him and get everything back to normal.

"What about Tuck?" asked Jade.

"What about him? He's barely ever there. Once Dixon's back, I'll never even have to see him."

Jade frowned. "But you kissed him."

"He kissed me."

"You kissed him back. I saw it. You kissed him back, which means you must be attracted to him."

Amber gave a shrug. "Maybe a little bit. He's a good-looking guy. And he's smart and funny. You should see the string of women lining up to date him. But nothing more is going to happen between us. He'll never really be interested in me."

She'd thought a lot about Tuck's kisses, concluding they were a power play, or a test like he'd said, or maybe it was just his habit to kiss any woman who happened to be around. If the tabloids were anything to go by, he did a lot of kissing with a lot of different women.

"You have to be careful of men," said Jade.

Amber didn't disagree, especially thinking about Earl and her mother's other boyfriends. Not to mention the stories about some of Jade's exes.

"Even when things start out well," said Jade, "they usually end badly."

Amber shifted from the bed back to the chair. "You and I agree on that."

"But lust is a funny thing."

"This isn't lust." Maybe it was curiosity, maybe sexual attraction, but what Amber felt for Tuck didn't rise to the level of lust.

"I've dated guys I knew were bad for me."

"You knew?"

"Yes, I knew. But it didn't keep me away. In fact it made them even more attractive."

"I'm not you," said Amber. She couldn't imagine herself setting aside good sense and taking up with a man who was clearly trouble.

Jade looked unconvinced.

"I have some other news," Amber said briskly, determined to move on. "I have to go away for a few days. It's for work."

Jade's eyes narrowed critically.

"For Dixon," Amber quickly added. She definitely didn't want Jade worrying about her. "He has a thing in Arizona, and I need to go out there. Do you think you'll be okay?"

"I'll be fine. I'm only going to lay here and study."

Amber congratulated herself on successfully switching the topic away from Tuck.

"Good." She came to her feet. "Because I have to leave tonight."

Jade's smile faded, but she gave a brave nod. "Are you sure you don't think I'm evil?"

Amber gave her sister a hug. "You're tough and brave, and a little bit brilliant. Take care of yourself. Feel good. And don't study too hard."

"Enjoy Arizona. Is Tuck going with you?"

Amber didn't have it in her to tell an outright lie. "Probably. For part of it anyway."

"Don't fall for him."

"I won't."

"He'll look sexy, and you'll want to. And I saw the way he looked at you. He wants to sleep with you."

An unwelcome wash of longing swept through Amber. “Too bad for him.”

“Just say no.”

“Well, I’m not going to say yes.”

Amber wouldn’t say yes. In fact, she doubted he’d ask again. He’d flat-out told her she wasn’t as attractive as his usual dates.

Deep down inside, she knew she wasn’t going to get another proposition from Tuck. He had far too many options in his life to even give her a second thought.

Seven

Tuck still wanted Amber. He wanted her very badly, and his desire was growing by the minute.

She was radiant in front of him, curled up in a padded rattan chair in the Scottsdale hotel courtyard. The gas fireplace flickering between them gave her face a gorgeous glow. Floodlights decorated the palm trees and rock garden behind her, while stars winked above them in the blackened sky.

"Do you have any ideas?" she asked.

There were any number of great ideas pinging around inside his head. But he doubted Amber was anywhere near his wavelength.

She was a picture of openness in a midnight blue knee-length dress and a cropped cardigan sweater with the sleeves pushed up. Her spiky sandals were dropped carelessly on the concrete patio in front of her. After her second glass of wine, she'd tugged her hair loose, and it flowed over her shoulders.

"I'm his brother," said Tuck, knowing she'd understand he was talking about their earlier conversation at Highland Luminance. "There must be someone who can authorize a release of information to me."

"The receptionist didn't seem encouraging." Amber referred to the woman who had asked them to leave the wellness resort.

"I can't imagine his yoga participation requires the same confidentiality rules as, say, an STD diagnosis."

"She did tell us the date he left."

"More than five weeks ago."

Amber took another sip of her wine, dark against her lush lips. Her face and shoulders were creamy and smooth. He remembered her taste, her scent and the feel of her lithe body enclosed in his arms.

"We should brainstorm about Dixon," she said.

Tuck shook himself out of a fantasy that had him kissing a shadow next to her collarbone. "What do you mean?"

"What do you know about him? Any unfulfilled dreams, secret desires?"

"He doesn't tell me his secret desires." Nor did Tuck confide in Dixon. And he was especially keeping quiet about his feelings for Amber.

"Toss out anything," she said. "What about when you were young, while you were growing up?"

"My desires have changed since I was young. I imagine his have, too."

"Play along," said Amber. "What else have we got to do?"

Tuck didn't dare voice his ideas.

The slight breeze rustled her hair and she brushed it back from her cheek. "Funny thing, I was reminded earlier today that childhood events can impact our entire lives."

He forced the sexy images from his mind. "You think Dixon is reacting to his childhood?"

"I think he's reacting to exhaustion and a cheating wife. But how he reacts could be influenced by his core self-perception."

"Core self-perception. Is that from the Highland Luminance brochure?"

"No." Her tone turned defensive. "It's from a documentary. But it's valid. It just means who you think you are."

"Who do you think you are, Amber? What's your core self-perception?" He was more interested in her than in Dixon.

"That's easy. I'm organized, a caretaker. I can't leave people to their own mistakes."

Tuck couldn't help but smile at the answer. "You left me to my own mistakes."

"Only after you fired me. Up until then, and against my own better judgment, I was helping you."

He knew that she had. "I was grateful."

"I could tell."

"I hired you back," he pointed out.

"Only because you needed me."

"True. But here you are."

"What about Dixon?"

"Don't you want to know about me?" Tuck knew the question sounded a bit needy, but he couldn't help himself.

"I already know your self-perception."

"Do tell."

"Talented, successful and good-looking. You know you're talented because so many things come easy, and the rest is reflected back in the mirror."

Her assessment was wholly unflattering.

"So I'm conceited?"

"I think you're singularly realistic."

"I was born into a rich family that had few expectations of me."

She didn't disagree.

"But that doesn't make me feel talented and successful," Tuck continued. "It makes me feel spoiled and useless."

Her expression turned decidedly skeptical. "Yet you don't do anything to change it."

He refused to argue. If she hadn't noticed how hard he'd been working lately, pointing it out to her wasn't going to change a thing.

"I'm here, aren't I?" he asked instead.

"To get back to the status quo."

"For the benefit of Tucker Transportation."

She seemed to consider that for a moment. "You're doing a pretty good job, you know."

At first he thought he must have misheard. "Excuse me?"

"You heard me. Don't fish for compliments."

"You took me by surprise with that."

She leaned slightly forward. "You're doing a pretty good job. This desperation to find Dixon is about you getting away again, not about the health of the company."

"You're wrong." Tuck might have been reluctant to come on board, but he was actually glad he had. He'd felt more useful in the past six weeks than ever had before in his life.

"I'm right," she said. "But we could go back and forth on it all night long."

Tuck bit back an all-night-long quip. He really had to get his craving for her under control.

"This is about Dixon," said Amber, her tone going crisp. "In the past, when he was young, what made him happy? What made him angry?"

"I made him angry," said Tuck.

She broke a grin at that. "Why does that not surprise me?"

"Because I'm the villain in this story."

"How did you make him angry?"

"I stole Nanny Susie's candies," he told her. "She kept a jar of them in the pantry as treats for good behavior. I dragged a kitchen chair into the pantry and piled a step stool on top, then I climbed up and filled my pockets. Dixon was freaking out. He was sure we'd be caught."

"That's bizarrely ironic."

"That I stole the good-behavior treats?" He grinned. "I get that now. I didn't get it then. They were delicious."

"Did you get caught?"

"No."

"Did Dixon eat the candies?"

"Yes. He held out for a while, but eventually he gave in. Maybe the experience scarred him? Should we be canvassing the local confectionaries?"

She rolled her eyes. "What else have you got?"

"I used to sneak out my bedroom window and meet girls in the middle of the night."

"Did Dixon sneak out with you?" she asked.

"No. By then, I guess he held firmer to his convictions. Or else he was loyal to his girlfriend. Which, now that I think about it, he really was. He only had two of them before Kassandra. Bettina Wright and Jodi Saunders. They were both gorgeous, but they also struck me as boring and a little stuck-up."

"You have different tastes than your brother."

Tuck let his gaze rest on Amber. "I do."

He knew that if he'd been working side by side with her for five years, married or not, his loyalty would absolutely have come into question.

The air seemed to thicken and heat between them. If he'd been closer, he'd have reached for her.

"So Dixon is dependable," Amber said into the silence. "He's honest, loyal and hardworking."

"You sound like my father."

"Even in the midst of an emotional crisis, first he tries to get your father's permission to leave. Then he leaves your father a letter of explanation and me as a fail-safe."

"You weren't much of a fail-safe."

"I told you I thought you could handle it. I still believe you could handle it if you'd apply yourself."

"Apply myself with no knowledge or experience to the running of a multinational conglomerate?"

"Whose fault is it that you have no experience?"

Tuck wanted to say his father's. He wanted to say his brother's. But he knew it was also his own fault. He'd sat back and allowed this to happen.

Had he always chosen the shortcut? Steal the candies instead of earning them? Make out with the girls without dating them?

"Do you think people can change?" he asked.

"I think we can try."

He felt the magnetic pull between them again.

Her expression turned guarded and she rose to her feet. "I should really go to bed."

He stood with her. "Any chance that's an invitation?"

"Tuck."

He immediately regretted the joke. "I know."

She looked up at him, eyes deep blue, cheeks flushed, the

breeze teasing her hair. Her lips were slightly parted and they looked so incredibly kissable.

"Is your flirting reflex really that strong?" she asked.

"It's not a reflex."

"Then, what is it?"

"It's you, Amber. It's all you."

"I'm not trying to send signals."

"You're not trying, but I know you feel it, too."

"Can you make it stop?" she asked, her voice a rasp.

He slowly slipped his arm around the small of her back, settling it there. "Why?"

She leaned slightly away, but she didn't break his hold. "Because it won't end well."

"We don't know that."

"One of us does."

"You can't predict the future."

"I can predict the next sixty seconds."

He gave a cautious smile. "I'm afraid to ask."

"You're going to kiss me, Tuck."

"That's a relief." He tightened his hold on her and leaned in. "I thought I was getting a knee to the groin."

"And then we'll—"

"Then nothing," he said. "Kissing you will take at least the next sixty seconds."

The sixty seconds passed, and then another and another. Tuck's lips were firm, his body taut and his embrace was sturdy and sure. The fire brought a glow to her skin, and the heat of passion built inside her.

She knew they had to stop. But she didn't want to stop. She didn't want to step away from the cradle of Tuck's arms or from the tendrils of desire weaving their way along her limbs. She decided she could risk a few more seconds, relish a few more moments of paradise.

They were both unattached, consenting adults. They could hug and kiss and generally test the limits of their endurance without bringing the world to a screeching halt. They were on a public patio, screened only by cactus plants and a latticework of vines. It wasn't as if things could get too far out of hand. Could they?

Tuck broke the kiss and dragged in a strangled breath. He buried his face in the crook of her neck. His palms slid lower, cupping her rear, pressing her into the V of his legs. His body was firm and aroused. The realization should have worried her rather than thrilling her.

"What happens next?" he asked between labored breaths.

She knew she had to get herself under control. It was time to say no, time to remind them both of who they were, time to politely retreat to her room and regroup for tomorrow.

"I thought I knew," she said instead.

"You don't?"

"I do," she said against his chest. "I should. I thought I did."

He drew back just far enough to look at her. "You're overthinking."

"I'm underthinking." If she was even contemplating letting things go further, she wasn't giving it anywhere near enough thought.

"That sounds promising."

"Tuck." She sighed, leaning against his strength for one last moment.

"I have a marvelous room," he responded, his voice rumbling deeply. "A huge bed, an enormous tiled shower and I bet room-service breakfast is fantastic. And I'm willing—no, *eager*—to share it all with you." But then his hold on her loosened and his tone changed. He drew back even farther. "But when a woman has to debate this long about whether or not to make love, the answer is already there."

She wanted to disagree. But he was right. And he was being such a gentleman about it.

It was chivalrous and admirable, and she was deeply disappointed. What had happened to the bold Tuck who'd stolen candies and sneaked out his bedroom window?

"You're saying no."

"I'm saying *hell yes*. But I don't want you to regret anything. And you would."

He was right again.

"You're nicer than people think," she said.

"I'm smarter than people think."

"Is this you being smart?"

"Responsible. This is me being Dixon. I've always known he was the better man."

"Yet you're here. And he's missing."

"Life is full of ironies."

She forced herself to take a step back, out of Tuck's embrace. "I'm really sorry."

He gave a self-deprecating shrug. "That you don't want to sleep with me?"

"That I let things get away from me. I didn't mean to lead you on."

"I'd rather have the shot than not." He reached out and smoothed her hair. "Kiss me any old time you like. And take it as far as you want. I can handle the disappointment. Who knows, maybe one day you'll be sure about what you want."

It was on the tip of her tongue to agree. But she didn't dare voice it. If she wasn't careful, she would convince herself she wanted him now, right now.

"Don't look so scared," he said.

"This isn't like me."

"It's called *chemistry*, Amber. It doesn't have to mean anything."

Her chest went hollow. Reality brought with it intense disappointment. "So you've felt this before? You've done this before?"

"All the time."

And it meant nothing to him. Good that they'd cleared that up. Jade was right. Getting involved with the wrong man inevitably ended badly.

"I'll never be sure." Then she realized it sounded as though she was waffling. "I mean, I'm already sure. The answer is no, and it's going to stay no. I'm here to work. I'm here to find Dixon. And that's all. Full stop."

"You want to add an exclamation point to that?"

"You're mocking me."

"I am. You have to admit, it was a quick turnaround."

"It took me a minute to get my head on straight. That's all. Good night, Tuck."

"Good night, Amber." The mocking tone was still in his voice.

She struggled to leave things on a professional note. "Jackson will be here in the morning?"

"You think Jackson will protect your virtue?"

"I'm thinking about finding Dixon. I've moved on."

She had. No more kissing Tuck. No more touching Tuck. No more flirting with Tuck.

She would keep her distance and keep it professional.

After a sleepless night fantasizing about Amber, and repeatedly asking himself why on earth he'd behaved like a gentleman, Tuck wasn't in the mood to care about corporate sales. But Lucas was on the phone asking, and Lucas was right. Robson Equipment was an important client and Tuck was only half an hour from Phoenix.

"Tell them yes," he said to Lucas. "Jackson showed up with a couple of guys. I'm sure they can spare me for a few hours."

Robson Equipment was hosting a black-tie business event and Lucas had arranged an invitation. It would be a chance to Tuck to touch base with the corporate brass and head off any moves Zachary Ingles might be making to poach the account.

"Take Amber," said Lucas.

"Jackson needs her help."

"Tell him he needs to share."

After her stance last night, Tuck couldn't imagine Amber agreeing to attend a dinner. "I don't need a date."

"She's not your date. She's your assistant. She knows the

account inside out and I'm beginning to think she's smarter than you."

"Ha-ha."

"That wasn't a joke."

"I doubt she'll agree," Tuck told him flat out.

"She's there to work, isn't she?"

Tuck didn't want to explain the complexity of their relationship, not that he was even sure how. The chemistry between them was combustible. He'd lied to her last night. What he'd felt with her didn't happen all the time. He'd never experienced anything like it in his life.

He could vow to keep his hands off her. But he was too smart to trust himself. He might have decided to behave more like Dixon, but it was definitely going to take some practice.

"Tuck?" Lucas prompted.

"She'll be working all day already."

"So pay her overtime."

"I'm not sure—"

"What did you do?"

"What do you mean?"

"You did something to upset her."

"I did not. Okay, I did. But it's not what you think."

"What do I think?"

"That I made a pass at her."

"That's exactly what I think. I bet she said no. And I hope you remember that for next time."

"She didn't say no. Far from it." Tuck checked his ego, but not quite in time.

There was a pause. "What did you do?"

"Nothing. But it's complicated."

"Uncomplicate it," said Lucas.

If only it was that easy. "You're such an armchair quarterback."

"Do I need to quote the Robson sales figures for last year?"

"No." Tuck knew they were significant.

"Are you going to argue that she doesn't know the portfolio?"

"I'm not." Tuck knew he was being cornered, but there wasn't a thing in the world he could do to stop it.

Lucas was right on all counts. Lucas was looking out for the best interests of Tucker Transportation, which is exactly what Tuck needed to be doing.

A knock sounded on the hotel room door.

"Get it done," said Lucas.

"I will."

"I'll talk to you after." Lucas ended the call.

Tuck finished buttoning his shirt as he crossed the living room of the suite. It was southwest in character, lots of rusts, browns and yellows, creating a warm atmosphere. The bed had been extraordinarily comfortable, the room temperature perfect with a fresh, fragrant breeze coming in from the desert side.

He'd returned here last night to find chilled champagne and chocolate-covered strawberries. Nice touch, but it was impossible to enjoy them by himself. He'd longed to invite Amber over to share, only to talk, just to listen to her voice, watch her expressions.

He blew out a cold chuckle as he reached the door. He wasn't kidding anyone, least of all himself. He wanted Amber in his bed, naked, smiling, welcoming him into her arms without a single mental reservation.

He answered to find her in the outdoor breezeway, Jackson by her side. Even without a smile, she was gorgeous, totally perfect.

"We've checked hospitals, morgues and police stations," said Jackson, heading directly into the room.

Tuck dragged his gaze away from Amber. "I take it you found nothing."

It wasn't a question. If there was bad news, Jackson's manner would be quite different.

"No leads from airlines, private or public. We've checked trains, buses and rental cars."

"Buses?" Tuck couldn't bring himself to believe Dixon would take a bus. "Have you *met* my brother?"

Amber marched into the room, expression schooled, her manner all business. He inhaled her subtle scent as she passed, feeling pathetic.

"He could have bought a car," she suggested.

"That would be more like him," Tuck agreed.

"We'll check to see if anything was registered in his name or in the company's. In case he stayed here in the Scottsdale area, we're also checking hotels, motels and resorts."

"Surely, he wouldn't buy a house," said Amber. She still hadn't looked directly at Tuck.

"Depends on how long he's planning to stay," said Tuck, willing her to meet his eyes.

"I suggest we have breakfast," said Jackson. "Then Amber and I will walk through everything she remembers."

"What about Highland Luminance?" Tuck asked.

"Their records are confidential."

"I know, but maybe you could—"

"Probably best if that's the last question you ask on that front," said Jackson.

"Got it." If Jackson was up to something less than legal, Tuck didn't want to know.

Amber looked puzzled. "What are you planning to—"

Both men shot her warning looks.

"Right," she said and shut up.

Tuck stuffed his wallet into his back pocket and located the room key. "Let's get started on what Amber remembers."

"It'll be better if she and I do it alone," said Jackson.

Tuck fought a spurt of jealousy. "No."

"She needs to be relaxed."

"She is relaxed. She will be relaxed."

"Given your history..." said Jackson.

Tuck couldn't believe she'd told him about last night. "Our *history*?" he challenged.

"You fired her."

"That?"

"Yes, that."

"I need to hear what she has to say," said Tuck.

"She doesn't want you there."

Tuck tried to catch her gaze again. He willed her to reassure Jackson, but she didn't.

"She might prompt a memory, remind me of something from our childhoods."

"You're going to use that against me?" Amber challenged.

"Do you or do you not believe Dixon's background might be relevant?"

Her blue eyes narrowed.

"It's not as if you're going to be naked."

"Oh, *that's* helpful," Jackson mocked.

"He's just being ridiculous," said Amber.

"She's right," Tuck agreed. "But I don't want to miss something because neither of you recognize its significance."

There was a beat of silence. "He's also right," said Amber, her shoulders dropping a notch.

Tuck would take the win.

"Don't gloat," she said to him.

"I'm not."

"You're such a liar." She started for the door.

"I'm going to need her tonight," Tuck said to Jackson.

Both Amber and Jackson swung their gazes his way.

"Robson Equipment is hosting a corporate event in Phoenix. Lucas said, and I'm quoting here, Amber has to attend because she's smarter than me, and we can't afford to lose the account."

"Fine by me," said Jackson.

Amber opened her mouth, but Tuck cut her off. "Double overtime. You'll be well compensated."

She hesitated. Then she nodded and turned for the door.

Tuck was surprised, shocked even. Money had swayed her again? This was starting to seem too easy.

Eight

Amber had dredged up every possible memory about Dixon's plans. Jackson was very good at his job, leading her down pathways that would have seemed insignificant to her, but clearly helped form the picture of Dixon's state of mind.

Tuck had been quiet throughout the conversation, excusing himself afterward without comment. She couldn't tell if he was pursuing a new lead or if he was annoyed with something she'd said. Jackson had immediately left to meet with his team, leaving Amber with some time to call Jade.

The news from the hospital was all good. Jade's blood pressure was stable and there were no other worrisome signs. They'd done an ultrasound and the baby still seemed fine. The technician had given odds on it being a girl.

Amber had also discovered that her signing bonus had been deposited into her bank account. It was a huge relief to know she was able to pay the hospital bills as they arrived.

Up next was the Robson party. After their kiss last night, she was nervous about spending the evening alone with Tuck. But she reminded herself that this was what she'd signed up for. Finding Dixon was one thing, but she also had to help Tuck keep the company running.

Lucas had said the Robson party would be formal—evening-gown and black-tie formal. She had a sleeveless, black crepe dress at home that would have worked. But she'd traveled light, with nothing but business and casual clothes in her suitcase.

Fingers mentally crossed, she navigated the hallway to the lobby shops, hoping the hotel boutique had something suitable.

She stopped at their display window, taking in a sublimely

beautiful cobalt blue dress. The cap sleeves were sheer netting and appliqué, with a fitted, crisscross bodice of supple, lightweight tulle. The dress was finished with an elegant, full skirt that glittered under the display lights.

It was perfect. It was also ten times Amber's price range.

She wandered inside, checking out the few formal gowns among an eclectic women's collection that ranged from hats and purses, to beachwear and jackets. She found a couple of dresses that would work without breaking her bank account and the saleslady directed her to a compact fitting room.

She started with an unadorned navy gown with three-quarter-length sleeves and a V-neck. It was neutral, and she could see how it would fit well on many body shapes. She moved out of the cubicle to look in the full-length mirror.

"A bit uninspiring," said a male voice behind her.

She turned to find Tuck, a plastic suit bag slung over his arm.

"Great minds think alike," he said, holding up what was obviously a newly purchased outfit for the evening.

She turned back to the mirror. "It's not bad. It's not as if I have a lot of choices."

"I do like the shoes."

Fortunately, Amber had tossed in a pair of silver spike heels that had just enough rhinestones to make them interesting. They weren't perfect with the navy dress, but she could get away with them.

"I've got a pair at home that would work better with this dress."

"I have no doubt that you do."

She peered at him in the mirror, trying to determine his level of sarcasm.

"Don't look so suspicious. Your extensive shoe collection is one of my favorite things about you."

"Nice save."

"It wasn't a save. I'm saying you need a different dress."

"There's not much to choose from."

He pointed over his shoulder at the display window. "What about that one?"

The saleslady was quick to pounce. "We do have it in her size."

"Great," said Tuck.

"Wrong," said Amber. She hated to be crass, but she didn't see any point in pretending. "It's too expensive."

"It's a business function," said Tuck.

"I know that."

"She'll try it on," he said to the saleslady.

"No, she won't."

"I'm not asking you to pay for it."

"You're sure not paying for it."

He was her boss, not her boyfriend. A few kisses notwithstanding, they didn't have the kind of relationship that allowed him to buy her clothes or anything else for that matter.

"Not me, Amber. Tucker Transportation."

"That's not how it works."

"That's exactly how it works. You're here on business. I'm compelling you to attend a *business* function. Your wardrobe is the company's responsibility."

"Did the company buy your suit?" she challenged.

"Yes."

"You're lying."

"Corporate credit card." There was a distinct note of triumph in his voice. He gestured to the navy dress. "You're not going in that."

"Yes, I am."

"Like it or not, Amber. Part of your function tonight is to be a billboard for Tucker Transportation's success."

She could barely believe he'd said it. "A *billboard*?"

"Don't get all high and mighty. It's part of the gig."

"You're saying I'm visual entertainment for your boardroom cronies? Do you want me to jump out of a cake, too?"

The saleslady had just returned with the dress and her mouth dropped open at Amber's jibe.

"It applies to me, as well," said Tuck. "Thanks." He smiled at the saleslady and took the dress from her arms. "I can't show up in a cheap suit."

"I don't imagine you own a cheap suit."

"Don't pretend you don't understand my point. You know full well what I mean. You and I both have to look the part tonight."

Amber hated that she did, but she got what he meant. And he wasn't wrong. She glanced at the rich cobalt blue dress. The irony was that it would be perfect with her shoes.

She looked for a graceful way forward. "Tell me this isn't the first time Tucker Transportation bought somebody a dress."

"This isn't the first time Tucker Transportation bought somebody a dress."

She gave him a skeptical frown.

"I think," he added. "Okay, I don't care. My rationale is sound." He glanced at his watch. "And we're running out of time. You might want to do something with your hair."

"What's wrong with my hair?"

The saleslady piped up. "We have a lovely salon in the hotel."

"Can you get her an appointment?" asked Tuck.

"Right away."

"This is ridiculous," Amber muttered. But she scooped the dress from Tuck.

It would be, by far, the most luxurious thing she'd ever worn. But if the man was determined to drop that much money for a single evening, who was she to fight him?

In the opulent ballroom, Tuck had to struggle to keep from staring at Amber. He'd expected the dress to transform her from her usual librarian look. But he'd had no idea the effect would be this dramatic.

The salon had styled her hair in an updo, wispy around her temples, showing off her graceful neck and highlighting her amazing cheekbones. Her makeup was subtle, but deeper and richer than she normally wore. Her thick, dark lashes and artfully lined eyes reflected the deep blue of her dress.

At the moment, he was trying hard to concentrate on Norm Oliphant's description of his newly evolving supply chain, but he was torn between watching Amber and glaring at the dozens of men checking her out. Didn't they realize she was with him?

Dinner was over and a music ensemble was filing into the room. Lighting was being subtly adjusted, dimmed around the perimeter, slightly brighter to highlight the polished wood dance floor.

"I hope there's some good news about your father," said Norm.

Tuck checked his wandering mind and told himself to behave like Dixon. Kassandra had been gorgeous as well, but he was certain his brother had never let that detract from business discussions.

"We're all encouraged," Tuck said to Norm.

"So you've seen him recently?" asked Norm's wife, Regina.

Tuck wasn't sure how to answer that. Truth was he hadn't seen his father since they'd move him to Boston. But how was that going to sound?

Amber smoothly and unexpectedly stepped in. "Tuck has become so pivotal to the day-to-day operations, Jamison is insistent that he focus on the company. Jamison has his wife with him, of course. She's been a stalwart support every day during his recovery. But he gathers peace of mind knowing Tuck is at the helm."

Tuck could have cheered. It was all lies, of course, made up on the spot, which made her explanation all the more impressive.

"Where's Dixon in all of this?" asked Norm.

Amber stepped slightly closer to both Norm and Regina, lowering her voice, throwing Norm off balance with the intensity of her gaze. "I'm sure you heard what happened. With Dixon's wife?"

"We did," said Regina, leaning in.

Amber nodded. "Tuck insisted Dixon take some time to himself. He left a contact number, but we haven't wanted to bother him. You know how brothers can be when one is betrayed. They value loyalty above everything."

Regina glanced at her husband.

"Loyalty," Norm agreed with a nod.

"In business as well as life," said Amber.

Her words were bang on, the inflection perfect. Tuck had to glance at her to convince himself she'd done it on purpose.

He caught her gaze and realized she had. She had skillfully and adroitly reminded Norm of his long-standing business arrangement with Tucker Transportation. She was frighteningly good at this.

Then Amber gave the man a dazzling smile.

Norm raised his glass to Tuck in a toast. "Good of you to come tonight."

"Good of you to invite us." Tuck took a drink with him.

The small orchestra came up with opening bars on the opposite side of the hall.

"We'll be in touch next week," Norm said to Tuck. "I hear Zachary Ingles moved on."

"I'm afraid he thought the grass was greener," Tuck said with a disapproving frown, deciding to stick with the loyalty theme.

"Don't like to see that," said Norm.

"I've promoted Lucas Steele to vice president. Good man. He's been with us for over a decade."

"Worked his way up through the ranks?" asked Norm, looking pleased by the notion.

"Absolutely," said Tuck, though he had no idea exactly how far through the ranks Lucas had worked his way up. "Corporately, we like to nurture talent."

Tuck was tossing things out on the fly, but it seemed like a vague enough statement to be true of most companies.

"Have Lucas give my guys a call," said Norm.

"First thing Monday," said Tuck.

Norm smiled at Regina. "Shall we dance, dear?"

"My pleasure, darling."

Tuck and Amber watched the two walk away.

"You were good," she said. "Very confident, very much in charge."

"Me? You're the one who deserves an acting award. My father gathers peace of mind knowing I'm in charge?"

"I'm sure he does. Or he would. If he knew what I know."

Tuck arched a brow. "Dixon left a contact number?"

She gave a sly smile. "He did. It didn't work in the end, but he did leave a number."

"Remind me to listen very carefully to how you phrase things."

"You don't already?"

Tuck started to smile, but then he caught another man eyeing Amber and sent him a withering stare.

"We should dance," he said.

"Why?"

Because she might not be his date, but she'd arrived with him. He wasn't used to having women poached from under his nose, and he wasn't about to start now.

"It'll look good," he said, taking her hand.

"To who?" But she came easily as he started walking.

"Norm and Regina."

"You think?"

"Sure."

Why wouldn't it look good? It was a perfectly acceptable excuse. They made it to the dance floor and Tuck turned her into his arms.

She fit perfectly. Of course she fit perfectly. And she smoothly matched his rhythm. Within seconds, it was as if they'd been dancing together for years. He immediately relaxed, drawing her closer.

"Thank you for all that," he said into the intimacy of their embrace.

"Just doing my job."

"You're doing it extraordinarily well."

"I guess that's what you get when you pay double overtime."

Tuck smiled at that. "You're a mercenary at heart."

She was quiet for a moment. "Money makes life easier."

"It can," he agreed. "But it can also be a burden."

Right now, Tuck felt the weight of every employee who depended on Tucker Transportation.

Her tone turned teasing. "Spoken like a man who just spent a mortgage payment on a dress."

"In order to ensure hundreds of other people can make their next mortgage payment."

"Do you have any idea how that feels?" she asked.

"To make a mortgage payment?" He wouldn't pretend he did. "The house has been in our family for a couple of generations."

"To worry about making your mortgage payment. To worry about paying for food, clothes, medical bills."

"You know I don't."

They danced in silence. He could tell she was annoyed with him. He didn't really blame her. From the outside looking in, his life must seem like a walk in the park.

Then it hit him, what she might be saying.

"Do *you* earn enough money?" he asked.

She glanced up in obvious surprise. "What?"

"Should I give you a raise?"

"Where did that come from?"

"It sounded as though you were having money problems."

"You pay me fairly."

He searched her expression. He could tell the conversation was hitting very close to home for her. If it wasn't now, then when? When had she been worried about meeting expenses?

"Your childhood?" he suggested.

"This isn't about me."

"Your childhood?" he repeated.

"Fine. We were poor. My mom was single. She drank. A lot."

He digested the information. "I'm sorry you had to go through that."

The orchestra switched songs, but he kept on dancing.

"It was a long time ago," said Amber. "Truth is, it impacted Jade more than it impacted me."

"How so?"

"She had a hard time settling into life. She quit school, left town. Then she bounced from job to job. She always picked the wrong men."

Interesting, but Tuck was far more curious about Amber than he was about Jade. "And you? Did you pick the wrong men?"

She gave a little laugh. "I didn't pick any men at all. Well, not many. I had a boyfriend in high school. But then I graduated and started working. I took a lot of night-school courses at community college, so there wasn't much time for a social life."

"You don't date?" Tuck couldn't help but contrast his own active social life.

"Occasionally. Casually." She glanced around the opulent ballroom. "I have to say, this is the most extravagant event I've ever attended. I guess I should thank you for the experience."

"Anytime." He was serious.

His brain ticked through the information she'd just given him. He liked the idea of what he thought she had to mean.

"So you're saying..." He tried to frame the question. "How do I put this..."

"Don't you *dare* ask me about my sex life."

As if anything on earth would stop him. "Tell me about your sex life."

"Shut up."

He gave a brief chuckle. "I'll tell you about mine."

"I've read about yours."

"Not the details."

"Nobody wants the details."

"I disagree. Reporters ask me about them all the time." He maneuvered them around the crowd to a quieter spot on the dance floor.

"Do you answer?"

"No. If I did, they'd be disappointed."

"Did you just tell me you're a bad lover?"

"What? No. I meant that I'm not as practiced as people assume." He hesitated, then went for it. "Not that you'd have a basis for comparison."

"You're outrageous." But her tone was laced with amusement.

"I won't argue with that. But I'm also available. You know, if you're in dire need of—"

The end of her fist connected sharply with his shoulder, startling him.

"Ouch."

"You better believe, *ouch*," she sniffed with mock offense. "I had a boyfriend."

"Not since high school."

"And I've had offers since then."

He knew that was true. "At least a dozen tonight alone."

She looked puzzled.

"You're not paying attention, are you?" he asked.

"To what?"

"To all the men in the room eyeing you up."

She seemed surprised. "It's the dress. And maybe the hair. Probably the shoes."

"It's all of that," he agreed. "But it's more than just that."

He couldn't help himself. He splayed his hand across her back, urging her close, molding their bodies together.

"Tuck."

"I won't pretend I'm not attracted to you."

The word *attracted* was the understatement of the century. He was wild about her, burning hot for her, growing more so by the hour.

"Jackson's here."

It took a moment for her words to make sense. He'd pictured their conversation taking an entirely different turn.

She signaled the direction with a nod and Tuck easily spotted Jackson in the crowd. He stood out in blue jeans, a white T-shirt and a worn leather jacket. It was easy to tell from his expression that he had some news.

Tuck quickly escorted Amber from the dance floor, meeting up with Jackson at the edge. The three of them made for the double doors that led to a quiet foyer.

"Dixon bought a car," said Jackson when they emerged into the relative privacy of the long, high-ceilinged, glass-walled room.

"When?" asked Tuck.

"Five weeks ago, a three-year-old Audi convertible. He paid cash."

"Is he still in Scottsdale?"

"Didn't stay here long," said Jackson. "We tracked the car to a marina in San Diego."

Tuck's anticipation rose. "Did you find Dixon?"

"There, he bought a sailboat."

Tuck waited for Jackson to elaborate.

"Forty-footer. Paid cash."

The situation was getting stranger by the second.

"I thought you were watching his bank accounts," said Tuck.

"We are. Does your brother normally carry that kind of walking-around money?"

Tuck didn't know. But that did seem like a lot of money to have at his fingertips. How long had Dixon planned this little adventure?

"Did you find the sailboat?" asked Amber.

"It left the marina weeks ago and hasn't been back."

They all stared at each other in silence.

"I doubt he sank," said Tuck. "There'd have been a distress call. We'd have heard from the authorities by now."

"Probably," said Jackson.

"Was it equipped to sail solo?"

"It was."

"Something's not right," said Amber.

"No kidding," Tuck agreed. There were plenty of things not right in this.

"When he headed for Scottsdale," she said, "even though it was a secret, he left a letter for your dad, and he left a number with me. He was that careful. There's no way he'd sail off into the Pacific without telling anyone at all."

"That's exactly what he did," said Tuck.

His worry about his brother was rapidly turning to annoyance. What had Dixon been thinking?

Amber was shaking her head. "Not without any word at all. I can understand that he didn't like it at Highland Luminance. And clearly he can afford a nice boat. But he's not irresponsible. He's trying to clear his head so he can do a good job at Tucker Transportation. He's not trying to harm it."

"Trying or not," said Tuck, "that's exactly what he's doing." He really wished Amber would stop defending Dixon.

"He..." She snapped her fingers. "That's it."

"What's it?" asked Tuck.

"Jamison," she said. "Dixon would have contacted Jamison. He didn't know anything about the heart attack. As far as he's concerned, your dad's still running the company. We searched through Dixon's accounts. And we've been monitoring Jamison's work email, but not his personal email."

Jackson swore under his breath. He was instantly on his phone giving instructions to one of his staff.

Tuck had to admit it was possible. It was even likely. It certainly made more sense than anything else right now. For weeks now, Dixon could have been operating under the assumption they knew his plans. He thought Jamison was running the show. He had no idea Tuck was making a mess of it.

Dixon was still gone. And Tuck still had to find him. But at least it made a little bit of sense now.

* * *

It was late into the night, and the three of them were back in Tuck's hotel suite when Jackson received a copy of an email from his investigator. The original had been sent by Dixon to Jamison's little-used personal email address. Amber was relieved they'd found an answer and happy there was a logical explanation for Dixon's behavior.

"It was sent from an internet café the day he left San Diego," said Jackson from where he was sitting at the round dining table. "He says he plans to spend a few weeks sailing down the Pacific coast. He apologizes but tells your dad to have confidence in you. He knows you can do it."

Tuck shook his head. "Not under these circumstances."

He'd parked himself in an armchair beside the flickering gas fireplace.

Amber had chosen the sofa. She'd kicked the shoes off her sore feet and curled them beneath her. The cushions were soft under her body, while the heat from the fire warmed her skin. Her brain had turned lethargic at the end of such a long day and she would have loved to let herself fall asleep.

"Can you answer Dixon's email?" Tuck asked Jackson.

"Easy. But he'll have to stop somewhere and log on in order to see it."

"He might not check," said Amber. "The point of the whole exercise was to get away from everything."

"He's been away from everything," said Tuck. "It's time for him to come back."

"Before he's ready?" she asked. She understood Tuck's frustration, but Dixon had a right to take some time to himself.

Tuck sat up straight and his voice rose. "How much time does the guy need?"

"You tell me." Her annoyance gave her a renewed shot of energy. "You're the expert. You've had nothing but time to yourself for years now."

He frowned. "Not by choice."

"They held a gun to your head?"

Jackson rose, closing his laptop. He muttered something about having work to do as he headed for the suite door.

Tuck didn't react to him leaving. His attention remained focused on Amber. "They did everything possible to keep me at arm's length."

She found that hard to believe.

"You think I'm lying," he stated.

"I know you had an office. You had keys to the building. Dixon invited you to meetings."

"Meetings where my father took great pleasure in setting me up for failure."

"How?"

"By cornering me with arcane questions to prove I didn't know anything."

"*Did* you know anything?"

He glared at her and she regretted the question.

"I mean," she said, attempting to backtrack, "you could have studied up, surprised him, turned the tables on him."

"That seemed like a lot of work to impress a guy who only wanted me gone."

"Why would he want you gone?" Tuck might be a bit of a rebel, but what father wouldn't be proud to have him as a son?

"Because he liked Dixon better. Parents aren't all perfect, Amber. They don't automatically love their children."

"Your father loves you."

Even as she uttered the statement, Amber realized she had no idea how Jamison felt about Tuck. She was under no illusions about automatic parental love.

She shook her head, regretting her words. "I'm sorry. I don't know that. I don't know anything about it."

Tuck blew out a breath. "It's okay."

She gave a little laugh. "I don't even know whether my own mother loved me."

His gaze turned sympathetic.

Uncomfortable, Amber sat up a bit straighter, attempting to explain. "I'm not sure my mother knew how to love anyone.

She said she loved us. I even think she wanted to love us. But she was so incredibly self-absorbed, she couldn't see past her own needs and desires."

"And your father?"

"Long gone before I had any memory of him."

"Did he support you at all? Financially?"

Amber couldn't help but cough out a laugh. "I'd be surprised if he stayed out of jail. My mother had extraordinarily bad taste in men."

"Where is she now?"

"She died. It happened while Jade and I were still teenagers."

Deeper sympathy came up in Tuck's eyes, softening his expression, making him look approachable, sexy. This was not good.

"How are we talking about me?" she asked.

They needed to get back to arguing.

"You helped raise your sister?"

"She was sixteen when it happened. I was eighteen. There wasn't much raising left to do." And by that time there hadn't been much of an opportunity to change any of Jade's habits.

"That's when she dropped out of school?" he asked.

"She took off after a few months. I didn't hear from her for a while."

Tuck rose and helped himself to a bottle of water, holding one out for her.

She nodded and accepted it.

He sat down at the opposite end of the sofa. "What did you do?"

"I graduated from high school and got a job." She twisted the cap and broke the seal. "With Dixon. He took a chance on me."

"That's surprising," said Tuck.

"I worked hard. I promised him I would, and I did."

"I believe you." Tuck stretched one arm along the back of the sofa. "No wonder you have no patience for me."

"I wouldn't say—"

"It's way too late to protest now. From where you're sitting, I had it all, every advantage, every privilege. My education was paid for, and I walked straight into a VP job in Daddy's company."

"I've never complained about my employment." She'd been grateful for it. "Well, up until you fired me anyway."

"You're back."

"I am."

He seemed to ponder for a moment. "You think I squandered my birthright."

"Those are your words, not mine."

"Then, give me your words."

She took a minute to come up with an answer. "I think you've always had a lot of options. And most of them were very pleasant options. It's not hard to understand why you'd choose the easiest path."

"Ouch."

"Who wouldn't?"

"Apparently not you."

"That's because I never had any easy options." The memories of her teenage years brought a knot to Amber's stomach. "I could work my butt off and only just get by, or I could give up and spiral down like my mother."

She took a drink, letting the cool water bathe her throat.

"Some might say spiraling down would be the easy path," said Tuck.

"To a point. But after a while, it gets a whole lot harder." The thought of living like her mother—the drinking, the smoking, crappy housing, used clothes, the carousel of shabby men—made her physically ill. She took another sip.

"What would you do?" he asked. "If you were me? If you had what I have?"

"I'm not trying to tell you that I'm morally superior."

"What would you do?"

Her instinct was to continue arguing the point. But instead, she considered the theoretical question. "Then or now?"

"Then. No, hindsight is too easy. Now. What would you do now?"

"If I were you," she said. "I'd go home. I'd leave Dixon alone, and I'd go home, work hard and prove to my father that he was dead wrong."

"Because that's the hardest path?"

"Because that's the most satisfying path."

Tuck stared into her eyes for a long time.

She grew uncomfortable, worrying she'd made him angry.

"Will you help me?" he asked.

The question surprised her. But there was only one possible answer. And she meant it sincerely. "I will."

"Will you like me?" As soon as he'd uttered the words, he looked away. But he wasn't fast enough to hide the uncertainty in his eyes.

She realized he'd made himself uncharacteristically vulnerable with the question. She knew she had to be honest. "I already like you."

His posture seemed to relax. "You're one in a million, Amber."

He couldn't be more wrong about that.

"I'm incredibly average," she said. "Thing is, in your world, you don't often come across incredibly average."

A knowing smile came across his face. "Stand up."

The request was abrupt and she wondered what she'd done wrong. Did he want her to leave? He didn't look angry. But then, it was getting late.

She stood.

"Put on your shoes."

She slipped her feet into the delicate high heels. But as she made to head for the door, he gently grasped her shoulders, turning her away, propelling her in the opposite direction.

"What are you doing?"

Before he answered, they were through a set of open double doors and into the bedroom.

"Look," he said, turning her toward a full-length mirror.

"What?"

There was nothing to see. The dress still looked great and it still went with the shoes. But her hair was coming loose and her makeup had faded. Her cheeks were rosy from the earlier wine and maybe from debating with Tuck. Her eyes were slightly shadowed with exhaustion. She really did need to get some sleep.

He brushed his fingertips across her shoulder, his tone going deep. "Is there anything about you that is remotely average?"

His words sent a tingle down her spine.

"You're amazing, Amber. You're flat-out amazing. You're gorgeous and smart as a whip. You're insightful and funny." He brushed her hair from the side of her neck. "And I can't get you out of my mind."

He eased slowly forward until his lips connected with the crook of her neck. They were soft and hot as she gazed at his image in the mirror. He kissed her again, lips wider this time, leaving a circle of moisture behind.

He planted a chain of kisses along her shoulder while his palms slipped down her bare arms. She watched his dark head, felt the air cool the moisture on her skin, let desire and arousal throb to life inside her. Then his hands came to rest on her waist, his blunt fingers splayed on her stomach, dark in relief against the glittery blue of the dress.

She leaned back against him. He was solid, a tower of muscle and strength. Their gazes met in the reflection, midnight blue and pewter gray. She let him in, not flinching, absorbing his obvious passion and returning it with her own.

He reached for the zipper at the back of her dress, watching her reaction closely as he drew it down. The air brushed her back and she quivered with the mix of sensations. He brushed aside the fabric and kissed her shoulder. His fingers delved into her hair, tugging at the clip and releasing thick waves.

She gasped in a breath and her hands curled into fists. It was the point of no return. No, it wasn't. She'd already passed no return when she'd met his eyes in the mirror. Her and Tuck, for now, at least for this small moment, were inevitable.

She shrugged her shoulders and the dress slipped down, the fabric cascading over her breasts, past her hips, pooling on the thick carpet.

His eyes darkened, his gaze pausing on her pink satin bra. It swept over her navel to the tiny matching panties, down the length of her legs to the sparkling shoes.

"One in a million," he whispered in her ear.

His hand closed over her breast and he kissed that first spot on her neck.

She knew she should look away, close her eyes and safely drown in the sensations of his touch. But she watched while he unhooked her bra. He set her breasts tumbling free. Then he let his fingertips roam from the curve of her hip, to the indentation of her naval, to the mound of her breast and her pearled nipples.

He touched and fondled while her temperature rose and her lungs dragged in air. When his hand dipped under her panties, urgency overwhelmed her. She turned in his arms, meeting his lips, tangling her limbs around him while his hand drove her to heights of passion.

"You are incredible," he rasped between kisses, peeling off the flimsy panties.

She pushed off his jacket, then struggled with his tie.

He tore off the new shirt and they came together, skin on skin, finally. He embraced her, held her tight, strong arms wrapped firmly around her as he explored every nuance of her mouth.

Then he lifted her and carried her to the big bed, yanking back the covers to deposit her on the crisp sheets. She lay on her back, watching as he stripped off his clothes.

When he was naked, he gazed down. He took in her disheveled hair, his eyes moving over her breasts to the shadow of her thighs, down the length of her legs. Then he smiled.

She realized she still wore her shoes.

She couldn't help but grin sheepishly in return.

"One of the things I love best about you," he said, coming to lie next to her on the mattress.

He renewed his exploration of her body, and she returned the favor, reveling in the taut muscles of his shoulders and arms, his washboard stomach and the strength of his hips and thighs. She kissed her way over his salty skin while he found her sensitive and erotic spots, the crook of her knee, the inside of her thigh, the tips of her nipples.

Then he rolled on top, his solid weight pinning her satisfyingly to the mattress. He took a second with a condom, then stared straight in her eyes.

She flexed her hips upward and felt him sliding inside. Her head tipped back and her eyes fluttered closed. Her world contracted to the cloud of sensation that was Tuck. His scent surrounded her. His heat enveloped her. His fingertips were magic and his lips were delicious.

His rhythm was slow and steady. First her bones melted to nothing. Then her limbs began to buzz. His pace increased and she couldn't contain her moans. Wave after wave of passion washed over and through her.

She couldn't move. She couldn't breathe. Her mind had gone into a free fall. And then the world burst open, and she cried out his name, hanging on tight, never wanting to let go.

Nine

Tuck knew that making love couldn't have been an easy decision for Amber. But for him it had been the easiest path, and definitely the most pleasurable path.

He eased onto his side, taking his weight from her and gathering her close. "I'm sorry," he whispered.

"For?" she whispered back. "Was that not your best work?"

He wanted to laugh, but he was afraid it would be the wrong reaction. "I know you weren't sure."

She turned her head and looked questioningly up at him.

"About making love," he elaborated.

"Did I not seem sure?"

"I guess you did."

"Should I have made you wait?"

"That might have killed me. I've been desperate for you since day one."

She smoothed her hand across his chest. "I've been resisting you for a while now."

He let his ego absorb the compliment.

She curled herself into a sitting position.

"What are you doing?" He wanted her to stay exactly where she was.

She moved to the edge of the bed. "Now that we've got that out of our system."

"Whoa, what?" His system was just getting started.

She rose and crossed the bedroom. "I realize it was inevitable. It might be nothing but chemistry, but it's still pretty powerful stuff."

Nothing but chemistry?

Okay, sure, he remembered saying that. Problem was he couldn't remember why.

She slipped into her panties, turning to face him while she dressed.

For some reason, he'd expected her to be shy. He wasn't sure why, maybe because of the clothes she usually wore.

He sat up, draping his legs over the edge of the bed. "You don't have to leave."

She stopped in the midst of fastening her bra, looking surprised. "We need to get to sleep. I assume we'll be leaving first thing in the morning."

"There's no rush."

They were flying in a Tucker jet. They could leave any old time they wanted. It didn't even have to be tomorrow.

"We've got a ton of work to do," she said. "I said I'd help, and I will. I'll do as much as I can. But you've got to do your part, Tuck. Dixon could be back soon. You might not have much time and you need to start proving yourself."

Wait a minute. "We *want* Dixon back."

"Sure we do. But not right away, not if you want to show your father you've got what it takes to run the company."

Tuck came to his feet. "I don't have what it takes to run the company."

Amber dropped the dress over her head, pushing her arms through the flimsy cap sleeves. "Maybe not yet."

"I don't know what you think I can do."

"You can start by hiring some new executives. Lucas needs help." She turned and presented him with the zipper.

He didn't want to zip her up. He wanted to strip her down again. He wanted her naked again, in his bed, in his arms, making love until neither of them could move and then sleeping until noon.

"I can't hire new executives."

"Zip me up. Yes, you can."

"That's a permanent decision. I'm temporary."

"You're a Tucker and you're in charge. Make a decision."

This was the first time Amber had struck him as being cavalier. She was normally careful and methodical.

"Is there something wrong with my zipper?" she asked.

"You don't have to go yet."

She reached back and zipped herself, making it most of the way up. Then she turned and gave him a quick kiss. "I'm exhausted."

"Sleep here."

She stilled, a stricken expression crossing her face. Just as quickly, it disappeared. "That's not going to happen."

"Why not?"

"This was a bad idea. I mean, it was a good idea, because it had to happen. But at its foundation, it was a terrible idea. We need to forget about it and move on."

"Move on to *what*?"

He didn't want to forget about what had just happened between them. It was the greatest sex of his life.

"Haven't you been paying attention?" she asked. "You're going to run Tucker Transportation. It goes without saying, but I'm saying it anyway, absolutely no good can come from a fling between us. It'll compromise your credibility and it'll destroy my career. You've fired me once. I'm not about to give you or Dixon or your father a reason to fire me again."

"Nobody's going to fire you."

She shook her head. "That's the *only* sure thing that happens when assistants get involved with their bosses."

"You can't know that."

She took a deep breath, squaring her shoulders. "Do you want to do this?"

He didn't dare hope she meant make love again. "Do what?"

"Do you want to *try*? Or do you want to spend the rest of your life as a self-indulgent playboy and a vice president in name only?"

"Those are my only two choices?"

"Yes."

"Then, I'm willing to try."

At least he could still spend time with her. And maybe he could manage to impress her. And maybe, if he was very lucky, their chemistry would rear its head again and she'd come back into his arms.

In the breezeway outside Tuck's hotel suite, Amber sagged against the wall. It had taken everything she had to pull off the act, to pretend that making love with Tuck hadn't thrown her for an absolute emotional loop.

She might not have been able to stop herself. But she knew she'd made one of the world's biggest mistakes. She had hopped into bed with her boss. She'd hopped into bed with her boss, and it was fantastic.

At least it had been fantastic for her. Who knew what it was for him? Maybe he had sex like that every Saturday night.

Maybe she'd been mediocre. Maybe he'd been disappointed. She forcibly stopped her brain from going there.

She wasn't going to do that to herself. If it hadn't been good for him, too darn bad. He'd have to get past it, maybe move on to someone else. She was moving on. She was definitely moving on.

She straightened from the wall, putting one foot in front of the other. Her room was along the courtyard and up one flight of stairs. She was going to shower and sleep, and then she was going back home to focus on Jade, the baby and Tucker Transportation.

Tonight was a lark. It didn't have to define her. It didn't even need to define her relationship with Tuck.

"Amber?" Jackson's voice came from a pathway at a right angle.

She stopped. Her heart sank and her stomach contracted into a knot of embarrassment and guilt.

She forced herself to turn and face him. "Hello, Jackson."

"I'm glad I caught you." His expression wasn't condemning, nor was it judgmental.

Maybe he hadn't guessed what had just happened.

She should play it cool. She could have taken her hair down for any number of reasons. From this angle, he couldn't see her zipper was partway down. She made a mental note to keep her back away from him.

"Did Dixon ever mention a woman?" he asked.

Amber forced herself to stay calm and collected. "What kind of a woman?"

She fought off the urge to smooth her hair. It would only call attention to the mess.

"Someone other than Kassandra."

"You mean a girlfriend?" She knew that wasn't possible.

"Yes."

"Dixon wasn't fooling around. He was as honorable as they come."

"I know you're loyal to him."

"That's not loyalty talking," said Amber. "Jackson, he didn't cheat on Kassandra."

"What about after they separated?"

"Nobody I ever heard about."

Jackson showed her his phone with a photo of a pretty blond woman. "Recognize her?"

"No. Who is she?"

"Is there any chance, any chance at all, that Dixon left Chicago to be with another woman?"

"He wouldn't leave Chicago to do that. His friends would be cheering from the rooftops. He wouldn't hide it."

Jackson was obviously deep in thought.

"What's going on?" she asked.

"I'm covering all the bases."

"Where did you get the picture?"

"She might be connected to the sailboat. We're tracking it down the coast."

"There might not be so much of a rush now."

Amber was warming up to the idea of Tuck proving himself to his father. He'd obviously spent his whole life riddled with self-doubt. She knew he'd feel good if he succeeded. And she knew he had it in him. He just had to apply himself.

Jackson's brow rose. "Why do you say that?"

"Tuck's going to run the company. It's the first chance he's ever had. This might even turn out to be a blessing in disguise."

Jackson didn't respond, but skepticism came into his eyes.

"You think it's a bad idea." She wished she hadn't come to respect Jackson's opinion.

"I think it's not Tuck's idea."

"It was. Kind of." She struggled to remember the exact details of the conversation. "He's always felt inadequate."

Jackson looked amused. "He's been too busy having fun to feel inadequate."

"You're wrong."

"You've known him how long?"

"A few weeks," she admitted.

Jackson gave her an indulgent smile. "He's not what you think he is."

"Don't patronize me."

"Then, let me put it another way. He's not what you want him to be." Jackson's sharp eyes took in her messy hair and what had to be smeared makeup.

In that second, she knew she was caught. And it was humiliating. Jackson thought she was going after Tuck. He thought she wanted to domesticate Tuck. She could only imagine he thought she was one of a long line of gold diggers out to become Mrs. Tuck Tucker.

She had to get out of here. "Good night, Jackson."

"I like you, Amber."

She gave a chopped laugh of disbelief.

"You're too good for him," said Jackson.

"I don't want him."

Jackson's smile was indulgent again. "You want him to be a better him."

She opened her mouth to deny it.

But Jackson spoke overtop her. "There's only one reason a woman wants that."

"There could be a hundred reasons why a woman wants that."

"You might not know it yet. But you're falling for him. Don't fall for him, Amber. You'll only get hurt."

"Advice to the lovelorn, Jackson?"

"Advice from a guy who knows Tuck."

"Well..." She had no good comeback to that. She truly didn't know what to say. All she knew was that she wanted the heck out of this conversation right now. "Thank you."

She turned sharply away, then realized he'd seen her partially undone zipper.

She swallowed. She lifted her chin and squared her shoulders. He'd obviously already guessed. He'd come to all the wrong conclusions afterward, but he knew full well that she'd just slept with Tuck.

When she looked up and saw Amber, Jade closed her textbook and pushed the wheeled bed tray off to one side. "Welcome back to the real world."

"I'm on my way to the office," Amber told her, moving closer. "We landed about an hour ago."

Taking a private jet to Scottsdale and back had been a surreal experience for Amber, but there was no disputing the convenience.

"How was it?" asked Jade with enthusiasm. "Warm? Great? I looked up the resort—*nice*."

"We were pretty busy working." Amber had struggled all night long, then especially during the flight back, to keep focused on the work and not to think about Tuck.

Jade gave a mock frown. "You didn't spend hours at the spa?"

"I'm afraid not."

"I was hoping to live vicariously through you."

"I could lie," Amber offered.

"Would you? That would be nice. I'm so bloated and tired and achy, I'd kill for a massage or a few hours in the hot springs."

"The weather was great," said Amber. "The hotel was gorgeous, the food, rooms. The beds were really comfortable."

"Was that a Freudian slip?"

Amber didn't understand Jade's point.

"Beds," Jade elaborated. "Plural?"

Amber realized it was a joke, but embarrassment made her mind go momentarily blank.

Jade's eyes went wide. "Wait a minute."

"It was a figure of speech," said Amber.

Jade's surprise turned to concern. "Tell me you didn't."

"I didn't do anything." At least nothing that was Jade's business, nothing that was anybody's business, except hers and Tuck's. And they were forgetting all about it.

"You *slept* with him?"

Amber didn't want to lie, so she didn't answer.

Jade reached for her hands. "Oh, Amber. You're usually so smart."

"It wasn't stupid."

"I don't want you to get hurt."

"I'm not getting hurt. It just…happened." Amber realized how trite that sounded. "It was only the once."

"He's your boss."

"Only for a little while. Dixon will come back and then it'll all be over. Tuck barely shows up at the office."

When Dixon got back, Amber fully expected Tuck to return to his previous life. He might want to impress his father, but he wasn't likely to give up the parties and vacations in order to work his butt off.

Last night she'd had a few moments of optimism. But she knew Jackson was right. Tuck liked his life exactly the way it was. Last night Tuck had told her what he thought she wanted to hear. He probably always told women what he thought they wanted to hear.

She lowered herself onto the bedside chair. "I don't know what I was thinking."

"You were thinking he was a superhot guy. At least, that's what I'm usually thinking."

Amber gave a helpless laugh. "He was. He is. Oh, man, he was good."

For the first time since it happened, she let the full bloom of their lovemaking rush through her mind. It had been amazing. And she wanted to do it again, so badly.

"At least there's that," Jade said softly.

"You say it as if it's a good thing."

"It's not?"

Amber straightened in the chair. "No, it's not. It would have been better to be disappointed."

"So you didn't want to do it again," Jade said with sage understanding.

"What is *wrong* with me? I'm no better than Margaret."

"Who's Margaret?"

"Tuck's father's secretary. Turns out she's having an affair with him."

"He's married?"

"Yes."

"Tuck's not married," said Jade.

"He's still my boss."

"True. But that makes it risky, not immoral. Those are two totally different circumstances."

"It was a mistake," Amber said, more to herself than to Jade. "But I'm over it. I can do that. I'm tough." She drew a bracing breath. "Now, what about you? Is everything still looking good?"

Jade's hand moved to her stomach. "She's kicking less. I bet it must be getting crowded in there."

"Is that normal?" Amber's gaze rested on Jade's bulging stomach.

"The doc says it often happens that way. My back is absolutely killing me." Jade moved and stretched in the bed.

"I'm sorry."

"And I've got heartburn and an overactive bladder. I'll be so glad when this is over."

"It won't be much longer," said Amber, feeling sympathetic. "I've been thinking I better get shopping. Have you thought about what you'll need? Can you make me a list?"

"You don't have to buy me things."

"You're going to need a crib and diapers."

"There's a secondhand store on Grand. We could check there after I get home."

"Sure," said Amber, knowing the least she could do was to buy her new niece a crib. She didn't want to make Jade feel bad about her financial circumstances, so she'd figure out the necessities on her own and get them ready.

"I should head for the office," she said, coming to her feet.

She wasn't looking forward to it, but she was confident that the more time she spent around Tuck in the office, the easier it would be to keep her feelings in perspective.

"In a way, it's reassuring," said Jade, a look of contentment on her face.

"What is?"

"To know you're not perfect."

"Who ever said I was perfect?"

"Mom, me, you."

"Me?" Amber couldn't imagine when or why she would have said that.

"You don't remember the straight As?"

"I didn't get straight As."

"You got a B plus in tenth-grade math."

"See?"

Amber remembered it well. It was a blight on the report card, as if someone had painted a black, hairy spider in the middle of a butterfly collage.

"You set your alarm for six fifty-three every morning."

It had made perfect sense to Amber. "I liked to lay there for two minutes before getting out of bed."

"You knew all the food groups. You talked about them at every meal."

"We didn't always have them."

"We never had them. But you knew what they were. I remember Mom giving us each five dollars for candy. She was drunk, of course, in an 'I love you, kids' mood."

Amber didn't like to remember her sloppy, tearful mother professing her love for them. It was inevitably followed by a monologue of self-pity, then a rant about how they didn't love her back. Then she'd vomit and pass out in the bathroom. More often than not, leaving a mess for Amber to clean up.

"Don't go back there," she said softly to Jade.

"I spent it all on chocolate," said Jade. "You bought chewable vitamins. I was baffled."

"I don't remember that," said Amber, searching her memory for the incident.

"You were perfect," said Jade.

"You make me sound pretentious and superior." What could Amber have been trying to prove?

"You didn't want us to die of scurvy."

But they hadn't been on the verge of malnutrition.

"We had juice with breakfast most mornings," said Amber.

"I hate to admit it, but part of me is glad you jumped into bed with your boss. If you're not all good, then maybe I'm not all bad."

"You're not bad, Jade."

"I'm pretty bad."

"No. And anyway, you're getting better."

"I'm trying."

"I'll try, too," said Amber.

"Try to do what? Be worse?"

"Be, I don't know… Normal, I guess, less uptight and judgmental. Those are not attractive qualities."

Jade grimaced as she shifted her back to a new position. "I realize now that you were trying to hold chaos together with your bare hands."

"Maybe I should have let it go."

Maybe if she had, Jade wouldn't have run away. Maybe if she hadn't been so morally superior, they could have worked together.

Then it came to her that she should do the same thing now—let things go. It was none of her business what Tuck did or didn't do with Tucker Transportation. Dixon's decisions were similarly his own. Why did she feel an obligation to control the situation?

"I can't see you doing that." Jade looked amused.

"A month ago, I wouldn't have been able to picture you writing your GED."

"Those are opposites."

"Not really."

"Don't change, Amber. I need you just the way you are."

For some reason, Amber's eyes teared up. She quickly blinked.

"I won't change," she promised. At least not so that Jade could see. But she wasn't going to badger Tuck anymore. Nobody needed that. She was surprised he'd put up with it this long.

Jamison's eyes were closed, his expression lax, and his wrinkled skin was sallow against the stark white of the hospital sheets. Machines whirred and beeped as Tuck moved cautiously toward the bedside, screens glowing and colored dots of LED lights blinking in different rhythms. There was an oxygen tube beneath Jamison's nose and an IV line in his arm.

It was odd seeing him like this. Tuck half expected him to open his eyes, sit up and bellow out orders.

"Dad?" Tuck said softly.

Sounds from the hallway drifted through the glass door and windows: a phone ringing, a nurse's voice, a cart wheeling by and the ping of an elevator.

"Dad?" he repeated.

Jamison's pale blue eyes fluttered open, looking cloudy instead of sharp.

"Hi, Dad," said Tuck.

He felt as though he ought to squeeze his father's hand or stroke his brow. But they didn't have that kind of relationship. There was no tenderness between them. Wary suspicion interspersed with crisp cordiality was more their style.

"Dixon?" Jamison rasped, then he coughed and grimaced with the effort.

"It's Tuck," said Tuck.

Jamison squinted. "Where's Dixon?"

"He's still away."

"Away where?"

"Sailing," said Tuck.

"On the lake?"

"Off the coast of California." Tuck paused. "I've been taking care of things while he's gone."

Jamison's frown deepened. Then he waved a dismissive hand, the IV tube clattering against the bed rail. "Where's your mother?"

Tuck pulled in a chair and sat down. "She's with Aunt Julie."

"Why?"

"Dad, you know you're in Boston, right?"

Jamison looked confused for a moment, then his brow furrowed deeply and he looked annoyed. "Yes, I know I'm in Boston."

"And you understand that you had a heart attack." Tuck was growing concerned with his father's apparent level of confusion.

"You must be feeling pleased with yourself." Jamison's voice seemed stronger. He gripped on to the bed rails.

"How so?"

"You got rid of me. And you've sent Dixon off somewhere. What have you been up to without us?"

Ah, yes. Tuck's father was back.

"I didn't give you a heart attack, Dad."

"I want to see your brother."

"Get in line," said Tuck. Then he regretted the sarcasm. "Dixon can't be reached right now."

"Of course he can. Call him."

"He's out of cell range."

"Then, send somebody after him, write a letter, use a carrier pigeon for all I care."

Tuck spoke slowly and clearly. "Dixon is gone. I can't find him and I can't get him back. That's why I'm here."

"This is nonsense," Jamison growled. "Just because I'm here in this hospital bed doesn't mean you can lie to me."

"I'm not lying to you."

"The business can't run without Dixon."

"It is running without Dixon, Dad. It's been running without Dixon for nearly two months."

Jamison opened his mouth, but Tuck kept on talking. "I'm here for your proxy."

Jamison's eyes bugged out. "My *what*?"

"I've held off as long as I can. But I need to make some decisions. I need to hire new executives and I need a proxy vote for your shares."

"It'll be a cold day in hell before I give you control of Tucker Transportation."

"It's only temporary."

"Where's Dixon?"

Tuck leaned slightly forward. "Dixon's gone. He left on his own and he hasn't come back."

"What's going on? Why are you doing this?" Jamison groped for the nurse call button and pressed it.

Tuck pushed back the chair and came to his feet. "I'm not *doing* anything. I'm jumping in to run your precious company."

"You don't know how to run the company."

"You're right about that."

The two men stared at each other.

A nurse breezed into the room.

"Mr. Tucker?" she asked. "Is something wrong?"

"Yes, something is wrong," Jamison stormed. "My son is telling me lies."

The nurse looked to Tuck and he gave a slight shake of his head.

"Are you in any pain?" The nurse checked his IV.

"I'm not in pain. My other son, Dixon, can you bring him here? I need to talk to him."

"I'm going to check your blood pressure." As she spoke, the nurse wrapped Jamison's arm in a blood-pressure cuff.

"Dad," Tuck began again, "you're in no condition to attend a board meeting."

Jamison tried to sit up.

"Oh, no, you don't," said the nurse, placing a hand on his shoulder. Her tone was calm but firm. "Your blood pressure is slightly elevated."

"Is that dangerous?" asked Tuck, wondering if he should leave.

"Only slightly," said the nurse. She frowned at Jamison. "You try to stay calm."

"I'm perfectly calm."

The nurse moved to the foot of the bed, making notes on the chart.

"Harvey Miller resigned," Tuck told his father.

"We have no finance director?"

"No."

"What did you do?"

"Nothing. He moved to a different company. People do that sometimes."

"Where did he go?"

"That's irrelevant. The important point is that I need to replace him. To do that, I need to formalize my position as interim president. So I need your proxy to vote your shares."

"You can't be president."

"Okay," said Tuck, thoroughly tired of this argument and every other one he'd had for the past decade. "I won't be president." He turned to leave.

"Dixon can be interim president."

"Sounds good," Tuck called over his shoulder. "Let me know how it all turns out."

"Bring him here," Jamison shouted out.

"Calm down," said the nurse.

Tuck stopped and turned back. "I'm sure he'll show up eventually. Until then, well, Tucker Transportation will have to survive without a finance director and without a president. I'm sure it'll be fine. After all, anything's better than having me in charge, isn't it?"

"Insolent," said Jamison.

"So you always say. I'm here. I'm offering to help. Take it or leave it. It's entirely up to you."

Jamison glared at him while the machines beeped his vital signs, the hospital hallway buzzed with activity and the nurse refilled his plastic water jug. Tuck almost felt sorry for his father—almost. Even when the man was all but desperate for Tuck's assistance, he'd only grudgingly accept it. How was that supposed to make a person feel?

"I'll give you my proxy," said Jamison. "Time limited."

"Fine," said Tuck.

He reached into his inside jacket pocket as he returned to the bed, producing the letter his lawyer had crafted. "We can both initial on an end date."

He approached the bed and maneuvered his father's tray into position. Then he jotted down a date one month away and stroked his initials next to the addition.

"I need my glasses," Jamison muttered.

Tuck spotted the glasses on the bedside table and handed them to his father. Then he handed over the pen and watched while Jamison signed over formal control of the company. Butterflies rose up unexpectedly in his stomach.

He didn't want this. He'd never sought it out. But now that he had it, he found he didn't want to fail.

Ten

"This was all your doing," Tuck said to Amber as he gazed at the aftermath of the party in the huge, high-ceilinged living room of his family's home.

Though staff had been ubiquitous throughout, she could see the mansion showed the effects of hosting two hundred people. The midnight buffet was being cleared away by the catering staff and the few glasses left on side tables were being dispatched to the kitchen.

"It doesn't look that bad," she responded.

He pulled at the end of his bow tie, releasing the knot. "I'm not blaming you for the mess."

"Then, what?"

He gestured to an armchair next to the marble fireplace.

Grateful, she sank down on the soft cream-colored leather. It was a relief to get off the four-inch heels.

Tuck sat in the opposite chair. "You convinced me I could do it."

"Throw a party?"

Tuck was nothing if not a party guy. She had to assume he'd thrown dozens, if not hundreds, of parties himself over the years.

"I meant run the company. If you hadn't pushed me to start making decisions, I never would have gone to see my father."

"And if you hadn't gone to see your father."

"I wouldn't have hired Samuel and Gena."

"I like Samuel and Gena."

"So do I. I'm not sure how my father's going to feel about them."

"Because they're too young to have such responsible jobs?" The two were both in their early thirties.

"I'm sure they won't fit his image of an executive."

"Do you think clients will care that Samuel wears blue jeans?" asked Amber.

"Lucas wears blue jeans."

"Operations and marketing are two different functions."

"True," Tuck agreed. "Thirsty? You want some ice water?"

"Sure."

Amber expected him to rise and pour some water at the bar. Instead, he subtly raised a hand and a staff member was instantly by his side.

"Yes, sir?" said the neatly dressed waiter.

"Can you bring us some ice water?"

"Right away, sir." The man withdrew.

Amber could only stare at Tuck for a moment.

"What?" he asked.

"Even knowing you were so rich, I didn't picture all this."

He gazed around at the soaring ceilings, wooden pillars and expensive oil paintings. "It is rather ostentatious."

"Flick of a finger and the ice water appears."

"I thought you were thirsty."

"I thought we'd pour it ourselves."

"Aah. You're uncomfortable with the household staff."

"I'm baffled by the notion of household staff."

"It's a big house," said Tuck.

"That doesn't mean you can't pour your own water."

"Are you calling me spoiled?"

"I always call you spoiled."

To her surprise, he shrugged. "Fair criticism. If it helps, I often pour my own water, and my own whiskey. I even go so far as to open my own beer bottle."

She couldn't help but grin. "Then, I take it all back. You're obviously a self-sufficient man."

The waiter returned, setting down a silver tray with two glasses and a pitcher.

"Shall I pour, sir?" he asked.

"We'll be fine, thanks," Tuck answered with a wry grin.

The man left.

"Okay, now you're just trying to impress me," said Amber.

Tuck sat up and leaned forward. "Is it working?" He poured them each a glass, handing one to her.

"Be still, my beating heart."

"You do know it's not always like this."

"Always like what?"

"This many staff members, hanging out in the living room, dressed in a tux." He tugged off the tie and undid his top button. "Other parts of the house are a lot less formal."

She found herself glancing around again. "I would hope so. I'd be jumpy if I had to live in this 24/7."

He took a sip of his water. "Want to know a secret?"

"Has anyone ever said no to that question?"

He chuckled. "I guess not."

"Then, yes, do tell me your secret." She took a long drink, realizing she was very thirsty after a martini and two glasses of wine.

"The place makes me jumpy, too."

"Yeah, right." She continued drinking the water.

"I never liked this room. Or the library. You should see the library. Talk about pretentious and forbidding. My dad's fortress. It's positively gothic." He lowered his tone. "Nothing good ever happens in the library."

"Now you really have got me curious."

"You sure you're brave enough to see the library?"

"Oh, I'm brave enough. Besides, your father's not here."

"Check out the lion's den while the lion's away." He set down his glass. "You're very smart. That's what I like about you."

She gave a saucy grin at the compliment, but it also warmed her heart. It was nice to think that Tuck considered her intelligent. She'd certainly gained great respect for his reasoning and judgment. She'd also come to respect his hard work.

The past two weeks, she'd found herself wondering if he'd always been industrious, but simply focused on things other than Tucker Transportation. There was no doubt he'd raised the bar on being Chicago's preeminent playboy bachelor.

He came to his feet. "Let's go."

She rose and grimaced as her shoes pinched down on her swollen feet.

"Something wrong?" he asked.

"Would it be terribly rude if I took off my shoes?"

His mouth broke into a mischievous smile. "Shoeless in the library. You're a maverick, Amber, no doubt about it."

"Good thing your father's not around to see this." She peeled off the shoes and dropped them to the carpet.

"I may send him a picture."

"And get me fired?"

Tuck headed across the room and she fell into step beside him.

"Nobody's going to fire you," he said.

"You did."

"I was mistaken. And I've learned my lesson."

"Jamison was about to fire me. Dixon's the only one who hasn't wanted to send me packing."

"What do you mean Jamison was about to fire you?"

"When he had his heart attack," she admitted. "When I wouldn't tell him anything about Dixon. I swear the next words out of his mouth would have been *you're fired*."

"But he had a heart attack instead."

"I wasn't glad," she hastily told him, assailed by a wave of guilt. "I mean, even to save my job, I would never wish a heart attack on anyone. Maybe I should have told somebody. I guess that would have been you. Should I have told you? Or… Oh, no, do you think it was my fault?"

"Wow." Tuck came to a stop in the hallway, canting his body to face her. "You just did a whole big thing there all by yourself."

He seemed unusually tall, unusually imposing and unusually impressive.

"I really hadn't given it enough thought before," she said. "The man had a heart attack because I refused to help him. I'm not sure I deserve to keep my job."

"My father had a heart attack because of one too many rib eyes, and a fondness for chocolate truffles and Cuban cigars. Don't beat yourself up." Tuck put his hand on the knob of a dark paneled door. "Are you ready?"

"I'm not sure I'm through feeling guilty."

"Yes, you are. Of all the stressors in his life, you'd be ranked near the bottom. If you want to blame anyone, blame Dixon."

"Dixon *had* to get away."

"Yeah, yeah. We all know your opinion on that. Then, blame me. Or maybe blame Margaret. Keeping his affair a secret had to be stressful."

Amber couldn't argue with that. Tuck pushed the door and it yawned open.

As she walked in, antique lamps came up around the perimeter of the rectangular room, giving it a yellowish glow. The ceilings were arched, the woodwork dark and intricately carved and the books were lined on recessed shelves, secured behind fronts of black metal latticework.

There were clusters of armchairs with worn leather upholstery. And in the center of the room was an oblong table, set on two massive pedestals and surrounded by eight antique chairs, upholstered in burgundy damask.

"I can picture him here," she said, her voice sounding small in the imposing space.

"I try not to," said Tuck. Then he unexpectedly took her hand. "Come here."

"Why?" A flutter of reaction made its way up her arm, crossing into her chest. She was instantly aware of Tuck as a man, her attraction to him and the fact that they were completely alone.

"I want you to sit."

"Why?"

"Here." He pointed to one of the armchairs.

"What are you doing?" She didn't know what he had planned, but something in his voice was arousing her.

"Sit," he said softly.

She did.

"I want to picture you there," said Tuck. "With no shoes." He unexpectedly reached around her and unclasped her hair, letting it fall around her face. "Perfect," he said.

Then he paused, his gaze squinting down.

"What?" She felt suddenly self-conscious.

"One more thing." He reached out again, sliding his index finger under the spaghetti strap of her silver-and-ice-blue cocktail dress, dropping it down off her shoulder.

Her arousal ramped up, sending pleasure impulses along her thighs. She gazed up at him, unable to speak.

He took a step back. "*That's* what I'm going to remember in this room."

Her entire body heated under his gaze.

He watched her intently for a full minute, his eyes dark and clouded with obvious desire.

"You want to see my favorite room?" he asked.

She knew she should say no. It was the only reasonable answer. His question could mean anything and everything.

But her lips stubbornly formed the word *yes*.

Amber looked surprised when they entered the second-floor sitting room. Tuck could only imagine that she'd expected something bigger and grander. She gazed at the earthy rattan furniture, the watercolors on the walls and the stoneware vases atop pale maple tables.

"Not what you were expecting?" he asked.

"Not even close." She ran her hand over the back of the sofa, moving farther into the room.

With her bare feet, loose hair and the spaghetti strap still drooping over her shoulder, she seemed to belong here. She'd looked great in the library, the juxtaposition of such a feminine woman in such a masculine room. But here she looked fantastic. He wanted to close the door, lock out the world and maybe keep her here forever.

"It keeps me grounded," he told her.

"I've never thought of you as being grounded." Her pretty smile took some of the sting out of the words.

"What do you think of me as being?"

"Indulged, cosseted, lucky."

"I suppose I'm all of those things." He saw no point in denying it.

"It's more complicated than that." She looped around and came back to him.

"Nice of you to say so."

"I'm only being honest."

"Then, nice of you to notice," he said.

"It took me a while to notice." She stopped in front of him, all fresh faced and adorable. Her skin was satin smooth above the dress, lips a perfect pink, her hair just mussed enough to be off-the-charts sexy.

He remembered her naked. He remembered every single nuance of her body, the curve of her hip, the swell of her breasts, the blue of her eyes as passion overwhelmed her.

"Took me about half a second to notice you," he said gruffly.

"What did you notice?" She was so close, it was about to drive him crazy.

The slightest movement of his hand and he'd be touching her waist, feeling the pulse of her skin. If he leaned in, just a few inches, he could kiss her. Or at least find out if she'd let him kiss her. He picked up the scent of her hair. His fingertips twitched with the memory of her skin.

"Your eyes," he said. "Your shoes and your sassy mouth."

"Somebody has to keep you in line."

He eased slightly closer. "You want to keep me in line?"

She didn't answer, but her eyes darkened to indigo.

"Know what I want to do to you?" he asked softly.

Her lips parted.

He moved closer still, twining one hand with hers. He brushed back her hair, leaned in close to her ear.

"Kiss you," he whispered. "Pull you into my arms. Peel that dress from your body and make long, slow love to you."

"That wasn't..." Her voice went breathless. "What I was expecting."

"No?" He placed a kiss on her shoulder, reveling in the sweetness of her skin.

"I'm lying."

He kissed her again, closer to the crook of her neck. "Yeah?"

"It was exactly what I was expecting."

"But you came up here with me anyway?" His lips brushed her skin as he spoke.

"Yes." Her palms touched his chest, warm and intimate. "I want you, Tuck. I keep trying to ignore it."

He drew back to look into her eyes. "I can't ignore it."

"I feel as if we need to..." She toyed with a button on his dress shirt.

"Make love?"

"Set some ground rules."

He tenderly kissed her lips. "Sure. Whatever you want."

"This can't impact our working relationship."

He cradled her chin with his palm, kissing her again. He didn't see how that was possible, but he wasn't about to disagree. "Okay."

"You can't fire me, or promote me, or give me any better or worse treatment because I'm..."

"Completely and totally blowing my mind?"

"Tuck."

"I'm not going to fire you."

"Or promote me."

"Maybe. Probably. I think I pretty much already have. You want a new title?"

"You're not listening."

He kissed her again. "You're very distracting."

She pressed against him, her body molding to his. "We have to get this straight."

"Keep the boardroom out of the bedroom." He wrapped his arms around her, sighing in complete contentment. Up against him, wrapped around him, that was where she belonged. That was where he wanted her to stay.

"Right." She sounded surprised.

"Then, shut up, Amber. We're a long way from the boardroom."

He kissed her and passion roared to life within him.

She kissed him back, coming up on her toes, her arms winding around his neck. He tipped his head to deepen the kiss, pressing the small of her back, arching her body, inserting his thigh between her bare legs.

She groaned his name. Then she went for his belt, his button, his fly, her small hand all but searing him with need.

"Amber, don't." He could feel his control slip away.

"I can't wait," she rasped. "I've waited, and I'm done waiting."

She didn't have to wait.

He reached beneath her dress and stripped off her panties. Then he dropped into a chair, sitting her straight and square in his lap. She loosened his slacks and eased herself down. She was hot and tight, and each inch was a straight shot to paradise.

He bracketed her hips and pushed himself home.

She braced her hands on his shoulders. Her head tipped back. "Oh, yes," she whispered.

"You're amazing," he told her. "Fantastic. Spectacular."

Her nails dug in and her thighs tightened around him. He lost track of time as their pace increased. His world contracted and then disappeared. There was nothing but Amber. He didn't end and she didn't begin. They were fused to one and he needed to hold on to that forever.

She cried out his name and the sound pierced straight through him. Her body contracted and pulsed, and he followed her over the edge in a cascade of heat and sensation. He dropped back on the chair, cradled her face with his hands, pulled her down for a kiss, tasting her, breathing her, feeling life pulse through her, willing the euphoria to last forever.

Then he cradled her close, thinking how perfectly she fit against him.

"Stay," he murmured in her ear. "I want you in my bed. I want you in my arms. The night in Arizona was sheer torture after you left me."

Her chest rose and fell against his, the sound of her deep breaths echoing through the silent room.

"Okay," she finally said.

He drew back. "Okay?"

She nodded.

"Okay," he said, his body relaxing with relief. "Okay."

Amber's ringtone woke her from a sound sleep. She was instantly aware of Tuck's naked body wrapped around her, the faint sandalwood scent of his sheets and the sound of a fan whirring above the big bed. The phone rang again.

She pushed up on her elbow and groped for the bedside table. Tuck groaned and moved beside her. A moment later, the room was flooded with light. Her phone rang a third time as she blinked to adjust her eyes.

"Did you find it?" he asked.

"Yes. It's here." She fumbled with her cell as she answered, clumsy with sleep. "Hello?"

"Amber Bowen?" The woman's voice was crisp.

"Yes. It's me."

"This is Brandy Perkins calling. I'm a nurse at Memorial Hospital."

Amber sat straight up. "Hi, Yes." She had met Brandy a number of times. "Is something wrong?"

"Can you come into Maternity right away?"

"Yes, of course." Amber swung her legs to the side of the bed. "Is Jade all right?"

Tuck sat up beside her.

"Her blood pressure has taken an unexpected spike."

Tuck's hand cradled her bare shoulder, his voice deep and soft. "Something wrong?"

"The baby has gone into distress, and we're performing an emergency C-section."

"I'm on my way." Amber rose from the bed as she ended the call.

Tuck's voice was sharper, more alert. "What's wrong?"

"I need to get to the hospital. It's Jade." Amber tracked down her panties, stepping into them and locating her bra.

He rocked to his feet. "I'll drive you."

"No. That's okay. I've got my car."

"You're upset. You shouldn't drive yourself." He was dressing as he spoke.

"I don't know how long I'll be."

"So what?"

"So I want to take my car."

Her dress on, she headed for the bedroom door. Her shoes were still down in the library. She was pretty sure she remembered the way back.

Tuck followed. "What happened?"

"It's her blood pressure. The baby's in distress and they have to do an emergency Caesarean. I knew there was a chance, but things were looking so good. I didn't expect..."

She knew Jade's condition could be life threatening, for both Jade and the baby. But she hadn't wanted to face that possibility. She'd been too optimistic, too cavalier about the potential danger.

She should have paid more attention to how Jade was feeling. Maybe if she'd spent more time at the hospital instead of throwing a party and sleeping with Tuck. What if she'd left her phone in her purse downstairs and didn't hear it ring? What if the battery had died overnight?

"Jade's already at the hospital?" Tuck asked as they took the stairs.

"She's been there for two weeks."

"Why didn't you say something?"

"Say what?"

Amber's personal life was another thing she was keeping separate. Tuck had barely even met Jade.

"Tell me something that big was going on in your life."

"Why?" She entered the library.

Luckily, the lights were still on, and she quickly located her shoes.

"Oh, I don't know," said Tuck. "Because we see each other every day."

"Only because we work together."

She marched toward the living room. Her car keys were in her purse. She was maybe thirty minutes from the hospital, twenty-five if traffic was light, which it ought to be at 3:00 a.m.

"Right," said Tuck, a strange tone in his voice. "We work together. That's all."

She paused to take in his expression. "I have to go to my sister right now."

"I'll drive you."

"No, you won't. Good night, Tuck."

"It's morning."

She didn't even know how to respond to that. She left through the front door, taking the long driveway past the brick entry pillars and onto the street.

Traffic was blessedly light and she was able to find a good parking spot at the hospital. She rushed through the lobby, going directly to Jade's room. She knew her sister wouldn't be there, but she hoped the nurses could give her some information.

Brandy was at the nurse's station.

"How is she?" Amber asked, realizing she was winded.

"Still in surgery," said Brandy.

Amber didn't like the look on the woman's face. All the way here, she'd been telling herself it was going to be fine. Jade was going to be fine. The baby was going to be fine.

Amber swallowed. "How bad?"

Brandy came around the end of the counter. "She had a seizure."

Amber felt her knees go weak.

Brandy took her arm. "Let's sit down."

"Is she…" Amber couldn't bring herself to ask the question. "What about the baby?"

"They're doing everything they can." Brandy led her toward a sitting area in a small alcove.

"I don't like the sound of that." It was not at all reassuring.

Brandy sat next to her on a narrow vinyl sofa. "The baby is very close to term."

"So she has a fighting chance."

"Very much so," said Brandy.

"And all I can do is wait."

"I know it's hard."

Amber nodded. She was sitting here wondering if her sister and her niece were going to live or die.

"Can I get you something?" asked Brandy. "There's coffee in the corner or water?"

"I'm fine."

"Would you like to freshen up?"

Amber glanced down at her dress and realized how she must look. She hadn't removed her makeup before tumbling into bed with Tuck. It was probably smeared under her eyes. Her hair had to be a fright.

"That bad?" she asked the nurse.

Brandy gave her a smile. "You'll be able to see Jade once she wakes up, not to mention hold the baby. You don't want to scare them."

"Yes," said Amber. "Let's think positively."

A woman in scrubs came through a set of double doors.

Brandy took Amber's hand and Amber's heart sank through the floor.

They rose together.

"Dr. Foster, this is Jade's sister, Amber," said Brandy.

"Jade is weak," the doctor said without preamble. "We had to restart her heart."

Amber's legs nearly gave way.

"She's in recovery," said Dr. Foster. "Her vital signs have stabilized and her blood pressure is under control."

"She'll be all right?" Amber felt the need to confirm.

"We expect her to make a full recovery."

"And the baby?"

The doctor smiled. "The baby is healthy. A girl."

"I have a niece?"

"She's in the nursery. You can see her if you want."

Amber gave a rapid nod, her eyes tearing up. Worry rose up from her shoulders and she felt instantly light.

Eleven

As soon as Amber had left the mansion, Tuck realized he'd been a total jerk. Her sister was having emergency surgery. What did it matter if he and Amber's relationship was up in the air? They could talk about it tomorrow, or the day after that, or the day after that.

She'd made love with him. Then she'd spent the night with him. He'd reveled in holding her naked in his arms, joking and laughing with her. He'd looked forward to breakfast together, mentally filing away another image of her in his family home.

Instead, he'd showered and changed, stopped to pick her up some coffee and a bagel and made his way to the hospital. She had to be exhausted, and distressed, and he was determined to make up for his behavior. She needed his support right now. She didn't need him arguing with her.

It took some time to locate the maternity wing. But once there, he was told visiting hours didn't start until seven and he had to wait in the lobby. He gave in and drank both cups of lukewarm coffee, finally getting on the elevator with the blueberry bagels for Amber.

As he approached the room, he could hear her voice. It was melodic and soothing.

"She's incredible," she was saying.

"Isn't she?" Jade responded, her voice sounding slightly weak.

Tuck paused to brace his hand on the wall, relief rushing through him. He hadn't realized he'd been that worried.

"Thank you," said Jade. "For being here. For helping us."

"Don't be silly," Amber responded. "Of course I'm here, and of course I'm helping."

"You always do."

"She has your eyes," said Amber.

"I thought of a name."

"You did?"

"After you. I'm going to name her Amber."

For some reason, Tuck's chest went tight.

"I don't know," said Amber.

"We owe you so much."

"I'm her aunt. It's my job, and she doesn't owe me a thing. Look at that face, those blue eyes, that tiny nose."

There was a silent pause.

"I think," Amber continued, "that she's her very own little person. She deserves her very own name."

"You think?" asked Jade.

"I'm sure. Thank you. Really, it's a wonderful thought."

There was a pause and Tuck took a step forward.

"What about Crystal?" asked Jade.

"Another rock?" There was a trace of laughter in Amber's voice.

"You're solid as a rock," said Jade.

"So are you," said Amber.

"And she will be, too."

"Crystal. I love it. It's perfect."

Tuck knew he should either walk away or announce himself, but something kept him still and silent.

"Do you think the three of us can become a family?" asked Jade, a catch in her voice. "The way we never were."

"Yes," Amber said softly. "You, me and Crystal. We can do that."

"No creepy boyfriends."

Tuck found he didn't like the sound of that. He wasn't creepy. Then again, he wasn't a boyfriend.

"No unreliable men," Amber stated firmly.

Did she think of him as unreliable? She probably did. She probably thought Dixon was more reliable, which wasn't fair, given the current circumstances.

He gave himself a mental head slap. If he didn't want to keep hearing things he didn't like, he needed to stop eavesdropping.

"She's never going to be frightened," said Jade, as Tuck moved for the door. "Or hungry, or lonely."

"We'll keep her safe."

"I'll get a job," said Jade.

"Not today, you won't."

He knocked softly on the open door. "Hello."

Amber looked up. She was sitting in a chair at the bedside covered in a pale green hospital gown, a pink bundle in her arms. He couldn't see the baby's face, but she had a head of dark hair—a brunette like her aunt.

Jade was propped up in the bed, looking exhausted, her face pale, her hair flattened against her head.

"Tuck." Amber was obviously surprised to see him.

"I wanted to make sure everything was okay." He glanced at the paper bag in his hands, realizing he should have brought flowers or maybe a teddy bear.

"Hi, Tuck," said Jade. She seemed less surprised and gave him a tired smile.

"Congratulations, Jade." He moved to get a better view of the baby. "She's beautiful."

"Isn't she?" asked Jade.

"Are you okay?" he asked, giving in to an urge to squeeze her hand.

"Sore. But I'm going to be fine."

"I'm very glad to hear that."

His attention went back to Amber and the baby. She looked good with a baby in her arms, natural, radiant.

"How did you know I was here?" asked Jade.

Amber's eyes widened.

Tuck paused to see how she'd answer.

She didn't.

"Were you with him last night?" asked Jade.

She was very quick on the uptake for someone who'd just had surgery.

"It was a corporate party," said Tuck.

"We spent the night together," said Amber.

Her answer thrilled him. Yes, they'd spent the night together. And he didn't care who knew it.

"Sorry to interrupt," said Jade, glancing between them.

Tuck grinned with amazement. "You had to have one of the best excuses ever."

Jade chuckled and then groaned with obvious pain.

"I'm sorry," he quickly told her.

"Don't apologize for being funny."

"I didn't mean for it to hurt."

Crystal let out a little cry.

"It does," said Jade. "I hate to whine, but it hurts a lot."

"Do you need me to get the nurse?" he asked.

Crystal wiggled in Amber's arms, emitting a few more subdued cries.

"Maybe you should," said Jade, holding out her arms to take Crystal. "I want to try to feed her again. You should go home," she said to Amber.

"No way."

"Get some rest. Take a shower."

"I don't need to rest."

"Yes, you do."

Amber hesitated.

"I can drop you," said Tuck.

"I have my car." She stood to hand the baby to Jade. "Okay, but I'm coming back."

"I would hope so."

Tuck started for the corridor to find a nurse.

Amber's voice followed him. "Goodbye, sweetheart."

He knew she was talking to the baby, but he loved the word anyway.

He located a nurse and then met Amber in the hallway.

"You look exhausted."

"I am *so* relieved." She pulled off the gown, revealing last night's dress. "Her heart actually stopped."

Tuck automatically reached for Amber, pulling her to him. "How can I help?"

"I'm fine. I was terrified, but I'm fine now."

"Let me take you home."

"There's no need."

"It'll make me feel better. I need to do something useful."

"You're very useful. You signed up four new accounts last night."

"I mean useful to you."

"You're keeping the company afloat, keeping me in a job, helping me pay my bills."

Tuck drew back, a bolt of comprehension lighting up his brain. "Twenty-eight thousand, two hundred and sixty-three dollars."

"Huh?"

"Jade was already in the hospital when you came back. That was the amount on her bill. You asked for a signing bonus. You agreed to help me. You did it all because of her."

He could tell by Amber's expression that he'd hit the nail on the head. Then he wondered what else she'd done because of her sister.

He backed off. "Is that why you're helping me with the company?"

"In part, yes. I need a job right now, Tuck. More than I've ever needed a job in my life."

He loosened his hold on her and drew back. "And the rest?"

Her expression narrowed. "The rest is the rest." She didn't elaborate and he didn't jump in. "I hope you're not asking if I slept with you to protect my job and support my sister."

He was. No, he wasn't. He wasn't, but he couldn't help but worry that her behavior with him was laced with complexities.

"Don't worry about it," she said.

"Don't worry about *what*?"

"I'm going home to change." She glanced down at her dress. "I look ridiculous. I'll see you at the office tomorrow."

She tossed the hospital gown in a nearby bin and turned for the elevators.

He wanted to call her back. He needed to understand where she was coming from, what she was feeling for him, what last night had meant to her. But he couldn't let himself be selfish again. She'd had a rough night. Jade needed her. And Tuck was simply going to have to wait to find out where he stood among everything else in Amber's life.

They might have spent the night together…well, half the night together. But everything Amber knew about Tuck remained true. No matter how tempting it was to let him drive her home and comfort her, she couldn't let herself pretend they were in a relationship. He was her boss, not her boyfriend. At best, they were having a fling. At worst, she was a two-night stand.

She had Jade and she had her new niece, Crystal. They were her family, her personal life, her emotional support. It wasn't Tuck.

In the office Monday morning, she steeled herself to see him. She dropped her purse into her desk drawer and plunked down on her chair. She told herself they'd worked the party together like a practiced team, picking up on each other's cues, making clients laugh and agree and, most important, closing the deal.

That had to be enough. It was *going* to be enough. She scrunched her eyes shut and gritted her teeth. She wasn't going to allow herself to want more.

"Good morning, Amber." Dixon's voice nearly startled her out of her chair.

"Dixon?" she squeaked, her eyes popping open.

He looked tanned and toned and totally relaxed.

"I'm back," he said simply.

"Where? How?"

Dixon wasn't the hugging type, so she didn't jump up to embrace him.

His smile faded. "I heard about my dad. I flew straight to Boston yesterday and then I came here."

"Welcome back." She was happy to see him.

She told herself it was an enormous relief to have him here. Things could get back to normal now. She could stop juggling so many problems and Tuck—

She swallowed. Tuck could get back to normal, too.

"He in there?" Dixon cocked his head to Tuck's closed office door.

"I think so."

"Great." Dixon's intelligent gaze took in the clutter on her desk. "Looks as if you're busy."

"It's been busy," she agreed.

"But you'll move back to my office?"

"Of course I will. Right away."

"Good."

"How was your trip?"

"Enlightening."

"You feel better? You look better."

"I feel better than ever. I can't wait to get back to it."

"Great. That's great."

Tucker Transportation would be in experienced hands once again.

Just then, Tuck's office door opened. He appeared in the doorway and instantly spotted Dixon.

From behind her desk, Amber could feel Tuck's shock. His expression seemed to register disappointment. But then it quickly went to neutral.

"Dixon." Tuck's tone was neutral, too.

"Tuck," Dixon answered evenly.

"You're back."

"You're about the twenty-fifth person to say that."

Tuck glanced at Amber.

"I said it, too," she said into what felt like an awkward silence.

"You know about Dad?" Tuck asked.

Neither man moved toward the other, and she was struck by the wariness of their attitudes. Dixon had to be wondering if Tuck was angry. She couldn't tell what Tuck was thinking.

"I saw him yesterday," said Dixon.

"But you didn't call? Didn't think to give me a heads-up?"

It was Dixon's turn to glance at Amber and then at Tuck. "Should we step inside your office?"

Tuck crossed his arms over his chest. "I don't know why. You seem to like to keep Amber more informed than you keep your own brother."

Dixon seemed taken aback.

"She didn't give you away," said Tuck, finally taking a step forward.

Amber found herself glancing anxiously down the hall, worried that other staff might overhear their argument.

"I fired her," said Tuck. "And she still wouldn't tell me your secrets."

Now Dixon looked confused.

"Where you were," Tuck elaborated. "Where'd you go?"

"*Why* would you fire Amber?"

"Insubordination."

"No way."

"To me, not you."

Amber couldn't stand it any longer. "Tuck, please."

Tuck gave a cold smile. "The loyalty's returned just like that." He snapped his fingers. "I guess it never really went away."

"Amber's as loyal as they come," said Dixon.

She moved from behind her desk. "I'm going to let you two talk." She nodded at Dixon. "Maybe an office or the boardroom?"

"Good suggestion."

"She's full of them," said Tuck.

"Has he been treating you like a jerk?" Dixon's question was for Amber, but he stared at Tuck as he asked it.

Amber met Tuck's gaze. "Not at all."

Tuck stared back. "Except when I fired her."

Dixon seemed to pick up on the tension between them. "How'd you get her back?"

"Money," said Tuck.

"A signing bonus," said Amber.

Dixon grinned at that. "Well, there's no doubt she's worth it. If she'd been permanently gone, you'd be answering to me."

Tuck's jaw tightened. "As opposed to you explaining *to me* where the hell you've been for two months?"

"I suppose I owe you that."

Amber moved again, determined to leave. "You have a ten o'clock with Lucas," she told Tuck.

"Maybe," he responded.

What did that mean? Was he heading out the door before 10:00 a.m.? Now that Dixon was in the office, would Tuck simply walk out?

Good.

Great.

It really didn't matter to her either way.

With the two men sizing each other up, she quickly made her way down the hall. She'd set herself up outside Dixon's office once again. Tuck could come and say goodbye or not. It was entirely up to him.

Tuck stared at his brother across the table in the meeting room.

"I told him I needed to get away," said Dixon. "He wouldn't listen."

"I heard." Tuck didn't see any point in hiding anything. "I overheard the two of you talking in the library. I heard what he said about me as a vice president."

"Were you surprised?"

Tuck hadn't been surprised. But he had been disappointed.

"Nobody wants their father to have such a low opinion of them."

"We're talking about Jamison Tucker."

"He likes you just fine."

"Yeah," Dixon scoffed. "Well, we all know why that is."

"Because you're the anointed one."

"I mean the other."

"What other?"

Dixon stared at him in silence and obvious confusion.

"I have no idea what you're talking about," said Tuck.

"The affair."

"With Margaret?"

Dixon drew back. "Who's having an affair with Margaret?"

"Dad."

"What?" Dixon was clearly shocked. "What on earth makes you say that?"

"Because it's true. Margaret gave it away to Amber."

"It's not like Amber to gossip."

"She wasn't gossiping. Wake up, man. Do you know what you've got in Amber? The woman will practically take a bullet for you. She has more character than you can imagine."

Dixon's intelligent eyes sized him up. "Got to know her pretty well while I was gone?"

Tuck was not about to give away anything that might embarrass Amber. "Got very frustrated with her at one point." Then his mind jumped back in the conversation. "What affair were *you* talking about?"

"Mom's."

"Whoa. No way."

"You knew about it."

Tuck knew no such thing. "Who thinks Mom had an affair?"

"Dad."

"What? When? And he's living in a glass house, by the way."

"Three decades ago."

"Clearly that's relevant." Tuck knew their father's affair had gone on right up to his heart attack.

Dixon carefully enunciated his next words. "Thirty years ago. In the months *before* you were born."

Everything inside Tuck went still. "Are you saying?"

"How do you not remember that huge fight we overheard?"

"Are you saying I'm not Jamison's son?"

"You are his son. He did a DNA test years ago."

"Then, how is that the thing? Why would it make him hate me?"

"He doesn't hate you."

"He has no use for me."

"My theory," said Dixon, "is that he looks at you and remembers you could have belonged to someone else."

"That's really messed up."

Dixon scoffed out a cold laugh. "Up to now, you thought we were a normal, functional family?"

Tuck came to his feet as everything became clear. He'd never had a chance. He'd been fighting for something he couldn't possibly win. He had to get out of here, leave the company, maybe leave the city. Maybe he'd leave the state and the money behind and find his own life and career.

There was a brisk knock on the door before it opened to reveal Lucas.

Lucas didn't miss a beat when he saw Dixon. "You're back."

"I'm back."

"Good. Tuck, Gena wants to join us at ten."

"Who's Gena?" asked Dixon.

"Our new finance director."

"Why do we have a new finance director?"

"Harvey quit," said Tuck.

"Why?"

"He missed you."

"What did you do?" Dixon's tone was decidedly accusatory.

"Nothing," said Tuck, heading for the door. "Hasn't that always been the problem?"

"I'll try to get him back," said Dixon.

Tuck halted, a flash of anger hitting him. Dixon intended to reward Harvey for his disloyalty?

Tuck opened his mouth to protest, then decided not to waste his breath. Dixon was back. Tuck's father was never, *ever* going to accept him. And what Tuck liked or didn't like no longer had any relevance.

"Whatever," he said without turning. To Lucas he said, "Dixon can take the ten o'clock."

Twenty paces down the hall, he came to Amber at her old desk outside Dixon's office. She was setting out her things, settling in.

"So that's that?" he asked, struggling to come to terms with his life turning so suddenly and irrevocably upside down.

"My boss is back." She didn't pretend not to understand.

"You bailed quick enough."

"He asked me to move here."

"And what Dixon wants—"

Amber glared at Tuck.

He wanted to tell her she couldn't, that she should march back to her desk at his office to work with him, not with Dixon. He wished he had the right. He wished he had the power. Against all reason and logic, he wished his brother had never come home.

"What about you?" she asked, adjusting the angle of her computer screen.

Unlike her, he did pretend to misunderstand. "My office has been in the same place for years."

"And what are you going to do in it now?"

"Nothing."

He could take a hint. Well, maybe he couldn't take a hint. But he could understand the bald truth when it was thrown up in his face. He wasn't wanted here. And there was nothing he could do to change it. He might as well have been born to a different father.

Two months ago, it probably wouldn't have mattered. But

it mattered now. Maybe it was pride. Or maybe he liked the sense of independence and accomplishment. Or maybe he just liked Amber.

He was going to miss her.

He wasn't sure he could leave her.

"You're walking away," she said.

"I am." He had to stifle the urge to explain.

He knew she understood dysfunctional families, and he knew she'd understand what he was going through. But he couldn't presume they had a personal relationship. She'd made that clear enough at the hospital yesterday morning. She was his brother's assistant, and that was all.

"I won't be your boss anymore," he said, determined to give it one last shot.

"We both knew that would happen."

That wasn't a hint one way or the other. She wasn't giving him any help here.

"We could," he said. "You know…"

She raised her brows and looked him in the eyes.

"Date," he finally said, wondering what the heck had happened to his suave, sophisticated style.

"Each other?"

Okay, now he was just getting frustrated. "*Yes*, each other."

"Is that a good idea?"

"I'm suggesting it, aren't I?"

"You're free now, Tuck. And you're practically running for the front door. And that's fine. I understand. You never said or did a thing to suggest otherwise. And you don't need to now. Dixon's here. You have your life back."

Tuck stared at her in silence.

That was how she saw him? Well, at least he knew the truth. Even after all they'd done together, how hard they'd worked to save clients and accounts, she thought he'd only been biding his time until he could go back to the party circuit.

"I'm free," he agreed between gritted teeth.

"Then, no reason to linger."

He stared hard into her eyes. "No reason at all."

Unless he counted how he felt about her, how much he wanted to be with her, how hard he wished she'd see something in him besides an irresponsible playboy.

"I'm going to be busy with Dixon," she said airily. "And with Jade, and with Crystal."

"I'm going to be busy getting my name back in the tabloids." As he said it, he willed her to call his bluff.

She didn't even hesitate. "Good luck with that."

"Thanks."

There was nothing left to say. But the last thing he wanted to do was leave.

He wanted to hug her. He wanted to kiss her. At the very least, he wanted to thank her for the help and for the amazing memories.

Instead, he left without a word.

Twelve

Amber missed Tuck, and the hurt was beyond anything she could have imagined. Each day she arrived at the office and promised herself it would be better. She'd think about him less, stop imagining his voice, stop thinking every set of footsteps in the hallway might be his. She was going to get past it.

Jade was home from the hospital and Crystal was adorable. Though the baby wasn't the best sleeper in the world. Amber told herself that living in a state of mild sleep deprivation had to be contributing to her depression. Surely, one man couldn't be the cause of all this.

Dixon had slipped right into the familiarity of his old job. He was definitely in a more upbeat mood, but he was just as efficient as always, no matter what the crisis.

It was coming up on eleven and the phone had been ringing almost constantly. There was a storm in the Atlantic and a major rock slide across one of the main rail lines between Denver and Salt Lake City. Everybody was rerouting and rescheduling.

"The Blue Space file?" Dixon called through the open door of his office.

Amber knew the Blue Space file was in Tuck's office. She'd been avoiding going in there, worried about triggering memories. Not that anything specific had ever happened in his office. They hadn't kissed and they certainly hadn't made love there. Thank goodness, at least, for that.

"I'll get it," she called back.

"They're phoning right after lunch," said Dixon.

"On my way."

She took a bracing breath and stood. She was going to do

this. In fact, she wanted to do this. Maybe it would be a turning point. Maybe she'd built it up to be something it wasn't. She could probably walk in there, get the file, walk back out and realize it was just another room.

She headed down the hall.

Tuck's office door was closed. But she refused to slow down. She reached out, turned the knob, thrust the door open and walked inside.

There, she stopped, gasping a breath, picking up his scent, her brain assailed by memories. Tuck laughing. Tuck scowling. His brows knitted together in concentration.

She could hear his voice, feel his touch and imagine his kiss.

"Amber?" Dixon's voice startled her.

"I'm sure it was on the desk," she said, pushing herself forward.

There was a stack of files on the corner of the desktop and she began looking through them.

"I'm meeting Zachary for lunch," said Dixon.

"Zachary who?" She tried to remember if there was a Zachary connected with Blue Space.

"Zachary Ingles."

She looked up. "Why?"

Dixon moved closer. "I'm trying to get him to come back."

"Why would you do that?"

"Because he's good. And he took a bunch of accounts with him when he left."

"There's nothing good about that."

She'd never liked Zachary. She didn't trust him and she'd been glad to see him leave. The new guy, Samuel Leeds, was much more professional. He was young, but he seemed to be learning fast.

Dixon chuckled. "I know Zachary's not the warmest guy in the world."

Amber continued sorting. It wasn't her place to criticize, and she didn't want to insult Dixon.

"Samuel's a bit too laid-back," said Dixon. "He's inexperienced. A director position isn't the place to learn the ropes."

"He's enthusiastic," said Amber.

"A little too enthusiastic."

Dixon had said the same thing about Gena, the new finance director. He hadn't replaced her yet, but Amber knew he'd been in contact with Harvey.

"Are you going to undo everything Tuck did?" As soon as she asked, Amber immediately regretted the question.

"You mean, am I going to undo the damage?"

She practically had to bite her tongue.

"It must have been bedlam around here." Dixon crossed his arms over his chest.

"Who says that?"

"Harvey, for one."

"Consider the source."

Dixon didn't respond and Amber realized she'd gone too far.

"What did that mean?" asked Dixon, a clear rebuke in his tone.

Amber straightened and squared her shoulders. She was loyal to Tucker Transportation and she'd been appropriately loyal to Dixon. She now found herself feeling some of that loyalty toward Tuck.

"Tuck worked hard," she said.

"I've no doubt that he did."

"He not only worked hard—he succeeded. Yes, Harvey and Zachary bailed. But you should ask yourself what that says about them."

"They couldn't work with Tuck."

"Or they *wouldn't* work with Tuck. Zachary stole your clients. He *stole* them. He was disrespectful to Tuck. He was disloyal to you. He was downright dishonest. And, by the way, he hits on your female employees. Tuck, on the other hand, came in here without the first idea of what to do. He could have bailed. He could have turned and run the other way. But he didn't. He dug in. Even knowing what your father thought of him, and how he'd been treated in the past, and how overwhelming the learning curve turned out to be, he stuck it out. Did you thank him? Did your dad thank him? Did anyone thank him?"

"We paid him."

"He didn't do it for the money. And he didn't do it to save the company. He has pride, Dixon. He had purpose. We won back half the clients and we signed up some more. He worked eighteen-hour days, threw his heart and soul into making sure the company didn't fail while you were off sailing. He hunted far and wide to get Gena and Samuel. Yes, they're both young. But they're well educated. They have some experience. And they're bringing new energy to the company. And that's thanks to Tuck, who was thrown in here without a lifeline."

Amber stopped talking. As she did, the magnitude of her outburst hit her.

"Amber?" Dixon began, clearly baffled by her behavior.

She was instantly overcome with regret. She knew she was about to get fired by the third Tucker Transportation owner. It was going to be a clean sweep.

"Yes," she said in a small voice.

"Did something happen between you and Tuck?"

She ignored the personal implication of the question. "I got to know him." It was an honest answer.

"You got to know him well?" Dixon was watching her carefully.

"Better than before. When he first showed up, I thought the same thing you obviously do—that he was a lazy playboy who was going to fall flat on his face and wouldn't even know it when he did. I wouldn't even help him. I mean, I helped him, of course. But I wasn't going the extra mile like I might have been. But then I saw how hard he worked. He truly was dedicated. And I started to understand that he hadn't chosen to stay away—your father had barred him entry."

"He has an office," said Dixon.

"That's what I said. And he does. But nobody wants him. He understands that full well."

"Amber?"

"What?"

Her fear was gone. Whatever was going to happen was going to happen. But she wasn't about to turn her back on Tuck. He'd worked hard and she wouldn't pretend that he hadn't, even to please Dixon.

"That wasn't my question."

She hesitated. "I know."

"What happened between the two of you?"

"Nothing."

Dixon waited, looking unconvinced.

"Okay, something," she said. "But it's over and done."

Silence settled thick in the air, but she refused to break it. She'd already said too much.

Dixon went first. "Are you in love with Tuck?"

She felt the world shift beneath her feet. "No."

She couldn't be. She wouldn't be. She'd made mistakes with Tuck, but she wouldn't make that one.

"I'm sorry," said Dixon.

"For what?" Was she about to be fired after all?

"That Tuck hurt you."

"He didn't hurt me."

And if he had, she'd get over it. She'd seen what falling for the wrong man could do, *would* do. She wasn't going to do that to herself.

Dixon gave a considered nod. "Okay. Tell me what else you know about Samuel."

"Why?"

"Because you just made an impassioned plea on his behalf. Do you want to drop the ball now?"

She didn't. "He works well with Hope. And I respect Hope. She has her finger on the pulse of social media."

"You think we need social media?"

"That's like asking if you need telephones or computers.

Yes, you need social media. Your father might not have seen it, but you need to think about the next twenty years, not the past twenty years."

"I'll give it some thought," he said.

She couldn't quite let it go. "*It* meaning social media, or keeping Samuel?"

Dixon coughed out a chuckle. "You know, Tuck went to great lengths to impress upon me how loyal you were to me. But what I'm seeing right now is how loyal you are to him."

"I'm not loyal to Tuck."

"Okay."

"I'm only being fair to him."

"Then, I'll be fair to you."

She swallowed. "You won't fire me?"

Dixon looked puzzled. "Fire you for what?"

"Insubordination."

"Is that a euphemism for offering your opinion?"

"In this case, it means offering my opinion forcefully and without provocation."

"That's not what I meant, but you're not fired, Amber. I'd hire fifty of you if I could."

She handed him the Blue Space file. "That was a nice thing to say."

"I'm hoping to win back your loyalty."

"You never lost it."

He glanced around the office. "Then, I can't help but wonder what exactly it was that Tuck gained."

She was about to say *nothing*, but Dixon turned and left her alone.

She stood for a moment, holding the atmosphere, remembering every little thing about Tuck until her heart throbbed and her chest ached, and she felt silent and alone and empty.

Tuck stared at his silent cell phone for a full minute before he slid it back inside his pocket. He was dressed to the nines, had a reservation at the Seaside, followed by tickets to a popular live comedy show, and he planned to end the evening at the Hollingsworth Lounge.

MaryAnn was a great date—bright, bubbly, lots of fun. But Tuck simply didn't have it in him right now. He didn't want to romance MaryAnn or anyone else. He didn't want to dine with them, dance with them or even sleep with them.

He was on the rebound from Amber. He got that, even though they'd barely dated. But the rebound had never hit him like this before.

The front door of the mansion opened and Dixon entered the foyer, doing a double take at the sight of Tuck.

"Hot date?" Dixon asked.

"Just got canceled."

"She get a better offer?"

"Something like that." Tuck wasn't about to tell Dixon that he was the one who'd canceled the date. He'd used a lame excuse of having a headache. As if a normal guy would give up a night with MaryAnn over a headache.

Trouble was, most normal guys hadn't fallen for Amber.

"Are you staying in?" asked Dixon.

"Might as well." Tuck loosened his tie.

"Drink?"

"Sure." Tuck followed his brother into the library.

He purposely sat down across from the chair where Amber had sat in her bare feet and sparkling dress. Then he smiled wistfully at the memory. She was so incredibly sexy with those luscious lips, simmering eyes, smooth shoulders and toned legs. He shifted in his chair.

Dixon handed him a crystal glass with two ice cubes and a shot of single malt. "What?"

"Nothing," said Tuck.

"You're smiling."

"I'm not sorry about the date." Tuck took a drink.

"That's an odd reaction." Dixon sat down.

Tuck gave a noncommittal shrug.

"I was talking to Zachary today," said Dixon.

"Why would you do that?" Tuck wouldn't have given the man the time of day.

"He's interested in coming back."

Tuck didn't bother responding. Dixon knew how he felt about Zachary.

Dixon seemed to give him a moment. "You got any thoughts on that?"

In response, Tuck scoffed. "You don't want to hear my thoughts on that."

"You don't think we should take him back?"

"I think we should drop him off the Michigan Avenue Bridge."

Dixon cracked a smile. "Let's call that plan B."

"Let's." Tuck drank again, pulling for plan B.

"Amber doesn't like him," said Dixon.

"Amber's not stupid."

"No, she's not."

Her image appeared once more in the chair across from Tuck.

"You're smiling again," said Dixon.

"Did she tell you her sister had a baby?"

"When did that happen?"

"Two weeks ago. Just before you got back."

"Is her sister in Chicago?"

Tuck nodded. "She is now." He found himself glancing around the library. "You ever give much thought to the way we grew up?"

"You mean with a controlling father and a distant mother?"

"I mean with gold-plated bathroom faucets."

"The faucets aren't gold-plated," said Dixon. "Though I'm honestly not sure about the dining room chandelier."

"We never worried about having enough to eat. Heck, we never worried about running low on gourmet ice cream."

"Rich people still have problems."

"I know that," said Tuck. "They never would buy me a pony."

He knew Amber's childhood challenges had been on a whole other level. Whenever he thought about that, it left him feeling petty.

"How about the fact that your father thought you were illegitimate?"

Tuck had given that revelation a lot of thought these past few days. It didn't change anything, but it did boost his confidence. He hadn't earned his father's disdain. It had been there all along.

"You said I knew," he said to Dixon. "Why did you think I knew?"

"Because of that night when we overheard."

"What night?"

"In the sitting room, listening at the air vent."

"We did that all the time."

Many nights, after their nanny had put them to bed, they'd sneak out of their room and listen to conversations going on downstairs. Usually they'd do it during parties, but they'd listened in on plenty of their parents' conversations, as well.

"They had a huge shouting match," said Dixon. "Dad accused her of fooling around. She denied it at first, but then admitted it. He said you had someone named Robert's hair and eyes."

Tuck sifted through his brain, but that particular fight didn't stand out. "I don't remember."

"You don't remember learning you might have a different father?"

"I must not have understood. How old was I?"

"Young," Dixon answered thoughtfully. "I said 'wow,' and you said 'wow' back. And I thought you got the meaning."

"I can only guess it went right over my head."

"Wow," said Dixon.

"I'm not going back to the way things were," said Tuck.

For some reason, the path forward crystalized inside his mind.

"Our father can like it or not," he continued. "But it's my company, too. I'm every bit as much his son as you are. I'm not going to be some token partner afraid of voicing my opinion. I'm going to fight you. I'm going to fight hard for what I know is right. Zachary is gone. He stays gone. Harvey, too. Amber..." He hadn't thought his way through what to do about Amber.

"Amber's great," said Dixon.

Tuck looked up sharply. He didn't like the tone of his brother's voice, and he didn't like the expression on Dixon's face. "You stay away from Amber."

"I will not. She's my assistant."

"And that's *all* she is."

"That's far from all she is."

Tuck found himself coming to his feet. "You better explain that statement."

"Explain it how?"

Tuck's voice rose. "What else is she? What is Amber to you? She won't date her boss. She can't date her boss. She would be supremely stupid to date her boss."

"Why?"

"Because it'll end badly for her. That sort of thing always does."

"So you didn't date her?"

"*No*, I didn't date her." Tuck would have dated her. But she'd said no. And she was right to say no.

"And you didn't sleep with her."

"What?" Tuck glared at his brother.

"You're acting pretty jealous for a guy who never dated her."

"I care about her, okay? Sure, I care about her. She's a nice woman. She's a fantastic woman. She's been through a lot, and now she's taking care of her sister. She does that. She takes care of people. She didn't like me, but she helped me anyway. And the whole time you were gone, she had *nothing* but your best interests at heart."

"She's loyal," said Dixon. "You've said that before."

"She is, to her detriment at times."

"Well, for a woman who's supposedly incredibly loyal to me, she sure talks a lot about you."

The statement took Tuck aback. "She does?"

"Almost as much as you talk about her."

"I don't—"

"Give it up, Tuck. You're obsessed with her."

"I like her. What's not to like?"

"You think she's pretty?"

Tuck could barely believe the stupidity of the question. "That's obvious to anybody with a set of eyes."

"You think she's hot?"

"Have you seen her shoes?"

"What shoes?"

"The… You know." Tuck pointed to his feet. "The straps and the heels and the rhinestones and things."

"Never noticed."

"There's something wrong with you, man."

"Why didn't you date her?" Dixon asked.

"Because I was her boss."

"Afterward—now—why don't you ask her out?"

Tuck sat back down and reached for the bottle on the table between them. He took off the cap and poured himself another drink.

"I did," he admitted. "She said no."

Dixon cocked his head. "Did she understand the question?"

"Yes, she understood the question."

"Did she give you a reason?"

"She doesn't trust me. She's got it in her head that I'm still an irresponsible playboy. She doesn't think she can count on me."

Tuck knew why she would feel that way. He also knew she deserved to feel that way. But she was wrong. If she'd give him half a chance, she'd find out she could count on him.

"So that's it? You're not going to fight?"

"How do I fight something like that?"

"How do you fight Dad? How do you fight his perception of you?"

"By standing up for myself. By taking my rightful place in this family."

Dixon cracked a smile. "And?" It was obvious he thought he had Tuck cornered.

"It's not the same thing. I have no rights to Amber at all."

"You do if she's in love with you."

"She's not—" Tuck froze. He gaped at his brother. "What makes you say that?"

"I asked her."

Tuck moved his jaw, struggling to voice the question, terrified to voice the question. "Did she say yes?"

"She said no."

Everything inside Tuck went flat. In that second, he realized he'd held out hope. He'd known it was impossible, but he couldn't seem to stop himself from dreaming.

"But she was lying," said Dixon.

Tuck blinked in bafflement.

"She's in love with you, bro."

"That can't be." Tuck didn't dare hope.

"I'm not saying she's smart or right. I'm just saying she is."

A million thoughts exploded inside Tuck's head. Was it possible? Should he give it another shot? Should he not take her refusal at face value?

"You need to fight," said Dixon. "You're tough, and you're smart and you know what you deserve. Fight Dad, fight Amber if she's being stubborn. Hell, fight me if you think I'm wrong."

Tuck tried but failed to temper his hope. "You are wrong. You're wrong about a lot of things."

"Then, fight me."

"But I hope you're right about this."

"You love her?"

"Yes," said Tuck, knowing it was completely and irrevocably true. He was in love with Amber and he was going to fight for her with everything he had.

Amber rocked Crystal in her arms while Jade worked on an English essay on her laptop. She told herself they were a family now. She had her job back, and the future was bright. Little Crystal was perfect, and she was going to grow up safe and happy, knowing she had a devoted mom and aunt to care for her.

Her gaze strayed to a glossy magazine on the coffee table. *Chicago About Town*. Jade had brought it home with the groceries. There was an inset photo on the bottom left, Tuck with a beautiful blonde woman. She didn't know who it was and it was impossible to know when the photo was taken. But Amber was jealous.

Tuck was back to his old life, while Dixon's words kept echoing inside her head. *Are you in love with Tuck?*

How could she have fallen in love with Tuck? How could she have been so foolish? She had so much going for her right now. Jade was working hard. She was going to pass her equivalency test. She was going to be a great mom.

Amber kissed the soft top of Crystal's head. The future was blindingly optimistic. All she had to do was get Tuck out of her head.

Her chest tightened and her throat seemed to clog.

"Amber?" Jade asked softly.

Amber swallowed. "Yes?"

"What's wrong?"

"Nothing."

Jade rose from her chair. "Is it too much?"

It was. It was far too much. Amber didn't know if she'd be able to get over him. She didn't want to keep fighting her feelings.

"Me and Crystal?" Jade continued. "Are we too much work?"

"What? No. No, honey. It's not you."

"You look so sad."

"I'm just tired."

"No, you're sad."

"I miss him," Amber admitted.

"Tuck?"

"How can I miss him? I know who he is. I know where it was going. But I couldn't seem to talk myself out of it."

Jade moved toward her, sympathy in her expression. "I know how you feel."

"Does it go away?"

A knock sounded on the door.

"Eventually, your head will overtake your heart," said Jade. "Though it can take a while."

Amber didn't like the sound of that. Her head was stronger than her heart, always. It was what had kept her safe and sane all these years. How could it be failing her now?

The knock sounded again and Jade brushed Amber's shoulder on the way to answer it.

Amber hugged her niece tight.

"I'm looking for Amber." Tuck's voice made Amber sit up straight. "Is she home?"

A buzzing started in the center of her brain, radiating to her chest then along her limbs. What was he doing here?

"What do you want?" asked Jade.

"To talk to her."

"Is it about work?"

"Yes."

Amber came slowly to her feet, careful not to disturb Crystal.

"It's okay," she said to Jade.

Jade sighed and opened the door wider.

Amber came forward. "Tuck?"

Jade gathered Crystal from her arms while Tuck smiled at the baby.

"She's beautiful," he said.

"What do you want?" Amber asked.

Tuck met her gaze. "I'm coming to work on Monday."

The words surprised her.

"Dixon's contemplating bringing Zachary back," said Tuck.

"He told me that, too," said Amber.

"It's a bad idea."

"I agree."

Tuck glanced behind her. "You mind if I come in?"

She hesitated, but she didn't want to be rude. "Okay."

"Did you tell him that's what you thought?" Tuck asked as she shut the door behind them.

"I did. Then I was afraid he might fire me."

"Dixon's not going to fire you."

"He didn't." But she'd made a mental note to keep her opinions to herself. She had grown used to being frank with Tuck, but her relationship with Dixon had always been more formal. She had to respect that.

Cooing to Crystal, Jade made her way down the hall, obviously deciding to give them some privacy.

"Are you planning to stop him?" Amber asked. "From rehiring Zachary."

"I'm going to try," said Tuck, moving to the middle of the room. "I'm going back, and I'm going to fight for what I want."

She was puzzled. "Why?"

"Because it's my company, too."

"It's a lot of work."

Right now, as he had in the past, Tuck had the best of all possible worlds.

"It is," he agreed.

"You don't need to do it."

"I disagree with that. Tucker Transportation can't run itself."

"But Dixon—"

"Dixon doesn't know everything."

"He knows a lot."

Tuck frowned. "What do you think of my brother?"

The question struck her as odd. "You know what I think of your brother. We spent weeks discussing what I thought of your brother."

"We spent weeks trying to keep our hands off each other."

Amber couldn't believe she'd heard right.

"Let me put that another way," he said.

"Good idea."

"What do you think of me?"

"Right this moment?"

"Right this moment."

Amber reached down and lifted the magazine, putting the cover in front of his face, reminding herself of exactly who he was.

"What?" He squinted.

"I think you're exactly what you seem."

"That's Kaitlyn."

"Nice that you remember her name."

"That's from last year. At the charity thing. The one for the animals. Pets, not the zoo."

"The humane society?"

"Yes."

"Did you have a nice time?"

"Why are you asking? What difference does that make now?"

"Because it's on the cover of a magazine."

He stared at her for a long moment. "I'm not dating anyone, Amber."

"I don't care."

But she was lying. She did care. She couldn't stand the thought of him with another woman. She wanted him for herself and she didn't know how to stop wanting that.

"You should care," he said. "You better care."

"I don't—"

"I asked you what you thought of me."

"And I told you."

He snapped the magazine from her hands and tossed it on the table. "Use words."

Her brain stumbled around. With him standing so close, she found she couldn't lie. "You're not good for me."

"Why not?"

"Don't do this, Tuck."

"Why not?"

"You know I'm attracted to you. You know we have chemistry. But we can't go there again."

"Why not?"

"Why *not*?" she all but shouted.

Why was he determined to make her say it?

"That's what I asked," he said.

"Because it's not enough."

"What would be enough?"

"Stop. Just stop." She wanted him to go away. Her heart was already shredded and he was making it worse.

"Me loving you?" he asked. "Would that be enough?"

His words penetrated and her brain screeched to a halt.

"Would it, Amber?" he asked. "Because I do. I love you. I'm *in* love with you. I want to work with you. I want to date you. I think I even want to marry you. Scratch that. I *know* I want to marry you. Now I'm asking again. What do you think of me?"

She worked her jaw, but no sound came out. "I…uh…"

He cocked his head. "I'm really not sure how to take that."

"You love me?" She couldn't wrap her head around it.

"I love you." He reached out and took her hands in his. "But I'm going to have to insist you answer the question. I swear, Amber, I don't know whether to kiss you or slink out the door."

"Kiss me," she said, joy blooming in her chest.

Tuck's face broke into a broad smile.

"I love you, Tuck. Kiss me, please."

He didn't wait another second. He kissed her deeply, wrapping his arms around her, drawing her close against his body.

"I'll be there for you," he whispered in her ear. "I promise I'll be there for you and for Crystal and for Jade. I'll protect you and fight for you. You can count on me now and forever."

"This doesn't seem real." She let the warmth of his body flow into hers.

"It's real, sweetheart. And it's definitely forever."

* * * * *

TAMING HER BILLIONAIRE BOSS

MAXINE SULLIVAN

With thanks to the fabulous Desire editors, Krista Stroever and Charles Griemsman, who worked so hard to make this series special.

And to friend and American author, C.C. Coburn, for her helpful advice on everything Aspen

One

"What are you doing in here?"

Samantha Thompson almost dropped her pen as her head snapped up, the desk lamp shedding enough light for her to see the handsome man standing in the doorway. "Blake, you scared me!"

Her heart didn't settle down once she knew who it was, it only increased pace as she looked at him in a dinner suit that fitted his well-toned body flawlessly. His commanding presence was of a man born to lead. This was Blake Jarrod, owner of Blake Jarrod Enterprises' Las Vegas hotels, and now the new CEO of Jarrod Ridge, his family's renowned resort in Aspen, Colorado.

And as his assistant of two years there was nothing unusual about her being in his office at ten at night. Just because they were now in Aspen at the Jarrod Manor and she was using the desk in his late father's office didn't change a thing. She had her reasons for being here.

And they concerned her boss.

Or soon-to-be-ex boss.

"It's late," he said, cutting across her thoughts in the way he usually did.

She took a steadying breath and looked down at the letter in front of her, giving herself one last chance to change her mind. Then she remembered this evening. The final straw had been watching a famous blonde actress flirt outrageously with Blake, and him sitting there enjoying it, taking it as his due.

Samantha couldn't blame him for wanting to sample what was on offer if he so chose. It was just that *she* wanted a little taste of him herself. She usually dressed sedately in finely tailored clothes whether she was in Vegas with Blake or here in Aspen, but tonight she'd outdone herself. She'd worn this slinky cream evening dress designed to grab his attention, putting her long, brunette hair up in a chignon when she usually wore it pulled back at the nape with a barrette, but it was clear now that nothing was going to happen between her and Blake.

It was *never* going to happen.

She'd realized that when he'd caught her eye and she'd smiled for all she was worth, looked the best she could be, and he'd turned back to the actress without a second glance, rejecting her just like Carl had rejected her. Her moment of epiphany had been that simple. She'd come to a decision then. The right decision for her. The *only* one for her.

She lifted her gaze. "Yes, it's late, Blake."

Too late.

He walked toward the desk, almost as if he sensed

something wasn't quite right. "I thought you said you were going back to Pine Lodge."

That had been her intention. She'd even stood in the lobby of the manor, her coat resting on her shoulders, waiting beside the doorman for the valet to bring the SUV around. She'd been determined to go back to their private lodge at the resort—she in her own room and Blake in the master suite.

Then someone had entered the hotel and the doors had slid open, and the cold night breeze from a midfall wind had slapped her in the face and chilled her to the bone, reminding her that it didn't matter what she wore or what she did, her boss would never take any notice of her except as his assistant. She'd spun around and headed for the private elevator, coming up here to the office in the family section of the manor.

"I needed to do something first," she said now.

There was an alert look to his eyes. "It's Friday night. Work can wait until tomorrow."

They'd been working every Saturday, trying to keep on top of things until they moved here permanently. And now that wasn't going to happen. Not for her anyway. "This can't wait."

He paused, those blue eyes narrowing in on her. "What can't?"

She swallowed hard. "My resignation."

Shock flashed in his eyes then went out like it had never been. "What are you talking about?" he said, his voice quiet. In control. He was *always* in control, especially where she was concerned.

"It's time for me to move on, Blake. That's all."

"Why?"

The question shot at her like a pellet but she managed to shrug. "It just is."

He put his hands on the desk and leaned toward her. "What's this about, Samantha? What's the real reason you want to leave?"

She'd faced him down over business issues occasionally but this...*this* was personal. Cautiously, she pushed the leather chair back and rose on her stilettos, then went to look out the large arched window behind her.

The scene below at the luxurious resort was surprisingly charming in October. Tonight, pocketed in amongst the tall peaks, the sleepy hamlet twinkled like fairy lights in the alpine breeze, a tapestry of winding streets, lodges, and village square. To a southern California girl who now lived in Vegas, this place had something nowhere else seemed to have.

It had heart.

"It's time for me to go," she said, keeping her back to him.

"You're unhappy here?"

"No!" she blurted out, swinging around, then winced inwardly, knowing she sounded contradictory and that he'd have to wonder why.

To be truthful, she'd been feeling slightly down ever since Blake's sister Melissa had announced her pregnancy a few weeks ago. She'd been happy for Melissa, so why it had bothered her she didn't know. Yet since then she hadn't been able to shake a feeling of being slightly depressed.

He'd straightened away from the desk. "So what's the problem?"

You are.

I want you to notice me.

Dammit, I just want *you*.

But how did you say that to a man who didn't even notice you as a woman? She was his trusted assistant and that was about it. She'd never acted overtly female around him. She kept everything businesslike between them. Looking back, perhaps occasionally she should have let her feminine side show. If she had, then perhaps now she might not be in this predicament.

Yet it wasn't that she was in love with him either. She was intensely attracted to him. He was an exciting, charismatic man who effortlessly charmed women like they were going out of fashion, but he was still discerning in whom he took to his bed.

She wanted to be charmed by him.

She wanted to be in his bed and in his arms.

Oh, God, it truly was hitting home that she'd never be in his spotlight. Until now a glimmer of hope had kept her going, but after his subconscious rejection of her tonight, she'd realized that if he knew her feelings about wanting him, then everything would change. She'd be totally embarrassed and so would he. She couldn't work like that. She'd be humiliated just like she'd been with Carl. It was better to leave with some dignity.

"Samantha?"

Hearing her name on his lips struck her like never before. She tilted her head at him. "Do you know something, Blake? You've never called me Sam. Not once. It's always Samantha."

His brows drew together. "What's that got to do with it?"

Everything.

She wanted to be Sam once in a while. Sam the

woman who'd left her ordinary upbringing in Pasadena to embrace the excitement of Vegas after a one-sided love affair gone wrong. The woman who wanted to have a purely physical affair with a man she admired, without ever risking her heart again. Not Samantha the personal assistant who helped run his office and his life and who kept the whole lot in check for him, all nice and neat and tidy, just the way he liked it. She couldn't believe she'd actually thought she'd had a chance with him.

And he was waiting for an answer.

"I have my reasons for resigning and I think that's all you need to know."

"Is someone giving you a hard time?" he asked sharply. "Someone from my family? I'll talk to them if they are. Tell me."

She shook her head. "Your family's great. It's…" She hesitated, wishing she'd given herself time to come up with a suitable explanation. Needless to say, she hadn't expected to be here tonight writing out her resignation, or that he'd even come upon her. She'd assumed he'd probably go off nightclubbing with Miss Hollywood. "I simply want something more, okay? It's nothing against you or your family. This is about me."

One eyebrow rose. "You want something *more* than first-class travel and a world-class place to live?"

"Yes." She had to tread carefully. "Actually I'm thinking of going home to Pasadena for a little while," she fibbed, then realized that wasn't such a bad idea after all. "Just until I decide what I want to do next."

"And that will give you more of what you want? I seem to remember you saying you'd left Pasadena *because* you'd been looking for more excitement."

She'd definitely said that—and she *had* been looking

for more than weekly piano lessons and weekend shopping with her girlfriends—but it had been so much more four years ago. Having fallen in love with a young architect who'd gone off to travel the world after she'd told him she loved him, she'd decided to find her own excitement. Her job with Blake had provided that excitement without any emotional involvement. Until now. And even now it was about lust, not love.

His eyes pierced the distance between them. "You seemed happy enough before to move to Aspen."

"I was… I am… I mean…" Oh, heck. She was getting herself tied up in knots. When Blake said he was moving back home and she should come with him, she'd been delighted. His estranged father's will had stated all the Jarrod offspring had to return to Jarrod Ridge for a year or lose their inheritance. Blake, being the eldest—only by a few minutes ahead of his fraternal and more laidback twin, Guy—had taken up the challenge of running the resort.

She'd looked forward to it, too, and they'd been traveling back and forth between Aspen and Vegas a couple of times these past four months, getting everything sorted. Blake would keep his hotels but would spend most of his time in Aspen. She'd been very happy with that. Until tonight.

She cleared her throat. "All my family and friends are back in Pasadena. I miss them."

"I didn't know you *had* any friends."

She pulled a face. "Thanks very much."

There was a flicker of impatience. "You know what I mean. You're always working or traveling with me and rarely go home except for the holidays. Your friends have never been a priority before."

"I guess that's changed." Thankfully Carl had never returned and she'd heard he'd married an English girl. Of course, time and distance had only shown her that she hadn't really been in love with him at all. She'd been in love with the *idea* of being in love with a man who'd talked of adventure in far-off places. She'd thought they'd do that together. God, what was wrong with her that she kept wanting men who *didn't* want her?

He held her gaze. "What are you going to do after Pasadena, then?"

"I'm not sure. I'll find something. Perhaps even one of those rare friends of mine might help me get a job," she mocked. All she knew was that she wouldn't continue working for Blake, not in Aspen nor in Vegas. A clean break was needed.

He eyed her. "You have plenty of connections. You could use them."

All at once she had an ache in her throat. It sounded like he was beginning to accept her decision. And *that* more than anything showed he really didn't care about her. She was just another employee to him. Nothing more.

"I'm thinking I might get right away from this type of work."

"And do what?"

"I don't know." She took a breath. "In any case, I'd really like to leave Aspen as soon as possible, so that I can wrap up things in Vegas before going home. It shouldn't take more than a couple of days." She'd make sure it didn't.

He scanned her face. "You're not telling me everything," he said, sending her heart bumping against her ribs.

"There's nothing else to tell. I do have a life and a family away from you, Blake, as hard as that may be for you to believe." She couldn't take much more of this. Going over to the desk, she picked up the letter. "So I'd appreciate it if you would accept my resignation." She walked toward him. "Ideally I'd like to leave here as soon as possible. Tomorrow even." Reaching him, she held out the letter.

He didn't take it.

There was a measured silence, then, "No."

The breath stalled in her throat. "Wh-what?"

"No, I won't accept your letter of resignation and certainly not on such short notice. I need you here with me."

His words sent a jet of warmth through her until she remembered this evening. It had been torturous watching him and that actress flirt with each other. How could she stay and keep up the pretence that she didn't want Blake for herself?

She continued to hold the letter out to him. "I can't stay, Blake. I really need to leave."

Now.

Tomorrow.

Certainly no later than that.

He ignored the sheet of paper until she lowered her hand. "I'm the new CEO here, Samantha. It wouldn't be professional of you to leave me in the lurch like this."

She felt bad but it came down to emotional survival. "I know, but there are others quite capable of replacing me. Just contact a high-end employment agency. I'll even do it for you before I go. Someone else would love to work here in Jarrod Ridge. They could be here by Monday."

His mouth tightened. "No."

She lifted her chin. "I'm afraid you have no choice."

"I don't?" he said silkily, inching closer. "You can't quit without a month's notice. It's in your contract."

She sucked in a sharp breath. "Surely you could waive that for me? I've given you two years of my life, Blake, and I've done the job exceptionally well. I've been at your beck and call 24/7. I think you owe me this."

"If you insist on leaving before your contract is up then I'll see you in court." He gave a significant pause. "I don't think that would look good on your résumé, do you?"

"You wouldn't!"

"Wouldn't I?

"This is business," he continued. "Don't take it personally."

She almost choked then. That was the problem. Everything was business between them. *Nothing* was personal.

Her hands shook with anger as she began folding the letter in four. Then she leaned forward and tucked it into his jacket pocket. "Fine. You've got your month. Two weeks here and then two weeks back in Vegas to finish up. After that I'm leaving for Pasadena." She went to step past him.

In a flash he grabbed her arm and stopped her, looking down into her eyes. It was the first time he'd ever touched her *with meaning* and something passed between them. She saw his spark of surprise before he dropped her arm. It surprised her, too.

"I never take no for an answer, Samantha. Remember that."

"There's always the exception to every rule. And I'm it, *Mr. Jarrod*."

* * *

She was still shaking when she got out of the SUV and back to her room at Pine Lodge. She was angry at Blake's refusal to let her go without giving a month's notice, and excited by the awareness in his eyes when he'd touched her. Was she crazy to look more into this than she should?

Her heartbeat stretched into a gallop at the thought that he was attracted to her. A split second was all it had taken and she'd known what it was like to have this man want her. Would he let himself take it further? Remembering the way he'd immediately dropped his hand and withdrawn, she knew he wouldn't.

Yet he'd wanted to, and that was the difference between him and Carl. Oh, she'd had a physical relationship many years ago as a teenager, but looking back, that had been so adolescent. Since then it had only been Carl, and he hadn't wanted her beyond a kiss or two.

But with Blake tonight, she'd known for a moment what it was like for a *man* to really desire her. And that gave her hope that with a bit of encouragement he might make her his. What did she have to lose now? If she went home without taking this opportunity to become Blake's lover she'd always wonder what it would have been like to be kissed by him, to be held by him, to have their bodies joined. And she'd always ache inside for what might have been.

She frowned. How could she capture his attention again and keep it? So far she'd tried everything and nothing had worked. She'd made herself as attractive as possible for him, to no avail. She'd even tried flirting over dinner earlier, but it had fallen faster than a lead balloon. Instead she'd ended up jealous of that actress's ability to flirt so naturally. If only *she* could act like...

Just then a thought clicked in her mind. She couldn't believe she hadn't thought of this before now, but if flirting with Blake hadn't made him sit up and take notice of her, maybe he needed to be stirred up. Maybe he needed an award-winning performance. And a little taste of jealousy.

Yet Blake wasn't the type of man who wanted things made easy for him. Making it appear at least a little difficult to catch her had to be the way to go. He wouldn't be interested otherwise.

And what better way to get his attention than letting him see that other men wanted her? Blake wouldn't be able to resist the challenge. This past week at least two good-looking men had asked her out to dinner but she'd turned them down. She hadn't wanted to be with any man but Blake. She still didn't, but he didn't need to know that.

Starting tomorrow, she'd let herself be wined and dined by men who desired her. She wasn't about to take it any further than that, but she wasn't going to sit around any longer and be uptight Samantha for the rest of her time here either. Sam Thompson was about to break out of her shell.

After Samantha left his office, Blake stood there for a minute, stunned by his encounter with his assistant, and not only because she'd wanted to resign. When he'd touched her he'd had the strongest urge to pull her into his arms and make love to her. She'd felt it, too. He'd seen an acknowledgement in her blue eyes she hadn't been able to hide. Strangely, it excited him. He wasn't used to beautiful women holding themselves back. Women usually *gave* themselves to him.

Clearly it had taken Samantha by surprise as much as it had him. Equally as clearly, she wasn't about to act on it. She probably didn't know *how* to act on it. Over the two years that she'd worked for him he'd rarely seen her date. She was a beautiful woman who socialized with grace and class at functions they both attended, but there had never seemed to be a permanent man in her life. Admittedly *he* kept her busy, but he'd often wondered if she'd had a bad relationship somewhere along the way.

None of that mattered right now, he told himself as he strode over to the window, catching sight of the SUV taking Samantha back the short distance to their private lodge. He waited until the car drove past the cabins and lodges then weaved around a corner and out of sight before letting his thoughts break free.

Damn her.

He didn't often feel thunderstruck, but she'd dropped a bombshell on him tonight. How could she think of leaving him at a time like this? She was his right-hand man. His assistant who made sure everything ran like clockwork. He couldn't do without her and certainly not after coming home to run the resort. He and his younger brother Gavin had already talked about building a new high-security bungalow for their most elite guests in a separate area of the resort.

So why, right when he needed her the most, did Samantha want to bail out on him? He'd expected better of her than desertion. Her excuse that she wanted to go home for a while hadn't made sense. She wasn't one to let her emotions get the best of her anyway and neither was he. That was what he'd liked about her from the start. Now his instincts told him she wasn't telling him the full truth.

Yet if she couldn't be truthful after working closely together, then something was definitely wrong. It just went to remind him to never trust anyone. A person thought they had everything, and in an instant it was gone. Hadn't that been the way since his mother had died from cancer when he was six and his father had withdrawn and blocked everyone out emotionally? It was like both his parents had died at the same time. He'd grown up determined to be totally independent from any emotional entanglements.

Okay, so Donald Jarrod had enough of himself left over to push his five children to be achievers, but at what cost? Four of Donald's offspring had departed years ago to make their mark in other parts of the country. Guy owned a famous French restaurant in Manhattan and ran another business venture. Gavin was a construction engineer. And Melissa was a licensed masseuse who had run a spa and massage-therapy retreat in L.A. Trevor was the only one who'd stayed in Aspen, but had chosen to have nothing to do with the resort, and instead built up his own successful marketing business.

Hell, Blake hadn't seen much of his four younger brothers and sister these past ten years. As his fraternal twin, he was closest to Guy, but he'd still kept a close eye on all his siblings. If they'd needed him, he would have been there. Of course his mind was still out on his half sister, Erica, who'd only recently shown up to become part of the family.

Unfortunately now he needed to rely on *all* of them to make sure the place continued to be a success. It wasn't a feeling he enjoyed. He didn't like relying on anyone, but he'd thought he could count on Samantha.

Obviously he couldn't.

Feeling restless, he looked out over the renowned ski resort that had always been the one place he called home. No matter how much he'd tried to forget it, Jarrod Ridge was in his blood.

He was now the CEO of Jarrod Ridge, for God's sake. His ancestor, Eli Jarrod, had started up the silver mine during the mining boom of 1879, and built himself one of the biggest houses in Colorado. Then "The Panic" of 1893 had closed many of Aspen's mines, and Eli had added to his house and made it bigger, turning it into a grand hotel that was now Jarrod Manor. This place had been through a lot, surviving right through to 1946 when the ski resort idea was born. Jarrod Ridge hadn't looked back since. It was a powerful feeling being in charge of all he surveyed.

And a big responsibility.

And dammit, he wasn't about to let Samantha walk out on him when he needed her most. Even in a month's time he would still need her by his side. It was important to the resort to make sure the changeover went as smoothly as possible, and only Samantha could help him do that. She was the best assistant he'd ever had and he wasn't about to lose her. He would find a way to make her stay, at least until the new bungalow was up and running.

He expelled a breath as he went over to his desk, where he sat down on the leather chair and took the resignation letter out from his jacket pocket. Under the lamplight, he read it, hoping to glean some hint on what was going on inside his assistant's mind. The letter was as professional as expected. No surprises there.

Frowning, he dropped the letter and picked up the pen, rolling it between his fingers as he tried to think. He didn't understand. Surprise appeared to be the name of the game with Samantha right now.

Why?

All at once the metal in his hand went from cool to warm in a matter of seconds, reminding him of his cool and remote assistant who'd soon warmed up at his touch. His heart took a sudden and extra beat. Would Samantha warm up for him if he touched her again? Remembering the electricity between them when he'd grabbed her arm, a surge of need raced through him. Samantha didn't seem to know what she wanted, but he *did* know women. She had wanted him. She had reacted to his touch.

And if that were the case, then perhaps he'd touch her some more and keep her around as long as necessary. He was sure he could persuade her to stay at least another six months. By then they'd both be ready to end the relationship. Sometime in the new year he'd more than likely be over needing her help anyway, and by then he would have someone to replace her, both in the office and the bedroom. No other woman had lasted longer than that. He wouldn't let them. Having affairs was the best he could offer.

As for Samantha, she was independent. She'd have no difficulty moving on when the time came. Hell, she'd probably even instigate it.

For now, it would be his pleasure to awaken the woman in her. Seducing Samantha was definitely going to be a priority task.

Two

Samantha felt more than a few moments of trepidation when she woke to the early morning light and remembered what she'd done. She'd actually handed Blake her resignation. She would be out of his life in a month's time. She tried to picture being apart from him for the rest of her life, but the thought brought silly tears to her eyes that she quickly blinked back.

Taking a shuddering breath, she tried to put all this in perspective. She'd moved on before, hadn't she? It wasn't so hard. Of course leaving Pasadena had been an adventure as much as an escape. It would be a long time before she escaped wanting Blake Jarrod.

Oh, God.

Then she remembered the plan she'd come up with last night. At the time she'd thought it was brilliant, but now she wasn't so sure she should go out with other men to try and make Blake jealous. It didn't seem right to manipulate the situation like that.

And that left her exactly…nowhere.

Remembering the sizzle of Blake's touch, she wondered if she really wanted to leave without giving them a chance. It was comforting to know that he would not want to get emotionally involved, but to become his lover, to be forever warmed by the memory of being in his arms, didn't she have to do this for herself?

She could do it. This was a goal that was achievable. She may not be a femme fatale but she was considered attractive and she knew how to flirt. And while it may not have worked with Blake at the dinner last night, she knew she could interest other men here in Aspen. Hopefully she'd grab his attention that way.

Tossing back the covers like she was tossing away her shackles, she jumped out of bed. She felt more lighthearted by the minute.

After her shower, Samantha figured it would be prudent to distance herself from Blake as much as possible from now on. She wouldn't capture any man's attention if she was with him all the time.

First things first.

Apart from the maids from the hotel who tidied up Pine Lodge each day, she and Blake had decided to be mostly self-sufficient. The refrigerator was usually stocked with food or they could eat at Jarrod Manor, the main lodge on the resort where some of the family chose to live.

Usually they ate a light breakfast together—surprisingly Blake hadn't brought any women back to the lodge while she'd been here—before they walked the short distance to his father's old office at the Manor. Anything to do with his hotels in Vegas was kept separate and done here in the office they'd set up in a corner of the large living room. That work was mostly done after dinner each evening. There was a lot to do with running both businesses, especially now that it was pre-ski season here. Samantha didn't mind keeping so busy. Besides, it kept Blake close.

But today was different. Fifteen minutes later, she quietly closed the lodge door behind her and left without waiting for him. The Colorado sun was making a shy return as she breathed in crystal air and walked the winding streets in picture-perfect surroundings. As she approached this grandest of hotels, a thrill went through her. With its main stone building complemented by guest wings on both sides, its peaked roofs and balconies with iron railings and its frosted windowpanes, it looked like an enchanted castle.

The doorman greeted her as she entered the hotel from under the stone arch leading off the driveway. She smiled and walked through the wide lobby dotted with tables and chairs. Being the off-season, it was quiet at this time of the morning with only a few guests up and about. A young couple stood viewing photographs of the mountains displayed along the wood walls. Older couples looked ready to go sightseeing the many popular tourist attractions, than pamper themselves in the spa.

It was no better in the casual eatery off the lobby, and Samantha sighed as she scooped scrambled eggs onto a plate from the buffet. Couldn't there have been one measly attractive man in sight this morning? So much for her plans to make Blake jealous. It wouldn't happen if she couldn't even find a man to flirt with.

She lifted her head and saw Blake's half sister, Erica Prentice, come out of the kitchen area and walk through the room with Joel Remy, the resort doctor. Joel was tall, blond and good-looking and he'd asked her out only last week and she'd refused, not giving it any consideration. Things had changed.

Erica saw her and blinked in surprise as she came over to her table. "Samantha, what are you doing here eating breakfast by yourself?"

Samantha liked Erica, who hadn't known she was a member of the Jarrod family until a few months ago. Since then, Erica had become engaged to the Jarrod family attorney, Christian Hanford, and everyone was happy about it. Everyone except Blake, that is, though Guy had taken a while to come round. Erica was a PR specialist who had thrown herself into the running of the resort, willingly giving a hand wherever it was needed, just like the other family members. Samantha didn't understand Blake's attitude toward her.

She smiled at the other woman. "I was up early so I thought I'd get a head start on the boss."

Erica laughed. "Yes, I think as Blake's assistant you'd need to do that occasionally."

Samantha let her eyes slide to the man beside Erica. "Good morning, Joel. You're here early, as well."

The doctor smiled. "One of the kitchen staff burned her hand, but thankfully it was only minor."

Samantha nodded, then, "Where are my manners? Would you like to join me for breakfast? Erica, you, too, of course."

As if she was getting a vibe, Erica glanced from one to the other and went to speak, but Joel got in before her. "I can't, I'm afraid, Sam," the doctor said. "I have to go out on another call. But how about I make it up to you? It's Saturday and my night off. If you're free I'd love to take you to dinner."

Samantha could have kissed him, but she managed to restrain herself. If Blake didn't get jealous over this, then at least she'd have some fun, right?

Thinking of Blake must have made him appear. He was at this moment striding through the lobby with a scowl on his face, heading for the private elevator. Her heart jumped in her throat when he glanced over toward them and saw her in the eatery. He changed direction and advanced toward her.

She turned back to Joel, waiting a few moments more for Blake to get closer. "Dinner tonight?" she said, raising her voice just a little. "Yes, I'd like that very much, Joel."

He grinned at her. "Great. How about I pick you up at seven-thirty?"

"Perfect."

Blake was almost at the table.

"I'd better go see my next patient," Joel said, then inclined his head as he passed by. "Good morning, Blake."

Blake nodded, then stopped at the table and practically glared down at Samantha. "You didn't wait for me."

She reminded herself how this man didn't like things made easy for him. "I slipped a note under your door. Besides, I do believe I start work at nine and until then my time is my own," she said, aware of Erica's speculative gaze.

Blake must have been, too. He darted an irritated look at his half sister, then away, jerking his head at Joel's retreating back. "What did the doctor want?"

Was he jealous already? She felt a thrill of excitement but before she could answer, Erica said, "Joel's taking Samantha out to dinner tonight."

Blake blinked in shock, but he recovered quickly, his blue eyes narrowing in on Samantha. "You can't go. I need you to work for a couple of hours tonight. I'm expecting an important call."

"I'm sorry, Blake, but I'm entitled to some time off."

He shook his head. "Not tonight, I'm afraid. I'd do it myself but as you know, I have a function to attend in town." He regarded her with a hint of smugness in his eyes. "That's why I pay you the big bucks."

Samantha's stomach started to churn. For all that she had wanted him jealous…for all that she anticipated him being difficult with the job…she still hadn't expected he would be quite so obstructive. It was obvious he was going to be exactly that from now on.

Well, she didn't like being told what to do, especially when it was out of spite. Oh, boy, she was going to really enjoy *not* making this easy for him now.

Her chin angled up at him. "Only for the next month," she pointed out smoothly, suddenly wanting to throttle him.

His mouth tightened. "Listen—"

"Blake," Erica's voice cut across him soothingly. "I really think you're being unfair here. If necessary, one of the staff can—"

"Mind your own business, Erica," he snapped, making both Samantha and Erica gasp. He grimaced, a pulse beating in his cheekbone. "Sorry. I shouldn't have said that." Then he looked at Samantha. "Go if you must," he said, then twisted on his heels and stormed off.

"Oh, my God, that was terrible, Erica," Samantha muttered. "I don't know what came over him."

Erica stood watching her half brother storm into the elevator. "I do."

Samantha sighed. "Yes, he seems to have a problem with you, doesn't he? I'm sure he'll be fine once he gets used to having a new sister."

"Half sister," Erica corrected with a wry smile, then sat down on the chair opposite. "Samantha, I don't think it's me who's upset him. What's going on between you two?"

Samantha was unsure how much she should confide in the other woman. When it came down to it, Erica was a Jarrod. Still, the others would have to know sometime. "I've given him my resignation. I finish up in a month's time."

"What! But why?" Erica cried. "I thought you loved your job." She reached across the table and squeezed Samantha's hand. "Please don't leave. I love you being here. You're part of the family."

Samantha felt her heart lift, then take a dive as fast. She'd only just begun to know Blake's family and now she had to leave. "It's time for me to make a change."

Erica gave her a penetrating look. "There's been something bothering you lately." She paused. "Blake needs you, Samantha."

For the job, that was all.

"Yes, he's made it quite clear that's why he's making me work out my contract for the next month." She couldn't stop her lips from twisting. "He told me it's nothing personal."

There was another pause, then, "I see."

Samantha realized she may have said too much. The other woman probably saw more than she should.

All at once Erica gave a disarming smile. "You know what I do when I'm feeling down? I go shopping. How about I take you into town after lunch and we buy you a new dress for tonight?"

Samantha knew Erica was trying to make her feel better. "It's a lovely thought, but I've already got enough dresses. And anyway, I have to work. Blake's going to make sure he gets his money's worth from me from now on."

Erica waved that aside. "I bet most of your clothes are suitable for Vegas, not here. And please…no woman ever has enough dresses," she teased, looking beautiful and happy but still slightly concerned. "Besides, I think it will do Blake good to do without you for a couple of hours." She winked. "He owes me now for being such a jerk."

Samantha appreciated it and she tried to smile but couldn't. "Erica, it's not a good idea." Despite being angry with Blake, she realized she'd probably pushed him a bit too much already today. She'd wanted to shock him into being jealous. Not give him a heart attack!

"Phooey! You want to look good for Joel tonight, don't you?"

Samantha thought about why she'd accepted the invitation to dinner with Joel in the first place. This was about making Blake jealous, she reminded herself, so she still had to keep trying. She couldn't give up after the first try.

She nodded. "Yes, I do."

"Then let's light a fire under him, honey, if that's what he needs."

Samantha did her best not to give anything away, but they both knew Erica was talking about Blake, not Joel. And seeing that this might be her one and only chance…

"Okay then, Erica. I'm in your hands. I have nothing to lose."

"Good girl! I'll come by the office after lunch." Erica got to her feet. "I'd better go and check on the staff member who burned her hand." She smiled and headed back the way she'd come.

As Erica left, Samantha sat for a few moments then looked down at the remains of her scrambled eggs. She just hoped she didn't end up like her breakfast—out in the cold and barely touched.

After lunch Blake's bad mood increased as he watched Erica leave his office, taking his assistant with her for the afternoon. They were going shopping, for Christ's sake! For a dress for Samantha's date tonight!

Damn Erica. His half sister was beautiful and smart, but, unlike his brothers and Melissa, he didn't totally trust her. After listening to her for the last five minutes, he hadn't changed his mind. She was unmistakably adroit at getting her own way, using his outburst this morning against him to make him feel guilty. It had worked like a charm, as she'd known it would.

But it was Samantha he really needed to fathom, he decided, leaning back in the leather chair. He'd woken up thinking he'd go after her with an enthusiasm he rarely felt for a woman these days.

And then it had all gone wrong. First, there had been the note slipped under his door that she'd already gone to breakfast and hadn't waited for him. She'd *never* done that before, not here in Aspen or anywhere else they'd stayed throughout the world.

Then he'd found her accepting a date with that gigolo doctor, Joel Remy. That was like going out with one of the ski instructors. Didn't Samantha know women were lined up to sleep with these guys? He'd seen it all his life.

Take a number, Samantha.

What the hell was going on here? She suddenly seemed a different person. It was like she'd decided to place being a woman first, his assistant second.

What had got into her? Was she trying to pay him back for not letting her walk out on the job early? Would she really *do* that? He grimaced. She was a woman, wasn't she? She'd probably decided to have a farewell fling just to rub his nose in it.

Thoughts of Samantha in bed with another man were suddenly anathema to him. He couldn't let her do it. He *knew* her and he knew she'd regret it.

And surely if she was going to make love to anyone, then she could damn well choose *him*. *He* was the one who'd worked closely with her for two years. *He* was the one who would appreciate her in bed. *He* was the one who had to save her from herself.

Three

As she descended the stairs that evening, carrying her clutch bag in one hand and her cashmere evening coat over her arm, Samantha's foot faltered on the next step. She'd been hoping to show herself off to Blake before he left for his business dinner, and now her heart began knocking against her ribs when she saw the man in question look up from the corner bar in their lodge and catch sight of her. His glass stopped halfway to his mouth and he stared…just stared…as she slowly came the rest of the way down.

Thanks to Erica, she knew she looked fantastic. She'd always taken pride in her appearance and in making sure she looked right for her position, but this long-sleeved dress—this piece of hot-pink knit material that stretched over her body like it had been lovingly cling-wrapped to every curve—made her feel a little naughty.

Without taking his eyes off her, Blake put his drink on

the bar and watched her walk toward him. "I'm stunned," he said in a deep, husky voice that held true admiration and sent her pulse skipping with delight. "I've never seen you look so…"

"Nice?" she gently teased as her confidence soared. She would forgive him anything right at this moment.

"Sexy."

The word took her breath away. She moistened her lips and saw his blue eyes dart to her mouth. "Thank you, Blake."

Then his gaze rolled down her, before slowly coming up again, his eyelids flicking briefly when he passed over her breasts both times. She had the feeling her nipples may have beaded with sexual excitement and one part of her wanted to hunch over and say "don't look," while another forced her to hold her shoulders back proudly.

His eyes—dark with a desire she'd never seen before—finally stopped at her head. "What have you done to your hair?"

She swallowed. It hadn't taken much to style the silky brown strands into bouncing curls around her shoulders. "I had a couple of inches cut off it."

"It looks terrific."

This was the reaction she'd been hoping for from him. "Thank you again."

He picked up his drink and took a sip. Then, "I have to ask you something."

Her heart took a leap. "What is it, Blake?"

"Are you sure you want to do this?"

She blinked. "Do what?"

Resign?

"Go out with Joel Remy."

His voice gave nothing away but her pulse started

to race even more. Dear God, could Blake be a little jealous? Had she actually managed to get through to him so quickly that she was a woman? A woman who needed him like she'd never needed any man before?

His eyes slammed into her. "He's not your style, Samantha."

Her heart almost burst through her chest. Blake *was* jealous. She tried to act nonchalant. She couldn't succumb and throw herself at him the minute he decided he wanted her for five minutes.

"How do you know *what* my style is, Blake?" she said, fluttering her eyelashes at him.

"I know what suits you and what doesn't and I know he's not the man for you."

No, this man in front of her was the man for her.

"Oh, so you're an expert on me now, are you?" she flirted, thrilled beyond her wildest dreams that he was finally noticing her. It was this dress. She had so much to thank Erica for. The other woman had…

"I'd like to think I know you very well, Samantha," he said, suddenly looking very superior, very arrogant. "You wouldn't be happy with Remy. Trust me."

Thud.

Clarity hit her like a bolt of lightning. What a fool she was in thinking anything had changed. This wasn't about Blake wanting her. This was about him being his usual conceited self. The man wasn't jealous. He was merely trying to stop her having a relationship with another man over the next two weeks so that she wouldn't inconvenience *him*. Frankly, she deserved better than this.

"That's your considered opinion, is it?" she said coolly now.

"Yes, it is." His eyes told her he'd noticed her change in tone. "Are you going to tell him you're leaving soon?"

She tried to think. She was *so* disappointed. "I'd prefer to keep that to myself for the time being. It's no one's business but my own."

"And mine, of course," he pointed out dryly. Then, "But you're probably right in not telling him. I doubt he's after a long-term relationship anyway."

"Neither am I," she said, taking pleasure in the way his face hardened. "In the meantime, I'm sure Joel and I will both manage to enjoy ourselves."

He looked all-knowing. "I doubt you'll have anything in common."

She raised one eyebrow. "Really? Don't forget I worked in a doctor's office before coming to work for you. And my family runs a medical transcription business, so I used to have quite a bit to do with doctors."

Blake's lips twisted. "So you'll talk about deciphering his handwriting? That'll be a laugh a minute."

Her fingers tightened on her clutch purse. He thought he was being clever, did he? She needed to wipe away that smirk. She gave him a sultry look. "Oh, I'm sure we'll have plenty of...*other things* in common."

The smirk fell off his face. "Dammit, Samantha, you shouldn't—"

The doorbell buzzed.

Samantha glanced over at the front door a few feet away and saw Joel through the glass panel. She tossed Blake an expressive look before going over to open it.

Joel stepped inside, his eyes sliding down, then up. "Wow! Don't you look like a million dollars." He grinned at Blake a few feet away. "I can't believe this beauty is going out with me."

"Neither can I," Blake muttered, then as quickly gave a smooth smile but Samantha heard him. "I mean, she's usually picky about who she goes out with."

She blinked. Was that still an insult? Joel had a puzzled look that said he might be thinking the same thing.

She hurriedly forced a smile. "Thanks for the compliment, Joel." She stood and looked him up and down, too. "For the record, you look like a *billion* dollars," she joked, then realized she'd overplayed her hand when Blake sniffed, though she suspected it was more of a snort. She turned her head slightly so Joel couldn't see her stabbing her boss with her eyes.

Blake ignored her. "So, where are you two dining tonight?"

Samantha was immediately suspicious. "Why do you want to know?"

He smiled. "No reason."

Joel then mentioned a restaurant in the center of Aspen. "It's only just opened and I know the owner. It'll be very hard to get a reservation in another month or so." He didn't sound like he was bragging, at least not to Samantha, but she saw a glint in Blake's eyes that told her he wasn't in agreement.

She smiled at Joel. "That sounds lovely."

He looked pleased. "And you, Blake? You're off to dinner, too, by the look of things."

Wearing a dark suit, Blake was the one who really did look like a billion dollars, Samantha had to admit, unable to stop herself from wishing she was going out with him instead of Joel, in spite of the fact that Blake was being an overbearing jerk.

"Just a business dinner in town." Blake looked at his

watch. "As a matter of fact, I'd better call a cab. I need to be on my way."

Joel frowned. "A cab? Don't you have a car?"

"I noticed it was leaking oil this afternoon so I thought I'd better not use it tonight."

Samantha sensed Blake was manipulating the situation for his own benefit again. Did he think she was stupid? He was doing this on purpose to try and keep her and Joel apart as much as possible to spoil her night.

She stared at him. "But you only bought the vehicle a few months ago and it's barely been used. How can a luxury Cadillac SUV have an oil leak already?"

He looked totally guileless. "I agree. It's the darnedest thing."

"We could give you a lift, if you like," Joel said, making Samantha want to rattle him.

"Oh, I'm sure Blake doesn't want to ride with us." She was determined not to give her boss any satisfaction. "The resort has a chauffeur service."

Joel frowned. "No, that's okay. I don't mind. We're going that way anyway."

She would have sounded mean-spirited to refuse. As Blake well knew, she decided, watching the satisfaction in his eyes. He was Joel's boss and he knew Joel wouldn't deny doing a favor for him.

She passed her coat to Joel. "Would you mind helping me on with this, please?"

"Of course." Joel held it open while she slipped into it, then he helped lift her hair out from under the collar so that it was once again bouncing around her shoulders. It was somewhat intimate and Samantha felt a little awkward at having a man touch her hair, but she soon felt better when she saw the steely look in Blake's eyes after he noted it, too.

"Thanks," she said, smiling brightly at her date, then deliberately linked her arm with his. She gave Blake a sweet smile as he put on his black evening coat, letting him know she didn't care that he wasn't pleased. Too bad!

"My car's out front," Joel said.

They left the lodge, then Samantha slipped onto the front passenger seat before Blake could take it himself. She wouldn't put it past him to try and make her sit in the back, and she wasn't about to let him play at being boss while she was on a date. This was *her* night out. Blake may have been the reason for it, but right now she wasn't about to give him an inch.

Soon they were driving off into the night.

"This is very good of you, Joel," Blake said, sounding grateful from the backseat, which didn't sound right to Samantha's ears. Blake *never* sounded grateful like other mere mortals.

"We don't mind, do we, Sam?" Joel said, shooting her a sideways smile.

"No, of course not. We have to keep the boss happy, don't we?" She smiled back at Joel, knowing Blake could see her from his diagonal viewpoint behind the driver's seat.

"By the way, *Samantha,*" Blake said, placing the slightest emphasis on her name, making her realize that Joel had called her "Sam" again—the name Blake had never called her.

"Yes, Blake?" she said, keeping her tone idle.

There was a tiny pause before he spoke. "Don't worry about that very important phone call I was waiting for tonight. One of the resort staff will sit in the office and wait for it."

"Good." She took her job seriously, but Erica's suggestion had been a good one, so she wasn't about to feel guilty about it.

"But I did have to give them your cell phone number, as well. Just in case. I hope you don't mind. Someone has to take the call if by chance it's missed at the hotel, and I'll have to turn my cell phone off so it won't interrupt the guest speaker tonight."

She could feel herself stiffen. He was trying to take advantage of her good nature for his own purposes again. This wasn't about taking the call. He wanted to put a spoke between her and Joel's budding relationship, freeing up her time for the job.

She turned her head to face him. "Actually I *do* mind. This is my night off. I don't want to work tonight."

He raised an eyebrow, like he was surprised. "I'm sure Joel won't have a problem with it. He's a doctor. He's used to being on call. You understand, don't you, Joel?"

"Sure I do." Joel glanced at her and smiled. "Leave your cell phone on, Sam. I don't mind if you take the call."

Her mouth tightened but she didn't reply. Her cell phone was already off and she intended it to stay that way. And Blake knew this had nothing to do with Joel anyway. Blake was just trying to make sure the job was in her face tonight.

Joel must have sensed something amiss because he started talking about general things for the rest of the way. Samantha could feel Blake's eyes on her from the backseat but she ignored him as she responded to Joel, relieved when the car slid to a halt outside a restaurant.

"Thanks for the ride." Blake opened the back door then paused briefly. "And don't worry about how I'll get home. You two have a good time, okay?"

Samantha bit down on her irritation. His sincerity was so false. He was just trying to get a ride back to the lodge to make sure nothing sexual happened between her and Joel. Ooh, it would do him good to wonder and worry what she and Joel were getting up to later in the evening.

She smiled tightly. "We'll be very late, so you'd best get the car service. Good night, Blake."

His lips flattened and he shot her a dark look. "Good night." He waited a second, but when Joel said good night, he got out of the car and shut the door. The last Samantha saw was him striding into the restaurant.

Then they drove off and she looked ahead, hoping Joel wouldn't say anything. He didn't, at least not until they were seated at their table and the waitress had left with their order.

"Excuse me for asking, but don't you like Blake?" he said.

She smiled to soften her words. "Of course I do, but I've worked with Blake a couple of years now. Sometimes he thinks everyone is there purely for his benefit."

Joel grinned. "As a successful businessman, he's probably right."

She laughed. "Yes, that's true." Then she forced herself to relax against the back of her chair. "Now let's talk about something else. I really don't want to talk about the boss tonight."

Joel smiled. "I'm more than happy to oblige, Sam. Now tell me..."

They had a pleasant evening after that. As predicted, they talked about her family's business and her experience in transcribing, though Blake's earlier derogatory comment about deciphering handwriting spoiled the discussion for her. Did Blake always have to be there at the back of her mind?

Unfortunately by the time the evening was half over, Samantha knew Joel wasn't for her. He was handsome and he was a nice guy, but they really *didn't* have anything else in common, much to her disgust. Not like her and Blake. She grimaced. No, she and Blake had nothing in common either—except the job and an attraction that she hated to think was really only on her side. Shades of Carl came to mind.

"Sam?"

She pulled herself back from thoughts of the past. "Sorry, I remembered something I forgot to do," she fibbed, then she smiled. "But it can wait. Now, what were you saying?" She would have a good time if it killed her.

It nearly did.

Her social life and her work life were the same thing, so she'd never lacked for company at business dinners and parties. But she wasn't used to being on a date and having to tune in to one person for hours on end. It was very draining.

Unless of course that person was Blake. He never bored her. Every minute of every day he challenged her like no other person on earth. Life with Blake was the adventure she'd always been after. One she soon had to leave, she remembered, her heart constricting. She pushed the thought aside. She would get through this.

"We should do this again, Sam," Joel said, holding open his car door for her on their return to Pine Lodge.

It was strange, but for some reason an evening of being called "Sam" had started to get on her nerves. It wasn't Joel's fault at all, but it was as if the shortened version of her name was an issue between her and Blake and therefore belonged only to them now. And that was rather pathetic.

"I've got plans tomorrow night," Joel said, dragging her from her thoughts. "But I'm free after that. Would you like to go to a movie on Monday night?"

She hesitated, feeling a little bad in using him. She didn't want to go out with him again, yet if she didn't continue with her plan to try and make Blake jealous, then Blake would think he'd won. She wouldn't give him the satisfaction now.

She got out of the car, with Joel doing the gentlemanly thing and assisting her. "I'd like that, but let me get back to you tomorrow, if that's okay."

"That's fine."

All at once she felt his hand move from her elbow to her chin. It was a smooth move and said this guy knew what he was doing, so perhaps using him shouldn't really cause her concern after all.

"But first..." he murmured.

She didn't resist even though his kiss wasn't something she wanted, and not because he wasn't an attractive man. Despite still being angry with Blake for trying to manipulate the situation earlier this evening, she wanted it to be Blake's lips—and *only* Blake's lips—on hers.

Suddenly scared that she might never want another man to kiss her, she raised her mouth to Joel. Perhaps Blake's attraction for her was merely in her mind? Perhaps she needed to be kissed by another man just to remind her—

"Don't let me interrupt," a male voice muttered.

Blake.

Samantha jerked back guiltily and Joel stopped, and they watched their employer stride past them and go inside Pine Lodge. He'd been walking from the direction of Jarrod Manor, where he must have gone after dinner.

"That was good timing," Joel said, over her thudding heart. Unfortunately her heart's thud wasn't for her date. It was for another man.

"Now, where were we?" Joel murmured, lowering his head and placing his lips on hers, making her conscious of one thing. She'd have to stretch her neck higher if it was Blake kissing her.

Blake sat on the couch and tried to get the image of Samantha about to kiss another man out of his head. She'd been swaying toward the doctor like she'd needed a shot in the arm. If she didn't get inside here pretty damn quick he was going looking for her. On the pretext of her safety, of course.

And he *was* concerned for her safety. That and other things. She was clearly ready to jump into bed with the first man who looked twice at her, and all to get back at *him* for not letting her walk away from her job. Hell, if he'd agreed to that she would have already gone from his life. His gut twisted at the thought.

The front door opened right then and in she walked. His pulse began to race when he saw she was alone.

Good girl.

She seemed distracted as she headed for the stairs, undoing the buttons of her coat as she walked. Then she saw him sitting on the couch and her eyes flared with pleasure before she seemed to catch herself.

For a moment his breath stalled. She'd never shown any sort of emotion toward him before. They got on well together but it had always been business between them. He should be perturbed, yet he knew he could use it to his advantage.

Then her mouth tightened as she came toward him. "Are you waiting up for me?" she said, her tone less than friendly, making him question if it had been a trick of the light before. He mentally shook his head. No, he knew what he'd seen.

"Can't a man have a drink before bed?" he drawled, relaxing. She was home now…with him…and that's all that mattered.

Her top lip curled. "You certainly didn't have to worry about drinking and driving, did you?"

He pretended ignorance. "No, I didn't." He indicated another glass of brandy on the coffee table in front of him. "I poured a nightcap for you. Sit with me."

An odd look skimmed across her face. "Perhaps I'd prefer to go straight to bed."

If one of his dates had said that he would have taken it as a come-on. But Samantha was a challenge in a different way. Did she know what she was inviting in that dress? Did she have any idea what she actually did to a man's libido? All at once he was enjoying what he now suspected to be her sexual naïveté.

"One drink," he coaxed. "And you can tell me all about your evening."

She paused, then put down her evening purse and began undoing the rest of her coat buttons. Slowly she began taking it off in an unintentional striptease, exposing the sexy pink material beneath. How had he never before noticed what a stunner she was?

She sank down on the opposite chair and gracefully picked up the glass, indicating the already poured brandy. "You were so sure I wouldn't take Joel up to my room, were you?"

He hadn't been, no. "Yes."

She took a sip then considered him. "You certainly tried hard enough to make it *not* happen."

"Did I?" He was feeling rather proud of himself for putting obstacles in her way tonight. It must have worked or she wouldn't be here now. With him.

"You know you did, and I don't appreciate it. You're trying to make sure you get every last bit of work out of me before I leave."

Is that what she thought? "Maybe I was protecting you?"

She gave a short laugh. "From what? Having a good time?"

He looked over at her kissable lips that had recently been beneath another man's…and something became even more determined inside him. If she was going to have fun, she was going to have it with *him*.

He forced a shrug. "I just think you need to look at who you go out with in future."

Her lips twisted. "Thanks for the tip."

He'd never known her to be sarcastic, not like she was lately. It was…energizing, he admitted, watching as she eased back in her chair, the soft silk stockings making a swishing sound as she crossed her legs. He'd give anything to reach out and smooth those long legs with his hands. Or perhaps his lips…

Before he could put words to action, he told himself he had to slow it down. He didn't want to frighten the lady by going too quickly. Time was running out but he had to let her lead. Tonight, anyway. Tomorrow—when she was in a friendlier mood—was another day.

He took a sip of his brandy and let it soothe his throat. "So. Did you have a good time tonight?"

Her eyes darted away briefly. "Yes, I did. Very much."

She was lying. "I bet."

She arched one of her elegant eyebrows. "I hope you didn't put much money on that bet, Blake."

"I didn't have to." He knew women, both in the business world and out of it. She was lying. And he was intensely relieved.

A soft smile curved her lips. "Joel really knows how to treat a woman."

She was still lying. And he found that fascinating. "Sure he knows how to treat a woman. The guy's a womanizer."

"I suppose it's easy enough to recognize one's own sort."

He had to chuckle. She made him laugh. Then he saw a touch of real amusement in her eyes and something connected between them. She quickly looked down at her glass, hiding her eyes for a second.

He started to lean forward. "Samantha…"

Her head snapped up. "For your information, Joel's a

very nice man," she said, making it clear she was trying to ignore the sudden sexual tension in the room.

It was a wasted effort. "I'm sure he is. Ask *any* woman in Aspen."

She sent him a defiant look. "Don't think I wouldn't go to bed with him if I wanted to, Blake."

She was all talk, but his gut still knotted at her words. "Obviously you didn't want to, or you would be in bed with him this very minute. Am I right?"

"No, you're wrong. I mean, yes… I mean, mind your own business." Her lips pressed together. "I'll sleep with whoever I want *when* I want."

"You're being very contradictory tonight, Samantha. They'd eat you alive in the boardroom with that attitude," he mocked.

She stiffened. "Listen, Blake, I'll sleep with any man I want when I'm good and ready. Tonight I just wasn't ready. And in case you didn't notice, this isn't the boardroom."

No, but he did want to eat her alive right now. He wanted to kiss her and take away the imprint of another man's lips, his hands itching to slide up over her hot dress and lift that hair off her nape himself, exposing the soft skin beneath to his lips.

Adrenaline pumping through him, he knew it was time to take action. He'd had enough playing games tonight. He wasn't one to sit on the sidelines for long. He needed to know if her lips were as good as they looked, if her body would curve to his touch, if the skin at her nape was soft and sensitive.

Surging to his feet, he removed the brandy glass from her hand and put it on the table. He heard her intake of breath as he pulled her to her feet, but nothing would stop him now. Already he could feel a mutual shudder pass between them.

"Blake?" she said huskily as he brought her into the circle of his arms, leaving mere inches between them. He'd never been this close to her before. Not close enough to see the rush of desire in her blue eyes. It knocked the breath from his body.

And then a sudden flash of panic swept her face and before he knew it, she had pushed against him and spun away. Scurrying toward the stairs, she left him standing there, his arms never feeling as empty as they did right now.

As hard as it was, he let her go. He could follow her and she would take him as her lover, but he knew all he needed to know for the moment. She wanted him. And he wasn't giving up. His plans for seduction were still very much alive.

Samantha closed the door behind her and pressed herself back against it, willing her racing heart to slow down so that she could let herself think. She'd gone and panicked just now. Blake had finally reached for her and she'd blown it.

What was wrong with her! Being in Blake's arms and in his bed was what she wanted most, wasn't it? So why had she run away like a frightened deer? He must think her green when it came to relationships, which of course she was. One lover in high school, then falling in love in her mid-twenties, did not constitute experience. Not unless that included the pain of rejection, she decided, quickly pushing that thought away.

Then she knew.

Despite the spark of electricity when he'd grabbed her

arm last night, this evening she'd managed to convince herself that his meddling was actually about the job and nothing more. But just now the desire in his eyes had thrown her for a loop again. He really *did* feel passion for her, and when he'd touched her they'd both felt that zip of attraction. It had overwhelmed her, that's all.

Oh, Lord, what did she do now? Go back downstairs and beg him to make love to her? She couldn't. She'd reached the limit to her little seductress act tonight. She didn't have it in her to face him again so soon.

She took a steadying breath. Right, she'd messed this one up tonight, but something positive had come out of this. She now knew that Blake really *did* want to have sex with her. So if she wanted Blake, and he wanted her, then next time there should be no further problems.

She hoped.

Four

"Blake, did you get a chance to read those documents I gave you?"

Blake was in a good mood as he leaned back against the marble countertop. It was eight on Sunday morning and one of his younger brothers had come by Pine Lodge to discuss an upcoming project, but it was Samantha who was on his mind. Anticipation coursed through him as he remembered how sexy she had looked last night. Soon she would be *his*.

"Blake?"

Reluctantly he dragged his thoughts away from his assistant who was still upstairs sleeping in her room, to look at the man propped against the kitchen doorjamb. He hid a smile as he raised the coffee mug to his mouth. Gavin may look laidback but *he* knew it was all a facade. Taking on the job of building a new and exclusive high-security bungalow for Jarrod Ridge meant a lot to his brother.

"Yes. I've put them in the safe up at the Manor," he said, deliberately misunderstanding him.

"And?"

Blake chuckled and put him out of his misery. "And I think you've done an admirable job of running with this project."

Gavin began to smile with relief. "You do?"

"The intensive feasibility studies, as well as the building site and sustainability analysis reports you've put together, are impressive. But then, so were the ones you did for my Vegas hotels."

Gavin's grin widened. "It means a lot to hear you say that."

Blake indicated the coffeepot on the bench. "Grab yourself a coffee."

Gavin straightened away from the door and went to get a mug. "You know," he said, pouring himself a drink. "I've really welcomed this challenge."

"I can see that."

Gavin shrugged shoulders made impressive by many hours working with his crew on various construction sites. "It's nice to be home and together again as a family after so long, but I'm glad I don't have to pamper people on a daily basis. It really isn't my style."

Blake nodded. "You're a first-rate construction engineer, Gav, but I agree. There's nothing like doing something you love."

Gavin smiled, looking pleased. "You said it, brother."

"Seriously. I'm proud of you."

"You getting soft in your old age, Blake?" he teased.

"Probably." Blake was proud of all his brothers and sisters. Well, his half sister, Erica, was another matter.

All at once, Gavin's smile left him. "You realize Dad would never have said such a thing."

Blake grimaced. "I like to think I'm not quite as cold as the old man."

There was a moment's silence as they both remembered their father. Blake refused to feel anything for the passing of a man who had shunned his children's emotional well-being and so badly let them down. Donald Jarrod's legacy had been more than the Jarrod Ridge Resort. It had been a legacy that his children keep their emotions on ice, avoiding personal commitment. And while both Guy and Melissa had found true happiness with Avery and Shane, Blake couldn't see it happening for himself. Not at all. Nor for Gavin or Trevor either. That was just the way it was.

"That reminds me," Gavin said. "You're working out of Dad's old office now you're CEO, so wouldn't it be more convenient to be living at the Manor, as well? Why are you staying here at Pine Lodge instead?"

Blake shrugged. "Actually it's more convenient to be staying here. That way I can keep my hotel operations separate from the resort stuff." His hand tightened around the coffee mug. "Besides, even though Erica's moved into Christian's place, they both spend most of their time at the Manor during the day. I don't want to encroach on their territory. You know what newly engaged couples are like."

Gavin shot him a mocking smile. "Since when have

you ever taken a backseat to anyone, big brother? Or are you still scared of our new half sister?"

Blake knew Gavin was riling him, getting him back for stringing it out a few minutes ago. "I was never scared of Erica, as you well know."

"You're going to have to get over your dislike of her one day, buddy."

Blake felt an odd jolt. "I don't dislike her. I just don't totally trust her."

Gavin's eyes narrowed. "She really doesn't have to prove anything more to us, Blake." He paused. "But I guess it's all for the best that you stay here anyway. Your new assistant might not get on with the rest of the family as well as Samantha does." A speculative look entered his eyes. "Yeah, whoever is coming in as your new PA, it'll be much easier for them to keep the two businesses separate if you both stay here."

Blake's jaw clenched. He refused to even think about Samantha leaving, or someone coming in to replace her. And why was he surprised that word had gotten around the family? Samantha had said she didn't want anyone to know, but obviously she'd told one person at least. It had to have been Erica. No doubt the two had shared some girl talk yesterday while they'd been shopping together.

"Samantha is *not* leaving," he said tightly.

"That's not what I'm hearing."

"Shut up, Gav." He slammed down his half-empty coffee mug. "Now, if you'll excuse me, I have some work to do." He strode past his brother and out of the kitchen.

As he entered the living room, he heard a noise outside. He glanced through the picture window.

Samantha wasn't in bed asleep like he'd thought. She was standing on the bottom step of the lodge, dressed in warm clothes and a woolen hat, talking to a man who no doubt was one of the guests at the hotel. She must have gone up to the Manor to eat breakfast, probably with her doctor friend, and this guy must have followed her back like a lost puppy. No, make that a raccoon.

He heard her give a lilting laugh and his mouth flattened. The guy was in his forties and looked sleazy to Blake. And hell, Samantha looked like she was flirting with him. Didn't she have any sense when it came to men? The sooner he showed her what it was like to make love to *him,* the better.

"Look at that," Gavin murmured in his ear. "I think someone else may be working today…*on* Samantha."

Blake glared at him, then strode over and pulled open the front door in a rush. If she was going to flirt it would be with *him.*

"How about us going for a scenic drive?" the man was saying. "Maybe even do lunch in town? I know it's pretty quiet at this time of year, but we should be able to find somewhere to eat. What do you think?"

"I—"

"I think I need to speak to my assistant," Blake cut across her as he stepped out on the porch. They spun to look up at him. "Samantha, I need you to make some calls to Vegas for me."

She sent him an annoyed look, making it clear she didn't like the interruption. "Blake, it's Sunday and most of the offices are closed. It'll have to wait until tomorrow."

He had the urge to remind her that last night he could easily have taken her to his bed. She wouldn't have minded *that* interruption, he was sure. "Then I need you to help me with something else."

Her lips tightened. "So I'm not going to get any time off now until I leave?"

"No." He turned to go inside and waited but realized she wasn't behind him. "Coming, Samantha?"

Her chin tilted stubbornly. "I'll be there in a minute."

Blake saw Gavin's look of amusement as his brother pushed through the doorway then descended the stairs two at a time, calling out a greeting to the pair as he left.

Blake went back inside. He didn't hear her following. Counting to ten, he waited but he could see her still standing there chatting. At that moment something occurred to him. Wasn't it strange that she'd been jumpy with *him* last night, yet she seemed perfectly at ease with Mr. Sleazy down there? And what about last night with the doc? She hadn't seemed nervous around the guy.

So what did that tell him? That she was flirting with men she considered *safe?* Which meant she must feel nothing for them, he mused. Nothing at all. The thought filled him with relief.

As for what she was feeling for him…there was definitely something between them. Yeah, she knew they'd be explosive together in bed.

And that begged the question. Just how far was she prepared to go to fight her desire for him? More importantly right now, did she have any idea what she was inviting by leading those other two men on?

Making a decision, Blake pulled on his jacket and boots, grabbed his car keys and strode back out into the chilly air. "I need to go check on something," he said, going down the stairs, "and I want you to come with me, Samantha." He bared his teeth at the other man in the semblance of a smile. "Sorry, buddy, but I need my assistant."

"Blake—" she began.

"This is important." He cupped her elbow and began leading her toward the side of the lodge to the garage where he kept his black Cadillac SUV.

She glanced over her shoulder and called out to the other man. "I'll talk to you when I get back, Ralph."

Blake gave a snort as he clicked the remote to open the garage door.

"What was that for?" Samantha hissed, hurrying to keep up.

"I hope you're not thinking of dating *Ralph*. The guy's old enough to be your father. Hell, he's even got a name to match."

She hid her satisfaction. "Perhaps I'm attracted to older men?"

He sent her a knowing look. "Then you'd better not dress like you did last night. He doesn't look like his old ticker could handle a woman, let alone a sexy one like yourself."

Her own "ticker" jumped around inside her chest and she tried not to blush. She loved hearing that Blake thought her sexy, though she wasn't sure why he was looking so confident all of a sudden. Still, this time she wasn't going to run away from him if he made a move on her. No repeat of last night, she told herself firmly.

They entered the garage, but it was only after she slid onto the passenger seat of the SUV and was putting on her seat belt did she remember something. "Didn't you say this vehicle had an oil leak?"

Blake smirked at her. "Here's the thing. I took another look earlier and it wasn't leaking after all. The problem must have been with someone else's car."

"Now there's a surprise."

"It was to me, too," he drawled, starting the engine.

No wonder he looked pleased with himself, she decided. He'd orchestrated the "poor me" routine last night over the oil leak, and now he'd put a stop to her going out with Ralph. Not that Ralph was her type, though he seemed very nice, but he *was* a man and one she could flirt with for Blake's benefit.

Once the vehicle had warmed up, she took off her gloves as he reversed out of the garage.

"Where are we going?" she asked, when he started along the narrow road lined with thick trees, and it became clear they were heading for the main entrance to the resort.

"You'll see."

For a second she dared hope this might be about spending some time alone together away from everyone else. "Is this really about work?"

"What else?"

Disappointment wound its way through her. They were clearly still employer and employee. Had last night merely been an aberration on his part because of the late night and close proximity? Was this once again about Blake trying to stop her from leaving her job, rather than him actually wanting her?

Back to square one.

Soon Blake was driving past the two stone pillars with the brass Jarrod Ridge Resort sign, and turning the SUV onto the main road but in the other direction of town. At this time on a Sunday morning there wasn't much traffic and further along he took another turn onto a side road. She wondered where they were going as they drove through stunning natural scenery filled with golden fall colors that would soon disappear under winter-white, but it was no use asking him again. Blake only did what he wanted to do and he would tell her only what he wanted her to know.

Remembering Gavin had visited Pine Lodge this morning, she suspected then where they were going. Farther along, Blake pulled over onto a slot of land that looked out over the Roaring Fork River weaving its way through a lush green picturesque valley between towering snow-dabbled peaks. The Jarrod Ridge resort was nestled like a crown jewel amongst it all.

He stopped the vehicle and cut the engine.

He didn't speak at first, just stared straight ahead, so she had to ask the obvious. "Why did you bring me here?"

He nodded his dark head at the majestic mountain panorama before them. "I wanted to show you where the new private bungalow will be built."

"I see." Her suspicions were correct, but the way he spoke made her heart sink. It was as if he had acknowledged she was leaving now. Like he was showing it to her—while he still could.

"Let's take a closer look." He started to get out of the car then glanced back at her, his gaze going to the woolen hat on her head. "Put your gloves on first. There's no wind but it's chilly."

A couple of seconds later they were standing in front of the black SUV, looking at the breathtaking alpine backdrop in front of them.

He pointed to a wooded area near the bottom of the

mountain to the right of the resort. "See that over there? That's our silver mine where we used to play as kids. One of my ancestors started up the mine but it's been out of use for over a hundred years."

"How interesting," she said, meaning it.

"The bungalow will be farther up the mountain but not too close. We don't want to destroy the historical significance of the mine."

She'd briefly seen the documents Gavin had given Blake, and heard them discussing it at times, but Gavin was the one running with this project. He was keeping it very much between himself and Blake at this stage, though she knew they were keeping the rest of the Jarrods up to date.

"See that rocky outcropping?" Blake continued. "That's close to where we'll build the bungalow. It's going to be super luxurious with top-of-the-line security. There'll be iris-recognition scanners plus the usual cameras and motion detectors. Personal safety will be a must, as will our guests' privacy."

She could picture it in her mind. "I'm really impressed. It'll be great."

He nodded. "It's just what Jarrod Ridge needs to stand out above the rest," he said, a proud look about him as he appraised his family's empire.

An odd tenderness filled her as she glanced up at his familiar profile. There was something so attractive about a man confident with himself. An aura that pulled a woman close and made her want to get under it, to become a part of the man no one else knew.

All at once he turned toward her, his gaze fixing in on her. "Why are you looking at me like that?" he asked quietly.

Caught!

She cleared her throat. "I was thinking how much you enjoy a challenge. You're suited to these mountains."

He looked pleased. Then, "You could be a part of all this, too, you know."

Her heart stumbled. Had he brought her here for another reason? "Wh-what do you mean?"

"You love it here. You won't be happy anywhere else." He paused. "Think carefully before you walk away from your job, Samantha."

The job.

She groaned inwardly at her stupidity. Had she really thought this confirmed bachelor had been about to pop the marriage question to his personal assistant? What on earth was the matter with her? Hadn't she learned her lesson with Carl? The thin air must be making her imagine things that weren't and could never be. Not that she'd ever consider it anyway.

She took a shuddering breath before speaking. "I *have* thought about it, Blake." Very much so. She hadn't stopped.

He turned to face her. "Stay, Samantha."

"I…I can't." If it had been a plea, she might have considered it. As it was, she knew this was basically still about him being inconvenienced.

She went to turn away. She couldn't face him fully. The last thing she wanted was him seeing she'd mistakenly assumed he was talking marriage a minute ago. What a fool she was for even thinking it, let alone believing he might be thinking it, too. This wasn't about anything more than desire, she reminded herself.

His fingers slid around her arm and tugged her back. "Why are you being so obstructive?"

She couldn't feel the pressure of his fingers through her thick jacket but she knew they were there. "Obstructive to what?"

"To me being concerned for your well-being."

She ignored the thud of her heart. "Oh, so *that's* why you won't let me finish up my job early?" she scoffed, knowing this was the only way she could handle him. "You're *concerned* for me?"

He froze.

Silence surrounded them.

Then, he said quietly, "I am, actually."

She gasped midbreath. "Why, Blake? Why are you concerned for me?"

"Why wouldn't I be?" As he spoke she could feel his eyes almost pulling her toward him.

"Um…Blake…"

He drew her toward him and bent his head. He was kissing her before she knew what was happening, instantly destroying any defenses she may have drawn on, regardless that she wanted him so very much. Like an avalanche rolling down a mountain, she fell—and it was just as devastating.

Then he slid his tongue between her lips and she opened her mouth to him fully. Hearing his husky groan, she wound her arms around his neck and held on to him, trusting him, knowing where he took her she would follow.

Time blurred.

And then, amazingly, he was slowing things down, giving her back herself, letting her regain focus. Finally, he eased back and they stared at each other.

"Oh, my God!" she whispered, awed by the sheer

complexity of the kiss that should have been simple and wasn't. It left her trembling.

He was feeling something equally as powerful. She could see it deep in his eyes. He truly desired her. Her dream of being in his arms was finally becoming a reality.

His cell phone began to ring.

He remained still, not moving, and she knew why. Nothing could take away from the strength of this moment between them. Here in the mountains it was like they were the only two people alive.

Then as quickly as she thought that, he blinked and turned away, breaking the moment. She heard him answer it, but she couldn't seem to move. She understood why he had turned away. Why he had broken the moment. It had been too much for him. For her. For them both. Without him looking at her, she could take a breath again.

She did.

And then she found she could move. She swiveled to go get into the SUV, needing to sit down for a minute and feel something solid beneath her.

She took a few steps but as she went to reach for the door handle, her feet slipped from under her on a patch of ice and, with a small cry, she felt herself falling backward…backward….

She frantically made a grab for anything within reach, but there was only the air and she felt her legs going up and her body going down, her back hitting the grass, then her head on something harder. She literally saw stars….

The next thing she knew Blake was dropping to his knees beside her. "Thank God!" he muttered, when he saw her eyes were open.

"What happened?" she managed to say.

He glanced back to where she'd been walking. "You must have slipped on that ice back there."

She started to lift her head, then winced at the pain.

"Take it slowly." He put his hand under her shoulders to help her up. "Is your back sore or anything? Are you hurting anywhere?"

"No."

Then he swore. "You're bleeding."

"I am?"

His hand came away with some blood on it. "You've cut your head." He helped her to sit up, then he checked the back of her head. "It's only small but it's bleeding like the devil and might need a stitch. There's a lump starting where you hit it, too." Snatching up her woolen hat that must have come off during the fall, he placed it against the cut. "Hold that on it. It'll help stem the flow of blood. We need to get you to a doctor."

"Joel?" she said, without thinking, not meaning anything by it.

His mouth tightened. "Yes." He waited. "Do you think you can stand up? Are you dizzy or anything?"

"A little, but I'll be fine."

He helped her stand, then walked her the few feet to the car. Soon they were heading back to Jarrod Ridge.

"How do you feel now?" he said a few minutes later.

"Okay."

They drove a little farther. "Talk to me, Samantha."

"I don't really feel like talking," she said, calling herself an idiot for slipping. If only she'd looked where she was going, then—

"I want you to stay awake. You may have a slight concussion."

"Oh." She realized this was the correct procedure.

"Come on, you can do better than that," he said, a serious look in his eyes.

"Okay." She tried to think. "What do you want me to say?"

"I don't know. Anything. What's your favorite color?"

She didn't need to think about that. "Yellow."

His brow rose in surprise. "Yellow? Any particular reason?"

She winced a little as she adjusted the woolen hat against the injury. "Because it's bright and happy."

He glanced at her again, noting her wince, his mouth turning grim. "Okay, so what's your favorite flower?"

"Tulips."

Another look of surprise from him. "Why?"

"They're so beautiful."

There was a tiny pause. "Like you," he murmured, and her breath caught, then she moved her head and winced again. "Not long now," he assured her.

After that Blake drove straight up to the clinic at the spa lodge. The middle-aged nurse immediately took control, putting Samantha in an exam room. She checked her over, mentioning it wasn't too bad but that she'd need to call the doctor anyway.

"No need to get Joel if he's busy," Samantha said, feeling bad for interrupting his Sunday morning.

Blake nodded at the nurse. "Get him."

The nurse nodded in agreement then looked at her. "The doctor really should see you," she said, then went and picked up the wall telephone as Samantha glanced at Blake.

He gave a short shake of his head. "He's paid to do his job, Samantha. Let him."

Before too long, Joel strode into the exam room, nodding at Blake and giving her a chiding frown. "What have you done to yourself, Sam?"

Samantha didn't look at Blake, but she sensed he'd noted the shortening of her name. Joel was professional in his examination. She didn't need stitches but he tidied up the cut and it finally stopped bleeding. Thankfully he hadn't needed to cut any of her hair in the process.

"I don't think the lump on your head is anything to be concerned about," he assured her, "but we still need to keep an eye on it for any signs of concussion." He considered her. "If you like, I can come to Pine Lodge and check on you a couple of times throughout the day."

"I'll take care of her," Blake said firmly. "I know what signs to look for."

Joel glanced at Blake, held his gaze a moment, then nodded. "Fine. But I'll drop by the lodge and check on her this evening. Call me sooner if you have any doubts."

"I will."

Samantha looked from one to the other. "Do either of you mind if I have a say in this?"

Blake shot her an impatient look, but it was Joel who spoke. "Sam, this has to be taken very seriously. Your brain's had a knock, and sometimes things can develop later on. You need to rest up and you need to have someone keep a close eye on you for at least twenty-four hours."

She swallowed, not sure she liked hearing that, but before she could say anything the clinic door opened and someone called out for help, saying something about a twisted ankle. The nurse and Joel excused themselves to go check.

Blake came to stand in front of her. “I intend to look after you whether you like it or not.”

“But—”

“It’s my fault you were out there today,” he cut across her, his eyes holding firm regret. “No arguments, Samantha. I owe you this.”

She melted faster than snow under a heat lamp. “All right.”

There was nothing in his eyes that said he remembered their kiss, and right now she was grateful for that. She would have plenty of time to go over it once she was alone.

He picked up her jacket. “Come on, then,” he said gruffly. “Let’s get this on you and get you back home.”

Home?

Why did that sound so good to her?

Five

By the time Blake brought her back to Pine Lodge it was almost noon. Not that Samantha was hungry. She wasn't. She was glad now that he'd decided to stay close today. She wasn't feeling ill, but she was still a little shaky, so she was appreciative of him cupping her elbow as they walked.

That shakiness increased as they went up the staircase and he told her that tonight she was to sleep in the spare bedroom in his suite—a spare bedroom separated from his bedroom by only a connecting bathroom.

Her stomach dipped as they reached the top stair. "I'm only across the landing there, Blake. It seems silly not to stay in my own room."

"No. I want you near in case you need me."

She *did* need him, but not in the way he meant. He was being nothing more than caring right now, while she was still stunned by the impact of their kiss back on the mountain.

"Fine," she murmured, not up to arguing anyway. She was a bit of a mess. Her jacket had mud on it, her slacks were still slightly damp in places where she'd fallen on the wet grass, and parts of her brown hair felt like it was matted with blood. Yuk! She must look a wonderful sight.

"I need to change my clothes," she said, wrinkling her nose. "Actually I might have a shower. My hair feels sticky."

He shook his head. "Not a good idea. You might faint in there."

Her heart thudded and she could feel her face heat up as she pictured him coming in to rescue her. She looked away as they walked toward her room. "You're right," she said, then could have kicked herself. Any other woman would have used that to her advantage, but no, not her. What was the matter with her? Then she remembered. That's right, she'd had a bump on the head, she excused herself, wincing.

"Are you in pain?"

"A little."

He pushed open her bedroom door and led her inside. "Here. Sit on the chair and let me help you take off your jacket."

"Thanks." She did as he said.

"Your sweater's got dried blood down the back of it," he said, after he'd eased her out of the padded material. "I don't know how you're going to get it over your head without causing pain." A small pause. "I'll have to help you off with it."

She gulped. "You will?"

"Yes." His voice was nothing but neutral.

She tried to appear nonchalant, too. "Trust me to wear a tight-necked sweater today," she joked, feeling dizzy again but not from her injuries. It was the thought of him undressing her, even though it made sense to do it this way. She didn't think she'd be able to get the sweater off without him. She had a long-sleeved T-shirt underneath to cover herself, but that had a wide neck and she could easily take it off herself.

"Right. This won't take long." His voice sounded tight and she wondered… "Keep still now."

He slid her arms out of the sleeves, then she felt him touch the hem of her sweater, and almost like it was in slow motion he started to lift it upward. She could feel him move close…closer still as he inched it up higher and higher…. She could feel his breath change as he neared her breasts, though not once did he touch her in any intimate way.

"Okay, careful now," he said, as he reached her nape, his voice huskier. "This will be a little tricky." He moved closer…. "There. That's it. Now let me ease it over your head." He moved around to the front of her and eased the knit material gently up over her head, and suddenly it was off and she was sitting there, her gaze level with his belt buckle. And then she raised her eyes to his, saw him looking down at her, and she dropped her eyes to where her T-shirt had ridden up and was revealing her breasts cupped in her lacy blue bra.

She lifted her head again and their eyes locked together. Something dark flared in his, and in retaliation her breathing became practically nonexistent as she remembered their kiss. Until that moment back there on the mountain none of this had been purely about *them*.

Things had changed.

Now it was.

All at once he twisted jerkily toward the small table and placed the sweater on it, saying over his shoulder, "I'll leave you to do the rest, but I'll be back soon to check on you." His voice sounded rough as he headed for the door. "You should get into bed."

She realized he was trying to be a gentleman and keep it all under control because she was injured, but what if she wasn't injured? Would he take her?

The thought was moot, she told herself, swallowing hard and concentrating on what he'd said. "I'm not staying up here all day, Blake. I can sit on the couch downstairs and do some work." It didn't feel right to go to bed in the middle of the day. Not unless…

He stopped at the door, his eyes firm. "I won't let you work, but you can lie on the couch."

"Good of you," she joked, trying to ease the tension in the room.

He didn't smile. He had a hard flush on his face. "I think so," he muttered, then left her to it, shutting the door behind him and giving her some privacy.

Swallowing, she had to move or he might come back and decide to help her undress the rest of her clothes. And that wouldn't be such a bad thing on her part, but clearly he didn't want to right now. She appreciated that he was thinking of her, even as her body craved to be a part of his.

First, she went into her bathroom, groaning when she saw a streak of blood on her cheek and the mess of her hair. Carefully she lifted the T-shirt over her head.

Unable to stop herself, she stared at her lace-clad breasts, her cheeks reddening as she thought of Blake seeing the invitation of her body like this.

Filling the sink with warm water, she grabbed a washcloth and cleaned as much of the blood out of her hair as possible, then very gently combed it into place over the cut. She was pleased with the result. If she didn't know better, and if her head hadn't been sore, it would be hard to believe she'd just had an accident.

But if she was going to be an invalid today, she may as well be comfortable. She changed into denim jeans and a long-sleeve blouse that buttoned up so she didn't have to lift it over her head. Blake tapped on the door as she stepped into a pair of slides.

"Come in," she called out, half-surprised he'd knocked, considering he'd appeared to have taken charge of her welfare.

He pushed open the door then stood there, inspecting her from the face up. "You look much better."

"I feel better. Thanks."

Then his gaze traveled downward and a curious look passed over his face. "I don't remember seeing you in jeans before."

One glance from him and she could feel how much the jeans hugged her figure. Her stomach fluttered. "I usually only wear them at home." If they were staying at a hotel, Pine Lodge included, she wore stylish clothes even when going casual. She considered dressing right a part of her job.

"You should wear them more often," he said, his eyes blank but his voice tight again. He stepped back. "Come on. There's a couch waiting for you downstairs."

She avoided his gaze as she walked forward, then

went past him in the doorway, but she could feel his presence like a soft touch.

Thankfully soon she was lying on the couch with cushions behind her back and a throw over her body. Did she want a book to read, he asked. A movie on the DVD player? A magazine?

"Perhaps some magazines," she said, though she didn't actually feel like doing anything but lying there and being with Blake. "You don't have to do this," she said as he went to get them from the rack.

He came back with a selection, his mouth set. "I told you. It's my fault you were injured in the first place. I shouldn't have taken you with me."

"But you were only wanting to show me the bungalow location before I left Aspen," she said in a flood of words, then saw his mouth tighten further. She understood. She didn't want to be reminded that she was leaving soon either. "Anyway, what's done is done. I don't blame you but if you want to make it up to me, then I'd love a hot drink. A hot chocolate would be nice. With marshmallows."

"No."

She blinked. "Why not?"

"Because you shouldn't be drinking or eating for a few hours. It could make things worse."

She realized he was right, but, "I'm really thirsty, Blake, and I'm feeling fine now. How about some peppermint tea? That shouldn't hurt." She watched him consider that.

He nodded grudgingly. "Only a very weak one, then."

She smiled. "Thanks."

He set off for the kitchen and she could hear him

moving about in there. Her family used to cosset her like this at times, and she had to admit she liked being taken care of by Blake.

He soon returned with her hot drink, then he moved to the table in the corner where they'd set up the office. For a time it remained quiet as she flipped through the magazines and sipped at her tea. Then she began feeling sleepy. Eventually she finished her drink and made herself more comfortable, being careful with her sore head as she curled up on the couch. Her eyes closed and she found herself thinking about her and Blake back on the mountain. She could still remember the feel of his lips against…

The phone woke her with a start and she heard Blake swearing as he snatched it from the handset. She sat up and tidied herself, listening to his conversation, knowing someone in his family was inquiring about her. He soon ended the call.

"Sorry about that," he told her. "It was Guy checking to see how you were. He'd heard about the accident from Avery."

"Oh, that's nice of him."

The phone rang again and Blake reached for it. "Yes, she's fine, Gavin, but I'll be keeping an eye on her anyway." She saw Blake listen, then dart a look at her, before turning away. "You're a funny guy, Gav." Then he hung up.

Curious, she asked, "What did he say?"

"Nothing much."

Had Gavin made a brotherly comment about keeping an eye on her? Not that she minded. It might work in her favor. "That's good of your family to be checking on me."

"You're supposed to be resting. I don't want them interrupting that."

His comment warmed her as she glanced at the wall clock, surprised to see the time. "I must have been asleep a while."

"An hour."

So he'd been keeping an eye on her. "That long? I didn't realize."

"I did."

The phone rang again and he muttered something low. This time it was Trevor. No sooner had he hung up than they heard car doors slam shut and Blake strode over to look out the window.

"Who is it?" she asked.

"Melissa and Shane."

She watched him start toward the front door and quickly called his name. He stopped to look at her. "You *will* let them in, won't you?"

His mouth tightened. "For a short while."

"Be nice," she chided gently, and he shot her a look saying that was a given. "You know what I mean, Blake. I think it's wonderful of your family to be concerned for me."

His mouth softened a little. "Yeah, they're pretty good when they want to be."

Soon Blake's sister Melissa and her new fiancé, Shane McDermott, came into the lodge, bringing a breath of crisp, fresh air.

Melissa's long, wavy, blond hair flew behind her as she made a beeline for the couch. "Samantha! We heard you'd had an accident. Are you okay?"

Samantha was touched that they'd thought to drop by. "I'm fine, Melissa. Thank you for thinking of me."

"She's fine for the moment," Blake said, standing closest to the door, as if ready to open it in a moment's notice. "But she needs to rest as much as possible."

Shane stood beside him but he at least smiled at her, unlike Blake. "Good to see you, Samantha," he said, inclining his head in the cowboy way.

Samantha smiled back at the handsome man. Shane was the architect who'd designed the resort's riding stables. He might look urban and sophisticated, but he'd been raised on a nearby ranch and his cowboy status couldn't be disputed. "You, too, Shane."

Melissa sank down on one of the lounge chairs and frowned at Samantha. "You do look pale. So tell me. What happened?" Without giving her time to reply, she glanced at the men. "Blake, I'd love a hot chocolate so be a dear and make me one, won't you?" She darted a look at Samantha. "What about you, honey?"

Samantha wrinkled her nose. "Blake won't let me."

Melissa seemed to consider that, then darted a look at her brother before nodding at Samantha. "Yes, that's probably best." She looked at her fiancé. "Shane, darling, would you mind helping Blake in the kitchen? I'm not sure he knows his way around it," she teased.

Blake eased into his first smile since they'd arrived. "You'd be surprised, Melissa."

Melissa patted the small hump of her stomach on her slightly curvy figure. "You'd better hurry. This baby is getting hungry." She winked at Samantha.

Samantha smiled but as the men left them alone and she looked at Blake's sister, she felt a tug deep inside her chest. Melissa had a radiant glow about her. She'd only recently announced her pregnancy to Shane and they were soon to be married. They'd had a few ups and downs but now all was well.

Samantha was very happy for Melissa, and yet she felt sad for herself, with this inexplicable ache in the region of her heart. One day she wanted a baby and a family of her own, but she couldn't imagine any man she wanted to father them—except for maybe Blake. That would mean he would have to marry her, but he didn't believe in happily-ever-after, and she wasn't ready for that either.

Still, she couldn't shake off the thought of cuddling Blake's baby in her arms. It was natural for a woman to think about having children with the man she was attracted to, right? Strangely, she didn't ever remember thinking about having Carl's children. Her notion of being married to him had merely been about them traveling the world together. It hadn't progressed further than that. Thank the Lord!

"Are you okay, Samantha?"

She managed a smile. "Apart from a small headache, I'm fine."

Melissa's piercing blue eyes suddenly seemed so like Blake's. "I hear you're leaving us soon?"

This was why the other woman had got the men out of the way. Melissa wanted to question her.

Samantha tried to look at peace with her decision. "Yes, it's time to move on to new pastures."

"Blake will miss you."

"So everyone keeps telling me," Samantha said wryly, but was grateful that Shane came back in right then to ask Melissa a question about how hot she wanted her drink. Once he left again Samantha changed the conversation to the ranch where Shane had grown up. Melissa was more than happy to talk about her fiancé.

The other couple stayed for a while, until Blake shooed them out, reminding them that a certain person needed to rest up.

"Right," Blake said, once they'd gone. "I'll get some more work out of the way, then how does an omelet sound for dinner? I don't think you should eat anything too heavy, just in case. It's not a good thing to have a full stomach."

She looked at him in mild amusement. "Is this Doctor Jarrod speaking?"

He didn't seem to find that funny. "Yes, so take note."

"I would, only you won't let me work," she quipped.

"Funny," he muttered, then went back to his paperwork. She sighed. He was taking it all so seriously, and while that was sweet of him, it wasn't necessary.

After that, Samantha was itching to get up and move around but knew it was best she take things easy. For something to do while she was waiting for Blake to finish working, she popped a movie in the DVD and began watching it with earphones so that she didn't disturb him. It was a romantic comedy she hadn't seen before and it made her giggle. She didn't realize she'd been laughing loudly until suddenly she became aware of Blake standing near the couch.

She paused the movie and looked up at him as she pulled out her earbuds. "I'm sorry. Is this interrupting your work?"

"No." He went still. "It's good to hear you laugh. You don't do it often enough."

Her pulse was skipping beats. "The job isn't exactly a laugh a minute," she joked. Then realized how that might sound. "That came out wrong. I didn't mean—"

"I know what you meant," he said easily enough as he leaned over and pulled the earplug cord out of the television. Picking up the remote, he turned the movie back on, only instead of going back to his work he sat down on the other chair.

She blinked in mild surprise, then tried to concentrate as he began watching the movie with her. He'd only missed about fifteen minutes of the story, so they both watched it together. It was amusing enough that she could feel herself relax, and when it was finished even Blake looked relaxed. She was glad about that. He worked too hard at times, and took his responsibilities too seriously.

Later, in spite of him telling her to stay on the couch, she followed him into the kitchen where he was going to prepare dinner. "I need to walk. My legs are getting numb."

His brows immediately drew together on full medical alert. "They feel numb? Are you getting any pins and needles? Is it hard to walk or are—"

"Blake, I was merely trying to say I wanted to move around," she cut across him, somewhat bemused by his agitation.

He grimaced. "Okay, so that was a mild overreaction."

"Mild?" she teased.

He gave a self-deprecating smile, then jerked his head toward the bench. "Go sit over there and take it easy."

She ignored that and turned toward the cupboard.

"I'll put out the place mats and cutlery first. We can eat in here."

He must have known it was a waste of time to argue because he nodded, then went back to preparing the omelet. It was a strange feeling watching him cook for her. It would be another memory to take away when she left.

Soon they were sitting down on the tall stools to eat and the next hour flew by as they chatted. As if they both didn't want to ruin the moment, neither of them spoke about her leaving.

Then he mentioned Donald Jarrod in passing, and that made her think. Blake had never spoken about his father while they were in Vegas, but now they were in Aspen she'd managed to put two and two together. "Your dad was pretty hard on you, wasn't he?"

He tensed even as he gave a light shrug. "After my mother died, he was hard on all his children."

She considered him. "But harder on you."

A flash of surprise crossed his face. "Yes. How did you know?"

"You were the eldest. He seems to have been a man who had set ideas about the order of things and didn't give an inch."

"He was. Very much so."

"Tell me more."

He paused and for a moment she didn't think he would tell her. Then, "Guy was only younger by a few minutes but it could have been years in my father's eyes. I was the oldest, so it was up to me to make sure I took responsibility for everything. None of us ever really got to play while growing up, but I suppose I got even less time than the rest."

The thought upset her. “That’s sad.”

He shrugged. “My father actually did us a favor. We grew up being very independent. We don’t need anyone.”

She could see that. And that was even sadder, but she didn’t say so. She tilted her head. “It still would’ve been hard losing your mother like that when you were just a small boy. And then having your father distance himself would have made it far worse. Children don’t understand why love has been withdrawn. They just know.”

His expression suddenly bordered on mockery and she knew she’d touched a nerve. “And you understand the way a child’s mind works when he loses a parent, do you?”

She pulled a face. He knew very well both her parents were alive. “Well, no, but—”

“I rest my case.”

“Blake, I don’t think it’s too hard to comprehend what you must have gone through.”

Anger flashed across his face. “Enough, Samantha. I don’t want or need your sympathy for something that happened a long time ago.”

“But—”

The telephone rang and he snatched it up from the wall beside him, almost barking into it. His mouth tightened. “Hang on, Erica. I’ll put her on.” He handed the phone over to Samantha.

“I see Blake’s being his usual talkative self,” Erica mused down the line. She didn’t wait for Samantha to agree. “I heard about your accident and just wanted to see how you were doing.”

Samantha appreciated her concern. “I’m fine, thanks,

Erica." She forced herself to sound cheery. "Blake and I just had dinner. He cooked me an omelet."

An eloquent silence came from Erica's end. "A man of many talents," she finally said. "I'd better let you go, then. I'll talk to you tomorrow." She hung up before Samantha could respond.

Samantha took her time placing the receiver back down, hiding her expression from him. She wouldn't tell Blake what Erica had been thinking. That his half sister was delighted the two of them were bonding, even if Blake did sound like a grouch. "That was really nice of her to call."

His lips twisted. "I wonder if I have any relatives left who might like to interrupt us tonight?"

Her brow creased with worry. "You really should give Erica a chance."

"To do what?"

Anger stirred the air, though she knew it wasn't directed at her. She tilted her head. "Do you blame Erica for your father's affair with her mother?" she said, coming right out and saying it.

He didn't look pleased by her comment. "I'm not blaming Erica for what my father did. I just don't want her coming in here and splitting up the family. I'm not convinced she'll stay in Aspen."

She didn't know how he could say that. Was he blind? "She and Christian are so in love. And she's in love with everyone here at Jarrod Ridge, too. Their hearts are here, Blake. They won't leave you."

He swore. "I don't give a rat's ass if they leave or not. This isn't about what *I* feel anyway. It's about her causing problems for the family and then walking away without a care in the world."

"I'm sure that won't happen. Erica isn't like that."

One eyebrow shot up. "You know her so well, do you?"

"Do you?"

A muscle began ticking along his jaw. "Thank you for your opinion, but I don't need it." He pushed to his feet and began collecting the plates, taking them over to the dishwasher. "Go into the living room. I'll bring in the coffee."

For a few moments she didn't move. She watched his rigid back and felt depressed by his remoteness and abruptness. She'd pushed him hard just now and she wasn't sure why, except that she somehow felt she was fighting not just for Erica's sake but for Blake's, as well. If she could at least get him to relent toward Erica then maybe when *she* left, her time here would have been of value. Maybe then something good would have come from all this. She sighed. Or was she simply looking for something to make herself feel good about leaving Blake?

And that brought her back to what she'd said before about Erica leaving him. Was that the crux of the matter? It occurred to her then that Blake may have abandonment issues with his mother dying, and now that made it difficult for him to get close to his half sister. Or to get close to anyone, including herself.

Someone rang the doorbell and Blake swore again.

"That'll be Joel," Samantha reminded him. "He said he would check on me."

"Stay there," he muttered and strode past her to let in the other man.

A couple of seconds later Joel breezed into the kitchen. She noticed he took in the homey scene, but he was all professional while he checked her over and announced he was pleased.

Then, "We have to get you better for tomorrow night," he teased, but she saw him dart a look at Blake and she suddenly had the feeling there was more to this. He seemed to be letting Blake know he was staking a claim.

"Tomorrow night?" Blake asked in a menacing voice.

Joel closed up his medical bag. "Samantha and I have a date for Monday night." He winked at her. "We're going to the movies."

Samantha wanted to say she hadn't actually accepted the invitation but the displeased look in Blake's eyes kept her quiet.

"Let's see how she feels first," Blake said grimly, then stepped back in clear indication that the doctor should precede him to the front door.

Joel hesitated, like he wasn't about to take orders, then he must have remembered that Blake was his boss. He inclined his head at Samantha. "I'll call you in the morning," he told her, picking up his bag.

He left the room and Blake saw him out, and Samantha couldn't help but wonder once again if Blake might be jealous of Joel. The thought made her heartbeat pick up speed. Blake had certainly *wanted* to kiss her back there on the mountain and surely that had to mean something.

Didn't it?

All at once she needed to know what he felt for her. "Joel finds me attractive, don't you think?" she said dreamily as Blake came back in the kitchen looking anything but relaxed.

His eyes filled with meaning. "Sure he does," he said cynically.

She couldn't let him get away with that. "What does that mean?"

"Just that any woman with the right equipment can attract a man. And believe me, you've got the right equipment," he drawled, slipping his hands into his trouser pockets, all at once looking very much in charge of himself, making her want to bring him down a peg or two.

"Thanks for the assumption that I'm only good for sex," she said with faint indignation.

His hands came out of his pockets and his complacency vanished. "I didn't say that," he retorted, then strode over to check on the coffee. He spun back around. "Dammit, what the hell are you doing with those men anyway? You don't need them. They're beneath you."

Startled, she gathered her wits about her. *This* was more like it. "Maybe I *want* them beneath me," she joked.

"Don't talk like that."

She hid a soft gasp. It *did* sound like he was jealous. She needed to push more. "I don't understand how you can say a doctor isn't good enough for me, Blake."

"That's because he's *not* good enough for you."

Her spirits soared. "What about Ralph? You don't even know what he does for a living."

"And you do?"

She did, then realized she'd set herself up here. She had to cough before she said, "He's a car salesman."

"Huh! That explains the slime rolling off him."

"Blake!" She hadn't expected quite such a response. "What's got into you?"

His mouth drew down at the corners. "Those guys aren't after you for your intellect."

She screwed up her nose. "How nice of you to point that out."

"You know what I'm saying."

Yes, she did. Unfortunately she knew it was true. And that would have been fine if she'd been the least bit interested in the other men. As it was, she still felt a little guilty using them, though no doubt they were big enough to look out for themselves.

She tilted her head and knew she had to say this. "If I didn't know better I'd think you were jealous."

"And if I am?" he challenged without warning.

She felt giddy but she couldn't let herself get her hopes up. "I'd have to ask why. Is it because you know I'm leaving soon and you only want what you suddenly can't have?"

"What the—"

"Or is it because you might actually want *me?*"

For a moment he looked like he would move in close. "You ask me that after the kiss we shared?"

Her breath came quickly. "I—"

And then something changed in his expression and his jaw thrust forward. "This isn't the time to discuss it. You need your rest. You should go lie on the couch."

Her throat blocked with disappointment, but then understanding dawned and she realized he was pulling back for *her* sake. If it hadn't been for her accident, she was sure he would be making love to her right now.

Frustration weaved through her, despite appreciating that he was doing the right thing. "I think I'll go read in bed. It's getting late." He went to come with her and she put her hand up. “No, I can manage by myself. Good night, Blake. And thanks.”

He nodded. “Make sure you sleep in the spare bedroom. I still want you close to me.”

She could feel heat sweeping up her face. Did he have to say it like that? “Okay.”

He seemed mesmerized by her reddening cheeks. “I’ll be checking on you a couple of times in the night.” His voice had a gravelly edge to it now. “So I apologize in advance for disturbing you.”

She looked away; the thought of him coming into her room during the night was enough to disturb her *now.*

Then she went up to bed with stars in her eyes. And they weren’t from the hit on the head either. Unfortunately she knew he wasn’t about to take advantage of her while she was injured, and certainly not during the night when she was sure he’d remain a perfect gentleman. But he’d better watch out when she was back on her feet.

Six

Blake looked at the bedside clock and grunted to himself. It was almost seven o'clock and still dark outside, but he needed to get up and check on Samantha before he did anything else this morning. Today he planned on working from Pine Lodge so he could keep an eye on her, but he needed to go to the Manor and get some things out of the way first.

He'd spent a restless night, getting up every couple of hours to check on a sleeping Samantha in the bedroom next door. Of course it was easy for her to sleep so peacefully. She didn't have to stand over an attractive member of the opposite sex who wore satin pajamas and looked deliciously alluring in bed. And she didn't have to reach out to touch that person's shoulder to shake them awake, nor rigidly ignore the urge to slide into bed next to her warm body and pleasure her senseless.

He would have done it, too—if he hadn't had to

wake her and ask questions to make sure she wasn't suffering any sort of confusion. Even now the thought of her having any sort of aftereffects from the head injury still managed to clench his gut tight. He'd hated seeing her hurt. If he hadn't been so focused on getting her away from that Ralph, then none of this would have happened.

Not even the kiss.

No, that kiss *would* have happened—if not there, then somewhere else. There was something going on between them now. It had started happening the night she'd handed him her resignation and it hadn't let up.

And it wasn't one-sided either. She'd dissolved in his arms so quickly yesterday he'd thought the marrow had melted in her bones. No woman had ever reacted quite like that for him before. It certainly made a man feel good.

Remembering the feel of her lips beneath his, he was tempted to just lie there and think about her, but he knew he'd never get out of bed if he did. And then Samantha would be bringing *him* breakfast in bed. The thought was more than pleasurable.

Giving a low groan, he tossed back the covers and shoved off the mattress in his pajama bottoms, then headed for the bathroom to take a shower. But as he opened the door and went to reach for the light switch, the light flicked on anyway and Samantha came through the connecting door.

She jumped back with a gasp. "Blake!"

A lick of fire sizzled through his veins as his eyes slid down over her slim contours, registering that what he thought had been green satin pajamas was an emerald midthigh nightshirt. It looked so sexy on her, suiting her complexion and rich brown hair.

He lifted his eyes back up to her face. "How's the head?" he asked huskily.

She seemed to become flustered. "Er…it doesn't feel too bad." Awkwardly she spun to face the mirrored wall, going up on her toes to stare at her reflection. "I came to see if it was okay." She lifted her long tousled strands to check the injury. "Yes, it looks fine," she chattered. "There's a bit of a bump and no sign of bleeding."

He appreciated that she was okay, but did she know that stretching up over the sink like she was, the side split of her nightshirt was showing him more of her long silken legs than he'd ever seen before? All the way up her thigh to the line of her panties.

Suddenly she seemed to freeze in position as she stretched up at the mirror like that, and he realized right then she was looking at *him* in the mirror, with a hungry look that drifted down over his bare chest and the pajama bottoms he'd worn last night for her benefit. He tensed with arousal and she must have noticed. Their eyes locked together in the glass.

And then she slowly pushed back from the sink and turned to face him with her body, her chin tilting provocatively, her eyes inviting him to take her. Caught off-guard by such an unfamiliar look from her, he swallowed hard. His assistant was certainly showing him a new side of herself lately.

"Samantha," he said thickly, galvanized into taking a step toward her. "Do you know what you're—"

"Yes, Blake, I do."

He reached her and she tumbled against him, her hands flattening against his chest, her mouth seeking his, her lips parting beneath his without any pressure at all.

Their kiss was hot and urgent and demanding, their bodies pressing closer and closer together, reveling in each other. Then a soft moan of hers breathed into him, and in a haze of desire, he deepened the kiss until he finally had to break away to suck in air.

But only for a moment, until he began planting quick, soft kisses down that creamy throat, before coming back up again to her lips, needing to be inside her mouth once more, needing to breathe her in once more.

He pulled her harder against him, running his hands hungrily over the satin material and feminine curves. She quivered all over from head to toe, wildly gripping his shoulders like she needed to hold on to him.

Mouth to mouth, he backed her to the full-length sink and lifted her up onto a folded fluffy towel. Her thighs fell open and he heard a button pop from the front of her nightshirt. He gave a groan of approval and wedged himself between her legs….

And the coldness of the marble touched his erection through his pajamas.

The shock of it made him still. Heaven knew he could do with cooling down…slowing down…but Samantha sat in front of him with her head tilted back and her eyes closed. Her cheeks were overheated, her breathing unsteady, and despite that come-to-me look she'd given him a short while ago, she appeared to be about to lose control. God knows he'd felt the instantaneous spiral of desire himself, but this was more and he really had to wonder just how inexperienced she actually was. He swallowed hard. Could she even be a *virgin?*

He wasn't sure how he felt about that, but he did

know he couldn't continue this right now. His previous lovers knew the score but this woman may not. And if he was playing with more than her body...if her emotions were more than involved...he could cause her a lot of heartache. He didn't want to do that to Samantha.

Yet this wasn't the moment to talk about it, with her looking all sexy and ready for the taking. There was too much hunger in the air in here. It would only confuse things. He liked her too much to do this to her.

Unwrapping her arms from around his neck, he lifted her down off the bench, hating that he had to walk away from her. "I'm sorry, Samantha."

Bewilderment spread over her face. "What's the—"

"I just can't do it," he rasped. "Not like this." As hard as it was to leave her side, he turned and went back to his room.

He badly wanted to turn right back around, sweep her up in his arms and carry her to his bed. He shuddered as he closed the door between them.

They would talk later and perhaps it would turn out that he'd have to keep the door closed permanently between them. Maybe she would be his road not taken. But he had to think what was best for Samantha. She deserved better than becoming his temporary mistress.

Samantha didn't know how she made it back to her own room. Humiliation scorched through her. She'd done exactly what she'd wanted to do and given Blake a come-on. She hadn't deliberately gone into the bathroom to entice him in there, but the opportunity had presented itself and she'd thought it had worked. Then he'd just upped and walked away and, despite his obvious arousal, he said he couldn't do it.

Couldn't make love with her.

She knew it had nothing to do with her having a minor head injury this time. He might say it was, but she knew this was about him not wanting her enough. His body had automatically responded to a female in his arms, but his mind had been elsewhere. As he'd said the evening before, any woman with the right equipment could attract a man. Unfortunately the attraction he felt for her hadn't been enough. Not for him.

It was Carl all over again.

She plopped down on her bed as her legs gave way. Had she unwittingly done something wrong back there? Something to annoy him physically? Clearly he hadn't been invested in the moment like she'd been. It had been wonderful in his arms but she hadn't realized he'd been feeling different. She thought he'd felt the same way. It was obvious now that he could turn himself on and off at a whim—just like he had after their kiss on the mountain.

Unlike her.

Her emotions whirled like a spinning top let loose on the floor. Oh, God, what was she going to do? How was she going to face him? Worse, would he insist on letting her out of her contract now? She had the feeling he would tell her to leave sooner rather than later.

At the thought, her emotions stopped spinning. They stopped dead. Her chin lifted. Right. Okay. If she was being given the heave-ho, then she would certainly leave without protest. It's what she needed to do anyway, she told herself. She regretted she would leave with this between them, but things had gone too far. It was a good lesson in being careful what she wished for. Now she simply wished this nightmare would go away.

Samantha took a shower and carefully washed her hair, but wasn't sure if she was dismayed or relieved after she came out of the bathroom and heard Blake's car leaving. Going over to peek out her bedroom window, she saw him driving toward the Manor in the early morning light. Evidently she was okay to be left alone now, she thought with a stab of hurt.

Then her heart dropped to her feet. Perhaps he was going to tell his family that she was leaving sooner? Would he tell them why? That she'd made a play for him and put him in an awkward position? Her cheeks heated at the thought and she wanted to curl up in a ball and not see any of them again.

Yet pride wouldn't allow her to do that. She'd held her head high when Carl had rejected her and she would do it again now. She would go up to the Manor and finish her tasks, and she would arrange her replacement. If she smiled at the others and acted carefree, then no one would know how bad she felt.

No one except Blake.

Half an hour later she sat at her desk at the Manor, relieved not to have seen anyone she knew on the way here. She didn't want to answer questions about her accident, or anything else for that matter.

Thankfully the door to Blake's office was shut, though the red light on the telephone told her he was making a call. Quickly she got herself organized, then found the number she was after and reached for the phone, hoping someone at the employment agency would be at their desk early like her. She knew that as soon as the red button on his phone lit up with her extension, Blake would learn she was here, but it couldn't be helped.

She got the answering machine. Having dealt with this employment agency before for other office matters, she decided to leave a message. At least that would get the ball rolling. "Yes, this is Samantha Thompson calling on behalf of Blake Jarrod Enterprises. Could Mary Wentworth call me back as soon as possible…" The red light on Blake's phone went off. Her heart started to race as a second later his door was flung open. "It's about a position that's become available." He strode to her desk. "It's—"

He pressed the button to disconnect the call, his eyes slamming into her. "What are you doing?" he demanded in a low tone.

She angled her chin as she looked up at him. "I'm trying to work."

"I thought you'd have enough sense to rest up today."

"I don't need to rest up. I did plenty of that yesterday." Calmly, she placed the telephone back on its handset. "I'm perfectly fine now."

His eyes narrowed. "And why the hell are you calling someone about your job?"

"You need a new assistant."

"I'm happy with my old one."

She arched one eyebrow. "Really? It didn't seem that way to me this morning," she said, staying cool when all she wanted to do was fall in a heap and cry her eyes out.

He swore.

"Don't worry, Blake. I'll be leaving Aspen soon, so

you don't have to worry that I'll attack you. I know you're not that into me."

He blinked, then, "What the hell!" He swore again. "We need to talk."

"It's a bit late for talking, don't you think?" She went to pick up the phone again. He grabbed her hand, not hurting her but not letting her make the call either. "Stop manhandling me, Blake."

He tried to stare her down. "No."

"Blake, this isn't getting us anywhere."

"Listen, Samantha. You're—"

Erica walked into the office and stopped dead, blinking in surprise as her gaze went from one to the other, then down at their hands gripped together. "Er… Blake, your car is here to take you to the airport."

He casually let go of Samantha's hand. "Thanks, Erica."

Samantha felt the blood drain from her face. "You're leaving?"

Like Carl?

He looked at her oddly. "Something cropped up overnight at one of the hotels and I need to go to Vegas and sort it out. I'll tell you about it later."

As fast as it had tightened, the tension unscrewed inside her. So he *was* coming back. It had been crazy of her to even think he wouldn't. Blake wouldn't give up all this because of *her*.

She went to get to her feet. "I'll come with you." Once she was in Vegas, she would start bringing her life there to a close.

"No, you stay here. You shouldn't be flying with a head injury," he said firmly, surprising her. She'd have thought he'd be eager to get her out of Aspen now.

He cast his half sister a look. "Erica, can you keep an eye on Samantha and make sure she doesn't stay here too long today? I don't want her overdoing things."

Erica looked startled then pleased. "Of course." It was obvious she valued being asked by her brother to help out, but Samantha was still surprised that Blake wanted *her* to stay in Aspen.

He nodded. "Thanks. I'll just grab my stuff." As he spoke he headed back into his office before coming out with his briefcase and coat. He looked at Samantha. "I'll be back tonight. I'll explain everything then." He started toward the door then hesitated. "You *will* be here when I return, won't you, Samantha?"

It hadn't occurred to her to leave behind his back, though she couldn't discount that it might have. Then she remembered how she'd thought he might have issues with feeling abandoned over his mother's death. Did he think *she* was about to abandon him, too? Tenderness touched a part of her that wasn't reeling by the latest events. "I promise."

He looked satisfied then he gave Erica a jerky nod as he passed by. He left behind a meaningful silence.

After a couple of seconds, Erica came toward the desk. "Are you okay?"

"My head's fine now, thanks."

She tutted. "You know I mean more than that."

Samantha grimaced. "Yes, I suppose I do." Then as she looked at the other woman, she wondered if Blake would eventually discuss her with his family. Would he even tell them she had made a play for him? Her breath caught. She'd never known him to talk about his affairs before to anyone. Huh! Affair? There *was* no affair. That was the problem.

"He's concerned for you, honey."

"He's concerned for the job."

"You're wrong." Erica paused. "Give him a chance to explain whatever it is he needs to explain."

The telephone rang then, and Erica said she had to go check on something but would be back later. Samantha answered it and heard Mary Wentworth's voice, and knew she needed to slow everything down a little. So she apologized to the other woman that she couldn't talk right now and would call her back tomorrow. By then, she should well and truly know the score between her and Blake. Either way, she still had to leave. It was just a matter of when.

After she hung up, the workday began with the phone ringing, then the mail arrived. Samantha worked through it all, but a part of her mind was on Blake's reaction earlier. He'd said he was perfectly happy with his old assistant.

Her.

And that made her wonder if he might still want her to work out her contract. Her heart raced at the thought, then came to a shuddering halt when she remembered this morning in the bathroom. She probably couldn't stay at Jarrod Ridge past tomorrow, but at least on his return tonight she might learn what had turned him off her. It may not be something she wanted to hear, but she needed to know or she would always wonder.

Erica returned an hour later, but Samantha still felt physically fine and convinced her not to worry. She'd decided to work until lunchtime, then she got a ride back to the lodge, where she made herself a light lunch. Afterward she felt tired, so she stretched out on the couch and took a nap.

The front doorbell woke her sometime later. It was a florist with a vase filled with the most gorgeous yellow tulips she'd ever seen. Something flipped over inside her heart. Her family wasn't into sending flowers, and only one person here knew she loved yellow tulips.

There was a card with them. "Dinner tonight. Pine Lodge. All arranged. See you at seven."

Her throat swelled with emotion as she carried the vase over to a side table and set it down. They looked so stunning that she was about to race upstairs to get her camera, but then wondered if that was a good idea. Did she really want to take away more memories of Blake?

The telephone rang then.

It was Joel. Oh, Lord. She'd forgotten her date with him tonight. The tulips caught her eye and she knew she'd rather spend her last hours here in Aspen with Blake than go to the movies with Joel.

She opened her mouth to speak but before she could say anything, he apologized and told her that his cousin was in town overnight and this was his only chance to catch up with her. Did she mind? No. Could they go to the movies tomorrow night instead? She said she would let him know. She had no idea whether she would still be here tomorrow night. Then he mentioned that he was in town right now and would get the nurse to check on her later today, but she thanked him and said it wasn't necessary.

More than relieved, Samantha looked at the tulips as she hung up the telephone, Joel already relegated to the back of her mind. Blake might just want to discuss her job tonight, but right now she didn't care. She needed to know where it had all gone wrong this morning. More importantly, she wanted to know if there was even a slim chance it was something that could be fixed.

Seven

Samantha hadn't been sure what she should wear for tonight. While the flowers and the dinner were very thoughtful of Blake, and while he'd said he would give her an explanation as to why he walked away from her this morning in the bathroom and that sounded promising, none of that meant he *wanted* her.

In the end she decided to keep it fairly low-key, just like she would if she were dining with him for business reasons. She wore a thin brown sweater over cream slacks and a pair of low-heeled pumps, adding a gold chain at her neck to make it a little more stylish.

Just after six-thirty one of the hotel staff arrived as sunset spiked through the lodge. He placed a cooked casserole in the oven to keep warm, dessert in the refrigerator, then lit the log fire before beautifully setting the table in the small dining alcove. Had Blake requested the two candles on the table? She was about to ask the young waiter when Blake came in the front door.

"Blake!" she exclaimed, her pulse picking up at the sight of him. Realizing she might be giving herself away, she pulled herself back and toned it down. "You're early," she said more sedately. "I didn't expect you quite so soon."

"We had a tailwind." He nodded at the waiter. "It looks good, Andy. Thanks."

Samantha wasn't surprised that he knew the man's name. Blake was good with people—as long as you did the right thing by him.

"No problem, Mr. Jarrod." Andy's smile encompassed them both. "I'll come and collect everything tomorrow." He nodded good-night, then went through to the kitchen.

Blake stood there for a minute looking at Samantha, his eyes flicking down over her outfit then away. "I could do with a shower," he muttered, and made for the stairs.

She felt nervous all of a sudden. She twisted away herself. "I'll just make sure the food's okay." She left the room and went into the kitchen, glad that Andy was still gathering a couple of things together before he left. It brought the world back into focus and took it away from her and Blake. She needed the balance.

Andy left and she busied herself unnecessarily checking on the casserole, then poured herself a glass of water and stood there sipping it to calm her nerves. She could only stay in there so long, and soon she wandered back into the lounge area and drew the drapes against the encroaching night, before switching on the lamps.

It was too quiet, so she put on a CD to fill the silence

and sat down on the couch to wait. The wood scent from the burning logs in the fireplace wafted throughout the room, and after a few minutes, she could feel the soft music begin to ease the tension inside her. And then it hit her and she realized how romantic the whole place looked. She groaned slightly. It hadn't been intentional but would Blake believe that? It all looked so intimate.

Panicking that he might think she was trying to seduce him, she was about to about to jump up and turn off the music when she saw Blake coming down the stairs. He wasn't looking at her and she ate up the sight of him. He was so handsome in light gray pants and a navy crewneck sweater, but it was his magnetic aura of masculinity that caught her breath.

He reached the bottom step and all at once he glanced up and his gaze quickly summed up the ambiance in the room. She could feel warmth steal under her skin. This guy never missed a trick.

"You must be tired," she said, hoping to ignore what he might think was obvious.

"A little. It's been a long day."

And then their eyes met—memories of this morning between them.

She moistened her mouth. "Blake, I—"

He shook his head. "Not yet, Samantha. Let's eat first. I'm starving and I need to relax a little."

"Of course." She swung toward the kitchen. "I'll serve the dinner."

"I'll pour the wine."

She hurried away, expelling a shaky breath once she reached the privacy of the kitchen. Blake wouldn't discuss the matter until he was ready, so she would just have to have a little patience. Perhaps it would be best if she had some food in her stomach first.

When she came back carrying the plates of chicken casserole, he was sitting at the table, having poured the wine. He stood up as she approached and took the plates from her. He'd always been a gentleman where she was concerned, holding out her chair or opening doors for her. She knew it was something he did on autopilot.

"You lit the candles," she said for something to say. "They look really nice."

He put the plates down on the table. "Andy knows his job."

She wasn't sure if that meant Blake had asked for them or if Andy had merely improvised. Did it matter, she asked herself as he held her chair out just as she'd expected.

As she sat down, she glimpsed the tulips on the side table. That was probably why he'd looked at her strangely before going upstairs to change. He must think her so ungrateful.

"Oh, Blake, I should have said something earlier. Thank you so much for the tulips. They're absolutely gorgeous."

"You like them, then?" He looked pleased as he sat down opposite her.

"I love them."

He considered her. "You getting hit on the head was very good for me."

She blinked. "It was?"

"I learned two things about you. What your favorite flower is, and your favorite color."

"Want to know my favorite perfume, too?" she joked, touched by his words.

Only he didn't laugh. "It's Paris by Yves Saint Laurent," he said with an unexpected thickness to his voice that made her nerves tingle.

"You know?"

"You bought some the first time we went to Paris together, remember?" He made it sound like they'd been together in Paris for something other than business.

Surprised he remembered that time two years ago when she'd first gone to work for him, she dropped her gaze and fanned her napkin over her lap, though she rather felt like fanning her face instead. "This looks delicious."

There was a slight pause. "Yes."

She could feel his eyes on her as she picked up her fork and finally looked at him again. "So, what was the problem in Vegas that you needed to go there in such a hurry?"

A moment ticked by then he picked up his fork. "There was a problem with one of the chefs. He was being a bit too temperamental, and the kitchen staff was threatening to walk out. It was beginning to escalate into a big commotion with the unions. It started to get ugly."

"And it's sorted out now?"

"Of course."

She had to smile. "Naturally. You wouldn't have come back otherwise, right?"

Suddenly there was an air of watchfulness about him. "What happened to your date with Joel tonight?"

She'd wondered if he'd mention it. And then something else occurred to her. Could he have arranged to get Joel out of the way tonight? The thought made her pulse race. "His cousin's in Aspen for the night and he wanted to spend time with her." She tilted her head. "You didn't have anything to do with that, did you?"

His brow rose. "Me? Am I that good?"

"Yes!" she exclaimed on a half chuckle.

A flash of humor crossed his face. "Believe me, I'm not *that* clever."

It did sound silly now. Blake could make things happen, but this time he'd have to find Joel's cousin and get that person to come to Aspen. Why would he bother? He knew he merely had to send her flowers and arrange dinner and she'd capitulate like every woman before her.

"Anyway, how are you feeling?" he asked.

"Terrific."

He searched her face, then inclined his head as if satisfied. "At least you only worked half the day."

Her eyes widened. "How do you know that?"

"I checked with Erica. She said you'd left at lunchtime."

She smiled wryly. "Did she also tell you she checked on me nearly every hour after that?"

"She promised me she would."

Why was she *not* surprised? "That was a bit over the top, wasn't it?"

"I don't think so."

She tried not to look more into it than there was. He probably wanted her all better so he could get rid of her faster. Then she knew that wasn't fair of her and she pulled her thoughts back into line. "You always were concerned for your staff, Blake. Thank you."

He looked at her strangely, as if he couldn't understand why she was putting herself in with the rest of his staff. But if that were the case, didn't that mean he was thinking she was something more to him than she actually was?

God, she had to stop thinking so much!

She picked up her wineglass. "You know, Blake. Erica isn't as bad as you imagine her to be. I suspect she'd still have kept an eye on me even without you asking her." She took a sip of her drink but watched him carefully over the rim of her glass.

His brows furrowed. "I guess so." As much as he appeared to concede the point, he didn't look totally convinced about Erica's intentions.

Samantha understood why. "You think she's only doing something nice for a reason, don't you?"

"Maybe."

"Has it occurred to you that the reason is *you?*" She let him consider that, then added, "Maybe she wants to get to know her brother, and she knows the only way she can do that is to show him she is willing to help him out?"

"Maybe." He paused. "But she cares for you, too."

She felt a rush of affection for Erica. "And that goes to show she's a nice person and worthy of your friendship… if not your love."

His lips twisted. "The hit on the head seems to have muddled your brain. You think you're a psychoanalyst now, do you?"

"Where you're concerned I have to be," she said without thinking, but knew it was her mention of the word *love* that had got his back up. Love and Blake Jarrod did *not* go hand-in-hand.

And neither did Samantha Thompson.

Not with love.

Certainly not with Blake Jarrod.

A curious look passed over his face. "Why would you want to psychoanalyze me anyway?"

This time she thought before speaking. No use giving away more of herself than she needed to. It was best she keep up a wall. He would appreciate her more for that.

She managed a thin smile. "A person likes to figure out how their boss's mind works. It helps with the job."

He leaned back in his chair. "Yes, you were always good at that."

Then…just as she thought she had it all under control, all at once everything rose in her throat. She couldn't take any more of this subterfuge and talking around things that mattered. "Blake, don't you think it's time we talked about last night? You took such good care of me, and then this morning…"

He stilled. "Yes?"

She swallowed hard. She had to ask the next question and she had to be prepared to accept the answer. "I'd like to know what I did wrong."

His face blanched as he sat forward. "Nothing, Samantha. You did nothing wrong."

"Then what—"

He drew a breath. "Samantha, are you a virgin?"

She felt her cheeks heat up. "No."

He looked surprised. "I thought you might be."

"Well, I'm not," she said, hunching her shoulders, wondering where this was going to lead.

His expression softened a little. "But you're not very experienced, are you?"

Okay, so it led to further embarrassment.

She could feel her cheeks redden further. "You must know I…er…haven't been with a lot of men."

"How many?"

Her eyes widened. "None of your business."

"You made it my business this morning."

She hesitated, then, "One lover when I was a teenager."

His brow rose. "And none since?" He must have read her thoughts. "You can tell me. I'm not going to tell anyone else."

So, okay, she would accept that. "Well, there was a man back home...."

He didn't blink an eye but she knew she had his attention. "And?"

"We didn't become lovers, but I was in love with him."

"What happened?"

Her lips twisted with self-derision. "He wasn't in love with me."

Blake nodded. "That explains why you haven't had any relationships since I've known you," he said, almost to himself. Then his eyes sharpened. "Are you still in love with him?"

"No. Carl left to go overseas and ended up marrying someone else. I realized I'd been in love with the *idea* of love and that's all it was." She sighed. "But it was a good lesson in learning that you can never be sure of another person's feelings." Realizing that she was suddenly giving too much away, she tried to be casual. "So, you see, I can only lay claim to one lover and that was a long time ago."

"I could tell."

Her composure lurched like a drunken sailor. "I'm sorry. I thought my enthusiasm might make up for any lack of experience."

"Don't apologize. Your enthusiasm was great. Damn great," he said brusquely. "I had a hard time walking away from you."

Her heart faltered. "You did? I thought you didn't want me."

He expelled a harsh breath. "Did my body *feel* like I didn't want you?"

She remembered the tense cords of his body burning her flesh through her nightshirt. "No," she croaked, then had to clear her throat before speaking again. "But what do I know anyway? I thought a man could easily turn it off and on." Carl certainly had been able to put a stop to anything beyond a few kisses.

"I'm not made of stone like that other guy," Blake scoffed, reading her mind, but his voice had gentled. "And all this goes to prove to me that I did the right thing this morning. I'm the experienced one here and that means I have a responsibility to you. I'm glad now I didn't take something from you that you might regret giving later on."

"You mean my virginity?" Her heart rose in her chest at the respect he'd afforded her.

"Yes."

"But I'm *not* a virgin," she pointed out.

"I know that now."

He'd rejected her all for nothing? It was admirable, but… "You should have asked me at the time."

He pursed his mouth. "It's not only that," he said, sending her stomach plummeting.

"I see."

"No, I don't think you do." He clenched his jaw. "You were so damn generous, Samantha. You were giving me everything and I was worried that you…er…might look more into this than you should. I just wasn't sure you could handle any emotional involvement."

She appreciated where he was coming from with this, but her heart still managed to drop at his words. What *was* it about her that every man felt they had to warn her off?

"Don't worry," she assured him. "I'm not planning on repeating history and losing my heart to anyone in the future."

His eyes searched hers. "Are you sure?"

"Positive." Suddenly she felt all-knowing. "Maybe it's *you* who can't handle it, Blake."

He looked startled, then scowled. "I admit it. I can't. And to be blunt, I don't want to even try." He paused. "But this isn't about me. I'm thinking of *you,* Samantha. Not me."

Her heart tilted. She appreciated his honesty but she could look after herself. And to be equally as honest, how could she give him up without a fight now that she knew he wanted her?

"Blake, thank you for that but you're doing me an injustice. I'm a grown woman. I know sex doesn't always mean commitment. I have needs and I know my own mind. I know what I want, and while I'm here..." She looked him straight in the eye. "What I want is *you.*"

"Hell."

She flinched. "I'm sorry if that makes things more difficult."

"Don't be. It's your directness, that's all. It blows me away."

She felt a rush of warmth. "I do want you, Blake. Very much."

"Your head—"

"Is on the mend." She paused, preempting him. "And yes, I'm sure."

His eyes flared sensuously. "Then do me a favor."

She moistened her mouth. "What?"

"Go upstairs and put your nightshirt on for me," he said, his voice turning heavy with huskiness.

She blinked in surprise. "My nightshirt?"

"You looked so sexy in it this morning. I've been thinking about it all day. It's been driving me crazy."

Sudden awareness danced in her veins. "Does this mean we're going to—"

"Have sex? Yes." A tiny pulse beat in his cheekbone. "But only if you're sure you can handle a purely sexual relationship," he said, giving her one last out.

Excitement washed over her. He still wanted her.

She nodded. "I can handle it, Blake."

"Then go change."

She got to her feet. It was now or never. And right now *never* definitely wasn't an option.

Samantha couldn't deny she was nervous as she came out of her room in her nightshirt and descended the staircase in a pair of high-heeled gold sandals she'd put on at the last moment. The bottom button was missing from her nightshirt, but the material covered her and what did it matter now anyway?

Blake had turned the lamps off and stood by the log fire, watching her in the flickering light with the same look he'd had on his face last Saturday night when she'd dressed for her date with Joel. She'd been trying to capture Blake's attention that night to make him jealous. Tonight she'd definitely caught more than his attention.

Tonight they both knew they would be a part of each other. The power of that thought stunned her.

"Come over here, Samantha," he said huskily when she reached the bottom step. The air throbbed between them and she quivered, moving forward without a falter as she made her away across the carpet to him.

His blue eyes moved slowly down over her, and something flared in them. "You're still missing the button," he said, as if to himself.

She blinked in surprise as she reached him. "You knew it was missing?"

"Oh, yes. It came off this morning in the bathroom… when I lifted you up on the sink."

She could feel herself go hot all over. "Oh. I hadn't realized."

"I know you didn't," he said, with a pointed look. He pulled her up against him. "God, you're so damn sexy, Samantha Thompson," he murmured, gathering her close. "My very sexy lady." His body was hard and she trembled. "Now, does that feel like I can turn myself off so easily?" he said thickly, his breath stirring over her face.

The solid warmth of him pressed against her stomach. "No." The word emerged on a whisper.

"There's no going back this time," he said, reassuring that this time he would not walk away.

The deepest longing stirred within her. "Kiss me, Blake."

He did.

Once…twice…long and slow…

And then he eased back and looked deep into her eyes.

She looked back at him.

Blue on blue.

"I want you in front of the fire," he murmured, sending her pulse jumping all over the place. "Here. Lie down on the cushions." She saw he had placed two big cushions near their feet. "Be careful of your head," he said, helping to lower her to the thick rug, so sweet and caring. She wanted to say it was too late, that she was about to lose her head anyway, only the words wouldn't come.

Soon she was lying there in her nightshirt and her gold sandals and he was standing over her in the firelight, his gaze scanning the full length of her, before stopping at the junction to her thighs. "You left your panties on," he mused throatily, telling her the front of her nightshirt must have fallen open at the hem.

She moistened her mouth. "I wanted to take them off, but…"

"I'll be happy to do the honors…" he said, and her heartbeat quickened, "but in a minute."

All at once she wanted him so much. "Take off your clothes first, Blake. Don't make me wait."

His eyes darkened and he dragged his sweater up over his head, along with his T-shirt, tossing them aside. He kicked off his shoes and his hands went to his belt.…

He hesitated.

"Your trousers, too." She was desperate to see him fully as a man for the first time, the thought making her lightheaded.

Another second, then his hands dropped away from the buckle. "Not yet." He dropped to his knees beside her, and let his gaze slide along the full length of her, like he was committing her to memory.

But his bare chest beckoned her and she reached

out to touch him, her fingers tingling as she came into contact with the dark whorls of hair over hard muscle. He groaned and slammed his hand over hers, stopping it from moving.

"Not yet," he repeated, putting her hand back down beside her.

And then with slow deliberation he began to undo her top button. She gasped as he undid another and slid her nightshirt off her shoulder a little. "I've wanted to do this since this morning," he murmured, lowering his head and trailing a kiss from the curve of her shoulder to her throat, then down to the valley between her breasts.

He inhaled deeply, then lifted his face and undid another button, exposing her breasts. Soon he was leaning over her, using his mouth to possess the tip of one nipple before moving to the other, gliding his tongue back and forth over them, imprinting them with his taste.

"Oh, my God," she muttered, shuddering at such an exquisite touch. "I..."

"Steady, my lovely." He shifted back a little. Another button undone allowed him to drift kisses along the exposed skin to her belly button. She shuddered again when he stroked his palm over her stomach, before the rest of the buttons were unfastened and the material finally parted, falling away to her sides and revealing her near-nakedness to him.

"Beautiful," he murmured, dipping his fingers under the waistband then peeling the panties down her body. By the time he'd finished, he'd moved to kneel between her thighs. She moaned faintly, suspecting a blush was rolling all the way down to her feet.

"So beautiful." He slowly reached out and slipped a

finger through the triangle of curls, making her gasp. "You like that?"

She moaned again. "Oh, yes."

For long, heart-stopping moments he toyed with her dampening skin, sending tremors through her. And then he slid his hands under her, cupping the cheeks of her bottom and tilting her lower body up to him, the satin material of her nightshirt falling away fully as his head lowered to the dark V at her thighs.

But before he touched, he stopped and looked up again, his eyes catching hers, holding still. He didn't speak or move a muscle, but there was a primitive look in his eyes that swept her breath away.

Slowly he lowered his head again and sought her out, his mouth beginning a slow worship of her femininity. She gasped as his tongue slid between her folds, teasing and tantalizing her, stroking her in erotic exploration, taking her to the brink, then bringing her back…once…twice…then finally he took her right over the edge, any remnants of her control disintegrating as she pulsed with the purest of pleasures.

Long moments later, she was still trying to recover when he rose to his feet and stripped off his trousers. She watched mesmerized as he put on a condom, thrilled that she had the power to make this man so hot and hard for her.

He was soon kneeling back down between her legs, and kissing his way right up the center of her until he found her mouth. He gave her one long kiss, then suddenly he was part of her.

In her.

She held him deep inside, finally one with Blake

Jarrod. She'd been waiting so long. It was the most wonderful feeling in the world.

He kissed her deeper as he began to thrust, long strokes time after time. Soon she began to tremble around him, toppling over the edge again, the flickering of the flames in the fireplace nothing compared to their own fire burning within.

Samantha lay amongst the cushions in front of the fire and watched Blake stride toward the downstairs bathroom. He'd covered her with the throw from the couch, and she enjoyed lying there watching his bare back and buttocks that were all firm muscle and arrestingly male.

She smiled to herself in the gentle glow from the fireplace. She couldn't believe it. She'd made love with Blake. She felt marvelous. He'd been so generous and loving and…

All at once, she found herself blinking back sudden tears. Their lovemaking had been so much more than sex. She hadn't admitted it to herself until now lest she back out, but when he'd said earlier they were having sex, something had gnawed at her as she'd gone up the stairs. It had sounded like they would merely be having sex for sex's sake. And while that was somewhat true, that wasn't what she was *only* about.

She'd known the same was true for Blake. He'd already proven that by not taking advantage this morning when he'd thought she was a virgin. She'd "made love" with Blake, despite love not being involved. There was respect between them and that was more important to her.

Right then she heard him coming back and she

quickly blinked away any suggestion of tears. He wouldn't want to know. Otherwise he'd think she *hadn't* been able to handle it, when it was merely because she hadn't expected to be quite so touched by all this.

He gave a sexy smile as he dropped down and leaned over to kiss her. "How do you feel?" he murmured, pulling back and looking into her eyes.

She was fully aware of his nakedness next to her. She could easily reach out and touch him. "Wonderful."

He looked pleased as he lifted the throw and slid under it to lie on his back, pulling her against his chest and kissing the top of her head but being careful of her injury. "Is that better?"

She was glad he couldn't look into her eyes. "Much."

He chuckled, his breath stirring her hair. "Who knew, eh?"

"What?"

"That we'd be so good together."

She'd never doubted it. "We work well together in business, so why not in bed?"

"True."

After that, they lay in quiet. The fire crackled and the clock on the wall ticked the seconds by. Samantha began to feel sleepy. There was no place she'd rather be in the world right now, she thought, as her eyelids drifted shut and she listened to the tick tock…tick tock…tick…*she loved him…*tock.

Startled, she jumped. Dear God, *she loved him.*

"What's wrong?"

Her brain stumbled. Panic whorled inside her. The ability to speak deserted her for a moment…and then somehow she pulled herself together. "What? Oh, nothing. I think I fell asleep too fast."

"Don't worry. There's no chance of that happening again just yet." He put his hand under her chin, lowering his head and lifting her mouth up to his. She quickly closed her eyes, hiding them from him, hiding her deepest secret. She'd betrayed him by falling in love with him. And she'd betrayed herself. She hadn't wanted to love him. She had never intended for that to happen.

Then he kissed her and the slow, delicious process of making love to her started again. She prayed to God for the strength not to reveal her love for this man who was leaving his mark on her like no one had ever done before. She couldn't afford to give her feelings away, or their relationship would be over before it had really begun. Wanting Blake had been hard enough.

Loving him was going to be intolerable.

Eight

Blake made love to her many times during the night, both downstairs and in his bed. Samantha had never known such bliss, but by the time the next morning rolled around and she'd gone back to her own room to get dressed for work, she had a thousand worries inside her head. She loved Blake and that presented so many problems. She'd virtually promised him she wouldn't fall for him. Now it seemed like she'd gone back on her word.

Worse, somewhere along the line she hadn't exactly "fallen" for him. No, she'd skipped that bit and had progressed straight to loving him. They'd worked together so closely these past two years, she already knew Blake was the type of man she admired and respected. And falling "in" love implied she could fall "out" of love with him—like she'd done with Carl. With

Blake, she knew there would be no retracting her love for him.

If only she could.

Oh, God, loving Blake had taken her further with her emotions than she'd ever dared venture. And now she had to survive until she could leave for good. She had to remain tough. She would constantly have to keep something of herself back. Last night during their lovemaking, she'd only managed to keep a lid on it through sheer terror—only by telling herself he would run in the other direction if he knew how deep her feelings went. Talk about emotional involvement on her part!

And now more than ever she had to leave at the end of her month's contract. She couldn't stay permanently. Blake had been honest enough to admit he couldn't handle emotional involvement and she believed him. If he discovered she loved him, he'd be horrified. He'd probably have her on the next plane out of Aspen before she could blink. Even if he didn't, she couldn't risk giving him such a strong emotive power over her. A power he might use in and out of the bedroom to get her to stay.

For all the wrong reasons.

Yet would Blake manipulate her in such a way? He was, after all, the man she loved. An honorable man. Would he really do any of those things? Her heart remembered his generous lovemaking and said no. Her head remembered the hard businessman and said maybe.

Making love to a woman certainly changed things, Blake decided as he watched Samantha eat breakfast in the hotel restaurant. He'd sat opposite her like this many times in the last two years but it had always been about work. Now all he could think about was being inside her again.

She'd been so generously tight last night when he'd finally buried himself in her softness. It had almost sent him straight into orgasm. Only the need to give her more pleasure had held him back. Never before had that happened to him. He'd always made sure his partner had been fulfilled before taking his own pleasure, but this time her pleasure had been totally his. It had been the ultimate experience for him. How could that other man—that Carl—not have wanted her in his bed? Idiot!

"Tell me something, Blake," she said, cutting into his thoughts as he buttered a slice of toast.

"Anything." Well, not quite anything. He wasn't up for a meaningful discussion this morning. He merely wanted to sit here and soak up this beautiful woman in front of him.

She tilted her brunette head to one side. "Did you tell Andy to add the candles last night at dinner?"

He was relieved at the simple question. "Sorry, no. I wasn't planning on seduction. At least, not until I was sure you could handle becoming my lover." He smiled. "I'll light you some candles tonight, though."

A feathery blush ran across her cheeks but she looked pleased. "I've just realized something. You're a romantic, Blake Jarrod."

"Sometimes." He liked to romance a woman as much as the next guy. "But don't get the wrong idea that I'm a softie."

She nodded. "Got it. Hard in business. Good in bed."

He gave a low laugh. "I like that assessment." He also liked to think he was both things in and out of bed, but he wouldn't embarrass her further. Not here.

But tonight…

"I keep forgetting to mention this," she said, "but I haven't thanked you for taking such good care of me the other night."

"Oh, I think you did thank me," he said pointedly. "And you can thank me again later."

"Blake!" she hissed, but he could see she was enjoying this sexual interplay.

"What?" he drawled. "I'm just saying—"

A figure appeared at their table. "There you are, Sam," Joel said, giving them both a smile but causing Blake's mouth to clamp shut. "I'm glad I caught you. How are you this morning? How's the head?"

"Fine, Joel. No aftereffects at all," she assured the doctor.

"You're taking things easy, I hope?"

Her eyes made a quick dart across the table then back up at the other man. "Yes." Her cheeks had grown a little warm and that in itself appeased Blake.

"Good. Then how about we take in that movie tonight?"

She looked at Blake again. "Oh, Joel, I'm sorry, I can't."

"Tomorrow night, then?"

Blake held his tongue. He wanted to lay claim to Samantha and tell the other man to shove off, but he'd first give her the opportunity to do it.

"Um, Joel. Perhaps not." She shifted in her seat. "I'm returning to Vegas in less than two weeks' time and then I'm going home to Pasadena for good once I wrap things up there. So, you see, there's a lot to be done here right now. I need to work full-on with Blake until then."

Blake was dumbfounded.

"You're leaving?" the other man said, sounding shocked, echoing Blake's thoughts. "I can't believe that."

Another echo of his thoughts.

She looked slightly uncomfortable. "Yes, I know. I'm sorry I didn't tell you, but it was something that hadn't been finalized until now."

Joel gave a small nod. "I understand. Maybe we can get together in Pasadena sometime in the future? We'll at least have to get together for coffee before you leave."

She slipped him a smile. "That would be lovely."

Blake was vaguely aware of the other man walking away from the table, but he only had eyes for one person. "Samantha," he growled. "What the hell is going on?"

Her look seemed cagey. "I didn't want him knowing the truth. Our affair is our business and no one else's."

Anger stirred inside him. "I'm not talking about our affair, and you know it. Dammit, don't tell me you don't know what I'm talking about."

She lifted her chin. "You're talking about me still leaving," she clarified. "I'm sorry, Blake. Did you think that I would change my mind?"

"Yes, I damn well did." He'd expected her to stay now, not because he'd enticed her into staying but because she *wanted* to. And hell, she didn't seem to understand that he'd made a big concession in not seducing her in the bathroom yesterday morning. Now it felt like she'd slapped him in the face. He'd given. She'd taken. And now she was giving nothing back.

"But why, Blake? Our lovemaking hasn't changed

anything. We both decided it would only be physical and nothing more. No commitment, remember?"

Her words appeared to be reasonable, but for all that she had a peculiar look in her eyes he couldn't decipher. "That's still got nothing to do with you leaving."

"Doesn't it? I was leaving before we made love and I'm still leaving, so what's changed?"

Damn her. She was right. Even so, he couldn't explain it. He just knew something *had* changed and he didn't want to decode it. He just wanted her to stay and enjoy what they had for a while. They could at least get a couple of months together. Why leave while the going was good?

She shot him an unexpected candid look. "Blake, you asked me if I could handle a sexual relationship, and I said I could. It sounds to me like *you* aren't handling it."

His mouth tightened. "I'm handling it."

She shook her head. "No, I don't—"

"Blake," a male voice called out, and Blake instantly knew who it was. He stiffened. Damn the world! His twin brother was the last person he wanted to see. Guy had always understood him—sometimes more than he understood himself. Right now wasn't a good time to put that to the test.

He shot to his feet, turned and headed for the private elevator. "It'll have to wait until later, Guy," he muttered, striding past his brother.

Guy's steps faltered as he approached the table. Then as he came closer, he looked at Samantha with mild amusement. "Was it something I said?" he quipped in that easygoing way of his.

Samantha couldn't smile if her life depended on it. "He's got a lot on his mind."

Guy sobered. "Yeah, I know." He sent her a penetrating look that reminded her of Blake. "I hear you're leaving."

She nodded, still surprised word had gotten around the family so fast, and even more surprised that they were genuinely sorry to see her go. It wasn't like she was a friend of the family…or marrying into it.

"I'm glad I saw you," Guy said, drawing her back to the moment. "Avery and I would like to have you around for dinner before you go."

Somehow she managed a faint smile. "That would be very nice."

"Blake, too, of course." Silence, then, "He'll miss you when you leave."

"Maybe." *Maybe not.* "I'll find him an excellent replacement."

"It won't be the same."

Her throat constricted. "He'll get over it." She stood up. "You'll have to excuse me, Guy. I need to start work. There's a lot to do."

Guy stepped back and let her pass, but he was frowning and she could feel his eyes on her all the way out the eatery. Thankfully she had a few moments of privacy as the elevator took her to the top floor.

If only Blake wanted her to stay because he loved her, then things would be perfect. But for him this was only about two things—the job and sex. It wasn't about love. She sighed. She'd have to be crazy to think he would make a commitment. And she hadn't wanted a commitment before anyway, so why the heck was she even considering it now?

She must have rocks in her head.

Or have been hit *on* the head with a rock. It must have caused more damage than she'd thought. Why else would she be unwise enough to love a man who wouldn't let himself love in return? That bruise must have addled more than her brain. It had addled her heart.

Thankfully Blake's door was shut when she entered her office so she sat at her desk. Come to think of it, she felt a little better knowing she had hoisted Blake with his own petard. That was rather clever of her. He'd sprouted all that talk about not getting emotionally involved, but clearly his emotions *were* involved, albeit not enough and not the ones that mattered most to her.

They didn't entail love.

God was merciful just then, when not only did the phone start to ring but one of the staff who had a meeting with Blake walked into her office. Samantha got busy, putting on her professional persona as she placed the caller on hold, buzzing Blake on the intercom to tell him his first appointment was here. At his request, she ushered the staff member into his office, all the while keeping her face neutral whenever she looked at her boss. He seemed equally as disinterested in her, though she knew otherwise. What he was and what he seemed were two different things. She could recognize that in another person. After all, wasn't she an expert at the same thing?

Midmorning while Blake was busy at a staff meeting in the Great Room, Samantha picked up the telephone with a heavy heart and did what she had to do. She called Mary Wentworth back and spoke to her about a replacement. The other woman was surprised to hear she was leaving, but was more than happy to help. Mary promised she would e-mail some résumés of suitable applicants within a few hours.

Blake returned after the meeting, formally asked if there were any messages, then strode straight into his office. Samantha's heart sank at how cold he was, but there was nothing she could do about it. She still had to leave.

At lunchtime she had some sandwiches sent up from the kitchen, and Blake made it apparent that he preferred to eat at his desk by himself, with his door closed between them. Usually they ate together while discussing work. Or if they ate at their own desks, the door remained open.

Not this time.

And that was fine with her, she decided, growing more and more upset. She needed a filter to stop the waves of anger coming out of his office anyway. To clear her head, she went for a walk in the fresh air. Blake didn't ask where she'd been when she returned and she didn't offer. It was plain to see he was no longer concerned about her.

By late afternoon, Samantha had had enough of his attitude. He'd chastised her after she'd put through a call he hadn't wanted to take. He'd found fault with a letter she'd typed up for his signature. And he'd told her to go recheck some figures on a report that she knew were correct.

When she brought the report back, she deliberately placed another folder on top of it.

His head shot up. "What's this?"

"Résumés. They all come highly recommended."

His lips flattened. "I didn't ask you to do this."

She angled her chin. "It's what you pay me to do."

"I pay you to do what you're told."

She gasped, then held herself rigid. "That's unfair of you. You don't mind me being proactive in other things with my job. It's why I'm such a good assistant and you know it."

"We're talking fairness now, are we? *You're* the one leaving *me*. How fair is that?"

"I'm not leaving *you,* Blake," she lied. "Anyway, don't take it personally, remember? That's what you said to me when you reminded me of my contract obligations."

He muttered a curse, but for Samantha the last straw had already broken the camel's back. "I can't continue under these conditions, Blake. If you won't treat me right, then I'll pack my things and leave tonight. And I don't care if you take me to court for breach of contract either." She hesitated, but only for a second. "I believe I could make a good case for justifying my leaving anyway, considering the personal turn our relationship has taken."

There was a lengthy silence.

His eyes challenged hers. "Would you go that far?"

She gave a jerky nod. "If pushed I would. Don't doubt that."

He held her gaze with narrowed eyes.

And then suddenly something happened and a suspicion of admiration began to glint in them. "Way to go!" he said softly, startling her. "You're a tough little madam. I always knew you could hold your own in your job, but I never thought to see the day when you used it against *me*."

A little of the tension went out of her. "So things will return to normal?" she asked cautiously.

"No."

Her heart dropped.

"Things can never be normal between us again. Not since last night." He drew a long breath, as if taking a moment before making a decision. "I don't want to see you go, but I don't want to keep you here against your will either. If you want to go then I have to accept it."

It wasn't what she wanted at all.

It was what she *had* to do.

"Thank you, Blake."

"But at least stay until your contract runs out." He waited a moment. "I'm not asking for the job and I'm not asking for the sex. I'm asking for *me*."

She caught her breath. This was the best she could hope for, the best it could get, and she wasn't about to argue with that. She would take her happiness where she could.

A whisper of joy filled her. "Okay, yes. I'll stay until my contract runs out, Blake," she said, and watched him let out a shuddering breath that touched her greatly. He really *did* want her to stay so that he could be with her.

Clearly satisfied now they were back on an even keel, he leaned back in his chair with a look she had no trouble translating. "Go over there and lock the door."

A tiny shiver of anticipation went down her spine. "Blake, I can't… I don't…"

"You can." His eyes turned deeper blue. "I seriously need to make love to you, Samantha."

Her heart tilted. Oh, she wanted that, too. She darted a look at the door. "The others—"

"Will think we don't want to be disturbed." He gave a crooked smile. "And they'd be right." He waited a moment. “You can always race into my washroom if anyone comes.”

Wanting this…wanting him…she went and locked the heavy wood door, but ducked her head out into her office first to make sure no one was there. “I can’t believe I’m doing this,” she muttered, turning the lock.

“Don’t think about it.” He looked amused and she decided that if he wanted her, then he was going to have her. And she would wipe that amusement right off his face.

Fingers going to the buttons of her long-sleeved blouse, she began to undo each one as she approached him across the plush carpet.

One eyebrow lifted. “Are you teasing me, Miss Thompson?”

“Actually I think I am.”

He smiled, and she smiled, then his smile started to slip as she completely undid the blouse, leaving it hanging open over her black bra. She marveled at where this seductress in her was coming from, but didn’t let it deter her. She wasn’t about to waste a minute of it.

She reached the side of the desk. “More?”

“Oh, yeah.”

“You’re the boss.”

Her hands were shaking a little as she slid the zipper of her slacks down, pushing them and her panties all the way to the floor, then stepped out of them. She heard a rasping sound escape Blake’s throat and there was a blaze in his eyes that seemed to emit from his whole body.

Gratified by his reaction…satisfied by his amusement now turned to desire…she climbed onto his lap, knees on either side of his thighs, her blouse covering her bra—and then only just.

After that, passion overtook all rational thoughts and the air hummed with soft, sensual sounds.

Nine

They dined together back at Pine Lodge, then made love again that night, and when Samantha woke the next morning she lay there and wallowed in a sense of occasion. Her memories of them together like this were all she could take away with her. Her heart, she would leave with Blake.

He woke up then and made slow love to her again. Afterward she put on a bright face and they went about their business as usual, neither of them showing any outward sign to the others that they were lovers. They hadn't discussed it, but Samantha was glad about it. Already his family seemed to have taken a special interest in them, and she didn't want anyone guessing she loved him.

Late morning, Samantha left her office and went down to the hotel kitchen to get some fresh milk for their coffee. She could have phoned down for it but she needed to stretch her legs.

In the hallway, she ran into Erica. They chatted a few moments but Samantha could see the other woman was preoccupied. “Erica, is something wrong?”

Erica wrinkled her nose. “Yes, unfortunately. I’ve been arranging a surprise party for tonight for this man who lives in town. It’s for his wife’s fortieth birthday and she thinks she’s coming here for dinner.” She clicked her tongue. “I’ve been working on this for weeks.”

“So what’s the problem?”

“We’ve got a DJ for later in the evening, but the husband particularly asked for someone to play piano music in the background during the meal, and now the piano player has come down sick.” Her smooth forehead creased as she began thinking out loud. “The DJ could probably play some soft music as an alternative, but I really don’t want to disappoint the husband. He said his wife loves the piano and he wants to give her the best party. I was hoping there might be someone in town I could find, but it’s probably too late.”

All the while she was talking, Samantha’s heart began thumping with a mixture of excitement and panic. “You may not believe this,” she said, not believing she was actually saying this, “but I can help.”

Erica’s eyes brightened. “You can? Do you know someone who plays the piano?”

“Yes.” *Did she really want to say this?* “Me.”

Erica stopped and blinked. “*You* play the piano?” She grimaced. “Sorry, that came out wrong. I just mean—”

Samantha smiled a little. “I know what you meant.”

Regardless, Erica still looked doubtful. "You *really* play the piano?"

Samantha nodded. "Yes, *really*."

"You're sure?"

Samantha chuckled as her anxiety faded. "Lead the way to the piano and I'll show you. Just don't expect perfection. I have to tell you I'm a bit rusty."

Erica began to grin. "As long as it's not 'Chopsticks,' then I'll be happy. Follow me."

A few minutes later, Samantha did a warm-up then started playing a quick medley of popular tunes. Her fingers felt a bit stiff because she hadn't played since last Christmas at home in Pasadena, but she was soon enjoying herself—and enjoying the look on Erica's face.

"That's wonderful!" Erica murmured, once the music ended.

Samantha smiled with relief that she hadn't lost her touch nor made a fool of herself. "Thanks, but it's nothing special."

Erica shook her head. "No, you're very good."

"Not really."

"Yes, *really*," Erica teased. "Good Lord, I didn't know we had Liberace living here at the resort."

Samantha laughed. "Just be grateful my mother made me take piano lessons growing up."

"Oh, I am. Play some more, Samantha." All at once Erica's eyes widened and she chuckled. "Oh, my God, I don't believe I'm about to say this but 'play it again, Sam.'"

Samantha laughed. She knew she needed the practice so she was happy to oblige and felt more confident with each touch of the keys.

Afterward, they talked for five minutes then Samantha continued on her way to get the milk. Blake had a business lunch in town and had already left by the time she returned to the office, so she didn't get to tell him about it all until late afternoon.

He fell back in his chair. "*You* play the piano?"

A wry smile tugged at her mouth. "Why is that so far-fetched?"

"I don't know." Then he shook his head as if he wasn't hearing right. "Let me get this straight. *You're* going to play the piano at a party here at the resort tonight?"

She shrugged. "It's just background music during dinner." But she wasn't quite so calm inside, and talking about it now was making her kind of nervous.

He tilted his head at her. "Why didn't you tell me you could play the piano?"

"It wasn't a job requirement," she joked, more to calm her growing anxiety than anything.

His mouth quirked. "No, I guess it wasn't."

Her humor over, she bit her lip. "Actually, do you mind if I leave a little early? I need to get myself ready and I'd like some time to myself."

He gave a wayward smile. "You creative types are all alike."

"Blake—"

"Feel free to leave early," he agreed. Then his eyes slowly settled on her mouth. "But before you go..." Hunger jumped the distance between them. "I do think there is one requirement of your job that needs revisiting."

She knew what he was getting at. Her heart raced with a growing excitement. "Blake, we can't make love in here every afternoon."

"Who said we can't?"

"But I have to go now," she said, knowing she was weakening.

"In a minute," he murmured, sending her an intimate look across the desk. "Come and give me a kiss goodbye first."

She wagged a finger at him. "That's all, Blake. One kiss and no more."

"Trust me."

She moved toward him. "Okay…"

Half an hour later she left the office a very satisfied woman, amused at how easily she had fallen for his trickery. Of course, she couldn't fully blame her boss. She'd *wanted* to fall for it.

"Lady, you're far too dangerous to let loose on our male guests," Blake said, watching Samantha step into high heels. She wore a beaded jacket over black evening pants that flattered her slim figure, and she'd curled the brunette strands of her hair into a bubbly halo around her gorgeous face.

"You think I look okay?"

"More than okay. You'll knock 'em dead." He stepped closer and went to pull her toward him but she put a hand against his chest, stopping him.

"Wait! You'll mess up my lipstick."

Blake was amused. "I'd like to mess up more than your lipstick, beautiful."

Her blue eyes smiled back at him. "You already did that this afternoon. 'Trust me,' remember?"

He gave a low chuckle. "I remember." Even now he felt the stirrings of desire, so he stepped away from temptation. "Come on. I'll drive you up to the Manor."

"I can call the valet."

"That's okay. I want to look over those documents Gavin gave me about the new bungalow. It'll be a good chance to study them without the phones ringing." It was an excuse but she looked so good that he wanted to make sure she got home okay. If anyone hit on her they'd be sorry.

Ten minutes later they walked down the corridor toward the ballroom, but as they got closer she suddenly stopped. "Blake, please. Don't come in with me. You'll only make me more nervous."

"Okay. I'll be in the office until you're ready to go home."

"But—"

He leaned forward and dropped a kiss on her forehead. "I'll wait for you."

He looked up and saw Erica and Christian coming toward them. They were a distance away so he nodded at them then turned and walked in the other direction, taking the private elevator up to the office. He didn't care that they'd seen the kiss. He *did* care that they might think Samantha was his weak spot.

Christian had proven his integrity months ago, but the other man had his own weak point—Erica. It could make him blind to whatever his fiancée was up to, Blake thought, then winced. She may not be up to anything at all, he corrected, aware his hard attitude toward his half sister was diminishing with each passing day.

Yet he couldn't discount Erica was fooling him as well as Christian, though he was feeling less and less that was the case. He was usually a pretty good judge of character—when emotions weren't involved. Unfortunately finding out he had a half sister *had* brought out an emotional response in him. He hadn't liked that.

And he didn't like the emotional response he was feeling now as he sat down at his desk and saw the file with the résumés. It all came back that Samantha was actually going to leave. It had either been let her go in three weeks' time or lose her now. He hadn't been able to bear the thought of the latter.

And he wasn't up to reading those résumés right now either, he decided, putting them to the side. He would deal with it when he had to and not before.

He wasn't sure how long he'd been working when he heard piano music drift up from the bottom floor. He sat back in his chair and listened. Samantha was clearly talented as she went from one tune to another, even throwing in some classical music. He heard clapping at the end of that one, though whether it was for Samantha or in honor of the birthday guest, he wasn't sure. The music started up in another medley of popular tunes, so he figured it was for Samantha.

And rightly so.

Unable to stop himself, he knew he had to see her play in person and not merely listen from afar. He got up from his desk and went downstairs, hearing the clink of glasses and cutlery and the murmur of voices, but it was the music that drew him as he approached the ballroom.

Pushing open one of the large doors, he slipped inside and stood at the back, watching people half listening and half talking as Samantha played another piece of classical music. She didn't see him, but she appeared totally at ease at the piano, concentrating on the music, her hands flowing across the keys, looking very feminine and beautiful. Suddenly he was so proud of her that a lump rose in his throat.

"She's good," a female voice murmured, and he glanced sideways at an attractive woman in her late thirties who'd come to stand beside him.

He wasn't interested. "Yes," he said, looking back at Samantha.

"You're new here." She thrust a manicured hand in front of him. "I'm Clarice, by the way."

It would have been rude not to shake her hand, but he still wasn't interested. "Blake." He wished the woman would leave him alone so that he could concentrate on Samantha.

"Do you know the guest of honor?"

For a moment he thought she meant Samantha, then he realized she was talking about the birthday lady. "A casual acquaintance." He didn't feel the need to explain.

"I went to boarding school with Anne. We've been lifelong friends."

"That's great." The music ended on a high note and everyone started to clap and it gave him the chance to move away. "Excuse me," he said, taking a step.

Clarice put her hand on his arm, stopping him. "Would you care to have a drink later?"

He'd been approached like this many times but for some reason now he found it distasteful, though he hid it. He only wanted to see Samantha. "I'm sorry," he said, being as nice as possible so as not to offend. "Not tonight." He walked away.

And headed straight for Samantha getting up from the piano. She was laughing as some people rushed to talk to her, and as Blake weaved his way through the tables he could only think how much she lit up the room.

Then she saw him. “Blake,” she murmured, her blue eyes lighting up *for him,* sending an extraordinary feeling soaring inside his chest.

He reached her and put his hand on her elbow. “I think the lady needs a drink,” he told the group at large, making no apologies as he led her away.

“What are you doing here?” she said as he took her over to the bar.

“I could hear the music upstairs. It drew me to you.” He paused. “I’m totally in awe of you,” he murmured, pleased to see a hint of dusky rose color her cheeks.

“Thank you,” she said in a breathy voice.

For a moment they held one another’s gaze.

“Samantha,” Erica said, rushing up to them and kissing Samantha on the cheek. “You were wonderful!” In her excitement she kissed Blake’s cheek, too. “Isn’t she wonderful, Blake?”

For a split second he froze at Erica’s friendliness, but then he found himself relenting toward her even more. Anyone who liked Samantha so much deserved a little more consideration.

He gave his half sister his first ever warm smile. “Yes, she’s pretty wonderful.”

Erica seemed a little taken aback at his friendliness, but her self-possession soon returned as she spoke to Samantha. “The minute you started playing this afternoon, I knew you were good.”

Samantha laughed as she looked from one to the other. “Do either of you have an ear for music?”

“We know a class act when we see it,” Erica said, then winked at her half brother. “Don’t you agree, Blake?”

Blake nodded, his gaze returning to Samantha and resting there. "I couldn't agree more," he said, as everything inside him went still.

Samantha was class all the way.

Just then, the real guest of honor and her husband came up to thank Samantha for playing so beautifully. Then Anne asked Samantha if she'd play her a special piece of classical music.

And as Blake watched Samantha start to play the piano again, he realized this woman could be destined for better things than being his assistant. He wasn't an expert at piano playing by any means, but he knew when something sounded good. It hit home then that he had no right to keep her here and hold her back from what could be her true vocation. He really did have to let her go. Somewhere at the back of his mind he'd still believed she wouldn't leave. Now he knew different.

"You're amazingly good at playing the piano," he said later, once they were inside Pine Lodge and alone together.

She sent him an amused glance as she took off her coat. "Don't start that again."

He frowned as he took off his own coat and hung it on the rack. "I don't understand why you didn't take your music further. I'm sure you could be a world-class pianist."

She lifted her shoulders in a shrug. "I'm an average pianist. I know my limitations."

He'd been raised to push himself to the limit. "Aren't you putting those limitations on yourself?"

She shook her head. "No, I don't think I am. There are lots of mildly talented people who don't take it all the way. It doesn't mean they're wasting their lives. They can use it in other ways. Some people teach. Some people play for themselves. Others play at parties," she said, her lips curving wryly.

"But—"

She put her hand against his chest. "I don't have the passion for it, Blake. Really, I don't. I like to play occasionally but that's all."

He finally understood what she was saying, but the world had better look out if she ever decided to further her talent.

He felt her palm still against his chest. "What *do* you have a passion for?" he said huskily, bringing it back to the two of them as much as he could. That's what he would focus on from now on. Them and only them.

She rubbed herself against him, seeming to delight in making him aware of her. "Right now? You."

By the time they reached the bedroom they were both naked. After they made love, he pulled her into his arms and let her sleep, but listening to her soft breathing, he admitted to himself that never before had he felt as comfortable after making love to a woman as he did right then. This woman felt right at home in his arms.

And he wasn't sure he should like the feeling.

Ten

One advantage of sleeping with the boss was that she didn't have to jump out of bed and hurry to get to work, Samantha thought lazily, after she woke late the next morning and lay in Blake's arms. He was still asleep.

Then he moved a little and she tilted her head back to look up at him. "You're awake?" she said unnecessarily.

He opened his eyes. "I have been for a while."

That surprised her. Usually the minute he woke up he made love to her.

"Is something wrong?"

"No," he said, but she felt his chest muscles tighten beneath her.

She saw that he had a closed look about him. Something must be on his mind, though she didn't know what. He'd been fine when they'd made love last night. Now he seemed…distant.

She could only think something had occurred to him during the night and upset him. For some reason a wall had been erected between them now. Then she remembered how Erica and Christian had seen him kiss her on the forehead before the party. It hadn't been a passionate kiss but it was clearly more than friendship. So perhaps Blake minded that his family knew about them now? As far as she could tell, it was the only thing that had changed overnight.

"Erica and Christian probably realize we're lovers now," she said, testing the waters.

"They'd be stupid if they didn't." It wasn't said nastily, but it still made her wonder.

She tilted her head back a little. "You don't mind?" He'd looked more at ease with Erica last night. He'd actually seemed to like his half sister.

"Why should I?"

"True." She swallowed. "I'm leaving soon so it doesn't matter anyway, does it?" she said, trying to get a reaction out of him. *Any* reaction. One that didn't lock her out.

There was nothing.

Feeling disheartened, she pushed herself out of bed and hurried to the shower, a tightness in her throat. Their remaining time together was so short. She didn't want to spend it like this.

No sooner had she stepped under the spray than he opened the sliding doors. "What's the matter?" he said, frowning at her.

She thanked goodness the water streaming over her head hid any tears that threatened. "Nothing."

His look said he didn't believe her as he stepped inside the cubicle and joined her. He didn't say a word, and he had a fixed look about him as he soaped them both up and then made love to her with an urgency that startled her. By the end of it she was none the wiser, but at least she knew he still wanted her.

Her heart twisted inside her then. As much as it was a compliment to her, was he still refusing to accept that she was leaving? If so, he was only making it harder for himself. They *both* had to accept it, she thought, her heart aching at the thought.

She managed a blank face as they went to the manor for breakfast. It was either that or cry, and she couldn't allow herself that luxury.

As they entered the lobby, a woman practically jumped out at them. "Blake Jarrod!" she exclaimed, in a you-are-a-naughty-boy tone. "You didn't tell me you owned this hotel." Her gaze slid to Samantha, "Or that your assistant was the piano player."

Blake put on a practiced smile but Samantha could tell he didn't like the woman. "It's Clarice, isn't it?" he said, making it clear he wasn't interested. "This is my assistant *and* piano player," he mocked, "Samantha."

Samantha inclined her head and the woman gave her a cool smile. "I'm Clarice Richardson. Mrs. Clarice Richardson, but I'm *divorced*." Her gaze slid to Blake, instantly dismissing Samantha. "I was wondering, Blake. How would you like to have that drink tonight?"

Blake shook his head. "Can't do, I'm afraid. I have a prior commitment tonight."

"Then how about a cup of coffee now?" the woman said, not giving up. "I have a free morning. In fact, I'm free for the whole day. I'm looking for someone to take me for a drive to Independence Pass."

"Sorry, but I have to get to work."

Clarice gave a tinkle of a laugh that grated on Samantha's nerves. "But you're the boss."

"Which is exactly why I'd better do some work," he said smoothly, then put his hand under Samantha's elbow. "If you'll excuse us."

"Oh. Of course," Clarice said, but Samantha saw her mouth purse with irritation as they walked away.

Then she realized Blake was walking her to the elevator instead of the eatery. "Aren't we having breakfast?"

"We'll get something sent up."

She gave a soft laugh. "Don't tell me you're scared of Mrs. Richardson?"

He shot her a wry look that said he wasn't scared of anyone. "No, but I don't want to deal with her."

"She's persistent, that's for sure." Samantha paused, thinking about something as they stepped inside the elevator and the doors shut. "So you're going out tonight?" She didn't want to sound demanding like Clarice, but as his lover she hoped *she* had a temporary claim on his time right now.

"No, I'm staying home. *You're* my prior commitment."

"I am?" Relief went through her.

He slipped his hand around her waist and pulled her hip against his. "And if I go for a drive to Independence Pass it will be with only one lady."

"Melissa?" she teased.

"You." He kissed her quickly on the mouth just as the doors started to open.

They met Erica as they stepped out of the elevator and into the corridor. She came hurrying forward with a big smile on her face. "Samantha, I want to thank you once again for the fabulous job you did last night."

Samantha returned the smile. "You're very welcome, Erica. I enjoyed it."

Erica considered her. "You know, I've already had a call from the president of the local music school. They heard about you and want to meet with you," she said enthusiastically, making Samantha's heart sink. "They have this huge summer festival where nearly a thousand students and faculty come together from far and wide. There's orchestral concerts and chamber music and—"

Samantha had to stop her there. "I'm sorry, Erica. It wouldn't be any use. I'm leaving soon." She felt Blake stiffen beside her.

Erica's eyes widened. "Oh, I thought—"

Blake muttered something about starting work and stalked off. For a moment Samantha wondered if he was still thinking about her not taking her piano playing seriously, but she soon dismissed it. This wasn't about her not playing the piano. It was about her leaving.

Erica looked at her and winced. "Sorry if I said something out of place."

Samantha tried to smile. "You didn't." She started to follow him. "But I'd better get to work."

Blake was closing his door behind him as she entered her office, and Samantha's heart sank. So. They were back to that again. Talk about a temperamental boss!

Shortly after, he buzzed her for coffee. When she took it into him he seemed okay if a little preoccupied, and she realized she was reading more into this than she should. He had the resort issues to concentrate on and was trying to get the feel for it, that's all. Besides, just because she was now his lover, it shouldn't upgrade her status from his assistant. On the contrary, here at work she'd be upset if it did.

Around eleven he opened his door and strode through her office, scowling. "I'll be with Trevor in his office." He left before she could make any acknowledgement.

Getting to her feet, she went to empty Blake's out tray. There were some letters he'd signed and…all at once she noticed he'd been reading through the files with the résumés. Her heart dropped. That file had sat on his desk untouched all day yesterday, but now he must be thinking ahead.

She should be pleased he wouldn't be left without an assistant, but she could only feel upset. And that was made worse as she went back to her desk and opened the agenda for tomorrow's meeting and saw one of the items was to discuss her replacement.

Oh, God.

So she didn't need Clarice to make a sudden appearance in her office about fifteen minutes later. "Mrs. Richardson, how did you get up here?" she asked, as the woman came toward her desk. A card key was needed for both the private elevator and the back stairs.

"I told one of the staff that I urgently needed to see the person in charge. And I do."

After seeing how Clarice had operated downstairs with Blake, the other woman would have refused to take no for an answer. More than likely she'd even given the staff member a monetary "donation."

Samantha frowned. She would deal with the security breach later. "This is a private area. You shouldn't be here at all. If you needed anything, you should ask at the front desk."

The woman sent her a haughty look. "I'd prefer to deal with Blake, Miss..."

"Thompson." Samantha recognized being put in her place. "Blake's not here at the moment," she said his name deliberately, "but I can pass on a message when he gets back. Now let me walk you to the elevator."

Clarice looked disappointed. Then, "I'll give you my room number." She picked up a sticky-note pad from the desk and wrote on it. "You'll make sure you tell him Clarice called, won't you?" she said, tearing off the slip of paper and handing it to Samantha.

"Of course."

Clarice went to turn away then spun back. "Tell him that I have a proposition for him," she said in a breathless voice.

"Fine." There was nothing to worry about with Blake, but it annoyed Samantha to have to deal with another woman who threw herself at him. There had been so many of them over the years. Clarice was very attractive, but so were the other women who had chased Blake.

Samantha stayed at her desk and waited for Blake to return for lunch. Knowing she was being contrary, she was still upset that he was looking at replacing her, and now she just wanted to spend more time with him. But he didn't return until after lunch, and she spent a quiet lunch break by herself.

"There's a plate of sandwiches on your desk," she said when he walked back through to his office.

"I ate lunch with Trevor."

It would have been nice to be told, she decided, then admitted to herself that as her boss, Blake didn't owe her his time.

She followed him into his office. "Here are your

messages. You'll see there's one from Mrs. Richardson." When his face remained blank, she said, "Clarice."

He let out a heavy sigh. "What does she want?"

"For you to call her. She delivered it in person."

He scowled. "How did she get up here?"

Samantha told him. "I've passed on my concern to the front desk. They're going to look into it."

He nodded. "Good."

"By the way, Clarice left her room number for you to call her back. She says to tell you she has a proposition for you."

"A proposition?" He grimaced. "I bet she does."

Samantha picked up the plate of sandwiches and put them in the refrigerator near her desk, feeling better that Clarice hadn't fooled him. Not that she expected he wouldn't see through it all. He knew more about women than she did herself.

It was fairly quiet for the next two hours as Blake returned messages and she typed up some reports. Then, he came out carrying his coat. "I have to go into town for a meeting. It'll take a few hours."

She almost asked if she could go with him, then stopped. Her place as his assistant was here.

Suddenly he came over and kissed her hard. "I'll see you later at the lodge. We can go out for dinner if you like."

She shook her head, pleased. "No, let's eat in. I'll get something from the hotel kitchen on the way home."

His eyes flickered, and she suspected he'd noticed her mention of the word *home*. "Okay." He left.

Not long after that, Samantha decided to go down to the kitchen to see about tonight's dinner. She took the plate of sandwiches down to the front desk, as one of the staff might appreciate them for later, rather than throwing them in the trash.

She was walking through the lobby toward the front desk when out of the corner of her eye she happened to glance over at the bar. Her heart stuttered. Blake and Clarice were sitting in there having a drink. Both of them were focused on each other, though she noted Clarice was leaning toward him and doing the talking, more with her cleavage than not. Was this where the other woman offered her "proposition?"

So much for his appointment in town, Samantha thought, not sure what she was doing as she spun around and headed back to her office, giving herself time to adjust to what she'd seen. She had to put this into perspective.

Okay, so there was probably nothing to it, but she just didn't like that Blake was telling her one thing, then doing another. And wasn't he getting Clarice's hopes up even by sitting with the woman? Then again, he was a free man and once *she* left Aspen he would get lonely. The other woman was certainly beautiful.

Samantha threw the sandwiches in the trash, unable to face going back downstairs again. Instead, she phoned the kitchen and ordered two meals for dinner, though she wasn't sure she would feel hungry.

Blake seemed lost in thought when he returned to the lodge that evening, so Samantha didn't mention it straightaway. Besides, she didn't want to sound like a harping wife.

She managed to wait until they had almost finished dinner before saying offhand, "By the way, Blake. Next time you *don't* plan on having a drink with Mrs. Richardson, don't do it in the bar."

His eyes narrowed. "What does that mean?" he said coolly, thankfully not looking the least bit guilty.

"I saw you with her," she said, still keeping her voice casual.

He frowned. "So?"

She lifted one shoulder. "I just thought it odd that you weren't 'free' to spend time with her…and then you were."

He had an arrested expression, before a look of male satisfaction crossed his face. "You sound jealous."

She tried not to look flustered. If he thought she was jealous then he might realize she was more emotionally involved with him than she was letting on. "It's not in my nature to be jealous," she lied, quickly disabusing him of that.

His eyes sharpened. "So you don't mind if I go out with other women, then?"

"While I'm here in Aspen, I *do* mind," she said, seeing his jaw tense. "I think a person should show respect for their lover, don't you?"

There was a moment's pause before he gave a brief nod. "I totally agree, Samantha. Lovers should be true to each other."

"Thank you."

He broke eye contact and took a sip of his wine. "Anyway, you have nothing to worry about with Clarice. She waylaid me as I was leaving for my meeting in town and I felt I had to hear her out. Her proposition is a business one. She owns a chain of high-end boutiques and she wanted to know if she can put one here at Jarrod Ridge."

Samantha digested the information. Now she felt foolish for jumping to conclusions about Clarice.

Yet not.

"It's purely about business," Blake assured her. "I'm going to speak to the family about it at tomorrow morning's meeting."

Her heart constricted at the thought of what else was on tomorrow's agenda—the résumés for her replacement. She noted he didn't mention that right now.

Trying not to think about it, she concentrated on what the other woman's proposition would mean. "Clarice will be here in Aspen a lot, then." And *she* wouldn't be. Clarice would have a clear field with Blake.

He frowned. "I'm not sure. I'd say while it's being set up, she'll visit on and off from L.A." His eyes caught hers. "Why?"

She schooled her features. "No reason. I was merely thinking out loud." She planted on a smile. "And of course I won't be here anyway, so it doesn't concern me."

His eyes turned somewhat hostile. "That's right. What do you care anyway?"

"Exactly," she agreed, her heart breaking. She stood up. "I'll get dessert." She hurried out of the room, aware that he still didn't understand why she had to leave and thanking God he didn't. She took comfort knowing he had no idea she loved him.

Unfortunately the marvelous chocolate concoction in the refrigerator wouldn't lessen her inner pain. She doubted anything ever would.

"…And now that the Food and Wine Gala is completely out of the way for this year," Blake said the next morning, looking down the boardroom table at his siblings, "let's move on to the next thing on the agenda.

Gavin, can you give everyone an update on the bungalow project."

Blake already knew the details of the project, so he found his mind straying back to Samantha. Last night at dinner he'd actually been pleased that she might be jealous of Clarice. Never before had he wanted a woman to feel jealousy over him. Samantha had soon disabused him of that, but appeared to deliberately bring up the fact that she was leaving soon just to goad him. And he'd retaliated by lashing out with an I-don't-care attitude.

Only trouble was…he *did* care. And he couldn't shake that feeling. It kept hitting him in the face no matter where he turned. She didn't seem to realize how much he was going to miss her. If she did, would she still leave? He'd already made it clear he didn't want her to go. Hell, she should be here at his side right now taking notes. Instead, he deliberately told her not to bother attending the meeting today. Not when *she* was on the agenda.

"Blake, I've finished," he heard Gavin say.

He blinked and saw the others staring at him. He had to get back to business. "Right. The next item on the agenda is mainly for you, Trevor. One of the wealthy guests has approached me about opening a boutique here at the lodge." He explained further.

Trevor nodded as he listened. "Sounds good. We could see—"

There was a tap at the door.

Samantha came into the room, looking slightly apologetic. "I'm sorry for the interruption, but Trevor's assistant asked me to give him a message." She walked toward Trevor and passed him a piece of paper. "I ran into Diana downstairs," she said directly to him. "She was on her way up here, so I said I'd hand it to you and save her coming up." Then she gave a general smile and turned to leave the room.

Blake watched her walk away with a slight sway to her hips that emphasized the soft lines of her body, but as she closed the door behind her, he heard Trevor mildly curse.

"What's the matter, Trev?" Guy was the first to ask.

Trevor looked at the note and shook his head. "I don't know what's going on. It's some woman called Haylie Smith. She left a message the other day saying it's important she speak with me but that it's private and she won't discuss it with anyone else. I've never even heard of her."

"Maybe she's got a crush on you?" Gavin mocked.

Trevor shot his brother a look that wasn't amused. "I don't mind a novel approach but this is getting ridiculous."

"Perhaps you should call her back," Melissa suggested.

Trevor shook his head. "No, if it was that important she could leave a message as to why." He grimaced. "I'll have to let Diana know not to interrupt my meetings in future."

"Maybe you should get a tap on your phone," Christian said, ever the lawyer.

Erica looked at her fiancé. "Darling, the woman's only left two messages. Hardly enough reason to put a stalking charge on her."

"Hey, who said anything about a stalker?" Trevor choked.

"I think—" Melissa began.

"People, can we focus here," Blake cut across her. "We have other matters at hand."

A few seconds ticked by.

Then Trevor nodded. "Yes, of course." His forehead creased as he thought. "Now, where was I? Right. I think we can give this Mrs. Richardson a short-term lease and see how it goes. I'm sure she won't want a long-term lease anyway."

Blake agreed. "Good idea. Perhaps you'd like to check out her business practices and financial situation before we decide anything further."

"Sure."

Blake turned to Melissa. "How's the spa going, Melissa?"

Melissa launched into a brief report.

"And now we need to discuss plans for the upcoming ski season." Blake looked at his half sister. "Erica, I believe you were going to prepare a report on how the Christmas bookings and the hiring of staff are going."

Erica inclined her head, looking very efficient. "Yes, Blake, that's right. I've drawn up a presentation, so if you'll all just look at the screen…"

Blake glanced at the screen, immediately impressed by Erica's attention to detail, and he couldn't help but surreptitiously glance at Christian sitting down the table on his right. The other man was looking at Erica with pride and admiration. But Blake saw something in the other man's features that reminded him of how *he* felt whenever he looked at Samantha.

Samantha.

Something twisted inside him. In less than ten days she would return to Vegas to wrap up everything. Then in another two weeks she would be out of his life and gone for good. He swallowed hard. There was nothing good about her going, he decided, dropping his gaze to the paperwork in front of him in case the others saw his thoughts.

The next agenda item jumped out at him.

Samantha's replacement.

Dammit, he had to do this. It was time to bring to the table a list of suitable applications for her position. It was only fair he keep his family up-to-date. After all, the new applicant would be mainly working out of here now and he wanted everyone to—

Just then there was another tap at the door and Samantha stuck her head around it, then entered the room farther. "I'm sorry, Blake, but there's an urgent message here for you from Mrs. Richardson. She wants you to call her back as soon as you can. It's to do with her boutique."

Here was the woman who was leaving him. The woman who could so easily walk away from what they had. Resentment rose in his chest and up his throat. He was tying himself up in knots for her and she was standing there looking so damn poised and polite.

And so damn beautiful.

Something snapped inside him right then. "I'm sure whatever Mrs. Richardson has to say can wait. Please keep any other messages for us until we finish this meeting," he dismissed, hearing himself talk in that harsh tone like he was listening to someone else talk to her.

Samantha flinched, then went to leave but turned back and squared her shoulders, a rebuke in her eyes. "Of course, Mr. Jarrod," she said primly and left the room with quiet dignity.

The door closed behind her.

All eyes were turned on him.

"I don't think there was any need for that, Blake," Guy said quietly.

Blake felt bad. If she hadn't come in at that moment then he wouldn't have verbally attacked her. It had been a reaction to her leaving him, not a reaction to *her.*

He looked at them. They were staring back at him with reproachful eyes that reminded him of Samantha. His mouth tightened. "I know, I know. I'll apologize later." He put thoughts of that to the side. "Now. Speaking of Samantha, as you know she's leaving. I'm looking at other applicants and I think one of them will be eminently suitable to replace her."

Guy arched a brow. "Can anyone replace her?"

"Guy," Blake growled.

"Blake," Melissa began, "don't you think—"

"No, Melissa," he said firmly, without being rude, knowing what she was going to say. "All of you listen to me. This is private between Samantha and myself. It's none of your business. Now. Let's talk about finding me a new assistant so that we can end this meeting and get on with other things."

The tension in the air was palpable, but he ignored both it and the looks on their faces. He owed no one any explanation. Hell, what explanation could there be anyway?

Samantha wanted to leave.

Samantha *was* leaving.

And he hated himself for embarrassing her just now.

"I apologize, Samantha."

Samantha had heard him enter the office but she'd

ignored him. Now she lifted her head to find Blake standing in front of her desk. Anger and hurt rioted inside her. She had to keep busy.

She rose to her feet and went to put some papers in the filing cabinet. "I'm glad I'm leaving now."

"Don't be like that."

She spun around. "Like what, Blake? Standing up for myself?"

His eyes clouded over. "Look, I know I embarrassed you in front of the family. I shouldn't have done that. I'm sorry."

She lifted her chin. "I was only doing my job. I'm not a novice at this. The woman said it was urgent, and seeing that her proposal was on the agenda for the meeting, I assumed you'd want to know any important developments."

"I know. And you're right. You did the right thing." His expression turned sincere. "You may not believe this, but the reason I snapped was because of you. I was angry because I had to bring up mention of your replacement. I don't want a replacement. I want *you*."

Her heart skipped a beat and she began to soften. She didn't doubt him. She never doubted what he said. If he said something, he meant it. He wasn't manipulating her. He'd accepted that she was leaving and he had nothing to lose by being honest. Why fight with him when time was so precious between them?

She thawed. "Oh, Blake."

He came toward her and slipped his arms around her waist. "Forgive me for being a pig? The others know I feel bad. Their sympathy was all on your side, believe me."

"Let's forget it." But it was nice to know his family had stuck up for her, especially against their big brother.

He lifted his hand and stroked her cheek. “Are you sure you don’t want to change your mind about leaving? It would be good between us.”

She drew a painful breath. “No, I can’t.” He wanted short-term. She wanted forever. And he wasn’t a forever type of guy.

His eyes shadowed with regret and he lowered his head and kissed her. She opened her mouth to him, knowing this was the only way she could let him inside herself.

The telephone rang just then and they both ignored it.

It stopped, then rang again.

She pulled back. “I should get that,” she said, and Blake nodded with a grimace.

It was Clarice.

Samantha looked at Blake as she listened. Then, “Yes, I passed the message on, Mrs. Richardson.”

Blake’s mouth tightened and he held his hand out for the phone. “What’s the problem, Clarice?” he said, after she handed it to him. There was a pause as he listened. “Look, I’m pretty busy right now.” He winked at Samantha and her heart soared with love.

Another pause.

“It was discussed at a meeting this morning. My brother, Trevor, is going to work with you on this.” He listened. “Yes. Fine.” He hung up, shook his head at it, then kissed Samantha quickly. “I need to go see Trevor and fill him in before Clarice gets to him. Unfortunately I’m not sure he knows what he’s coming up against with that woman.”

Samantha considered him. “You really worry about your brothers and sisters, don’t you?”

"Yes, I suppose I do."

She went up on her toes and kissed him briefly. He looked a little surprised as he turned and left the office. He was a good brother, she decided, her heart beating with love for him.

And a good man.

Eleven

Just before lunch, Melissa popped into the office as Blake was discussing a letter with Samantha. "I've booked you in for a spa treatment with me at four, Samantha. You need some major pampering."

Samantha blinked. "Oh, but—"

"No arguments. I don't give many massages these days but I've decided to give you one." Melissa smiled slyly at her big brother. "Anyway it's Blake's treat."

Blake lifted his brows. "What is it with my sisters bullying me?" Then he smiled at Samantha. "Keep the appointment."

"Okay, thanks." Samantha smiled at Melissa. "And thank you, too, Melissa."

"You're very welcome. See you at four." Melissa started to leave then stopped to consider her big brother. "It would do you good to have one, too, Blake." Her face lit with mischief. "You could share with Samantha. I'll even throw in a bottle of chilled champagne and some chocolate truffles. It's quite decadent."

"Not right now, thanks. I've got a lot to do."

"And that's exactly why you *should* have a massage."

"Soon."

"I'll keep you to that."

After she left, Samantha looked at Blake. "I wish you could come with me."

Heat lurked in the back of his eyes. "So do I, but I've got that meeting in town this afternoon."

His look warmed her through as she tilted her head. "You don't realize, do you?"

"What?"

"That you said *sisters* before."

Not *sister* and *half sister.*

Sisters.

Something flickered across his face, then he shrugged. "Yeah, well, don't make a big deal out of it." He went back into his office and Samantha went back to work, but she felt he'd made a big step in his relationship with his family and she was pleased for them all.

At four, Samantha walked over to the Tranquility Spa. Just stepping into a place that exemplified sophistication and sheer indulgence in a mountain setting relaxed her. It was gorgeous.

Melissa was waiting for her and led her to one of the treatment rooms that had serene music playing in the background. "I'll leave you to take off your clothes. Then slide under that sheet there and lie facedown on the bed. It's heated. I'll be back in a minute."

Samantha did as suggested and five minutes later, Melissa came back. "Good. Now I think a gentle massage should do the trick." There was the sound of her moving about. "Hmm, I'll have to be careful with your head. How is it, by the way?"

Samantha appreciated that Melissa remembered her injury. "Much better, thanks. It's healing well."

"I'm pleased. It could have been so much worse." Melissa started to rub oil on Samantha's back. "I hear Blake was quite upset about it."

"He blamed himself because he insisted I go with him for a drive."

"My brother's deep at times."

"I know." Samantha groaned as Melissa began long strokes to help soften the muscles.

"Am I hurting you?"

"No, not at all. It's exquisite."

Melissa laughed. "There's nothing like a massage." She continued working wonders, finding the right spots with unerring accuracy. Then, "Blake was pretty hard on you in the conference room today."

Samantha was glad she was lying on the bed with her face turned to the other side. "He apologized later."

"I knew he would. He's a man who knows when he's in the wrong."

"A rare boss," Samantha said, trying to make light of it.

"And a rare man."

"Right on both counts," Samantha just had to agree, then gave a little moan of pleasure as the massaging reached the base of her neck. She hadn't realized how badly she needed this.

Conversation ceased for a bit, before Melissa said, "I think Blake might be getting used to Erica."

Samantha wasn't surprised by the comment. "So you noticed that he said *sisters,* did you?"

"Oh, yeah."

"Erica's really nice."

"I love her already." Genuine warmth filled Melissa's voice. "It's like we're full sisters, not half sisters. We connected together right from the start."

"You've been really great at welcoming her into the family, Melissa. Erica must have appreciated that, especially when it came to the cool attitudes of her brothers."

"Those guys are so stubborn at times, and now look at them. They'll protect her to the death. I suspect even Blake would, too."

Back to Blake.

It always came back to Blake.

Time to change the subject. "So how is business doing at the spa?"

"Quiet right now, but next month it'll start picking up. And in December we'll be run off our feet. Of course, Shane worries about me and the baby, so I've promised him I'll put on extra staff."

"I can understand that."

There was a tiny pause. "This baby means so much to us," she said, with a little catch in her voice that tugged at Samantha's heartstrings.

"Pregnancy suits you. You're glowing."

Melissa cleared her throat. "Thanks. I can highly recommend it." All at once there was a slight change in the air. "What about you, Samantha? Do you plan on having children one day?"

Samantha swallowed the despair in her throat at the thought of having Blake's baby. She forced herself to sound natural. "Yes, I'd love to. But only when the time is right and with the right man."

There was no immediate reply. Then, "Forgive me for saying this, but isn't Blake the right man for you? Wouldn't you like to have his baby?"

Samantha's heart constricted as she was forced to face something she hadn't dared let herself think about now that she knew she loved Blake. This was dangerous territory for her. Loving him like she did and having his baby would be so absolutely wonderful, but knowing it was never going to happen was like a knife through her heart.

She swallowed hard again, then somehow said calmly, "You should know your brother by now, Melissa. Blake isn't into commitment, and having a baby would be a *huge* commitment."

Besides, Blake was already a father figure to his brothers and sisters, and he was already married to his job. There wasn't room for her, even if he actually *wanted* her to be a part of it all.

"Is that why you're leaving?"

She didn't hesitate. She couldn't afford to. "No. I'm leaving because it's the best thing for me."

There was a short silence, then, "I see."

Much to Samantha's relief, Melissa changed the subject and they talked about more desultory things on and off until the massage was over.

"Now," Melissa finally said, after she'd tidied up. "How do you feel?"

"Like I'm about to slither off the bed."

Melissa laughed. "That's what we aim for. Right, I'm going to leave you to get dressed. Take your time and don't rush. And make sure you drink lots of water for the next couple of hours. The massage releases toxins and if you don't flush them out you'll end up with a toxic headache."

"That sounds lethal," Samantha joked as she managed to push herself into a sitting position and wrapped the sheet around herself. "Thank you so much for this, Melissa," she said sincerely. "I didn't know how much I needed it. I really do feel wonderful."

Melissa smiled as she headed for the door. "Then I've done my job."

Samantha watched her leave, her smile fading as soon as the door closed, leaving her alone. Her body might feel better, but how did a person continue with a broken heart? Unfortunately no one could fix that.

"How was the massage?"

Samantha closed the front door behind her and saw Blake leaning against the kitchen doorjamb, as if he'd been waiting for her to come home. This was how it would be if she were to stay here with him. Yet how long would it last? Certainly not forever. Eventually things would become awkward between them and he would start to avoid her.

And then she'd know he would no longer want her.

"Wonderful," she said, giving him a smile that somehow felt empty.

"What's the matter?"

She looked at him and her heart felt sore. She couldn't seem to shake herself out of her despondency. "I think I need you to hold me, Blake."

"Why?"

"I just do, okay?"

He pushed himself away from the wall and came toward her, pulling her close. “Is that better?”

She slid her arms around him. “Yes.” But a shiver went through her.

His brow wrinkled as he looked down at her. “What’s going on with you?”

She drew a breath. “We won’t have this for much longer.”

He stiffened. “And?”

His reaction told her all she needed to know. “I feel…sad it’s coming to an end.”

“It’s your choice to leave, Samantha.”

She kept her face perfectly straight. “I know.” He didn’t understand and she couldn’t say any different. “I want to go to bed, Blake. Let’s make love until the sun comes up.”

It could have sounded silly but he didn’t smile and she was glad about that. It was as if he knew this meant a lot to her. And regardless of him avoiding any type of commitment, she hoped it would mean a lot to him, too.

In his bedroom she kept her eyes closed as she made love to him with everything in her heart. The thought of leaving him…of never having his child…of not sharing his life forever…was utmost in her mind. She’d never before felt such profound depth of emotion and she cried softly afterward. It would be so much worse once she left Blake for good.

Blake carefully eased out of bed the next morning just before sunrise, drew on his pajama pants and robe and left Samantha to sleep as he went downstairs to make himself some coffee. He felt restless, with a hard knot in his gut that he couldn't shake. Samantha had cried last night after they'd made love. She hadn't done that before. And it made him wonder. It was obvious she had strong feelings for him and he was certain now those feelings were the reason for her leaving. She hadn't said the words out loud, but he'd felt it every time she touched him and in her cry of release. Could she *love* him?

He couldn't love her back.

Hell, he should have seen this coming. *He* was the experienced one after all. Okay, so he'd invested more of himself in this relationship than he'd planned, but falling in love with Samantha, or any woman, wasn't on his agenda. It never had been and never would be. He'd never allow any person that much control over him.

Never.

So where did they go from there? Exactly nowhere. She'd leave and he'd let her go. End of story. There would be no happy ending for them. He couldn't give her that. He wished to heaven he could. He hated hurting her like this, especially knowing her last boyfriend had rejected her, too. She must feel so totally unwanted. Cast-off. Discarded and abandoned. God, how he hated to do this to her. It really pained him to do this. He shuddered, then reminded himself. He *had* warned her. And now that it came down to the crunch *she* had to be responsible for her own reactions.

Just then, the security light came on over the back decking and he saw a figure coming up the steps. The man was wrapped up to ward off the pre-sunrise chill, but he'd know that gait anywhere.

He opened the back door just as Gavin reached for the handle. "I see you smelled the coffee."

His brother smiled as he stepped inside the kitchen. “Sure did.”

Blake went to get another mug down from the cupboard. “What are you doing out and about so early?”

Gavin began taking off his thick gloves. “I was going for a walk to clear my head and saw the light on.”

Blake frowned a little as he poured coffee into the mugs. “Anything in particular bothering you?”

“Not really.”

He handed one of the mugs to his brother. “Is the bungalow project worrying you?”

“Not at all.” Gavin shrugged. “I guess it just feels strange being back home again. It hits me most at this time of the morning, and that means I usually need to get some fresh air.”

Blake understood. “I know what you mean.”

Gavin shot him a curious look. “I’m surprised. Don’t you have a lovely lady warming your bed, helping keep those thoughts at bay?”

Blake kept his face blank. “Do I?”

Gavin shook his head. “You always were the same about never sharing your feelings with anyone.”

Blake’s lips twisted. “Yeah, like *you* do?”

“All I can say is that you must be losing your touch where Samantha is concerned.”

“Why?” He knew he shouldn’t bite, but Samantha was so much on his mind this morning.

“I thought for sure you wouldn’t be dumb enough to let her go.”

Blake immediately went on the defensive. “Why would I want her to stay?”

“You need to ask?” Gavin shook his head. “How about she’s excellent at her job, she’s a looker and a nice person to boot, and as much as I hate to say it, she's damn good for you, that's why. You'll never find an assistant who anticipates your needs the way she does."

Blake dropped his gaze to the mug of coffee in his hands. What Gavin said was true, except the bit about Samantha being good for him. He didn't need any woman to make him feel good.

And he didn't like his brother getting too close and figuring out something that didn't need figuring out. Certainly he didn't want his brother figuring out that Samantha was in love with *him,* and that he couldn't return her love. He had to protect her. He didn't want anyone talking about her even after she left here. He owed her that much.

"Yeah, she's more than competent at her job and she's beautiful, too, but so are many other women. As for being good for me…yeah, we've had some fun while it lasted but it's coming to an end now and I'm more than happy with that."

Gavin sent him a challenging look. "So you feel nothing more for her?"

"No," he lied, feeling like Judas.

"I'm sorry to hear that," Gavin said slowly.

Suddenly a figure stepped into the doorway. "Don't be, Gavin," Samantha said quietly, hurt in her lovely eyes but dignity in her face. "I'm not."

Blake's heart cramped. "Samantha, I—"

"No need to explain, Blake. I shouldn't have eavesdropped but I'm glad I did. I would never have guessed you felt so little for me," she said, a catch to her voice.

He took a step toward her. "Samantha—"

She put up her hand. "No, Blake. You've said more

than enough." She turned and hurried away so fast all he saw was her shadow.

Shit!

Gavin lifted a brow. "Seems to me she might mean more to you than you think."

Blake tried to focus. "No, you're wrong."

Gavin stared hard, then put his mug down on the bench. "I'll leave you two to sort things out."

Blake gave a jerky nod as his brother headed for the back door and left him to it. He stood there in the kitchen for a minute as regret washed over him before he took the steps to follow her. He'd do his best to mend this damage as much as possible, but if he were to be honest, things between him and Samantha really couldn't be fixed. It was probably best this had come to a head.

Samantha could barely see as she fled up the staircase for the sanctuary of her room. After waking up, she'd gone downstairs in her nightshirt looking for Blake, surprised to hear Gavin's voice and never dreaming they were discussing *her.*

Oh, God. She couldn't stay in Aspen any longer. Not now. This was it. She was leaving as soon as possible, come hell or high water.

She grabbed her suitcases out of the wardrobe and threw them on the bed. She'd always been neat and tidy and fast at packing, but who cared anyway, she decided, swallowing a sob. All she wanted was to throw everything in her bags and get to the airport. She was going home to Pasadena where she would lick her wounds. Beyond that she couldn't think.

"Samantha?" Blake's voice came gently from the doorway.

Refusing to let him see her cry, she blinked back her tears as she carried her sweaters over to one of the suitcases.

"Samantha, stop. We need to talk."

She looked at him but continued what she was doing. "No. I'm leaving. It's time for me to get out of your hair."

And out of your life.

He swore low. "I'm sorry."

She dumped her clothes into the case. "You're only sorry that I overheard you," she said tightly, then took a shuddering breath as humiliation and hurt swelled inside her. "You made it sound so…cheap. You made *me* sound cheap. As if I don't matter."

"You *do* matter," he said, looking pained, but she knew better.

"Just not to you, right?" she derided, despair wrapping around her heart and not letting go.

"I didn't mean to speak like that about you. I just didn't want Gavin to know what was going on between us."

She snorted. "Of course. How silly of me? We can't have the great Blake Jarrod show any feelings now, can we? Not to his family and not to me." It was never about his feelings anyway, and that was the hardest part to take. She'd dared hope he might at least have a high opinion of her. "Your words show me that you never even respected me as a person, Blake. And certainly not as your lover."

His face blanched. "Don't say that," he growled. "I respect you. There's no one I respect more."

"It didn't sound like that to me back there." All at once she took a shuddering breath and admitted that she couldn't blame him for everything. "But I'm doing you a disservice. You made me no promises, I'll allow you that. You tried to warn me not to get involved with you."

His gaze sharpened. "And did you?"

What did she have to lose now? "Of course I did. I..." She couldn't say she loved him. She just couldn't. That would be too humiliating. "...I thought we had something special."

"We do."

She shook her head. "We *did*. It's over." Suddenly she caught a subtle change in his face—a change that Carl hadn't shown when he'd rejected her. She stilled. Her breath stopped. Did Blake have feelings for her after all? "Unless..." *Dare she ask?* "Can you give me one good reason to stay?"

Silence fell.

She waited. She couldn't say the words but he must know what she was asking. If ever there was a time he might let down his guard...a time when he could allow her into his heart...it would surely be—

His face closed up. "No, I'm sorry. I can't give you a reason to stay."

As hard as it was to pull herself together, she recovered her breath. "That's what I thought."

"Sam—"

A hard laugh escaped then. "Too late to call me that, Blake. Far too late." She held her head up higher. "Now, please leave me to pack in peace. It was good while it lasted but it's over between us now."

He stiffened, withdrawing into himself. "I'm really sorry I hurt you."

She held his gaze. "So am I. And as horrible as this

sounds, I wish I *was* capable of hurting you back." It would at least show she had meant something to him.

Turning away, he stopped and said over his shoulder, "The family jet is at your disposal. It'll take you wherever you want to go."

The words stung her heart. "Thank you."

He strode down the hallway to his suite, going inside and quietly closing the door behind him, shutting her out of his life. For good.

Samantha made herself move. She walked to her door and closed it, then went and sat on the bed and picked up a pillow to muffle her sobs. She figured this time she was entitled to cry.

Twelve

Half an hour later, Blake had showered and dressed and now sat in his office at the Manor, his leather chair turned toward the picture window. An early fall snow that wasn't unusual at this time of year had begun covering the resort, and now a weak sun was shining on the surrounding mountains. Usually at this time he was back at Pine Lodge making love to Samantha. All he could think now was that she was leaving.

God, she'd been so hurt back there. It had pained him to realize how much. And yet he hadn't been able to say the words to get her to stay. He'd known what she wanted, of course. She wanted him to say he loved her, but those words were no longer in his vocabulary. The last time he'd used them had been all those years ago to his mother—just before she died. He'd never said them again to anyone. He'd accepted he never would.

His upbringing—his whole life since—had been about avoiding commitment.

And now Samantha had to accept that, too.

Just then he heard a noise behind him and his chest instantly tightened. She'd come to say her final goodbye.

"What happened with Samantha, Blake?"

Erica.

He twisted his chair around, forcing his brain to work as he looked at the unhappy face of his half sister. Clearly she'd spoken to Gavin not too long ago.

He picked up a pen. "She's packing to leave."

"So you're just going to let her go?"

He gave a shrug. "She wants to go. I can't stop her."

She came closer to the desk, frowning. "What's gone so wrong with you two?"

He shot her a hostile look. "It's none of your business, Erica."

"You're my brother. I'm making it my business."

"Half brother," he corrected.

"I'm so sick of this," she snapped, drawing her petite frame up taller than she was, glaring down at him, standing her ground. "We have the same blood in our veins and that makes me a Jarrod, Blake. You're my brother, like it or lump it."

He stared up at her, a growing admiration rising inside him as he looked at this woman who was related to him, no matter how much he didn't like it. The angle of her chin. The light of battle in her eyes. That stubbornness in her mouth. Oh, yeah. Erica *was* a Jarrod, through and through.

"Blake, for God's sake, when are you going to drop your guard and let people in?"

He tensed. "I don't know what you mean."

"I mean, you won't let a half sister into your life because you think I might let you down like your mother did when she died. And you won't let Samantha into your heart because of the same thing. You're frightened you'll get hurt."

"That's ridiculous," he snapped. Sure, he wasn't willing to get involved with anyone and lay himself open to hurt, but that was only because he couldn't be bothered with the ramifications of it all. He was too busy to introduce any complications in his life.

"Then tell me why you're letting a beautiful woman like Samantha walk away from you?"

"She wants to go."

"No, *you* want her to go and she knows it."

His jaw clenched. "This has got nothing to do with you, Erica."

"Look at yourself, Blake. You're deliberately making it hard for Samantha to stay. You're pushing her away and abandoning her before she can abandon *you*."

He swore. "Just stay out of this."

"Think about it. Your mother died when you were six, so it stands to reason that you would be affected by her death. And what about your father? Donald Jarrod shut up shop with his emotions when his wife died, and the only way he could cope was by focusing on his offspring. He pushed all of you to be the best you could be, and none more than you as eldest."

"Erica…" he warned.

"I suspect he wanted his kids to be fully reliant on themselves. He didn't want any of you to get hurt. Not like *he* got hurt."

"That's enough."

"So you effectively lost not only your mother when you were little, but your father, as well. Is it any wonder you don't want to let anyone get close to you?"

He opened his mouth again....

And then somehow, without warning, her words began to hit him right where it mattered. But still he had to say, "What I want is not to listen to this drivel."

Her eyes said he wasn't fooling her. "People have their breaking point, Blake. Your mother's death was your—I mean, *our* father's breaking point. A person can do silly things in their grief. Everyone reacts differently. Our father turned to my mother, looking for solace. Who's to say you wouldn't do the same thing?"

"I would never want another woman after Samantha," he growled. "Never."

"Do you hear yourself?"

He stiffened and blinked. "What?"

She stood there watching him in silent scrutiny for a moment. "If Samantha died how would *you* feel?"

"Don't say that," he rasped, the thought slicing down through the middle of him.

"You love her, Blake."

His head reeled back. "No."

"Yes. Don't let yourself realize it too late. You may never get a second chance."

He swallowed as something deep inside him lifted up like a shade on a window and he finally admitted what was right there in front of him.

He *did* love Samantha.

And right then, he finally understood the depth of his father's loss. He still didn't understand how Donald Jarrod could have shunned the children who were a legacy of his beloved wife, nor how his father had turned to another woman, but the idea of Samantha dying squeezed his heart so tight he could barely breathe.

He surged to his feet. "I have to go to her."

"Thank God!"

He glanced at his watch. "She may not have left the lodge."

"She's already taken the valet car. I saw her leaving." Erica made a gesture toward the door. "Go. I'll make sure they stop the plane. And hey, take it easy getting to her, okay? We've got our first snow, and she'll want you in one piece."

"I will." He was almost at the door by the time she finished speaking. All at once he stopped, conscious that he had to take a moment more for something else. He returned to Erica to kiss her on the cheek. "Thanks, sis."

She beamed at him. "You're welcome. Just remember you'll have a few brothers and sisters who'll expect your firstborn to be named after them."

He grinned. "That's a lot of names."

"Well, maybe you can have a lot of kids."

He chuckled as warmth filled him at the thought of Samantha carrying his child. But first things first…he wanted only one person right now.

Samantha.

As he raced down to the lobby, he remembered how after their lovemaking the other night he'd felt so at home in her arms. Now he knew it was more than that.

In Samantha's arms he *had* come home.

"Is it going to be much longer, Jayne?" Samantha asked, after she'd boarded the Jarrod private jet and nothing seemed to be happening. They hadn't even taxied out onto the runway yet.

"I'm sorry about this, Ms. Thompson," the stewardess apologized. "It's the weather. There's a storm ahead. We have to sit tight until it passes."

Samantha swiveled her leather chair around on its base a little to glance out the cabin window to the snow-dusted airport. A few weeks ago, before she'd decided to resign, she'd been eagerly looking forward to the first of the snow falling over Jarrod Ridge. Now she had to return to the warm California weather and try not to imagine how magical it would have been here in Blake's arms.

Somehow she faked a small smile back at the other woman. "Okay, thanks, Jayne."

The stewardess smiled, then went to the back of the plane, leaving her alone to stare out the window. She'd done her best to repair her face after her crying session back at the lodge, but the longer she sat here the more likely she might burst into tears.

And if she did that she would be humiliated in front of Jayne. She wanted no one knowing how painful this was for her. Blake knew she'd been hurt, but he really had no idea at the depths of her despair. How could he? He didn't love her. He was going to move on. He'd probably already written her off as a bad debt, she thought with a touch of hysteria.

Oh, God. This was it. She was actually leaving Aspen…leaving Blake for good. Fresh tears were verging in her eyes when there was a sudden flurry of movement near the doorway. She quickly took a shuddering breath and glanced ahead to check what was happening.

Blake!

He stood there looking at her…so dear to her heart. And then he moved toward her through the wide cabin, and her thoughts kicked in. Was he here merely to make sure she left? She dared not think otherwise.

He stopped in front of her seat and looked down at her. "You didn't say goodbye, Samantha."

She moistened her mouth. "I didn't think you wanted me to."

"I didn't," he said, and her heart twisted tight at his honesty. "The fact is…I didn't want you to say goodbye at all. I still don't want you to leave. I want you to stay with me." He pulled her to her feet, looking at her with an emotion in his eyes that almost blinded her. "I love you, Samantha."

She knew in a heartbeat he was telling the truth. "Say that again," she whispered.

"I love you."

She threw her arms around his neck. "Oh, my God! I love you, too, Blake. So very, very much."

He kissed her then and she clung to him, loving him with every ounce of her being, feeling the pounding of his heart in time with hers. Forevermore.

Finally he pulled back, but kept his arms around her. "I love you, Samantha. I love you more than life itself."

She sighed blissfully. "I feel the same."

He gave her a soft kiss. "After we made love last night, I suspected you loved me."

At the time she'd hoped she'd masked her feelings well. "I gave myself away when I cried, didn't I?"

"Yes, I'm afraid you did, darling."

She went all sappy inside at the endearment, so she

could forgive him anything. "Yet you were still going to let me go."

"You can thank Erica that I didn't. She made me see sense about a couple of things."

"Thank you, sweet Erica," she mused out loud.

He smiled, then it faded on his handsome face, making him more serious. "I hope you can forgive me for what I said to Gavin. You were right. I didn't want anyone knowing my feelings for you. I was even hiding them from myself," he added with self-derision. "And I hope you can believe this, but I was trying to protect you. I didn't want them realizing you had feelings for me either." He lifted his shoulders. "Loving someone is a private thing."

She thanked him with her eyes. "I agree, though they probably suspected anyway. And yes, I do forgive you, darling," she said, loving the sound of that on her own lips and seeing his eyes darken. "If you hadn't said what you did to Gavin, then all this may not have been resolved."

He chuckled. "Erica would have made us resolve it, don't you worry about that. My sister is a very determined woman."

Her heart swelled. So he'd let Erica into his heart, too. How wonderful. Now he could be the man he was meant to be with his family.

And with her.

All at once there was so much to talk about. She'd have to tell him about when she'd actually realized she loved him, and she'd have to come clean about trying to make him jealous. He was bound to get a laugh out of that.

"Samantha," he cut across her thoughts. "I insist you

don't give up your music. I want you to contact that person Erica mentioned at the music school as soon as you can."

"Oh, Blake, I'm not giving up anything," she said softly, and ran her fingers along his chin, loving the feel of its masculine texture. "I've got all I ever wanted right here."

His brows drew together. "But—"

She smiled at the worried look in his eyes. "Okay, I'll contact them. Perhaps sometime in the future I'll be able to help out in some minor way, but please believe that playing the piano isn't important in my life. I enjoy it. I might even take some more lessons, or give lessons for that matter, but living here with you, and being part of your family, will be more than enough for me."

He gave her a searching look, then his shoulders relaxed. "While we're being honest…"

Her heart caught. "Yes?"

"I know you feel I'm letting you down in some way, but…"

She swallowed hard. "But?" What wasn't he telling her? Was he actually in love with someone else? Was she his second choice? Perhaps he—

"Forgive me, Samantha, but I don't think I'll ever be able to call you Sam."

It took a moment to sink in. She laughed and lightly punched his chest. "You think that's funny, don't you?"

He put his hands on either side of her face and looked at her lovingly. "You're Samantha to me. *My* Samantha. Do you mind?"

She blinked back silly tears of happiness. "Of course not." Not anymore. "It makes me feel very special."

"You *are* special, my darling." He placed his lips on hers, then, "Let's go to Vegas right now and get married."

She blinked. "Married?" As crazy as it seemed, she hadn't thought that far ahead. She'd been too busy taking in that he loved her. "You really want to marry me, Blake?"

He stroked her cheek. "Yes. I want your kisses for the rest of my life."

She drew his mouth down to hers and kissed him softly. "Here's one to start with."

When the kiss finished, he said, "Speaking of giving, you haven't *given* me my answer. Will you marry me?"

"Is there any doubt?"

"Not really."

"You're a conceited man, Blake Jarrod," she teased.

"And that's a good thing in this situation, right?"

She sent him a rueful glance, then something came to her. "But don't you want to get married in Aspen with your family present?"

"No. I'm an impatient man. I want to marry you now. Today." He scowled. "Unless *you* want a big wedding?" He didn't wait for her to answer. "I suppose I shouldn't cheat you of a wedding with your family."

She shook her head. "No, I don't need my family there. I love them dearly but they'll understand. All they want is for me to be happy."

"I can guarantee that."

"Then a wedding for two will be just perfect, my love," she murmured, a flood of emotion making her voice husky.

Blake lowered his head to place his lips against

hers. Outside the plane more snowflakes fell in a hush, blanketing everything in a fairy-tale setting. And that was appropriate. Their love was, after all, a fairy tale come true.

* * * * *